LITTLE
DISASTERS

SARAH VAUGHAN

**SIMON &
SCHUSTER**

London · New York · Sydney · Toronto · New Delhi

A CBS COMPANY

First published in Great Britain by Simon & Schuster UK Ltd, 2020
A CBS COMPANY

1 3 5 7 9 10 8 6 4 2

Simon & Schuster UK Ltd
1st Floor
222 Gray's Inn Road
London WC1X 8HB

Simon & Schuster Australia, Sydney
Simon & Schuster India, New Delhi

www.simonandschuster.co.uk
www.simonandschuster.com.au
www.simonandschuster.co.in

A CIP catalogue record for this book
is available from the British Library

Hardback ISBN: 978-1-4711-6503-0
Trade Paperback ISBN: 978-1-4711-6504-7
eBook ISBN: 978-1-4711-6505-4
Audio ISBN: 978-1-4711-6789-8

Excerpt from 'Morning Song' by Sylvia Plath.
Reprinted by permission of Faber & Faber Ltd.

Typeset by M Rules
Printed and bound by CPI Group (UK) Ltd, Croydon, CR0 4YY

To my husband, who sparked the idea.
With love.

LITTLE
DISASTERS

Love set you going like a fat gold watch.
The midwife slapped your foot soles, and your bald cry
Took its place among the elements.

Our voices echo, magnifying your arrival. New statue.
In a drafty museum, your nakedness
Shadows our safety. We stand round blankly as walls.

I'm no more your mother
Than the cloud that distils a mirror to reflect its own slow
Effacement at the wind's hand.

All night your moth-breath
Flickers among the flat pink roses. I wake to listen:
A far sea moves in my ear.

One cry, and I stumble from bed, cow-heavy and floral
In my Victorian nightgown.
Your mouth opens clean as a cat's. The window square

Whitens and swallows its dull stars. And now you try
Your handful of notes;
The clear vowels rise like balloons.

'Morning Song', Sylvia Plath

I have given suck, and know
How tender 'tis to love the babe that milks me;
I would while it was smiling in my face
Have plucked my nipple from his boneless gums
And dashed the brains out

Macbeth, Act I Scene VII, William Shakespeare

PROLOGUE

The cry builds. At first it is pitiful. A creak and a crackle. Tentative, tremulous, just testing how it will be received.

The doubt quickly flees. The whimper becomes a bleat, the catch hardening as the cry distils into a note of pure anguish. 'Shh . . .' her mother pleads, reaching into the cot and holding the baby at arm's length. The sound buttresses the space between them. 'It's OK, baby. Mummy's here now. Mummy's going to make it OK.'

The child stares at her. Eleven weeks old; in the fierce grip of inconsolable colic; her eyes two beads that glower, incredulous and intense. *Don't be ridiculous*, these eyes say. *I am livid and I'm livid with you.* Her face folds in on itself and her Babygro dampens as if the rage that is turning her body into a white-hot furnace is so intense it must escape.

'Shh, shh. It's OK,' the mother repeats. She is suddenly wary. Sweat licks the child's brow and her fontanelle pulses like some alien life form just beneath the surface of her skin. Evidence of her pumping heart, of the blood which courses through her veins and could burst through this translucent spot, as delicate as a bird's egg, so fragile the mother daren't touch it in case it ruptures. The beat continues, insistent, unrelenting. Like this baby's uncontrollable rage.

The cry cranks up a gear and she draws the baby close. But the child writhes against her, fists balled, torso arching backwards in anger or pain.

'It's OK.' Who is she trying to convince? Not this baby, who has been crying for the past eight weeks. And not herself because every time she thinks she's found a fresh solution – a hoover sucking at the carpets; an untuned radio hissing white noise – the rules of this particularly cruel game shift and she has to think again.

'Shh, shh.' Her eyes well with self-pity and frustration and an exhaustion so entrenched she is sometimes knocked off balance. *Please be quiet, just for a minute. Be quiet. Just SHUT UP!* she wants to say.

The wails seem to mock her. *A terrible mother. Not even your first. You're meant to know how to comfort your baby. What will next door think?*

'OK. *OK!*' She is shouting now. The baby squirms. She is pressing too tightly: frightened, she releases her grip. And as she does her baby's lungs expand so that she erupts in a blast of fury that turns her tiny body rigid, fierce energy pulsing from the tips of her toes all the way along the length of her spine.

'OK, OK.' Like an addict desperate for a fix, she will do anything now for silence, and so she stumbles to the bathroom; strips down to her bra and pants. Then she flings a heap of clothes into the washing machine, switches it on and, huddling in the darkness, pulls her daughter close.

The machine starts up: a rhythmic swish as the drum fills with water then turns, noisy and repetitive. White noise that is the most potent balm. The cries catch, falter, stop, as the swish and the slosh and the dull clunk of the spinning clothes fill the damp, dark room.

She risks glancing down. Two eyes stare back. *Please don't cry, please don't cry*, the plea is automatic. The baby's bottom lip quivers and the uneasy quiet is broken with a bleat. Great gulps of rage soon drown out the heavy lullaby. *Please be quiet. Just be quiet. Be quiet, won't you? Just be quiet, for God's sake!*

It's no good. The walls push in; the heat bears down and the noise – the terrible crying that has been going on for three hours – engulfs her. Her eyes burn and she feels like joining in. She cannot cope with this: she *cannot* cope. She does not know how much more she can bear.

They say you should leave your baby when you feel like this. Put her down, close the door, and walk away. Remain elsewhere until you feel calmer. But then the crying will continue; the baby quivering more with anger than a cause that can be fixed, like a wet nappy or pain. Doesn't it make sense to hold her tight, to plead, to bargain, perhaps to shout? To try to shake a little sense into her? No, not that: she knows she mustn't hurt her baby – though if she could shock her into silence, if she could stifle that noise again . . .

At moments like this, her mind fills with toxic thoughts. *You're a bad mother. She'd be better off without you.* And then, insidiously, the more shameful ones that she tries to shake away.

Thoughts she can barely acknowledge, let alone express, about the desire – just for a moment – for this child to be silent always.

LIZ

Friday 19 January, 2018, 11.30 p.m.

One

It is definitely the short straw of hospital medicine. A&E in a trauma centre on a Friday night in late January; almost midnight, and the waiting areas are rammed. Patients glazed with boredom slump on every available chair, a queue is waiting to be triaged and we're nearing the mayhem that descends when the drunks and the lads whose fights have turned a bit nasty roll in, lairy, disruptive, laughing in the face of reason. If the abuse turns physical – walls punched, a nurse shoved, a Sri Lankan doctor spat at – security will have to be called.

A cold January means that the hospital is already busy: filled to ninety-nine per cent capacity. A&E is on the brink of turning away ambulances: almost on red alert. Many patients don't need to be here: not least those who couldn't get – or didn't *think* to get – a GP's appointment and who now realise that a long and uncomfortable weekend stretches ahead of them unless they hotfoot it to A&E in the belief that doing so will make their virus swiftly better. They're the ones who are the most vocal about the long wait, who hover by the nurses' station ready to harangue them. The properly sick don't have the energy to complain.

I wouldn't go near an A&E in a busy trauma centre on a Friday night unless my life depended on it. Nothing short of a cardiac arrest, a stroke, a fracture or a massive haemorrhage would force me through the automatic doors. So why am I here, breathing in the fetid fumes of others' illnesses; tramping the corridors; peering at the faces of the frustrated, and those with life-threatening conditions who wait, two, three, four hours – or sometimes more?

Well, I don't have a choice. This is my job. Senior registrar in paediatrics at St Joseph's, west London: a major acute general hospital and trauma centre at the cutting edge of clinical care. My career hasn't been meteoric: two babies and two six-month maternity leaves plus disappearing down a cul-de-sac of research mean I'm still not a consultant, unlike the men I studied with at med school. But I'm only a year off and then I'll have reached the giddy peaks of medicine's hierarchy. Twenty years of study and I'll finally be there.

I'm not a doctor who works full-time in A&E. I'm here because I've been called down from the children's ward to see a patient. But I'm the sort of doctor on which every hospital depends. Sufficiently senior to make crucial decisions; sufficiently junior to be based in the hospital during long nights and weekends on call. Dressed in periwinkle blue scrubs, what you see is what you get: someone pragmatic, no-nonsense, approachable, empathetic; occasionally a little blunt, according to my teacher husband, but a good person. (I work with sick children and deal with distressed parents, after all.) Physically unremarkable: five foot six, wiry dark brown hair scraped into a ponytail, a permanent crease between my hazel eyes. Negligible make-up, no jewellery except for a thin gold wedding band, worn and scratched. White hospital crocs: good for running. Easy to wash when splattered with blood.

I'm anonymous, dressed like this. Androgynous, too. No one's going to assess the size of my hips, a little wider than I'd like thanks to night shifts when I don't get a break until after ten and rely on vending machine chocolate or canteen chips. No teenage boy's going to spy my cleavage when I bend over to examine him on a hospital bed. I'm a doctor, this pyjama-type uniform says, as does the lanyard round my neck. *Hello. I'm Dr Trenchard. I'm here to do a job, and to do it well.*

Wearing scrubs, like any uniform, also bonds you with your colleagues. We're all in it together: an army working for a greater good we still believe in – the dysfunctional, fracturing, only-just-about-coping-because-of-the-goodwill-and-professionalism-of-its-staff, free-at-the-point-of-need NHS. And if that sounds sentimental or sanctimonious, I'm neither of those things. It's just that when it's your daughter's tenth birthday and you can't put her to bed because it's impossible to swap a Friday night shift, and she's said, piling on the guilt in a way that only your firstborn can: 'It's all right, Mummy. I understand that you need to work.' When *this* is the background to your fourth late shift in a row, and you're exhausted and would really like to be in bed, curled around the husband you only grunt at during the week. When that's what you're missing and your reality's very different: when you know your colleagues are racing to a crash call – hearts pumping as they run, shoes squeaking on the shiny floor, curtains whooshing around a bed; that fierce concentration as they crack ribs or apply paddles to shock a patient back into life ... When, more prosaically, you haven't had time for a wee ... Well, you have to cling onto some belief in what you're doing; you have to believe there's a point in being committed to this sort of career. Because otherwise? You'd give up medicine, or emigrate to Australia, New Zealand or Canada, where the weather, hours and pay are all far, far better.

Oh, don't get me wrong. I love my job. I believe what I'm doing is important. (What could be *more* worthwhile than making sick children better?) It's stimulating; and, coming from my background – I'm the child of a single parent who ran a seaside café – I'm immensely proud to have got here at all. But this shift comes at the end of a string of nights preceded by an academic course last weekend and I'm shattered: my brain so befuddled I feel as if I'm seriously jetlagged. Adrenalin will carry me through the next few hours. It always does. But I need to focus. Just ten more hours: that's all I need to get through.

I'm thinking all of this as I trot along the shiny corridor from the children's ward to A&E, my mood not enhanced by the art on the walls: a mixture of seascapes and abstracts in bright primary colours that are supposed to soothe patients and distract them from the unpalatable fact that they have to be here. I pass the oncology and radiology departments; and think of the lives being fractured, the hopes and dreams evaporating; for some, the lives ending; then shove the thought aside.

I'm on my way to see a patient. Ten months old: fractious, irritable. She's vomited, according to A&E, though she hasn't a fever. She may be no more ill than Sam, my eight-year-old who's just had a chest infection, though it's odd to bring in a child who's not genuinely poorly at this time of night. The junior isn't happy to discharge and asked me to come down. My heart tips at the thought of a complicated case.

Because I could do without another terrifyingly sick child right now. My shift started with a crash call to the delivery suite to resuscitate a newborn: a full term plus thirteen days overdue baby; blue, with a slow heartbeat, and a cord pulled tight around his neck. I got him back: stimulation, a few breaths – but there was that long moment when you fear that it could all go horribly wrong and the mother who has managed to carry her baby beyond term might end up mourning the child she has dreamed of. As every obstetrician knows, birth is the most dangerous day of your life.

Then a child with an immunosuppressant condition and a virus was brought in by ambulance, and just after he'd been admitted, I had to deal with a three-year-old with croup. The mother's anxiety made the situation far worse, her panic at his seal-like whooping exacerbating the condition until it became dangerous, the poor boy gasping for breath as she distracted our attention. Often parents are the most difficult part of this job.

So I've had enough drama tonight, I think, as I squeak along the corridor and take in the chaos of paediatric A&E, filled with hot, disgruntled parents and exhausted children. A boy in football kit looks nauseous as he leans against his father in a possible case of concussion. A waxen-faced girl peers at a blood-soaked dressing, while her mother explains she was chopping fruit when the knife slipped. From the main A&E, where the aisles are clogged with trolleys, there's the sound of drunken, tuneless singing: 'Why are we waiting' half-shouted increasingly belligerently.

I check with the sister in charge, and glance at the patient's notes: Betsey Curtis. My heart ricochets. Betsey? Jess's Betsey? The baby of a friend I know well? Jess was in my antenatal group when I was pregnant with Rosa and she with Kit. Together we navigated early motherhood and stayed close when we had our second babies, though we've drifted apart since Jess's third. Perhaps it's inevitable: I've long since left the trenches of early babyhood, and work, family life and my suddenly vulnerable mother are all-consuming. Still, I've only seen her a handful of times since she's had this baby and I've let things slip. She didn't send Rosa a birthday card and I only noticed because she's usually so good at remembering. Far better than me, who sometimes forgets her son, Kit's, a week later. Of course it doesn't matter – but I had wondered, in a distracted, half-conscious way as I scooped up the cards this morning, if she was irritated with me.

And now she's brought in Betsey. I look at the notes again: 'Non-mobile, irritable, drowsy, tearful, has vomited . . .' they say.

'Ronan, is this the patient you were concerned about?' I double-check with the junior doctor.

He nods, relieved at deferring responsibility.

'I'm not sure what's wrong,' he says. 'No obvious temperature but her mother was concerned enough to bring her in. Wondered if you'd keep her in for observation for twenty-four hours?'

I soften. He's been a doctor for less than eighteen months. I've felt that uncertainty, that embarrassment of asking a senior colleague.

'Of course – but let's have a look at her first.'

I pull the curtains aside.

'Hello, Jess,' I say.

'Oh, thank God it's you.' My friend's face softens as I enter the bay, tension easing from her forehead. 'I didn't think we should come but Ed was adamant. It's so unlike him to worry, it panicked me into bringing her in.'

I look up sharply. *Panicked*'s a strong word from an experienced mother of three.

'Poor you and poor Betsey.' Examining a patient I know is really not ideal, but with no other paediatric registrar around, there's no other option. 'Let's see what's wrong with her.'

Jess's baby is lying on the bed, tiny legs splayed against the paper towel coating its blue plastic surface; large eyes, watchful, her face a tear-streaked, crumpled red. I'd forgotten how pretty she is. Almost doll-like, with thick dark hair framing a heart-shaped face, a cupid's bow of a mouth and those vast blue eyes peering at me. A thumb hangs from the corner of her mouth and her other fist clutches a dirty toy rabbit. It's the toy I bought her when she was born: the same make as Sam's, an unashamedly tasteful, French, velveteen rabbit. Her bottom lip wobbles but then the thumb sucking resumes and she manages to soothe herself. She is heavy-lidded. Looks utterly exhausted.

'Hello, Betsey,' I say, bending down to speak on her level. Then I straighten and turn to Jess, whose hand rests lightly on her little girl. It still surprises me that someone this beautiful could be my friend. She's one of those rare, effortlessly striking women, with copper, pre-Raphaelite curls and slate grey eyes, now red-rimmed and apprehensive – perfectly natural, since no one wants their baby to be this sick. She has fine bones, and slim fingers garlanded with rings that she twists when nervous. A tiny gold star nestles in the dip of her neck. Her glamour is incongruous in this world of specimen containers, rolls of bandages and stainless steel trolleys. I think of the shadows under my eyes, the rogue grey hair kinking at my forehead I found this morning. I look a good five or six years older than her, though we're the same age.

'Can you run through what you think is wrong?'

'She isn't herself. Grizzly, clingy, listless and she was sick. Ed freaked out when that happened.'

'Is he here, now?'

'No, he's at home, with Frankie and Kit.'

I imagine her boys lost to the depths of sleep; her husband unable to settle; and Jess's loneliness as she sits in A&E with a poorly baby who can't tell her what the problem is.

She gives me a quick, tense smile, and pulls a charcoal cardigan around her. Her top slips, revealing a black bra strap, sleek against her blanched almond of a shoulder, her improbably smooth skin. The top of her ribs and her clavicle are exposed and I realise she is noticeably thinner than when I last saw her just over a month ago at the school nativity. Under the glare of the fluorescent strip lights, she seems more vulnerable; less assured. And very different to the woman I first met ten years ago, who buzzed with excitement at the thought of having her first child.

LIZ

Thursday 22 November, 2007

Two

'Shall we give him another five minutes – and then we'll need to start?' Cathy, the antenatal teacher, tilts her head at Jess, the only expectant mother with an empty chair beside her.

'No, let's begin. He's in a cab now, but he'll be a while longer.' Jess smiles at each couple. *I'm so sorry*, her expression says. That look dispels any momentary irritation and I feel a rush of sympathy for a fellow mother-to-be whose partner hasn't been able to make the 7.30 start. Beside me, Nick shifts in his seat and I am grateful that his job as a secondary school teacher means that, though he will never be rich like Jess's hedge fund manager husband, he is unlikely to ever be late for such things.

We have been waiting for Ed Curtis for nearly fifteen minutes now and the very pregnant woman who introduced herself as Charlotte is breathing heavily: possibly as a result of having the largest bump among us, though it's difficult not to read bad temper in each sigh.

Charlotte strikes me as someone who is always five minutes early. A corporate lawyer, she has already told us it is imperative she quickly establish a routine. She favours Gina Ford and will be pumping breast milk to stimulate her supply and provide her husband, Andrew, with enough to do the night feeds. 'It's the least he could do,' Charlotte says with a sardonic, surprisingly sexy laugh, and it isn't clear if Andrew will be doing this to compensate for getting her pregnant or because so much of the burden of early parenthood lies with a breastfeeding mother. 'He'll be doing all the nappies too,' she says, and she doesn't appear to be joking.

There are nine expectant parents, sitting on black plastic chairs and smiling nervously at each other, this Thursday evening. Five women, all over seven months pregnant, expecting their first babies in the new year. Three of the fathers have rushed straight from work and look out of place in this preschool nursery decorated with collages of dried pasta and finger paintings. Andrew's suit trousers ride up to expose red silk socks and an inch of hairy ankle, and it seems unimaginable that this man, who looks a good ten years older than me, will be getting down on a floor with a baby any time soon.

But it is going to happen to us all. The tiny pegs in the hall with their laminated labels and names in Comic Sans font tell of a world we are going to have to get used to.

One filled with human beings so alien even their names differ from those of our childhoods: Olivia, Ethan, Jade and Ayaan; Callum, Chloe, Mia, Zac. There are small icons on those labels – an umbrella, a football, a butter-fly – and pairs of bright wellington boots, neatly stacked under each bench. And it is something about the care with which these have been placed, and the sense that each pre-schooler is seen as an individual – Millie with her fish; Ollie with his cricket bat – that reinforces the magnitude of what is going to happen. These aren't babies we are having but small people for whom we will feel responsible for the rest of our lives.

'Well, if you're sure?' Cathy, neat and grey, a mother of three girls in their twenties, looks relieved to be getting started. 'Let's begin by introducing ourselves properly and explaining why we want to do this course.'

She turns to the pregnant mother on her right: a slight, blonde woman with rosy cheeks, an eager smile, and a partner whose body language – crossed arms and legs, eyes fixed on a spot in the distance – suggests he'd rather be anywhere but here.

'I'm Mel,' the woman says, 'and this is my husband, Rob. I'm a primary school teacher and I want as natural a labour as possible with minimal intervention.' She beams as if she knows she's given the right answer. 'Ideally a home birth.' She turns to her husband, who grunts his assent. 'Rob?'

'I work in the City, and I'm here because my wife told

me to be,' he says. A ripple of laughter from Charlotte and Andrew, and from a younger man with a broad physique and reddened skin.

Mel's cheeks redden but she smiles, indulgent. 'As you can see, there's no pretence with Rob.'

'Supporting your partner's very important,' Cathy says, as she fiddles with the felt beads around her neck. 'Birth, and the whole perinatal period – the time around the birth – can be deeply unsettling. It's crucial mothers feel supported by their partner. Now.' Her tone brightens. 'Who's next?'

'Me. I'm Susi,' the girl sitting next to the youngest man says. She smiles broadly and, like her partner, speaks with an Australian accent. 'I'm in HR; Andy's in IT. We're over here from Oz, half a world away from our families. So being taught how to give birth, and meeting some other mums, seemed like a good idea.'

'Do you have any friends who are having babies?' Cathy frowns slightly. Susi looks younger than me, perhaps twenty-five or twenty-six; tall, strong and wide-hipped. She shakes her head.

'No! They're all out on the lash and having a fine old time!'

'Getting pregnant was a bit of a surprise,' Andy adds. 'But people have been having babies forever without much hassle, and I'm sure we'll manage just fine.'

He smiles broadly at his wife and I wish I could view birth and motherhood as this easy. I know too much about the potential difficulties of childbirth and the lottery of a happy childhood to relax about it all.

I shift uncomfortably while Charlotte introduces herself and her husband, who looks genuinely embarrassed as she describes him as a leading intellectual property lawyer. ('Not *leading*, Charlotte.' 'Well, that's what *The Times* said.')

'And why did you want to take this course?'

'Well.' Charlotte looks as if she has practised this answer. 'I suppose one always wants to prepare for things: finals, law exams, marriage, children. Parenthood's a major change, isn't it? But no one learns how to do it in any detail. And I just want to get it right.'

I smile at her. Perhaps we aren't dissimilar, after all. I'm specialising in paediatric medicine and had to deliver a baby to qualify as a doctor but I'm anxious about being a mother. I effectively brought up my younger brother but I have no positive role model: my relationship with my mother is problematic and I've no sister or older relative to ask for help.

I've always sought answers in books but the medical textbooks and child-rearing books feel inadequate. Yes, I understand the theory of routine versus attachment-based parenting, I know about developmental milestones and the whole host of childhood illnesses, but there has been nothing to prepare me for how I might *feel* when I first hold this child. I don't know if I will love it unconditionally, or be able to interpret, or understand, its emotions. I need to learn how to mother if my maternal instinct – a nebulous concept that's supposed to be natural but what if it isn't? What if I lack it as clearly as my mother? – fails to kick in when I hold my child.

'What about you, Liz?' asks Cathy.

'Well,' I stall, because I can't admit to any of my fears out loud, 'I'm a junior doctor, so I'm not too anxious about the birth itself: I'll take any pain relief including an epidural I'm offered. I'm here to meet other mothers with babies the same age.'

'You've certainly found some potential friends here. All your babies should be born within a month or two, so you can provide vital support during those first few weeks.' Cathy turns to the only woman who hasn't spoken. 'And what about you, Jess?'

Jess smiles. Mine is far from a 'glowing' pregnancy – I've had severe morning sickness and have still managed to balloon out of all proportion – but there's no better word to describe Jess's state. Her hair shines under the unforgiving light, and she has managed the ideal: a perfect pregnancy silhouette of full breasts, neat bump, sharp cheekbones and slight frame. In any group of women, there is always one who is the most effortlessly cool. That's Jess, but the fact she is so obviously the Queen Bee doesn't alienate. Her enthusiasm is so infectious I want to share it. This is how I should be feeling, isn't it? As if motherhood is the most fantastic adventure – not something about which I am apprehensive at best, fearful at worst.

19

'I just want to be the best mother I can,' Jess says, and her voice is low with the hint of a rasp to it as if she's entrusting us with a delicious secret. She strokes her bump, and looks down at it as if talking to her unborn child. 'We know we're having a boy and I want him to know he'll be so cherished, and so very important.' She hesitates, picking her words carefully. 'I don't think we need to parent as our parents did . . .' and her voice suddenly turns bright so that any unease is fleeting, like a cloud passing over the sun. 'I want my boy to know that he is the centre of my world.'

Perhaps it's the hormones, but what should sound unbearably trite and painfully obvious is exquisite, and moving. We sit in silence for a moment, in this room with its crates of plastic cars and Duplo blocks and its smell of Milton disinfecting liquid, and sweat.

'That's lovely,' Nick says.

'Yes,' I manage. 'Being that sort of mother, or feeling confident that I'll be able to be that sort of mother, that's what I'd like to take away from here.'

Jess smiles back at me then, with the clear-eyed anticipation of a woman who has no reason to expect anything but the best for her child. And, as the rain pelts against the windows, Jess's optimism transforms that nursery. I feel a tentative hope that I will be an adequate mother. I won't be perfect but I will be good enough.

The door bursts open, a skittering of leaves blasting into the room on a vicious draught.

'Ed!' Jess's smile grows broader.

'Hello, darling. Hello, everyone. I'm so, so sorry.' Ed Curtis moves fluidly, briefcase in hand, as he bends to kiss his wife and settle into the empty chair.

'Huge apologies. I couldn't get away and then the District Line was delayed. What have I missed?' He leans forwards, palms on his thighs, legs apart, a broad smile on his face. It is impossible not to be charmed by this other half of a golden couple. Not to forgive his delay, because of course his job is high-pressured. He glances around the group and, when he spots Charlotte, his brow furrows in sudden recognition and his smile grows even wider.

'Charlotte?'

'Ed.' She has flushed a deep red, the blood rushing up her throat from her fussy, pussy-bow collar.

'Charlotte Fitzgerald?'

'Charlotte *Mason*, now.'

'How *are* you?' He looks delighted, Charlotte noticeably less so. 'Sorry, sorry, everyone. Jess: Charlotte and I were at uni together. What a small world!' He shakes his head, unable to get over the coincidence. 'We must catch up properly.'

'Yes, yes we must.' She is still flushed but looks surprised, even flattered. Her husband glances at her enquiringly and she squeezes his hand.

'Well, how lovely – but perhaps you could chat later?' says Cathy, irritation catching her voice. 'I'm conscious that time is ticking on and we've lots to get through today.'

'Yes, of course. I'm sorry. I've interrupted. Where were

21

we again?' Ed smiles at her and Cathy visibly softens as if she's been caught in a sudden shaft of soft, warm light.

'Jess was just telling us all about her hopes for motherhood – and how very excited she is.'

Liz

Friday 19 January, 2018, 11.35 p.m.

Three

Jess looks afraid. Hospitals put her on edge, I understand that: it's hardly surprising given her traumatic experience giving birth to Betsey. But she looks more than wary: she seems acutely scared.

'How long has she been like this?' I ask, my tone soft and conversational, as if my examining a friend's child is a perfectly normal scenario.

'On and off all evening. She usually settles easily, but she didn't tonight.'

'Has she slept at all?'

'A little. She woke at nine, crying . . . and she was still unsettled when Ed checked on her, a little later . . .'

'And that's when she was sick?'

'Yes.'

'Just the once?'

There is the slightest hesitation. Half a second but it's enough for me to notice. 'Yes. Just the once,' she says.

I look at her closely. Her smile is forced: not an expression I've ever seen her make but then this is an unprecedented situation. 'Is that something that's happened before? Is she a sickly baby in general?'

'No.' Jess shakes her head. 'I know you haven't seen that much of her but she's not a baby who throws up a lot. She can be grizzly and bad-tempered, particularly when she's teething, but I can't understand why she would be like this.'

I shrug off the hint of reproach – I don't know this baby like I know her other children; work this year's been partic- ularly busy – and slip a thermometer under Betsey's armpit.

'I'm just going to have a look at her while we carry on talking,' I explain. 'Can you put your arm up for me, Betsey?' She bleats, her bottom lip quivering as she looks to Jess for reassurance.

'It's all right, darling. It's Mummy's friend, Liz.' Jess removes her hand from Betsey's to make it easier for me, but I sense her reluctance. She's never liked anyone else handling her children, not even when Kit and Rosa were learning to walk and I'd automatically pick up her boy if he fell near- est to me.

I remove the thermometer.

'Her temperature's normal. Has she had any pain relief?'

'Ed gave her some Calpol after she threw up.'

'When was that?'

'Just after ten. Before we came in.'

'And you hadn't given her any before then?'

'No ... Perhaps I should have but, well, you know how I feel about giving them drugs ...'

Jess is suspicious of any medicine. It's one of the things we've clashed about. Betsey hasn't had her MMR, Jess erroneously believing that the vaccine is linked to autism, and I was both incredulous and angry when she told me about this. It partly accounts for our recent distance: I can't bear the fact she's relying on the 'herd' effect: other people's children being vaccinated to protect her own. But I can't be irritated now. I've more immediate concerns.

'Because I know you and Betsey I'm going to call my colleague, Ronan, in while I examine her properly, OK? There's nothing to worry about. It's hospital protocol. Then I'm going to look at your tummy, Betsey.' I speak in my soft, no-nonsense voice to the baby, who is whimpering raggedly, a bead of spittle on her lips.

'Ronan?' I pull back the curtain and half-duck out. The junior doctor looks terrified, either of making a mistake or of me. 'Could you join us?' He slides into the cubicle beside me, his long, gangling limbs folding into the space.

'I'm just examining Betsey's chest,' I explain to both of them, as I unbutton her Babygro. There's no rash on her torso. No indication of meningitis. But my immediate relief is temporary. Betsey is grizzling properly, now, and her cry intensifies as my fingers caress the crown of her head. She flinches. A head injury? It's something I'm automatically concerned about. I stop and part her mass of dark hair.

'Did you know there's a slight swelling at the back of her head?'

It's not an obvious bump but I can feel a slight bogginess obscured by Betsey's damp, dark curls. I watch Jess closely.

'Umm, no I didn't.'

I'm surprised. It feels like rolling your fingers over a waterbed. Was she really so distracted she didn't notice when she'd placed Betsey in her car seat, or transferred her to her buggy? Surely she would have felt it, or Betsey would have cried out, just as she did when I tried to examine her now?

But Jess looks at me blankly. Her face is closed as if she's blocked off her emotions. A chill of unease creeps up my spine.

'Is she crawling?' I ask.

'She's just started – and pulling herself up.'

'It looks as if she's knocked it . . .'

My friend looks – there's no other word for it – *shifty*.

'Oh,' she says, her tone bright and high.

And then she clears her throat as if she's suddenly thought of something she should have mentioned at the start. 'Look. She did bash it earlier.'

'She bashed it earlier? Oh, Jess, why didn't you mention it? This could explain the sickness. When did this happen?' Relief flows through me, in a sudden flood. Jess – always so perfectionist when it comes to parenting – will have feared being judged. But there's no need for that because it sounds as if there's a perfectly innocent explanation, after all.

'It was around four o'clock,' she begins. 'Just after we'd

26

got back from picking up Frankie. She was crawling in the kitchen and she slipped and hit her head.'

'So how did she fall, exactly?' I perch on the side of the bed, the paper towel puckering under my bottom. *I'm listening and I've all the time in the world*, my posture says. I haven't, of course – I'm concerned that we might need to scan Betsey, but I need to take a comprehensive history first.

'I was getting Frankie a snack,' Jess says. Her voice is constricted, as if she's about to cry. 'Betsey was crawling around. The floor was clean but slippery for some reason. I wasn't really concentrating; I was getting things ready for the kids' tea. And then I heard a sort of gentle thud, and Betsey was lying on the floor, pulling the kind of face she does when she's wondering whether or not to cry.'

She pauses. It's a perfectly adequate explanation and yet she watches me as if to check she's given the right answer.

'I just turned my back for a moment. I can't be watching her every second!' She is suddenly strident in her self-defence.

'It's all right. I know what a good mum you are. It's just – it's quite a bang: not something that would happen from crawling and falling. I'm wondering whether she hit anything when she fell? If she could have struck anything?'

'I don't know. I assumed she just hit her head on the floor but she was right by the fridge ... I suppose she could have pulled herself up on the edge of it and hit her head on that as she fell ...'

'Yes, that's possible.'

I look at the back of her head again. I don't like this. I don't like it all. It's Jess's evasiveness and defensiveness that bothers me. Why is she behaving like this? As if this accident is an afterthought? As if there's something that she needs to hide?

'I'm just going to check the rest of her, but there's absolutely nothing to worry about: it's standard practice,' I say, and I peel away the arms and legs of Betsey's Babygro, scrutinising her body thoroughly. There's no sign of bruising: no bluish hues; no greens or yellows; no redness either. Not a single indication that she has been harmed. Slowly, methodically, I ease off her heavy nappy and lift up her legs. Her bottom has an angry pimpling of nappy rash, a smear of Sudocrem, but – thank God – there's nothing sinister around her vagina or anus.

'What are you doing? Betsey hasn't been *interfered* with!'

'We just check babies all over. It's completely routine,' I try to reassure her.

'My God! You think she's been *molested*!'

'No. No, I don't at all. There's a little nappy rash but there's nothing to worry about. She's absolutely fine.'

She is momentarily relieved.

'And she will be OK, won't she?'

I pause.

'With any head injury we have to be careful and so I'd like to run a couple of tests.'

'What tests?'

'Blood tests, and probably a scan to check if her skull's been damaged.'

'That's really necessary?'

'I think so, and I'd like to keep her in a little longer, just in case she's sick again.'

She hasn't anticipated any of this. She glances at her baby, then ducks her head and starts fiddling with her rings. Is she embarrassed? Perhaps if I tread carefully she'll tell me what's wrong.

'I know you, Jess. You're protective. Perhaps even a little overprotective – is that fair?'

She nods.

'But you left it a while before bringing her in, which seems *uncharacteristic* . . . I suppose I'm wondering why you didn't think to bring her in before?'

Fiddle, fiddle with her rings.

'I suppose I didn't think it was that serious,' she says at last. 'You know what toddlers are like. Kit and Frankie have had worse bangs – so have Sam and Rosa, haven't they? They fall over all the time when they're that age. It didn't seem that bad compared to knocks the boys had when they were starting to crawl. There wasn't a bump. I didn't think there was a problem. It was only when she started to be sick that we thought we should bring her in.'

'That makes sense,' I say, and of course it does, but I remain uneasy as Ronan begins to take Betsey's blood and I arrange for her to be admitted to the ward.

Because when any parent presents with a child with an

injury, I'm trained to be alert to the possibility that it may not be accidental. That the parent may have harmed their child. Of course I don't want to think this of my friend. I've trusted her with my own children, and I know how she parents; but still, I'm conditioned to ask that question, and it nudges at me, at the back of my mind.

And so I find myself running through my checklist: am I happy with the interaction between parent and child; was there a delay in presentation; is the parent overly defensive or strangely unconcerned? Do I suspect them of lying? Most importantly: does the mechanism – the way in which the accident is said to have happened – match the injury? Does the story fit?

I stand by the desk, waiting for the paeds team to pick up the phone and I feel troubled. Why was Jess so shifty when I pointed out the trauma to the back of the head? Why did she hesitate when I asked if Betsey had only thrown up the once? And why – given how conscientious she is about all aspects of parenting – did she wait six hours to bring in her baby, and only then when Ed suggested it?

I twist the lead of the phone around my fingers, creating welts. With any other parent these would be clear red flags signalling that we should be concerned, but this is someone I know well. A long-term friend. The woman who looked after Rosa when she and Kit had chickenpox and the hospital nursery still deemed her infectious; the friend who searched for obsolete Lego for Sam's birthday then insisted I give it to him; the mother who loves her children beyond all else; who's ferocious in her defence of Frankie, once accusing Mel of demonising him when she suggested he'd been too rough with her son Connor, turning on her with a flash of surprising anger; the mother who is so proud of sporty, good-natured Kit.

I know all this as deeply, as instinctively as I know that Nick won't be unfaithful. I'm almost completely sure of it, that is to say.

And yet here I am, admitting her daughter for a suspected skull fracture and perturbed by her behaviour.

Am I seriously thinking the very worst of Jess?

LIZ

Saturday 20 January, 12.15 a.m.

Four

Betsey has been admitted and is now lying in a bed by the window, the sides up to prevent her falling. An infant in a protective cage.

Jess has left the ward to ring Ed. Her daughter's been crying for her, though: 'Mum-mum' the only words she's uttered. Kath, the nurse in charge of this bay, administers some liquid ibuprofen, the drug and perhaps her gentle reassurance easing her pain.

I need to ring my boss. A head injury in an infant is something my consultant will want to know about, even though he'll hate me for waking him to discuss it. At sixty-two, Neil Cockerill's had enough of the NHS; has no desire to have to come into hospital in the early hours of the morning, or to have his sleep broken by a registrar who should be able to stand on her own two feet. You could argue that's fair enough: he's dedicated forty years of his life to this job; has had his fill of departmental politics, not to mention the bureaucratic demands of a government hell-bent on raising expectations beyond what their money can buy. He's tired, too, of the relentless grind that comes with looking after sick, sometimes dying children. I understand, and I could accept his hands-off attitude if I rated him as a colleague. But I don't – and the feeling is mutual: unfortunately, he doesn't rate me.

I first came across Neil when I was twenty-five and a very junior doctor, just a year into the job, and doing my obligatory six months in this hospital's A&E. I heard him before I was introduced: a tall, patrician man with thick, swept-back hair (he was in his late forties by then and this was his vanity) bellowing across the department at his reg.

'In my day, registrars ran the show – they didn't scamper to their consultants at every opportunity!' he blazed as he stormed out of paediatric A&E and all the parents in the waiting room craned their necks to see who was so furious. 'JFDI!' he'd added. Justin, the registrar who'd been mauled, was puce with embarrassment.

JFDI? *Just fucking do it.*

My perception didn't improve when I came back to the hospital and worked for Neil, three years later. I'd had the temerity to get pregnant and two months of my maternity leave coincided with the end of my attachment with him. The trust didn't replace me, which doubled his workload in clinics and on the wards, and even when I returned to work, he thought me unreliable and not a team player. It didn't help that Rosa had glue ear when she was tiny and so I was forever being called to the hospital nursery, where she spent each day from 8 a.m. to 6 p.m.

Perhaps if Neil had liked me he'd have been more tolerant but he didn't understand me. I wasn't like the nurses who flirted with him or indulged him; and I wasn't like him: a self-confident man from a dynasty of doctors, with a broad cultural hinterland and the ability to converse about cricket and fine wine. I was a nervous young woman from a working-class background who had made his life more complicated and his workload more onerous by becoming a mother.

And he resented this. There was no reason for him to empathise with me because he had never experienced the tug between work and parenthood. His wife stopped nursing when she had their first son and so never had to walk that tightrope nor ask him to make compromises in his career. *I want a wife*, I think, when I note his crisply ironed shirt; when he mentions a holiday – something Rosie's organised in Italy, he's not quite sure where, that's her domain, he just pays for it (this said with the self-indulgent chuckle of a man who bought his west London home thirty years ago and has paid off the mortgage). *I want a wife*, I think, when, at the end of a long shift, I know he's returning to a freshly cooked meal. *I want a wife*, whenever the fact that I am a mother, and the subsequent occasional rota swap to accommodate a parents' evening, prompts him to wrinkle his nose as though he smells something noxious. *This is real life with all its messy demands*, I want to tell him. But of course I don't because I don't want to rock the boat; I need a good reference; and I need a consultant's post, preferably his when he reaches retirement in a couple of years.

More than anything, though, I want to impress him. He's never forgotten a very early mistake I made: the sort of bad call that follows you round in this profession. I desperately want him to think I'm good at my job.

But this phone call – required because no one wants to give a ten-month-old a dose of radiation unnecessarily – will do nothing to endear me.

'Cockerill,' he growls, when I finally steel myself to dial his number.

'Dr Cockerill.' I lower my voice, intensely deferential. 'I'm sorry to disturb you this late at night.'

'It's morning now.' His voice bristles with bad temper. 'It's nearly half past midnight. *Christ*, I was asleep.'

'I'm so sorry' – I keep my voice low and calm – 'but I wanted your advice. I've admitted a ten-month-old with bruising and a suspected skull fracture to the back of her head so I thought we should scan her to see what's going on.'

'Mmm.' His irascibility hums down the line. He asks if there is any sign of a rare fracture to the base of the skull – black eyes; bleeding from the nose and ears – or of a leakage of cerebral spinal fluid, and we discuss her GCS rating, a neurological measure of how conscious she is.

'Anything else we should be concerned about?' A pause, pregnant with irritation, and I imagine his knees jiggling as they do when he's frustrated in a departmental meeting: energy pulsing through his legs.

'She has vomited,' I say. 'Mum says just the once.'

'And did she say how it happened?'

'She didn't see it – she had her back turned – but the baby was crawling and either slipped, or fell after pulling herself up on the side of the fridge.'

'It would be quite some fall from that low height to create a skull fracture with, what, some bogginess?'

'Yes.' I need to be honest. 'There's something else. Mum didn't notice the trauma, or mention she'd fallen, until I pointed it out to her.' The words rush from me as if they will sound less incriminating said at speed.

'And you've put a call in to social services?'

'No I haven't. Not yet.'

'You don't think it's a safeguarding issue?'

'No. I know the mum. Don't worry: I won't treat the baby once you're in, and Ronan was present at all times, but she's a good mother. I just can't imagine that she would harm her child.'

His disbelief is clear from his too-long silence.

'And she came in immediately?'

'No. It happened around four … She came in at some point after ten.'

Another pause, steeped in suspicion.

'I don't like the sound of this, Elizabeth.' No one calls me Elizabeth, except Neil when he's angry. 'I don't like the sound of this at all. A delay of six hours in bringing the baby

in; Mum's failure to notice a trauma to her head; a mechanism – falling from crawling – that doesn't necessarily fit
with the injury, and a skull fracture to the back of the head?
You do realise what that could indicate?'

I remain silent. Of course I bloody well know what this
indicates.

A fracture to the back of the head is commensurate with a
child being slammed down hard on a changing table.

'She should be scanned, and I'll take over at eight.'

The radiology pictures are available shortly after Betsey is
wheeled down for her scan.

They seem unequivocal. A depressed fracture to the back
of her skull, some bruising, and a subdural haematoma: a
pool of blood accumulating beneath the skull and pushing
inwards, compressing the brain.

I so wanted this not to be the case. For there to be no
break and the bruising to be superficial. For Betsey to be
discharged as soon as possible, and for neither she nor Jess to
have to go through this.

But now this scan, viewed through a series of filters on
the computer, confirms this is a head injury and makes the
situation far more serious. I flick back to the bone filter.
Indisputable: a textbook case. Instead of the nice, curved
white line of the skull, there are two black cracks, and a cres-
cent of white, a segment of bone, which has slipped from the
skull like a jagged piece of a jigsaw dislodged from its space.

I switch filters to the one that lets me assess any damage

to the soft tissue and shows whether there's bleeding inside or outside the brain. The white cracks fade out of focus as I assess the patches of grey. Again, it's incontrovertible: a grey oval blob, one centimetre across, is pushing outside the surface of the brain. I phone the radiologist on call just to check there's nothing I'm missing and he talks me through his report as we assess the scan together. There's no anodyne explanation. It's all as the pictures suggest.

I feel very cold and simultaneously conscious that I need to remain calm and professional: to not be swayed by the emotions provoked by this. We have this scan showing an unequivocal skull fracture and we have Jess's odd, evasive behaviour but that doesn't mean we have to think the worst of her, does it?

Because most skull fractures are caused by accidents, and though I suspect Jess is lying, there'll be a reason she has done so and an innocent explanation for all of this. But there's only a tiny window in which I can help, before Neil sweeps in and claims Betsey as his patient.

If there's something Jess needs to tell me, she must do it now.

Jess is waiting in Betsey's bay, and sits straight up as I walk towards her. She's been crying. A silt of mascara clings to her bottom lashes. 'Is she OK?'

'The CT scan showed what we thought: that Betsey has a skull fracture. There's no long-term damage but obviously it's worrying.'

'Oh my God,' she whispers. 'Oh my God, oh my *God.*' She bends over as if to retch. The vertebrae at the top of her back form a string of small, tender bumps. I want to hold her close to me, just as she held me in those first awful months of motherhood, when I couldn't cope with Rosa's inability to sleep. Instead, I crouch down next to her, as she might with her children, and look her straight in the face.

'Jess,' I say. 'Look. There's no easy way to say this but when a child sustains a head injury like this it raises questions, and we have to think about whether this was an accident or whether it could have happened some other way.'

'I don't understand.' She looks at me blankly.

'The thing is, it's quite unusual to have an injury like this caused by this mechanism,' I plough on, reverting in my embarrassment to doctorese.

'This mechanism?'

'I'm sorry. It's unusual for this injury to be caused like this. Are you sure that nothing else happened? That nothing was different from how you described? I know it's hard to think about but could someone have hurt Betsey?' I pause – and she looks stunned that I could suggest it. I touch her on the forearm, and try one last time: 'Or is there anything else you want to tell me?'

And this is it, her chance to open up. To say: *Look – I didn't want to say but she was crawling up the stairs and she tumbled when I wasn't watching, when I wasn't focused, when I was distracted by the boys arguing.* Or, quite simply: *Oh, Liz, I'm so embarrassed but she rolled off the bed.*

And, then I would reassure her; would say: *Don't worry. You know you shouldn't leave her even for a moment at this age, but we all know that accidents happen. We know it's just an accident. But, perhaps this is a wake-up call, a reminder that it can happen, even to a mother who's already had three kids.*

But she doesn't say any of this. She just looks at me, her wide, sensual mouth in a straight line, her defensiveness swapped for a weird blankness as if her usual emotions have shut down.

She plays with her rings, twisting them round and round the third finger of her right hand, and I realise that her look of blankness is really an expression of denial, motivated by fear. It's the same look she had when I tried to raise the issue of Frankie's hyperactivity and whether he should be assessed for a possible diagnosis of ADHD. A look that says she has absolutely no intention of taking on board what I'm saying.

Her mouth twitches.

'No, there's not,' she says.

LIZ

Saturday 20 January, 8.30 a.m.

Five

Neil is spoiling for a fight.

I can tell from the way in which he comes into the room where we hold the handover meeting: all bristling energy and brisk movements

'So – Betsey Curtis,' he says, flinging himself into his chair.

Fousia, the registrar who's taking over my on-call, and Rupert, the most junior member of the team, look at me enquiringly and I fill them in on Betsey's history, detailing the results of the scan, my discussion with the radiologist, and my conversations with Jess.

'And you've put in that call to social services?' Neil says, his tone light as if he's mentioning this in passing because of course I'll have done so.

'Um, no. I haven't.'

'You haven't?' He raises an eyebrow. He has particularly

bushy eyebrows, like a horned owl's, and while this might sound grandfatherly, they just make him seem more formidable than ever.

'I wanted to discuss it further. I'm still not convinced there's a safeguarding issue here.'

He leans back in his chair and rolls his Cross pen in and over his fingers. Most of us use biros: Neil has this glossy black fountain pen which he fiddles with whenever he's thinking or irritated, his two regular states of mind. Over and over it goes now. It's both annoying and strangely mesmerising.

'So let's get this straight . . .' His voice drips sarcasm. 'Mum delays bringing baby in; she claims *not to have seen* the trauma to the back of the head; her explanation for how it happened doesn't necessarily fit – and yet you don't think it's a safeguarding issue?'

Put like this, my judgement sounds skewed. But Neil's determination to think the worst of Jess makes me want to defend her. If medicine's a science, it's also an art: one in which personal judgement and intuition play a part in determining how you act. And I've known Jess for a decade. Surely I would have an inkling if I thought she might harm her own child?

'I hope you're not letting your personal feelings for your friend get in the way of your professional responsibilities?'

'No, of course not.'

And yet that's precisely what I am doing.

'I have to say I'm concerned about your judgement here,' my consultant says. A pause. 'It's not the first time, is it?'

At that moment I think I might actually hate him. That he would do this to me in front of my colleagues is mortifying. Rupert is sniggering – the nervous laugh of a new boy trying to ingratiate himself with the boss – and even Fousia looks embarrassed. She shoots me a look of sympathy that I fail to acknowledge, wary of appearing weak in front of Neil.

'I have never made an error of judgement over safeguarding,' I manage to say.

'Not over safeguarding,' he concedes. 'But none of us are infallible. We all make mistakes and your judgement's been off before.'

And here it is. That mistake I made when I was a very junior doctor in that first A&E job, just twelve months after finishing medical school. A potentially fatal error that he can use as collateral and that even now is proving hard to shake off.

The meningitis rash is harder to detect on darker skin and I didn't spot it on eighteen-month-old Kyle Jenkins, misdiagnosing the markings on the soles of his feet and his hands as a common virus: hand, foot and mouth disease. With the memory of Neil's JFDI still fresh in my mind, I didn't want to bother him and was about to discharge Kyle when Kate, one of the senior paediatric nurses, recognised the rash for what it was and called Neil herself. Being saved by a nurse is something that's always remembered. An indelible black

43

mark. But I was just relieved Kate spotted my mistake in time. And I learned *never* to put my fear of being humiliated before my concerns about a patient again.

'I acknowledge I made a terrible mistake then but I think my judgement has been sound ever since.'

He raises one of those intimidating eyebrows and glances at the others as if to shore up his argument. Rupert simpers; Fousia looks steadfastly down at her lap.

'If you're not being swayed by personal loyalty, I can't for the life of me see why you don't believe this merits investigation. I'd argue it's *negligent* not to do so. Let's not forget to whom we owe a duty of care. Referring this on doesn't mean we think someone fractured this baby's skull. All we're saying is that we think there's something that needs investigating.'

And he's right; much as I hate to admit it, of course he's right. Putting in that call doesn't mean we're blaming Jess – just that red flags are fluttering fiercely. And, deep down, I can't be one hundred per cent certain that no one hurt this child. I can't imagine it was Jess or Ed – but parents can do terrible things in a moment of frustration, as I know from my own mother. Is it completely inconceivable that something like that happened here?

I rub my eyes. My mind tilts with tiredness, those four consecutive night shifts weighing down on me so that my brain feels smudged.

'All right,' I say, swallowing down a lump that feels like a physical manifestation of my betrayal. I know that if I don't

Neil will put in that call to social services anyway. But, in his not-so-subtle power play, he wants consensus. This is a decision that will impact dramatically on this family. If we all shoulder the responsibility, it will feel a little easier.

'All right,' I repeat, looking at Neil, and hating myself for doing this. 'I'll make the call.'

JESS

Saturday 20 January, 9 a.m.

Six

'Would you like some tea, love?'

A healthcare assistant pushing a trolley with a vast metal pot hovers near Jess.

'Toast?' She gestures to pieces of dried white cardboard-like bread and sachets of margarine and Marmite.

'Tea, thank you.' Jess takes a cup, teak in colour, and puts it by the side of Betsey's bed.

The tea and toast are reassuringly ordinary in this world where nothing feels normal. Not the wires and buttons, or the rest of the hospital paraphernalia: the oxygen canisters and drips. Not the children, either. Very old people should be in hospital, or pregnant women – or, occasionally, as she knows herself, postnatal mothers. Not children. That subverts the natural order of things.

She hates hospitals. That was part of the reason she resisted bringing in Betsey. The stench, the institutionalism, the uncertainty, the knowledge that the place reverberates with sickness – and she can sense bacteria and viruses multiplying a thousand-fold each second, burgeoning through the air. When she rang Ed, she had to stop at each hand hygiene station to slather antibacterial gel in between her fingers. An elderly man was slumped on a plastic chair by a pump, the sweet stench of urine emanating from him, and she imagined his germs rising up towards her. And this was just part of the problem. Beyond the swing doors, in the unknown world of the operating theatres, she knows there is anarchy: blood spewing, hearts stopping, bowels and stomachs emptying in a chaotic mess of bodily fluids. So different to the calm and order required by a hospital. So different to everything she craves.

She reaches into her bag for some more gel; welcomes the stinging. This acute fear of hospitals began ten years ago, when she had Kit. 'Take Dettol wipes,' Liz had told her, but with no knowledge of the shock and awe of childbirth, of the sheer bloody mess of it, she hadn't seen the need. The hospital was a flagship one: gleaming, state of the art, with an atrium and two coffee chains; and a prime minister's son among its recent deliveries. She had been unprepared for another woman's blood studding the shower floor. Unprepared, too, for the sound of other women in the late throes of labour: guttural, animalistic noises she'd not been warned about in those antenatal classes. She had thought she would give birth with lavender candles burning and the slow movement of Bach's Double Violin Concerto in the background, the strings lifting her to a birthing climax. How incredibly naive.

In the end, Kit's was a textbook delivery: apt for her easy, uncomplicated eldest. And so she insisted on having Frankie at home. It was an ideal birth. She had the soft lighting, the music playing, and Ed, who had vigorously opposed a home birth, was so proud, so supportive as this slight, slender baby – a different child entirely from his placid, nine-pound brother – slithered out of her. She felt . . . well, she felt as if she had got it right for once.

She had wanted to have Betsey at home, too. But then things started to go wrong: the baby was bigger than anticipated, Jess panicked, was blue-lit to St Joseph's, the head got stuck and they had to cut her and use forceps; were brutal – or so it felt at the time. Then things grew worse. A rush of people in the room, an urgency once they realised Betsey's shoulders were held fast. The focus on the registrar's face as he rummaged inside her so aggressively she felt violated. The pain. The sheer, *burning* pain.

They had between three and five minutes to get Betsey out, she later learned. It's a fact she can't forget. Other aspects she can't remember and had to be told later: having a massive haemorrhage tends to distract you, to muddle your mind. She only knows that as soon as she could be discharged, after a hefty blood transfusion, she was frantic to get out of there.

And now she is back. In this ward filled with over-used

air and slumbering children. Sitting by her baby, who she dare not leave in case her condition gets worse. Disorientated and exhausted, her mouth tastes metallic and her calves tingle. Gingerly, she flexes her ankles and pushes down to ease out the cramp.

A tall, grey-haired man is tramping down the ward towards her.

'Dr Neil Cockerill, paediatric consultant,' he says, and holds out his hand. She stands and takes it uneasily. 'I'll be taking over Betsey's care, since I understand you and Dr Trenchard are friends?'

She nods. Liz has distanced herself these last few hours. It's the nurses who have roused Betsey, every hour, and Jess isn't stupid. Her friend might be preoccupied – in work mode – but still, she would hardly say she seemed particularly warm.

'As I'm sure you're aware, it's not good practice to treat patients we know.' Dr Cockerill is still talking. 'We'll arrange for Betsey to be scanned to check for any retinal haemorrhage, and for a possible skeletal survey. These are all standard tests in a situation like this.' He smiles, his eyebrows knitting together. 'Now, all OK?'

She nods. Is he asking for her consent or just checking she understands? His words blur, the medical terminology and the supposedly familiar phrases that string them together all meaningless. Betsey being here, and this torrent of information, feels unreal.

His next question makes absolutely no sense at all.

'I'm sorry,' she says, and her scalp prickles with apprehension. 'I didn't quite catch that. Please could you repeat it?'

'I need to ask if there has ever been any social services involvement with your family at all?'

She is blindsided; her chest tight; her mind befuddled as if she's been knocked over by a colossal wave and all she can hear is the thud and rush of water.

'No. No, of course not,' she manages eventually.

He gives a quick, business-like smile as if he doesn't believe her.

'Betsey has a skull fracture and we are concerned about how this might have happened,' he says.

She doesn't react.

When he continues, his tone is soft, his speech slow. 'I'm sorry, Mrs Curtis, but we have to look at the possibility someone harmed your little girl.'

Somehow she gathers that she will need to be seen by a police officer. 'It's standard practice when we're looking into this. They need to check what happened,' says Dr Cockerill. He or Liz must have contacted the police because by ten o'clock, two officers have appeared.

They're detective constables. One male, one female. Neither seems threatening. They're almost mundane. And yet the sight of them, with their innate authority and their intention of seeing right through her until they get to the heart of the matter, makes her crumple like a marionette whose strings have been dropped abruptly, and she finds she is fumbling towards a chair.

'Jess? May I call you that? Jess? Are you OK?' The female detective lowers her into it, watching her intently. Somehow, through the fog of her anxiety, she nods her head.

'I'm DC Cat Rustin and this is my colleague, DC Steve Farron.' The officer pauses. 'We need to ask you a few questions about what happened yesterday afternoon to Betsey. Is that all right?'

Jess nods again then starts to shake as they take her to a side room. A voice singsongs in her head, like a child desperate for attention – *you're a bad, bad mother* – and she tries to shove it away.

'I'm wearing a Body Worn camera on my chest,' DC Rustin says. Her hair's parted severely in the middle and hangs to her shoulders; she wears no make-up; looks competent, officious. 'It will record our interview, so that there's no dispute about what's happened if we ever need to refer to this.'

If you ever need to refer to it as evidence – that's what she wants to say.

Her colleague, DC Farron, clears his throat. Tall and slim, with hair the colour of weak Earl Grey and a spray of sandy freckles across the bridge of his nose, he asks if she would like a glass of water. His voice is soft with a faint West Country burr and, as he places the plastic cup in front of her, he seems quietly courteous. Perhaps he will treat her more gently, she thinks.

'If we can go back to the beginning: when Betsey sustained her injury,' DC Rustin begins, and Jess tries to reorder her thoughts, to think back to her narrative.

'I was making a smoothie. She was crawling around on the floor. She must have slipped or maybe she tried to pull herself up on the fridge and fell ...' Is that what she told Liz? Tiredness turns her thoughts sluggish but DC Rustin is watching, and her directness forces her to focus. 'I'm sorry. I had my back turned so I can't say exactly.'

'Where was she when you found her: in what position?'

'Um ...'

'Take your time,' DC Farron intervenes.

'I think she was raising herself up on her front ... hence my thinking she was crawling and slipped forwards.'

DC Rustin does not let her gaze shift. 'And yet the skull fracture is to the back of her head?'

The air is heavy with suspicion. Jess can taste it: earthy, ferric. Her skin goosefleshes, the fine hairs on her arm standing on end.

'I ... yes ... You're quite right. I was confusing it with her slipping forwards, the day before. She was on her back.' The bruising was to the *back* of Betsey's head. She knows that. She mustn't forget it. 'She was lying on her back,' she says, more confident this time.

'And what made you turn to see her?'

'Well, there was a thud and she started crying. I *was* in the same room with her: I'd just turned my back for a minute while I was cooking. I picked her up immediately ...'

Never over-explain, Ed once told her, after she was stopped for speeding and had three points added to her licence. And yet she can't help it. Her explanation floods out, casting doubt on what she previously said.

DC Rustin leans back and she can feel the waves of disbelief rolling off her: a gentle lapping at first, but building in intensity.

'So we know that she banged the *back* of her head . . .'

'Yes.'

'And yet you didn't mention this when you came into A&E and saw the first doctor, Dr O'Neill, nor when you were seen by Dr Trenchard?'

'No.'

'Why was that?'

'I . . . I guess I didn't think it was important. I didn't think it was *connected*.' She weighs each word like ingredients for a recipe she must get right.

A pause. DC Rustin glances down briefly then looks straight back at her, her eyes a dull, dishwater grey.

'And you didn't notice that the back of her head was tender: that it felt – I think Dr Trenchard describes it as squishy or boggy?'

'No, I didn't,' she says.

Another few seconds of silence while DC Rustin assesses her, and heat threads up Jess's neck.

'Presumably you would have cradled Betsey's head when you got her into the car seat, or held her in the hospital?'

'Yes.'

'But even then you didn't notice this tenderness?'

'No, I didn't, no.' Her voice swoops and catches, and she knows she sounds flaky. 'I was in such a rush to get here.'

'You were in a rush to get here, and yet you left it six hours I think to bring her in?'

'Yes.'

A pause during which DC Rustin does not let her gaze shift.

'I think earlier you said Betsey may have pulled herself up on the fridge and then fallen?'

'Yes.'

'But you didn't see her do that either?'

'No.'

A pause.

'So why did you say it?'

'I just . . .'

DC Rustin's tone has segued from quizzical to confrontational and Jess hears herself faltering.

'I just . . . I suppose it was an option. She's started to pull herself up quite a lot, recently, and I thought that if she'd done so that might account for the thud. If she'd fallen from standing, she'd have fallen more heavily. That's what usually happens because there's further to fall.'

'So this has happened before?'

Jess gives a short laugh, harsh and off-key. It sounds mad, even to her. 'Well, yes. I mean, of course it's happened before. All babies fall over when they're pulling themselves up or crawling.' She forces herself to smile. 'I have three

children and they do fall over, they *do* slip and hurt them-
selves. They're more robust than you might think.'

DC Rustin smiles encouragingly. Perhaps they'll be sat-
isfied now. But no, the questions keep coming, and with
each one, the detectives' scorn increases. *A mother who doesn't*
watch her baby. Who can't even accurately describe how she found
her. Think, *for God's sake, think.*

'Please,' she appeals to DC Farron, and she is suddenly
engulfed by a fresh fear. She has no idea what is happening
to Betsey or if her injury has got worse. 'Please. Could I find
out what's happening to my baby? I just want to see how
she is . . .'

DC Farron's young face softens. Perhaps saying that was
canny, though the request was instinctive.

But DC Rustin is in no rush. She doesn't like Jess: that's
pretty evident, and it feels as if she is relishing this power she
has over her.

'In a minute. We just need to clarify a further couple
of things.'

ED

Saturday 20 January, 3 p.m.

Seven

The police officers move swiftly and efficiently, the kitchen no longer the hub of Ed's home but an area that must be photographed. He swallows, remembering a recent TV drama. They're behaving as if it's a crime scene.

Jess has gone to bed. He'd insisted. Had told her quite firmly that she was no help to him or the children, if she continued to watch the detectives with such fear, her desperation to be rid of them plastered across her face.

He didn't add that she risked incriminating herself. But he felt it acutely. She's been unpredictable, lately. Overemotional. Increasingly prone to becoming upset at the slightest thing. It hadn't occurred to him that she wasn't managing to hold things together, until very recently.

He turns his back on the scenes of crime officer. He can't face watching him; feels exposed as if both he and the detectives view him with suspicion. All this could have been prevented if he'd taken Betsey to the hospital himself. This police interest must have been caused by some inaccuracy, some glitch in Jess's explanation, and he would have smoothed away any wrinkle and stopped things progressing this far. She has never liked explaining herself. Perhaps she'd not been sufficiently clear in her explanation, not understood the magnitude of what was going on?

He risks glancing at the scenes of crime officer, conscious that any reaction might be noted, then runs a glass of water, welcoming the cool liquid coating his dry lips. He should have gone in. *He* was the one who noticed Betsey's distress. The way she'd turned from him, twisting her neck, flinching from his touch; her teariness when she'd seen him – because she was usually so sunny, at least with him, a bone of contention with Jess. And then there was the vomit, the smell of which, he realises now, had partly drawn him into the nursery.

He feels ill at the memory. He'd never found any of his children like that before. A trail of sick spooling from her mouth and pooling on the cot mattress; her eyes gleaming with tears. Thank God he had checked on her. He wouldn't normally have after a night out and, though he was home by ten, it had felt like a heavy session – a few beers drunk fast at the end of an exhausting week in a desire to delay facing Jess, and perhaps try to kid himself he wasn't just a parent and the breadwinner; to pretend he was still the right side of forty.

It was Jess's job to deal with the kids but she was in bed

for some reason and he could hear Betsey crying. A sporadic whimper, more like a bleating lamb. He wasn't really into babies. Far preferred children when they were properly mobile and you could kick a ball around with them – Kit was the perfect age; even Frankie, who could be hard work, had his moments – but still, this insistent demand for attention had wrenched at his heart strings. *Humans are clever,* he thought, as he pushed open the door to the nursery, which was closed for some reason. This cry was of just the right pitch and timbre to ensure a baby survived.

'What's up, Bets?' He had crept into her room, less steady than usual, and peered into her cot, anticipating an end to the crying and a gummy smile. But she didn't give her usual response and, instead, her big blue eyes filled with tears. Her bottom lip wobbled and a cry – more half-hearted now that she'd caught his attention, but still anguished – burst out. He snatched her up as the source of the smell hit him and he finally registered the reason for her distress.

He hadn't taken her to the hospital because he clearly wasn't sober and he knew that he must reek of alcohol. But it was also because on some level he assumed that Betsey would want her mum. The children were very much Jess's domain. That was one drawback of having a baby at forty-two: a baby he hardly knew; that he'd never even bathed, for God's sake. As his career had become more demanding, so the family had run along increasingly traditional gender lines. His job was to bring in the money; Jess's, the children and home.

But now this has happened. A scenes of crime officer is photographing the corner of the fridge for any sign of a baby banging against it and recording the state of the floor: unnaturally shiny, as if cleaned with some sort of slippery spray. He will have to be interviewed, DC Rustin, the rather dry, unsmiling officer, has said: she and a DC Farron will do that; will video it, too, he discovers later, and then require a written witness statement. And she, and a social worker, a Lucy Stone, will have to talk to Frankie and Kit.

He scrubs at his face, as if to erase the tension of the last twelve hours. A throbbing headache clamps his temples and he is aware of his lack of sleep: three hours at most, something he can cope with if work demands it but here there's no deadline, no sense that this is finite and eventually he'll be able to relax. He needs to get a grip. This nagging anxiety isn't something he – usually so calm, so ordered and in control – has previously experienced. But then he has never had police officers in his home before.

All he wants to do is to go and see Betsey. His last memory is of her with her face scrunched up and tearful, her breath sour, her little body twisting from him; resisting all attempts to be comforted and held. He hadn't noticed that there was a bump to the back of her head. Had been too preoccupied with trying to get the Grobag and Babygro off her and with trying, ineptly, to clean her up. He wants to reassure himself that Betsey is as he always thinks of her: frequently beaming, always sunny, her face breaking into a smile when she sees him. *Christ.* He needs to get real: she's in hospital with a skull fracture, for God's sake.

He starts to shake. It surprises him, the depth of this need to see her: to check for himself if she's getting better, or at least that she's not getting worse. He has always been relaxed when the children have been ill; has never felt anxious when they've had high temperatures. He supposes Jess has always just dealt with it. But now? This is different. His baby is lying alone in hospital with a head injury no one seems able to explain.

He needs to check that Jess's assessment of her condition is accurate – and he needs to talk to Liz. He's always liked her and she'll give him a straight answer, won't she? A quick word in her ear and perhaps she'll manage to stop this nightmare that's been set in motion: will reassure the police and social services that this is a run-of-the-mill accident and everyone is overreacting. Why didn't Liz curb this at the start? She knows Jess, knows how much she adores the kids. Jess said that the consultant seemed suspicious but Liz is no pushover: Ed's always liked her for seeming so assured of her opinion, for holding her own in discussions. She would have argued ferociously against her boss, he knows that: so why wasn't this consultant convinced?

He tries Liz's mobile again, almost jabbing at the redial. Nothing. He's already left a message; can't harass the poor woman. He's rung her landline, too. He tries one last time; redials the number; hangs on, and on.

The scenes of crime officer is still snapping away. He

seems particularly interested in the layout of the kitchen, photographing the units where Jess apparently told them she made the smoothie and the kitchen table where Frankie drank it; measuring the distance from both to the fridge. Ed watches, every part of him wanting to tell the man to leave the room. For his suspicion not to contaminate the space.

Instead, he busies himself with ensuring the boys are occupied: Kit playing *Fortnite* on the Xbox, Frankie plugged into his addiction, *Minecraft*, settled on separate sofas in the snug. Two bent heads; one a tousled blond, the other, a silky dark brown. Two very different pairs of legs, too: Frank's, jack-knifing in dark skinny jeans; Kit's, lolling and muscular in football shorts. You wouldn't know they were brothers. Kit, so clearly his boy; and Frankie – the child he doesn't understand properly; that he doesn't know how to handle. Two boys, dissimilar not just in looks but in temperament.

He has already told them that Betsey is in hospital and will remain there for the day; that Jess is in bed, and he will tell them what's happening later.

'You mean when the police have gone?' Kit, a child who never usually makes a fuss, who accepts explanations without rancour, had looked at him, a look of trust on his open face.

'Yes. But there's absolutely nothing to worry about, understand?' He gave him a look. The one that said, *I'm not discussing this, I'm the adult and you need to accept it.* Kit nodded, and went back to the screen. Frankie, predictably, started to kick off – 'But why can't I be with Mummy? I want to be with Mummy . . .' His voice soared, high-pitched, and Ed gave him a different sort of look. He can't handle Frank's tendency to dramatise, at the moment – though, for once it was merited. 'Mummy was at the hospital all night. She needs to sleep,' he told them, once again.

'Can we ask you a few questions?' DC Rustin approaches him now, with a thin smile.

'Of course.' He gestures her back to the kitchen and the dining table. *Keep calm; keep focused. Above all, remain courteous.* He thinks of the advice he would give Jess; that he wishes he could have given her yesterday if only she'd told him what was happening. *Be open. Be helpful. Don't give them any grounds for suspicion. We've done nothing wrong.*

'This is just a fact-finding exercise at the moment. A chat to try and find out what went on here,' the detective begins but he isn't fooled. He cringes at her 'at the moment' with its implicit threat of a more formal interview, under caution, later; winces too as she explains about the Body Worn camera, used to record exactly what he says. 'We're just trying to find out who was in the house when Betsey was injured,' she goes on. 'Were you here yesterday afternoon from about four?'

'No. I was at work. I was there until around six p.m. and then I went for a couple of drinks with some colleagues. I can give you their names if you like and the bar we drank in?' He provides both, conscious that it sounds as if he's providing an alibi. 'I didn't get home until around ten.'

'And what happened then?'

'I came in and Jess appeared to be in bed. Both the boys were in their rooms – I assumed they were sleeping – but Betsey was crying, whimpering, really. So I went and looked in.'

'And how did you find her?'

'Fractious, teary, and she'd been sick on her mattress. I picked her up and tried to comfort her but she was clearly uncomfortable. She strained against me; twisted her head. I suppose I'm more cack-handed than Jess, less used to getting her to stop crying.' He pauses. 'I couldn't stop her crying.'

'Was this unusual for her?'

'Well, yes.'

'Have you ever found her like this before?'

'No, not at all.'

'Just to be clear: you'd never found her sick in her cot?'

'No.'

'And what about her crying like this. Was that usual?'

He thinks, conscious that he's not around for the majority of the day; aware too that he does not want to say anything that might raise suspicions. In the end, he decides to be honest.

'She does cry – like any baby – but this was different. I couldn't settle her; couldn't stop her, as I said.'

The band around his head tightens as he remembers his shame, his sense of impotence, at being unable to do this. Why hadn't he snapped on the nursery light? He supposes he didn't want to shock her with its brightness: Jess was obsessed with blackout blinds and with not making the children wired. Instead, he'd pushed the door open so that the landing light splayed into the room. She had craned away and that had shaken him. Wasn't straining from the light a sign of meningitis? Jess hadn't had her inoculated, something he'd been livid about but which, as with all domestic things, he hadn't thought to organise. He had put her down in the cot to wrestle off the sodden Grobag and see if there was a rash on her stomach. She'd screamed and writhed, furious at his manhandling – or in pain, he now realises. He'd been out of his depth and had bounded up the stairs to Jess.

'And your wife? Where was she while this was going on?' DC Rustin says.

'In bed.'

'Asleep?'

'No. But I think she had been. She was coming round. Was dozy. She'd had a long day.'

'Could she hear the crying in your room?'

'I don't know.'

'Could *you* hear it up there?' DC Rustin tries again.

He pauses. 'Yes.'

'How loud was it?'

'It was the sound of a baby crying. It was ... insistent when I was there, but I don't know how loud it was before. I imagine it was gentler and more sporadic, as it was when I came into the house.'

'Did you ask your wife why she hadn't gone down?'

'No.'

DC Rustin tilts her head to one side.

'Did you wonder *why* she hadn't done so?'

'Not really.'

The detective taps a biro three times on a pad of paper: a dull, rhythmic knocking. The sound of her palpable disbelief.

'I was more concerned with getting Betsey to hospital,' Ed says.

'You were sufficiently concerned at this stage?'

'I was worried about her straining from the light, and the fact she'd been sick. I was worried it might be meningitis.'

'And did your wife agree she was sufficiently poorly to be taken in?'

'Yes – when I told her about her reaction to the light. Of course she agreed she should go to hospital.'

'Did she mention that Betsey had banged her head?'

'I don't think so, no. We were just preoccupied with how she was at the time.'

'Would that have made you worry more if she had?'

'I suppose so.' He's not sure what they're getting at and so how to answer. 'But it wasn't an issue because she didn't mention it.'

'And did she go to the hospital straight away?'

'Yes. As soon as she got herself ready.'

'How long did that take?'

'Five minutes at most.' He feels a frisson of irritation. There's no way he is going to tell them of his frustration as Jess brushed her hair. He had gone and put Betsey into a fresh Babygro, found her changing bag, fumbled in her drawers for clothing and nappies, not quite sure if he'd assembled everything; embarrassed by how little he knew of the minutiae of his daughter's life.

Jess was jittery when she came down, her eyes bright, her expression cagey. He'd assumed his unease was contagious: she'd been dismissive, and sharp. 'Can you pass me her bag?' she had asked as she had taken Betsey from him, her screams ragged now, the poor child utterly exhausted. He was left feeling not just inadequate but disturbed.

And as DC Rustin's questions continue, with DC Farron chipping in, this sensation grows and hardens, until his doubts, barely acknowledged when she told him the police were coming, begin to multiply. Why had Jess buried herself under the duvet, ignoring Betsey's cries? Why the inexplicable delay as she prepared to go to the hospital, not sharing his sense of urgency until he had shouted at her in frustration and threatened to call a cab to take Betsey himself? Why had she argued against going to the hospital in the first place? Because he wasn't frank with DC Rustin: Jess had taken quite some persuading; had insisted that Bets must just have a virus and initially accused him of overreacting. And he was thrown because, apart from her aversion to vaccinations, she is so vigilant about the children's health. The amount she spends on organic food and herbal supplements, her obsession with the house being hygienically clean, her reluctance to leave the children with other people, all indicate how seriously she takes being their mother. A role she pursues diligently, determined to compensate for not having one who was particularly maternal herself.

Jess adores their children, he has no doubt about this, even if she hasn't appeared to enjoy motherhood – or to be as engaged with it – since Betsey's birth. Recently he has itched to tell her that loving them is enough. That the perfectionism that drives the way in which she feeds and clothes their kids is unnecessary; that her care – attentive, thoughtful – is sufficient. But it's not in Jess's nature to do anything by halves, and, until Thursday at least, he had been wary of broaching the subject. He hadn't even thought it through properly; had just inched towards this realisation. Then he tried to raise it and made everything so much worse.

He is struggling to find the words now. To balance the truth with his need to protect Jess from this dour detective, because something here doesn't quite fit.

The truth chafes against the version of events he offers up, not out of a desire to mislead – because he is not stupid; he knows you're not supposed to lie to the police – but because his instinct is to shield his wife, whom he loves even if he no longer seems to understand her.

But he is not entirely honest, and the truth is hidden in the things he leaves unsaid.

Liz

Saturday 20 January, 10 a.m.

Eight

I close my front door gently behind me and wait in the hall, savouring the moment.

I've never felt more grateful to be home.

The radiator hiccups heat. Nick thinks it's mad, my obsession with keeping our house warm. Brought up in an Edwardian house, he sees draughts as inevitable. But if you've never taken being warm for granted, then you crave it. It's one of our basic needs, followed by safety and security. Then comes love. Well, at least I had my brother Mattie for that.

I shrug off my coat and move through the hall towards the kitchen and Nick, who I met in my first year of university, and who, with his reassuringly ordinary background – two teacher parents who were kind to each other; one younger sister, who seemed to like me – made me realise I was lovable, after all.

We met at the university swimming pool, and grew close manning a student telephone counselling service. That sounds hideously earnest but even then there was this shared desire to help. It took a while for me to trust him: why did he want to be with *me*? Wouldn't he prefer someone from a background more like his? And then we did a sponsored hike in the Yorkshire Dales, during which he saw me at my worst: exhausted, tetchy, vomiting – I had a stomach bug I didn't want to admit to – and he still seemed to want me. I remember him holding me after I'd retched all night, and parting the hair from my face with such tenderness I finally listened to what he was telling me. *I love you*, he whispered in that dank, sodden tent, as he shielded me from the water-logged canvas, and it was a revelation that someone not only desired me – there'd been a couple of boyfriends before – but wanted to be with me unconditionally. We've been together ever since.

I get that familiar but oh-so-welcome kick in the stomach as he smiles at me now.

'OK night?' He stops clearing the detritus of breakfast.

I shrug, unable to convey the array of emotions I've felt since contacting social services: a deep concern for Betsey, and guilt at what feels like a betrayal.

'Bit shit?' He puts the dirty plates down and holds me close. I sink into him, enveloped by his heft. Not that he's heavy but his shoulders are wide and his six foot two frame reassuring. Encased, surrounded, I feel safe. I breathe in coffee and the wool of his jumper, the faint, male saltiness of his skin.

I kiss the dip above his clavicle and am surprised by a flicker of desire. I revised for a first-year anatomy paper by working my way down his body. *Clavicular fossa*: just a few of the terms are lodged in my brain. He nuzzles my neck. 'Oh, that's lovely,' I say, enjoying the warmth of his lips, and I run my hands down his back, reading his spine like Braille. Ordinary life is suspended for a moment. He whispers something suggestive and I laugh out loud. 'Not very practical,' I say, as I pull away. He gives me a look and I smile, rueful. But in truth I'm distracted not just by the thought of the children barging in but by my nagging anxiety about what's happening to Betsey and Jess.

'Jess came in with her baby,' I say, filling the kettle. I speak blankly as if this will neutralise what happened. 'She had a nasty bang to the back of her head.'

As a teacher, Nick knows what this might mean.

'I had to call social services.'

'You think one of them hurt her? Are you sure?' Nick is far less cynical than me: has never had any reason to think the worst of a parent, though his work means he's been exposed to the reality. Like me, he won't want to think this of a friend.

I shrug. 'Neil's sure. And there are grounds for suspicion: Jess's story was dodgy, her manner evasive, and there was a delay in bringing her in.'

'And you think Jess did it? Or Ed? Christ . . .'

'I don't know. I just don't know.' The words rush from me like a sigh.

'It's just, if anything, Jess is overprotective, isn't she? And cautious ...'

'Yes. Yes, she is.'

'And gentle, and in control.'

'That's what I thought. I'd describe her as a loving parent. A good parent. I still want to think she is ...'

'Do you remember how calm she was when Rosa had her tantrums? How she'd give you a break and just sit beside her while she screamed it out?'

'I know.' I remember reading to Kit one wet afternoon while Jess sat patiently by a prostrate Rosa; and my sense of inadequacy as my daughter screamed, puce with indignation, and Jess waited for her to stop.

'Ed as well,' my husband goes on. 'I mean I know he finds Frankie tricky but I've never seen him lose his rag – never seen him snap at the children, not really.'

A wave of weariness picks me up and drops me back down. It only takes a moment to harm a baby. Could one of our friends have momentarily acted on their frustration? I can't articulate this thought.

'I'm sorry – I need to get some sleep.'

'Of course. You go up. I'll take the kids out.' He smiles and I see that he looks tired, too: there are flecks of grey dusting his sideburns and the spokes at the corners of his eyes have deepened, though his swimmer's physique has barely changed since he was eighteen.

'Try not to beat yourself up,' he adds.

'Mmmm.'

'If you think there were grounds for it – well, your duty of care is to Betsey.'

'I know, I know … Doesn't make me feel any better about it, though.'

I put a herbal tea bag in a mug but Sam bowls in before I can fill it with boiling water.

'Muuuuuuum!'

'Careful!' I put the kettle down as he barrels towards me and grabs me around the waist. 'Gosh! You seem better!'

'I've eaten *loads*!' He clutches his flat stomach, a strip of flesh where his top rides up. He's invariably hungry, my boy, and he's often in motion, his centre of gravity close to the ground as he spins like a breakdancer. He reminds me so much of my brother at this age: the endless energy, the constant hunger, the reckless need to do things the second he thought of them: to live in the moment, whether it was clambering up walls, or jumping in at the deep end of the pool when he could barely swim. That early childhood willingness to chance things; to push the boundaries. A frisson of unease runs through me, and I pull my boy close.

'Dad says I'm well enough to go to football,' he says, looking up at me, and I smile down at his hopeful eyes, his unblemished, peachy skin.

'Sounds like a plan,' I say as he breaks free and races upstairs. I listen to him thundering along the landing, making the wooden floorboards of our Victorian ter-race creak.

'Must remind him not to run,' I mutter, but half-heartedly

because I love his noise and vibrancy: the perfect antidote to working in paediatrics. Sometimes I look at my children and think: *this is what childhood should be like.* I feed off their energy, their fearlessness, reminding myself that this – rather than chronic illness, or acute injury, or abuse – is most children's normality.

'Sam—' Nick calls up the stairs after him, though he tells the children not to do this. 'Please don't thud. The walls are shaking.'

The pounding stops.

'I'll keep them out for lunch,' Nick says.

'Don't worry.' My job places such impositions – spilling way past my rota-ed hours, dictating holiday dates and even whether I'm around for birthdays or Christmas – that I don't want to disrupt their lives any more than I do already. 'I doubt I'll sleep much, anyway.'

But as I crawl under the covers, my limbs are leaden and I realise that sleep, however disjointed and troubled, is what I need.

It's nearly 3 p.m., and the dull January light behind my curtains is dimming by the time I wake. Downstairs, Rosa has started her piano practice. A door slams, and Sam's footsteps pound down the stairs.

For a moment I try to kid myself that nothing is wrong. But it's no good. I dozed off agonising over Betsey; have woken thinking of her and Jess.

I reach for my mobile but it's not by the side of my bed: I

left it in the kitchen. I heave myself up against the pillows, contemplating getting up and joining my family, when there's a gentle tap at the door.

'Thought you might like a cup of tea?'

Nick places a mug on the bedside table and perches on the edge of the bed.

'Oh I love you,' I say.

'Should hope so, too. Did you sleep?'

'A bit.'

'Want something to cheer you up?'

I nod. I feel sick; doubt anything will make me feel better but I've got to make an effort for him and the kids.

'Just watch this video a second. It's from Matt. He got Rosa's birthday wrong: thought it was today.'

He holds out the family iPad and taps an attachment. My brother's face fills the screen against a backdrop of a snow-capped Ben Nevis and dark, glassy water. Mattie works at an activity centre for deprived kids near Loch Eil: almost the furthest he could flee from us, in the UK. My throat thickens as he starts singing 'Happy Birthday' alongside two wild reindeer. The deer are majestic: imperious, and impervious when he pretends to interview them about their birthday wishes for Rosa. He pulls a look of mock-surprise for the camera as one doe tosses its head. 'Well, ignore them, Rosa: I'm wishing you the happiest of birthdays.' He crosses his eyes quickly then gives a wide, open grin: so different to the guarded expression he wears in London. He is happy in this environment. I can't help but smile, even as I automatically notice the angry sheen, the scarring, that runs from his right ear to his torso, rippling down his neck.

'Very good,' I say, acutely aware of his absence. 'Have you shown her?'

'Yes,' says Nick. 'She loved it. Asked when she could next see him ...'

'Good question. I meant to ask him for some dates.'

'I suggested we see if we could go up there in the summer?'

'I'd really love that – and we won't get him down here.'

'You've a lot of missed calls, by the way.' Nick fishes my phone out of his pocket and hands it over.

'Work?'

'I'd have woken you if they were.'

I glance at the screen. There are missed calls from Ed, Mel and my mother, plus four new voicemails. I tilt the screen to show him.

'Take your time. The kids are just doing their homework,' he says, leaving the room.

I grimace, wishing I were helping them with something as familiar and constructive, rather than dealing with this.

With some trepidation, I play my mother's message back first. She rarely rings me – and only then when there's a problem.

'Lizzie? Lizzie?' She's only sixty-six but the voice down the end of the line sounds disarmingly frail. 'Lizzie? Are you there? Why aren't you answering me? I want to speak to you.' Then, frustratingly, nothing. I play the message again. For her to ring, it must have been important. I'll call her back after I've listened to Ed and Mel.

There's no doubt about the reason Mel's phoned. Her words spill from the phone in a torrent.

'Oh my God. I've just heard: about Betsey being in hospital and you calling the police? Ed's trying to get in contact with you: can you call him? He says Jess has done her closed-off thing: that he can't understand what's happening, and what she has said doesn't make any sense.

'I told him you wouldn't have called the police but, if you have, you will stop this straight away, won't you? You know she couldn't have harmed her. It's completely crazy! I know we all lose our rag sometimes but Jess is so child-centric, so calm and yogic, she's the *very last* person who would harm her kids.'

She continues for another minute or so. I hold the phone away from my ear, listening to her spiralling bemusement, catching a few lines that snag: about her surprise at my not showing my customary emotional intelligence, my compassion, if this is the case. It's not that I'm detached: more that I don't know how to deal with this. As a teacher, she knows you have to follow safeguarding protocol; understands that however personally uncomfortable a decision you can't try to protect, or be seen to protect, a friend. She's having a tough time – Rob left her for his young PA eight months ago – and she's understandably emotional at the moment. I itch to ring her back, and chat to her properly about this, but my phone starts vibrating in my hand. I let it ring out four times before I trust myself to answer.

'Liz?' Ed sounds breathless. 'Oh, thank God! Sorry for the barrage of calls. Did you get my messages?'

'I'm sorry. I haven't had the chance to play them back.'

'Oh.' His voice dips with disappointment.

'I've just done four night shifts on the trot. I left my phone downstairs while I tried to grab some sleep.'

'Sorry, sorry.' His voice is that of a man in a rush to get some answers. He's used to being listened to, and to being answered in a confident, forthright manner. Now, for the first time since I've known him, I sense a certain hesitation and uncertainty.

'I just can't get a handle on what's happening,' he says. 'A skull fracture? That sounds pretty serious.' A pause and the strain of the past eighteen hours is encapsulated in his next question. His voice cracks. 'She will be all right, won't she?'

'She should be.' I can't promise anything. Which of us can do that? But I so want to do so. I think of the scan: the crescent-shaped piece of bone; the two distinct cracks. He doesn't need to hear this from me.

'Christ.' His voice swells with emotion. 'I just can't make out what happened.'

'Didn't Jess tell you she banged her head?'

'Yes – but she's, well, you know how she gets when she's distressed, she shuts down a bit. Gives you the bare minimum. It didn't seem *that* serious at the time.'

'Look.' I'm a little confused. 'I'm not meant to discuss any of this with you, but I thought it was *you* who suggested she bring Betsey in?'

'Yes, yes, it was. But I didn't realise the outcome would be so dramatic. That a simple tumble would mean she'd cracked open her head!'

'Hold on. It's not an open fracture. There's no blood seeping out.' Poor man. He hasn't seen his baby since Jess brought her into the hospital. Perhaps he's catastrophising.

'The bone's cracked, though, is that right? Jess said you saw that on the scan? And her brain's been bruised.'

'Yes, but there's no apparent long-term damage.'

'Oh, thank God!' The breath rushes from him like air from a balloon, but his relief is short-lived.

'It doesn't feel right, though,' he continues. 'Her being so badly hurt that she's in hospital and the police are crawling all over us. It just doesn't make sense.'

I shift against the pillow. We've strayed into territory I shouldn't talk to him about. But Ed is like a terrier with a stick.

'Is this usual? Getting the police involved in an accident like this?' he goes on. 'It seems like an overreaction. Something really excessive ...'

'Look, I shouldn't be discussing this. I can't be involved because I know you and Betsey. But whenever there's a head injury in a child under one the hospital get very anxious,' I try to explain. 'And if the explanation doesn't make sense, then alarm bells start to ring. I'm sure there will be a perfectly innocent explanation: that it was an accident and that the police and social services will realise this very quickly. But until then I'm afraid you just have to answer their questions. I'm so sorry you're going through this, but it's not uncommon, it really isn't, however horrible it must seem.'

'Hmm.' He sounds unconvinced but is a little chastened. 'I'm sorry. I didn't mean to question you. I know you'll have done your best to dissuade your boss from contacting social services and the police.'

There is an uneasy silence. I want to concur with his assumption but I can't lie to him.

'Liz?' Another pause. 'You *did* argue against this, didn't you?'

'I'm sorry, Ed. I did – of course I did – but in the end, I had to agree with my colleagues. Professionally, we have to follow protocol, and if there is *any* concern we have a duty of care to Bets.'

'You mean *you* thought the police and social services should be contacted as well? Jesus Christ, Liz! They're here at the moment: they want to interview Kit and Frankie – will do, when the social worker gets here. Frankie's absolutely bloody *terrified*, as you can imagine. How could you think that getting them involved was a good idea?'

'I'm sorry – but please don't get angry with me . . .'

'How could you *think* they should be involved?'

'Believe me, their involvement was the very last thing I wanted but it would have been unprofessional, *negligent* of me even, not to do this.'

With my professional integrity at stake, I'm defensive,

my heart rate increasing to a rapid, syncopated thud. I try to calm it by using the sort of legal language I know he will understand and respect. But he's boxed me into a corner, and in squaring up to him I sound far less empathetic than intended.

'I'm sorry, Ed, but Jess was holding something back from us. She's not telling the whole truth here.'

ED

Sunday 21 January, 2 a.m.

Nine

He doesn't mean to spy on her. That's what Ed keeps telling himself as he opens Jess's laptop and sits, hunched in the darkness, deciding whether to tap in her password or not.

He's not the kind of husband who keeps tabs on his wife, and he hasn't the time – or inclination – to fret about what she gets up to all day. He isn't worried that she's being unfaithful, and there's nothing on their credit card or bank statements to perturb him.

And yet here he is.

It's two in the morning and, while Jess is knocked out by a sleeping pill, he is poised to use her not-so-secret password. To dig around, scrutinising her search history, trying to discover something, *anything*, that might help him understand his wife. The blurred outlines of their children glow, and he briefly considers just closing the lid and going back to the warmth of their bed and the comfort of her body. That's what he ought to do, rather than committing this pretty fundamental betrayal. And yet he knows that he can't.

He can't because the Jess he married, and even the Jess who was a confident, seemingly exemplary mother to Frankie and Kit, is not the woman sleeping upstairs. This new Jess is as slippery as water. Secretive. Guarded. Her tone clipped; her expression inscrutable. Someone he can't get a handle on at all.

Of course, she's always been a bit like this. Locking him out's a protective mechanism learned from early childhood, when she and her three siblings were dispatched to boarding school and learned not to bother their parents with anything disturbing. He thinks of her brother, Charlie, who thoughtfully broke his arm during term. By the time he returned home, his cast was off and his right forearm two shades paler than his left. Jess's mother, Frannie, never mentioned it – just as she apparently never acknowledged her eldest daughter Martha's teenage abortion. As far as she was concerned, her children's pain or trauma was an irrelevance, a distraction. God knows how she'd have coped with anything more sinister.

So Jess has always been prone to shutting him out when she's distressed and that's never been particularly perturbing – until now, when the stakes are suddenly so horribly high. Their baby daughter is in hospital with a skull fracture that the police think is so suspicious they've interviewed the boys and arranged for them to stay at Mel's for the night. And Jess has not merely turned frosty but is behaving in a way that unsettles him deeply. For the first time in their fifteen years together, he'd say she is being cagey. As if there is something she is trying to hide.

Take her reaction when she came down this afternoon to discover that the police were about to question the boys. It wasn't just her distress that they would have to go through this. It was her fear when DC Rustin told her she couldn't be present: almost as if she was terrified they would betray her in some way.

'Remember I love you. Remember that, won't you?' she had told Frankie, fiercely kissing the top of his head. And then she whispered something. Perhaps it was only Ed – so attuned to her body language – who picked up on it. But Frankie gave just the tiniest inclination of his head.

He hasn't been able to shake that suspicion away, and so here he is, in the cool of the night, ready to hack into her laptop and justifying that decision because in the light of what's happened, Jess's behaviour seems, if not callous, then certainly *odd*.

Of course, his sense that he doesn't know her is partly his fault. He's hardly at home in the week, and weekends are consumed with the boys' sport, with further work, with the occasional run or rugby match. There has never been the time or, if he is honest, he never has the emotional energy to try and consider how Jess has changed or how he might improve things. Sunday night comes around too fast, and another week flits past: a week of leaving the house at 5.30 a.m. and not being back until 9 p.m. Of existing, rather than living. Taking her for granted, because that's what happens

83

by this stage of your relationship, when you're this busy, isn't it? Isn't that part of the deal?

But her detachment is more than resentment on her part, some petty unwillingness to share things with him. She's keeping something back from him because she's scared, he knows her sufficiently well to see that.

Take how she behaved when she rang him from the hospital last night.

'They're keeping her in for observation,' she'd said and made no mention of further tests. Crucially, she hadn't mentioned that they'd discovered Betsey had banged her head; that it had been scanned and found to be a skull fracture. OK, she was preoccupied, but it was the first thing he would have told her. He had even asked if they suspected concussion, given that she'd been sick.

'Did they give any indication of what they're looking for? They must have said *something*?'

But: 'No,' she had replied, and her voice was firm and definite. 'They haven't said anything specific at all.'

She'd behaved oddly earlier on Friday, as well, before the accident happened. He'd surprised her by coming home from work at lunchtime. Perhaps he should have rung her but he'd wanted to be spontaneous; had hoped to smooth things over after Thursday night's argument. Maybe – and here he realises he got this completely wrong because this never happened these days – they might even go to bed?

Jess had been absorbed by something on her laptop; had been so distracted she didn't seem to notice Betsey, who was whimpering, upstairs, where she'd been put for her nap. When he'd walked into the kitchen, she'd snapped the lid shut, and had looked – there was no other description for it – guilty.

'Are you spying on me?' Her posture was ramrod straight like a child hiding something behind her back.

'No. Of course not.'

He'd been carrying roses, wrapped in crisp brown paper and raffia ribbon, and they suddenly seemed inappropriate, and he, intrusive, like a guest who turns up at a dinner party on the wrong date.

Their argument – the terrible argument from the previous night – had flared up again and he had forgotten about the expression on her face, the swift closure of the laptop, until he lay in bed this evening and started obsessing about all the ways in which she has been defensive or evasive in the past thirty-six hours.

He had thought of Betsey too, of course. He'd only managed to get to the hospital after the boys went to Mel's. Had seen the pressure bandage wrapped around her head, in brutal contrast to her paper-thin eyelids. He'd been frightened of what might lie beneath.

'It's all right. You can touch her,' the registrar on call – not Liz but a young woman called Dr Hussain – had said, and he had placed his right palm gently on Betsey's back. His hand was so large it had almost spanned the width of her, little finger and thumb touching each side. He was aware of how vulnerable she was and how easy it would be to damage her

85

tiny body. Her torso was warm, though, and this grounded him: reminded him that this wasn't some alien child, but his baby. His breath had juddered, almost in a sob.

He feels like crying now. You're supposed to protect your children, aren't you? And fathers, well, they're allowed to be almost overprotective of their daughters. But he hadn't been there for her: something had happened, and he'd been in a pub with colleagues, avoiding coming home. Guilt, bemusement, anger: they all churn away at him, but he refuses to give into them – or rather he's going to funnel his guilt and his rage and use it coldly and clinically to work out what is going on.

Because, as he ran over everything that had happened during that painful, discombobulating day – the police interview; the social worker's request that the children stay with Mel; his hospital visit; Jess's behaviour – he kept homing in on his wife's furtive expression when she snapped shut her laptop: that potent combination of guilt and fear. And, as he lay in the dark, his thoughts circling around that point, he realised how little he knew about what the woman lying beside him *did* for fifteen hours a day.

And he wondered what it was that she wanted to hide.

And so here he is. Password – *kitfrankbets3* – typed in; her virtual fingerprints exposed, or ready to be pored over. He feels like a hacker unearthing dirty secrets as he imagines what he'll find: a gambling addiction? A clandestine chat room? Surely not something as innocuous as porn?

His stomach cramps. Let there be an innocent explanation.

An ex-boyfriend she's looked up; a birthday present for him that's a surprise; an extortionate pair of shoes she covets and has bought? Seen through the prism of the last thirty-six hours, he will laugh with relief if it's anything as harmless as that.

The password's worked, and her recent searches cascade in a rapid flickering. She's logged out without closing all the pages and the first that comes up is a parenting site. Netmummies: organic weaning for fussy eaters. Perhaps she was just embarrassed at being caught looking at this: she, who knows how to mother with her eyes shut; an experienced parent who's had three kids?

Maybe she merely doubted herself. Given their row on Thursday night, maybe he'd crushed her confidence. Christ, he hadn't meant to. He'd been fumbling towards the realisation – expressed cack-handedly – that the extra baby might have tipped the balance. That she wasn't enjoying motherhood as much as when they just had the two boys. But would a lapse in confidence really mean she was embarrassed at being caught looking for recipes like this?

Her search history: that's what he needs. He pulls down the History bar. The latest page was opened at 4.03 p.m. on Friday but he had come home and surprised her earlier. It was shortly before 1.30 p.m.: he remembers hearing the time stated on the radio as he came in.

He clicks on Show Full History. There's butternut squash recipes, an online internet shop, then reams of Netmummies pages: 'How to deal with a crying baby'; 'How to deal with an unsettled baby'; 'Can a baby still have colic at ten months?'

Can they? He pauses to skim this page. He had no idea she searched for things like this. Is this where she goes for advice and support? Didn't she used to ask Liz or Mel, or even Charlotte, at the stage where Charlotte allowed some chink in her parenting armour? (He can't *remember* Jess confiding in his old friend, whom Jess has never found particularly empathetic, but presumably she could have done.) She hasn't mentioned any new mum friends, unless he wasn't listening properly (always a possibility). Perhaps she's lonely? That must be it. And he – cretinously – has only made things worse.

He carries on scrolling, heart lifting slightly at the thought that he's discovered her secret: that now that he understands her sense of isolation he can make things better. And then it dips. There are more pages, the ones she glanced at in the early afternoon, after he left abruptly to return to the office, even more Netmummies threads: 'I think my husband wants to leave me'. 'My husband thinks I'm incompetent'. Christ! That was straight after their argument.

And then he finds it. A line she typed into Google at 1.27 p.m., just before he came into the house; a line that makes his heart constrict into a fist that punches hard, a quick one-two, against his ribs.

Here it is. The thing that embarrassed her. That she didn't want him reading:

'Why do I want to harm my baby girl?'

JESS

Monday 13 March, 2017

Ten

The first time Jess imagines hurting Betsey she has been home from hospital for three days. Ed is back at work. Paternity leave isn't really recognised in the City and there is a crucial merger. She doesn't mind, does she? The boys are at school, and it will be lovely for her to have some time with Betsey on her own.

Of course not, she murmurs. She is up and into her jeans already, a loose linen shirt and undone button the only signs her tummy is still sore. She's sleep deprived and fragile; the horror of the birth nudging at the edges of her brain. But Ed doesn't need to hear this. 'No point both of us looking after a tiny baby,' she reassures him. 'Besides' – and here she half-laughingly trots out their familiar line – 'we need you to earn some money. Now go on: get back to work.'

But getting three children up and ready to go out for

school is harder than she imagined. Kit and Frankie are excited, Frankie bouncing off the walls at the thought of showing off their new sister, or maybe it's the realisation that he'll have to fight two siblings for her attention that's making him belt out the latest Taylor Swift and gurn at the baby, his face pushed into hers.

She'd forgotten she could feel so bone-achingly tired: this tiny baby, who wanted to be fed at one, three, and five, throughout the night, had drained her of all her energy. Perhaps she hadn't been given enough blood? She hates thinking about the transfusion, though she owes her life to that anonymous B negative donor.

It might help if she puts the baby down, but she doesn't want Betsey out of sight, doesn't want the boys to play with her like a dolly: she's already had to talk to Frankie about not being rough. She doesn't want to alienate him; she needs him to bond with, not resent, this new sister who's usurped his place as the youngest sibling, but she doesn't quite trust him. And so she carries the baby everywhere, remembering how to pick up a mug at the same time, or some dirty washing, to pull open curtains or close a door; managing to organise and tidy and maintain the order that is in danger of slipping from her grasp.

'Muuuuuummm,' Kit calls up the stairs from the hall. 'Where's the butter?'

She had asked him to make breakfast: had hoped that at nine he might be able to manage this, but he has already called for bagels, a knife and milk.

'Just a minute. I'm coming down,' she says as she reaches the top of the stairs, her right hand on the bannister – *hold on tight* – her left carrying the baby. But suddenly she can't move: she is rigid with fear.

The stairs are slats of golden oak with gaps in between: slivers of warmth suspended between the wall and the frosted glass bannisters. A feature staircase: something she hadn't considered a risk to young children when they moved in, two years ago, because both boys could navigate the stairs safely and she hadn't imagined having another child. Now, they tip towards her, the March light tilting them upwards, and she sees herself dropping Betsey and watching as she bumps down each step. *Bang. Bang. Bang.* Her baby's delicate skull bashes against each slat, until she comes to rest, her body bent, her head like a deflating football. The stair-well is eerily quiet: after the initial shriek, there is no sound.

The vision intensifies, and changes: now, she drops her because she stumbles, her foot slipping on the first, shiny step, both arms reaching for the bannisters as Betsey slips from her grasp. Now, she throws her, hurling the baby viciously down the stairs. The vision consumes her as she stands there, swaying. Utterly incapable of putting one foot in front of another, of moving onto the first step.

'Muuuuuuum.' Kit is peering up at her now. 'Are you OK, Mum? Are you coming?'

His voice brings her back to the real world.

'Yes, just a minute.'

Somehow, she shuffles back from the top of the stairs and

sits on the floor, still clutching Bets. Removing her socks, to give herself more traction, she inches back towards the staircase until her feet are dangling down. Shaking, she turns around and, like a toddler, navigates the stairs backwards, left hand clutching the bannister, right clinging to this mewling child. Later, she leaves Betsey on a play mat downstairs and counts the steps, then practises the manoeuvre without her: thirteen, fourteen, fifteen steps back down to safety. For a few months, she rations how frequently she carries her baby: not risking bringing her up and down too much.

She starts to see danger everywhere. Ed insists on having a knife block with a few wickedly sharp blades scabbarded inside. She has always worried that the boys might climb up and use them against one another, but now she fears using them against her girl. Dicing beef, she leaves a Sabatier on the chopping board to answer the door. Returning, she sees herself picking it up to drive it through Bets, who sits benignly in a bouncy chair. Just a neat, vicious strike, and her three-month-old's white Babygro turns crimson, blood pooling on the floor.

She reruns the scene as an accident: sees herself stumbling over the bouncer and plunging the knife straight into Betsey's tender crown, or her eyes, or her heart. A freak occurrence – but isn't that what most accidents are? She takes precautions: the knives hidden in a kitchen drawer, padded with tea towels, each one individually swaddled. But she can never guarantee Betsey's safety because the greatest threat to her baby is *her*.

There is danger posed by a kettle of boiling water. If she pours it into a mug, she risks the water tipping: gushing onto the floor and scalding her girl. She can't put the bouncer or a Bumbo chair close to her on a surface because Bets might wriggle to touch the kettle, or grab a rogue knife. The copper implements and steel pans that hang from a ceiling rack are a constant source of anxiety. She sees them falling, no *flying* across the room like child-seeking missiles. And so she skirts around them, constantly aware they could bludgeon her baby's head.

She keeps quiet about this, of course. Covers her tracks. Makes sure that the knives are back in their block and the heaviest saucepans, which she unhooks from the rack at the start of the day, are hanging back up again before Ed gets home. The boys don't question her behaviour: she has always been particular. A visit from a friend – Liz or Mel, and just the once Charlotte – means putting Bets in a different room as she moves the knives and puts the saucepans back up, then repeating the process once they've gone. She can't relax when Liz makes an impromptu visit, and is hyper-conscious of the potentially fatal implements and their proximity to her baby girl.

Eventually, she tries to raise this with Mel.

They have been for a walk with the younger boys and have had to cross a relatively busy road. Mel holds onto Connor and Frankie's hands, and runs them through the Green Cross Code – 'left, right, left; then we'll walk, not run' – leaving Jess free to push the Bugaboo. There is a gap in the traffic and the others cross but Jess remains rooted on the spot, not breathing and growing increasingly light-headed. All she can see is herself pushing Betsey into the path of a speeding car.

'Aren't you coming?' Mel on the other side of the road, looks bemused.

'It's not safe.'

'It's perfectly safe.' Mel frowns and looks mildly irritated. They wait a full three minutes until the traffic lights change further up the road, then Mel darts across and pushes the pram.

'I thought a car would come racing towards her.' Jess can't convey her paralysing terror, her utter conviction that if she steps off the pavement, she will kill her own child. She feels rather stupid. 'Have you ever felt like that?'

'Nope. I know my Green Cross Code – look left, look right, look left again. "Charlie says ..."' and she mimics the adenoidal cat of the 1980s children's advert for safe road crossing. 'No?'

Jess hasn't a clue what she is talking about. How can she admit that she imagines dropping Bets, or stabbing and scalding her? That she sees danger around every corner; a potential murderer in the driving seat of each car?

'Probably just sleep deprivation,' Mel suggests, as they continue towards the park. She gestures to Betsey. 'How long a stretch does she go for now?'

'Four hours on a good night – between ten and two.'

'And then you're up again at five?'

Jess nods, bleakly.

'Well, there you are. Sleep deprivation's a form of torture: they use it in SAS training. God, I thought I was going completely loopy after Connor was born.'

'Really?' She can't remember Mel being anything other than her usual, pragmatic self. She's certainly never mentioned having intrusive thoughts, or disturbing visions. She hesitates, then risks asking: 'What do you mean by *loopy*, exactly?'

'Oh, you know. Ratty. Absent-minded. I once lost the car in Tesco's car park, don't you remember?' She laughs at the memory. 'Wandered around, unable to find it, for half an hour.'

And Jess cannot say: *Yes, but did you ever imagine killing your baby? Did you check and double-check you hadn't overdosed her on Calpol; that you hadn't poured bleach into her bottle; that she wasn't being suffocated by soft toys in her cot? That you hadn't inadvertently smothered her?* There seems such a chasm between her and Mel's experiences.

Luckily her friend seems oblivious, and is distracted by their arrival at the park.

'Right – let's run these puppies around, shall we?'

Mel has always maintained small boys are like dogs who need ample exercise to be biddable. Frankie has never seemed biddable – parenting him is like balancing on a high-tension tightrope – but perhaps that is a failure of Jess's parenting rather than anything else.

'Yes,' she says, her voice strained, as she focuses on being hyper-vigilant, on not letting that old man sitting on the bench anywhere near them. (Potential paedophiles are a new source of concern; she suspects any man who smiles at her baby daughter.) 'Let's run them around.'

Liz

Monday 22 January, 2018, 7.10 a.m.

Eleven

'Bad night?' Nick asks as we dance around each other in the kitchen, buttering toast, slurping tea, warming milk – all with an eye on the clock and the knowledge we have less than ten minutes before we're out of the door.

'I woke about three-thirty: couldn't stop thinking about Jess.' I gulp my hot drink then wipe crumbs from the surfaces, my actions brisk and efficient. *Come on,* my body language tells my family. *I haven't got all day.*

The children eat languidly, Rosa licking the butter off a crumpet, eyes closed as she enjoys the sensuous experience.

'Oi – I'm using that knife,' Sam protests, spoiling the moment as he leans across.

'There's another one *in front* of you,' she says, glowering at his apparent incompetence.

'Oh – OK.' He is quickly mollified and resumes buttering. They both look as if they could sit here all day.

'I kept thinking about Jess,' I continue, one eye on Rosa, who is skilled at picking up on adult conversations. 'It's the strategy meeting this morning.'

'To decide if they should investigate further?'

'Yep.' I start stacking the dishwasher, clinking a mug and almost chipping a plate. 'Not that I'm allowed to attend. The detective's pretty tough – I've met her on a previous case – and Neil's so hardline.' I drop my voice to a whisper, glancing at the children, but they're bickering over who has the Marmite. 'I feel so bloody impotent: I want to tell them about the family we know – but that's not possible because I can't even be there.'

Nick drops a kiss on the top of my head, and I lean against him a second, gaining some comfort from his warmth, his familiarity. He smells of granary toast and I breathe this wholesomeness in.

'Any decision is not your responsibility,' he says. 'You had to agree to refer her. There was no other option – that's what you told me, isn't it?'

I draw away and continue loading the rest of the dirty crockery. It's what I've told myself all weekend, what I discussed with him on Saturday night once the children were in bed, but it sounds too pat repeated back like this.

'It doesn't feel that simple,' I say as I fill the children's water bottles and grab them both an apple I know will be forgotten in the bottom of their bags.

My husband smiles at me.

'What? I need to go.' I shouldn't have brought this up again.

'You need to stop being so hard on yourself.'

He's right, of course, and normally I'm able to compart-mentalise home and work. I have to. I wouldn't be able to survive if I obsessed about each patient. But Betsey's injury feels more personal, and it's stirred up half-hidden memories. I hardly slept last night: duvet twisted round my body, limbs greased with sweat as I imagined Jess screaming that she hated me, her mouth a tunnel I fell into until I woke, heart pound-ing. I can't pretend I'm viewing this dispassionately.

'OK, I'll try,' I say, neutrally, because I'm running late now and I know he's only being protective. I give him a kiss.

'It'll be all right.'

'Yeah – I know.'

But as I pull on my coat, I can't shake the feeling I'm largely responsible for causing Jess and Ed this grief.

I'm properly late when I get to the hospital, just after eight-thirty. My phone rings with my mother's number. I answer it the moment before it cuts to answerphone, wrestling with my spilling bag and jamming it against my ear. I'm in the Victorian part of the building, all vents and pipes discharging steam, and swing doors leading to labyrinthine corridors. A patient, wearing pyjamas and attached to a drip, stands puffing on a cigarette, and I move away, wary of being heard.

'Lizzie? *Li–zzie?*'

'Mum. Are you all right?' I'd left a message for her on Saturday and had meant to try again yesterday. It's unusual for her to call me this early in the morning. She sounds panicked, her speech a little slurred.

'I've just bashed my face.'

'You've just bashed your *face*?'

'I must have opened a cupboard door into it, in the kitchen.'

'Oh, Mum, I'm so sorry. Is it badly bruised?'

'My eye is, and my cheekbone's cut.'

'That must have been scary. Was there much blood?' Faces can bleed profusely.

'Oh …' A pause while she thinks about it. 'Well, not too much.'

'And has it stopped bleeding, now?'

'Yes. I've put a bit of tissue on it.'

'OK. Do you think you need to come into A&E for stitches? I'm at work but I could call a taxi for you.'

'Oh no. I don't want to make a fuss.' She makes it sound as if I'm overreacting. 'I just thought you'd want to know.'

'I do. Of course I do. Do you want me to drop round tonight?' She only lives three miles away but Nick has a staff meeting and I'll have to wait until he's finished. I don't take our children to her flat.

'Oh, I don't think so. No.' She audibly recoils from the idea.

I breathe deeply, balancing my automatic concern with

my need to maintain some distance. 'I'll call you when I'm finished but will you promise me you'll get a taxi here, or go to your GP, if you feel worse?'

'I'll be fine. I wish I hadn't called now.' Her irritation is palpable. She has always been like this: prone to swerving from one response to another. As a child, it was impossible to know where I stood.

'I'm glad you did. I want to know. You hadn't hurt yourself when you called me on Saturday, had you?'

'I didn't call you on Saturday!' She is affronted. 'Why on earth would you think that?'

'Well – you . . .'

'I *didn't* call.' She is emphatic. 'I think I'd know if I called or not, wouldn't I? Or do you think I'm losing my marbles, is that it?'

I remain silent. There's no point in arguing with her, particularly when she's like this.

'Ridiculous,' she chunters, having failed to goad me into a reaction, and then, as if I'm keeping her: 'Look, I need to go now.' And she hangs up abruptly.

I feel aggrieved, as I often do at the end of our conversations. Without meaning to, I pick at a hangnail, ripping it so that it throbs angrily. I must maintain my boundaries and not get sucked into her usual games. This one feels like an emotional version of Grandmother's Footsteps: me, trying to inch my way closer, only to be chased furiously away.

I'm relieved to be at work, where I can immerse myself, and where I know I'm valued. Shoulders back, head up,

I thrust open the hospital's door. It swings forward with a clatter, the handle whacking the wall, and denting the plaster. And I realise that, in my anger and frustration, I've applied too much force.

Betsey lies in her cot by the window, dozing and no longer unsettled. I watch her, after the ward round and once Neil's retreated to the strategy meeting, wondering if there's an innocent explanation for what's happened here.

She looks so peaceful, now she's asleep: her cheek flat against the mattress, her bottom in the air like a sheepdog at rest. She *will* get better, I remind myself: the haematoma should resolve although there remains the risk of seizures, as this collection of clotted cells congeals, dries and breaks down. Will this happen – and will they be fleeting, or an ongoing issue? There's no way of knowing, quite now.

I massage my temples as I run through whether we could possibly be missing something crucial. Something that means any suspicion could be lifted from Jess and Ed. Maybe she bleeds easily from haemophilia? Could she have brittle bones or rickets? Back at the computer, I check her blood results: her platelet count and clotting profile is normal and so is her bone profile and levels of vitamin D.

Neil and Fousia are still in their meeting with Cat, Lucy and the safeguarding lead, Kate Walsh, and so I watch Betsey a little longer, regretting not knowing her in happier times. She's such a delicious baby – dimple-cheeked, with delicate features – and I imagine her chortling, kicking her creased thighs up high. Then I imagine her screaming. Rosa was mercurial at this age, her sunniest moods changing in an instant. A delayed sleep, a late meal, a missed feed: any of these were enough to trigger tears or a tantrum. Before she was admitted, was Betsey like this?

I must get on with my work but as I leave, the mother of the baby in the next bay catches my eye.

'He's so much better,' says Tania Bryce, nodding to the cot where seven-month-old Daniel lies on his back, blowing bubbles and flexing his Babygroed legs. His parents rushed him in late on Thursday after he appeared to have stopped breathing. He'd contracted bronchiolitis. But his oxygen SATs levels are now back to normal and he should be discharged in the next couple of days.

'You gave your mummy quite a shock,' I tell her baby now as he smiles with delight.

He gurgles back as if he can't quite believe life can be this exciting.

'Yes, you did.' I smile down at him and he starfishes his fingers, twisting his hands against the light.

'You can say that again!' His mother blows out her cheeks in exaggerated relief, and then her voice breaks. 'I thought we would *lose* him.'

'You did absolutely the right thing in bringing him in. And he was much better overnight, wasn't he?'

Tania, who has barely left his bedside since he was admitted, nods. A first-time mum, she delayed coming in for fear of being perceived as fussing. Now, she can't forgive herself for not listening to her instinct.

'I just wish I'd brought him in earlier . . .' she says.

'Hey, it's OK,' I say, crouching down. She gives me a watery grin, tears welling at their ordeal being over. 'Daniel got exactly the right treatment,' I tell her. 'He's off the oxygen. We'll monitor him but he'll be fine.'

There's a bustle of activity down the corridor, and I look up to see Lucy and Cat leave the paediatric meeting room. I say goodbye to Tania and get to the nurses' station as they walk down the corridor, Cat walking decisively, Lucy scurrying to match her pace. A skinny woman with long, shiny hair, Lucy dresses like Sam's teacher: black trousers, a bottle-green crew-neck with a polka dot scarf that hangs loosely, and bangles that jangle when she gesticulates. She seems too gentle to deal with potentially abusive parents, and yet she must have an inner steel: something that drove her to choose this profession, and enables her to stand up to parents, including articulate middle-class ones like Ed and Jess who might threaten to sue. Though she's not harsh like Cat – who once told me 'we'll get the bastards' when referring to parents in a previous case – Lucy wields some power. She's the person who could take Betsey, and Kit and Frankie, from Jess's care.

'Anything you can tell me?' I smile winningly at Neil, who has followed them and is now looking up a patient's notes on the computer.

'Hmmph?' His eyebrows knit in disapproval.

'About Betsey Curtis? Can you tell me anything about the plans for her care?'

'We'll keep her in for another twenty-four to forty-eight hours to ensure she doesn't knock herself and risk a further bleed, or experience seizures.'

'And then?'

His cool blue eyes assess me and he makes me wait. He is such a stickler for procedure that he's not going to give me any hint of police suspicions.

'Then it's a matter for our good colleagues in the police and social services,' he says. 'But suffice to say, the mother should not be given unsupervised access to her children – either at home or in the hospital. When she visits, access should continue to be prearranged and she should be accompanied by another social worker or Miss Stone.'

He stalks off, and it feels as if he sucks the oxygen from the room, leaving me light-headed. Jess still can't see Betsey unscheduled or alone. She will have signed a police undertaking not to do this over the weekend, but now it's been shored up: confirmation that they suspect her of inflicting harm.

I sidle up to Fousia.

'He's in a foul mood,' I whisper, conspiratorially.

'When isn't he?'

'He seems convinced it's a non-accidental injury.'

'Yep.' She nods in the direction of the doctors' room, where there's little risk of our being overheard.

I follow her, hugely grateful that she's prepared to fill me in.

'You didn't get any of this from me, OK?' she says, her expression stern. Childless and five years younger than me, she has so far managed not to antagonise Neil in her six months working in the department, and understandably wants to keep it this way.

'Of course not. Can you just tell me what's driving this? Is there evidence from the other children's medical examinations?'

'They were fine and there's nothing sinister in the records – no previous contact with social services, no indication of chaotic behaviour, no evidence of historic fractures from the skeletal survey, either.'

'Oh, thank God.' I have been wondering if I'd shut my eyes to sustained abuse but this is hugely reassuring. 'So why do they think this justifies further investigation?' I say.

'It's Cat Rustin. She argued strongly for this. She thinks Mrs Curtis's story doesn't stack up.'

'But why?'

Fousia checks that no one is likely to come in.

'Look – promise I didn't tell you?'

'Of *course.*'

'They interviewed the brother who was in the room when Betsey fell over.'

'Frankie, the younger boy?'

She nods. 'Apparently, he was hugely distressed, very distracted, and not very forthcoming, but he did contradict something his mother said.

'According to Cat, Mrs Curtis said he was sitting looking

out towards the garden when Betsey slipped so didn't witness what happened. But *he* said he was in his usual seat at the table, so looking towards the fridge and his sister – and yet he saw nothing. He didn't see her slip or fall.'

My stomach tightens. Frankie is a very literal child, and he'll want to please any figure in authority. He'll have been scared of them, however gently they took the interview, and he wouldn't contemplate lying. However much he adores his mother, his instinct will have been to tell the truth.

'You can see why they're concerned, right?' Fousia peers at me, her smooth brow wrinkling.

'Yes, of course.'

'One of them is lying. The boy or the mother. And the police think that it's her.'

JESS

Monday 22 January, 11 a.m.

Twelve

'You want my *sister* to look after *my children*?'

When Lucy Stone breaks the news to her that her sister Martha is willing to move into the family home and look after the children as an 'approved adult', Jess can't believe what she is saying. She tries not to sound unreasonable, but her tone betrays her disbelief.

Lucy fumbles for a tissue in her bag. She has a cold. Jess hears the phlegm bubble up in her nose as she blows it with a fruity squeak. She moves her own chair back, flinching at the sudden, nails-down-the-blackboard scrape against the kitchen floor. The social worker tucks the tissue up her sleeve and looks up, her face blanketed in compassion. 'In cases where there are safeguarding concerns, we have to look for alternative care for any other children in the family,' she says.

'*Safeguarding* concerns? You think I might harm Frankie

or Kit?' Though the phrase was used on Saturday, when the boys were sent to stay with Mel, and when she signed the undertaking not to see Bets alone, it is only now that its meaning swims into focus. Jess hears her voice rise in incredulity as Lucy fails to answer and blows her nose again.

The boys have stayed with Mel the past two nights. Lucy had suggested that they go there on Saturday once it became clear that there would be further meetings, but Jess had told herself their absence was for largely practical reasons. *They think you're a bad mother.* Yes – but not to Frankie or Kit, surely? It's her mothering of Betsey they're concerned about, not of them.

She glances from Lucy to her husband, her disbelief caught in her chest like something she needs to cough up, and waits for him to defend her; to insist this is nonsense.

Ed tries to smile. He knows he should be smoothing the situation down; charming the social worker into being reasonable and seeing things from their point of view as he is usually so adept at doing, when there's been a mix-up with a holiday booking, for instance, or a waiter brings the wrong meal. But there's no rulebook for a scenario like this. The terrain is so unknown, they are both floundering: him not knowing how to handle this professional, who he has failed to charm or impress with the veiled threat of having spoken to a friend who's a solicitor; her not knowing how to react at all. It's as if they've stumbled into a patch of boggy moorland, and with each cack-handed, tremulous step, risk sinking deeper.

'Look we know you are only worried for the children,' he begins. 'But is it really necessary to have Martha staying here? I'm here if there are any real concerns about my wife's parenting.'

'We need to have another adult, an approved adult, here because your family is the subject of a police investigation,' Lucy explains in the gentle tone she might use for a child. She pauses but what she says next shifts the balance of power so emphatically that any hopes of Ed dissuading her vanish. 'If you aren't happy with the idea of this then the other option is for us to apply for an order for the children to be placed in foster care.'

The room is suddenly hot, as if one of the boys has spun the dial on the thermostat without Jess noticing. Heat creeps up her face, flushing her cheeks, and her throat is dry. She wants to plead with this girl, but the words are stuck because this has always been one of her biggest anxieties: the thing that taps into her belief she is a hopelessly inadequate mother, incapable of looking after her babies. *The children could be taken away from us.*

'You're saying that if we object to Martha coming here you would do that?' Ed's jaw juts a little. Perhaps without realising it, he has put weight on his front foot, as if poised to strike.

'Yes.' Lucy swallows. Fear creeps up Jess's spine like the point of a knife. She can feel each prick, each nudge; a gentle, inescapable pressure that could fillet her flesh and that is pushing her towards a total meltdown where she risks losing all sense of her self and succumbing to her bleakest fears.

She clears her throat. She must say something. Must acknowledge what Lucy has said to prevent things getting even worse than they are at the moment. Because, just as her thoughts can spiral at the slightest provocation, so the act of taking Betsey to hospital has caused her life to spiral out of control.

'And Martha's agreed to this?' she asks.

'Yes. Do you remember we discussed the possibility of asking her on Saturday?'

Jess doesn't. Saturday was dominated by her fear for Frankie, as he was taken to a specialist police suite to be interviewed, and her terror of what was happening to Betsey. It was Ed who provided Martha's details and discussed the possibility of her helping while Jess busied herself with getting the children ready to stay with Mel.

'She's been very supportive,' adds Lucy. 'She's keen to help in any way she can.'

'Well, we're very grateful,' Ed says. 'Of course we are.' Jess nods. They should be grateful, shouldn't they? Relieved that she's prepared to be so selfless, and yet, much as she loves her sister, she doesn't want anyone taking her place — or even living in their home.

For a moment, she imagines her sister spreading out in the place; sees Martha's disregard for her sense of order. The way in which she injects colour and clutter — bags spilling open, scarves dropped, mugs leaving damp coffee rings.

And then she imagines the children, and Frankie in particular, uprooted and living at Martha's, Mel's, or some unknown foster carer's. Wrenched from the place where, despite her failings, she has always tried to make them feel safe.

They have no option. She knows this, though every part of her wants to rail against it.

'If Martha's really willing to do this for us,' she says, 'then of course we would love to have her here.'

'Bloody hell.' Ed paces the kitchen once Lucy has gone. Nervous energy radiates from him like static. When he finally comes to a halt, he sits, head buried in his hands, fingers pressed into his eye sockets as if by exerting pressure he will find the answer there.

Jess doesn't know what to say.

Her husband can barely look at her. Ever since she woke yesterday, he's been assessing her whenever he thinks she's not looking, but now he won't risk eye contact. She wants to touch him: to remind him that she is still his Jess. But he doesn't know her now, he said that on Thursday; and things have only worsened since that argument. Nothing will ever be the same again.

It doesn't help that he's spending as much time as possible at the hospital: sleeping there last night after staying there all of yesterday; keeping a vigil by Betsey's bedside – perfectly understandable since he has to work this week. Betsey needs a parent there, but it's hard not to feel he's also avoiding being with her as much as possible. That he suspects her in some way.

If he looks up and smiles, even slightly, then perhaps he doesn't suspect her? She waits. Nothing happens. That was a false bargain: she must think of something else. Or make it the best of three. And still she doesn't risk going to him because what would it mean if he failed to respond? Even worse, what would it mean if he shrugged her away?

She turns aside, her thoughts shifting to Betsey, who she will see later, at a prescribed time with Lucy. Her chest aches at the thought of her baby alone in that institutional cot in the paediatric ward, confused, in pain, with no one to comfort her, and she forces the thought away. Better to do something practical like preparing for Martha. Sluggish, as if wading through deep water, she trudges upstairs.

The fear, the pure, body-quaking fear, comes as she dusts the spare bedroom, arranges flowers, checks that the clean sheets don't need re-ironing. It's a beautiful room; the walls a muted Farrow & Ball grey. She lights a candle, hoping the winter jasmine will create an air of serenity, and re-plumps the white towels so they resemble fat pillows. Rechecks that the crisp white sheets are smoothed; that the basin in the en suite bathroom really is without a smear and there are no stray hairs curled behind the cistern; that there's no fuzz of dust coating the skirting boards behind the bed.

She had taken her rings off to clean but now she puts them on and begins to fiddle, to spin them round her fingers. *One, two, three. One, two, three*, she aligns the tiny gems. And then, suddenly: wham. Her hands are shaking so badly she cannot get it right. *One, two, three; one, two, three; one, two, three.* It's just not neat enough. She tries but fails to resist the ritual. She must do it again, until they're perfectly neat, and her fingers jab as she becomes more frantic. *One, two, three. One, two, three.*

She is a child on a beach, smashing up stones to excavate fossils. The bone-white pebbles are hot; her toes dry with salt as she pushes down against them, adjusting her weight as she squats, tilting from hip to hip. She probes with the chisel blade. She mustn't shave the layers away too fast, mustn't force it as she prises open the rock in her desire to find a fossilised spiral. An *Echioceras*. One, two, three: *tap*; one, two, three: *tap*. It's not working, and the rhythm grows faster and more frenetic. One, two, three, *tap*; one, two, three, *tap*; one two three.

And as she probes, the strikes increasingly quick and careless, her thoughts run in a riff of anxiety. If she can only excavate this ammonite then the never-ending spiral of invasive thoughts can be contained. If she can extricate it perfectly, everything will be OK. Her mother might spare her some attention, and her father might not rage. (And here she remembers the ugly look on her father's face as he turned on her mother the previous night; his words spat out in a voice so warped with hatred, it was a growl.)

The chisel skids and skitters. And the ammonite, hidden

and preserved for two hundred million years, is damaged as the rock falls away.

She thinks of this now, as she sits with her back to the wall, arms wrapped around her knees, hands clasped, her body packed up tight as if she is trying to take up the least space. The impotence that consumed her on that beach grips her like a vice. She can't control this situation. She isn't even allowed to mother her own children.

And yet perhaps it's only what she deserves.

They all doubt her:

Her sister, who must feel some suspicion, will believe the authorities wouldn't investigate without reason.

Ed, who can no longer look at her.

Liz, who suspected her from the start and helped usher in this social worker and the police.

And maybe they are right to do so.

Because she did something terrible, didn't she?

Liz

Monday 22 January, 5.45 p.m.

Thirteen

I'm going to be on time to pick up my children from after-school club. In fact, I should be early. That may not seem a cause for jubilation but today it feels like a major triumph.

I managed to leave the hospital on time. Nick has his staff meeting and I've incurred the wrath of the childcare workers too many times to risk arriving late. Besides, the children hate me not getting there by six – 'It's *so* embarrassing,' Rosa said on a previous occasion when they were the last to leave, while Sam's large eyes filled with pained disappointment. So I was assertive: told Neil that I had to leave at five, and did. It feels strangely liberating, as if I'm playing truant.

I quicken my pace. With any luck I'll be there by ten to six: time to watch Rosa in the last few minutes of her netball match. (She does netball club on Mondays.) I imagine how thrilled she'll be: her surprise, and her smile of delight. All too often she compares me to mummies who help on school trips, or with baking or reading. Mummies like Jess – or Jess before she had a third child. *Why can't you be at school more, Mummy?* is a frequent refrain. *Because I have to work and help other children*, I reply, with a smile I work hard on not letting slip. Well, I'm going to be that sort of mummy today.

Five forty-five p.m. My breath mists the cold air, my bag slips from my shoulder and bangs against my hip as I race along, imagining my daughter's beam and Sam's fierce hug. I'm winning at the juggle: being there for my children, *and* staying on top of a challenging job. Work was manic today: a flurry of admissions requiring calm, decisive thinking and quick action – the most potentially worrying, a six-year-old suffering from severe asthma. We treated her with nebulisers and intravenous steroids; corrected her potassium level – which had dropped dangerously low on the multiple infusions she needed – and then escalated her to high-flow oxygen before getting a space in ICU. Asthma sufferers come in daily but we're never complacent. Tonight, I feel the quiet satisfaction of knowing we acted swiftly, and did the very best for this little girl.

My phone buzzes: a text message from Mel. 'Five mins away. Cd u hang on 2 mine if netball's finished?' Normally it's me calling in the favours and I'm pleased she's asked me, particularly since I didn't return her call on Saturday. There's no kiss, though, kisses being her trademark payoff, and no 'please', again atypical.

'Of course, xxx' I text back, thinking of her torrent of unbridled anger. What was it she said? *You will stop this straight away, won't you? It's completely crazy.* It's the first time I've been to school since Betsey was admitted and I'm apprehensive. Of the babies in our original antenatal group, three – Rosa, Mel's Mollie and Charlotte's George – play netball, and so I'm going to have to brave their mothers for the first time since Bets was admitted.

It's Charlotte who sees me first.

'Can I have a word?' she says, once I've picked up Sam and Mel's son Connor from after-school club and arrived at the netball court. St Matthew's have just beaten another team and the children are triumphant, George trying to jostle between Rosa and Mollie, who ignore him with a contempt due to having known him their entire lives.

Charlotte watches, biting her lower lip. She's keen George gets as much female company as possible before he goes to a boys' public school for secondary. But despite him being athletic – a good footballer and competent at netball – the girls are increasingly dismissive. As Charlotte says now, somewhat sadly: 'They're leaving him behind.'

'Oh – it's just a stage,' I try to reassure her, although I wonder whether we'll all stay in touch once he forges new friendships.

'I'm not so sure.' She looks unsettled. Then her mood switches as she looks at me directly. It's an unnerving gaze. She's physically striking, with her strong brows and nose and those dark eyes that seem to penetrate. I do like her – she's been particularly supportive when I've done exams; she's generous; and has a dark, sardonic humour – but I wish she were a smidgeon warmer. Irrationally, I feel as if she's a head teacher and I, a problematic child.

'Can we talk about Jess?'

'I can't,' I say between clenched teeth, as I start to cross the playground. Sam and Connor have raced ahead to join their sisters. We are briefly childless, but that doesn't mean I can discuss this here.

'I'm not asking you to tell me what's happening with the case,' she says, stopping still.

'It's impossible. I'm not involved in any way. Betsey's no longer my patient. It would be highly unprofessional, not to mention unethical, for me to discuss it.' I continue walking, hoping this fellow professional who knows all about client confidentiality will get the message. But she's taller than me, and her strides longer: before I know it, she has engineered it so that she is blocking my path.

'It's just that I'm concerned.' She puts one hand on my forearm and her voice softens, so that she manages the curious trick of sounding both mellifluous and assertive. 'There's something that's worrying away at me and I wonder—' and here she drops her voice so I have to come close. 'Well obviously I don't want Ed to think Andrew and I are anything but supportive – but I wonder if it's something I should tell the officer handling the case, or something you should hear?'

She tips her head to one side and I feel the knots in my shoulders tighten. At this moment I think I might hate

119

her. She's putting me in an impossible position and she clearly doesn't care. Of course I shouldn't be listening to this, should direct her towards Cat Rustin if she has any real concern, but there's something competitive about her relationship with Jess — borne of her knowing Ed before his wife, or perhaps, on some childish level, because Jess will always be cool, and Charlotte, despite her professional success and hefty salary, never will be. If she wants to talk to DC Rustin, I'd rather filter what she wants to tell her.

'Go on, then,' I say.

'Well, to start with: I'm worried that she seems detached from Betsey. I haven't seen much of them together, it's true, but do you remember how absorbed she was with Kit? How she was almost nauseatingly child–centric?'

'Charlotte . . .' I'm reproving.

'Oh, come on. You know what I mean. We all parent differently. She and I were probably at different ends of the attachment continuum but, to be honest, I always felt she was a more "natural" mother; that it came to her more instinctively. Don't you remember how she'd get down on the floor and really play with Kit and his cars — and how I couldn't do that? How I was too self-conscious? But I don't think she seems that engaged now.'

'I don't know how you can know this. *I've* barely seen her properly since she's had this baby and you must have seen her even less.'

'I'm not so sure about that.'

'Well, when did you last see her?'

'At the Christmas production a month ago: that's what I'm talking about. She seemed uninterested in Betsey. Don't you remember? *You* noticed it, too.'

I was late for the Key Stage 2 Nativity at which our youngest were angels. A meeting that overran and Tube delays meant I hurtled into the packed hall on the dot of 2.15 p.m. – only just in time. I caught a glimpse of Sam, then made my way to the one remaining seat, feeling the eyes of several parents sweep over me, some filled with sympathy, others with censure. 'You made it!' Charlotte whispered as I squeezed next to her on the end of a row. 'Can't see Mel but there's Jess,' and she nodded to a mass of curls three rows directly in front of me. Betsey's vast red buggy was parked in the aisle at an angle, and was already quivering with boredom or rage.

In between my children's appearances, I was mesmerised by that pram. I could see Betsey's legs, stuck out in front of her, and watched as she showered the floor with rice cakes. Jess didn't seem to notice, her attention on Frankie and our boys on the stage.

Then Betsey began to whimper. I felt tense on Jess's behalf, remembering my hot shame when a two-year-old Sam screamed at a similar event. Betsey's legs were rigid, and the buggy canopy was shaking, but Jess just held an iPad out in front of her. Fair enough, I told myself. Don't be judgemental. Anything to keep the peace.

Because the angels were singing by then: the purity of their voices transforming the hall, with its tang of boiled mince and sweaty feet, and making my throat tighten. All around, the faces of parents softened, their bodies relaxing at the sight and sound.

Frankie, jiggling his tinsel halo frenetically, was particularly exuberant and I glanced down the aisle at Jess, hoping she'd seen. But my friend was looking down at a smartphone, focused neither on her grumbling baby nor her boy singing his heart out but on something of far more importance on her screen.

Charlotte, leaning across me to peer at her, raised her eyebrows, and I felt a surge of disloyalty that only intensifies now she has brought it up again.

'Look,' I say, 'we're all preoccupied in the Christmas rush. Perhaps it was something important: a toy she was trying to find.'

'We'd been asked to switch our phones *off*, and she was on it *all the time*. How often is Frankie going to be an angel, or Kit a shepherd? The old Jess would have been taking photos or watching as if they were the centre of her world. She would never have behaved like that.'

'OK. I understand your concern, but I don't think this is anything with which to bother the police.' I give a quick laugh to show we should dismiss this, and start walking briskly. I can't admit that I was surprised by this change in Jess's behaviour, too.

'There's something else.'

Has she a list of Jess's wrongdoings?

'If it's something along those lines then I think you're being unfair.'

'It's not. It's more serious. This relates to Friday night. It's the thing I'm considering mentioning to the police.'

'Go on, then,' I say reluctantly.

'I didn't drop the boys back after football. Jill, Ben's mum, wanted to swap, so that she could go on a work night out next week or something, and so after I'd left them at the pitch I had some free time. I'd been thinking about how little I'd seen of Jess since she'd had Betsey – and so I thought I'd be spontaneous and pop in . . .'

'OK . . .' She is making me nervous.

'Well, I rang the door but no one answered. I tried the landline but it just rang out. Then I thought that perhaps she'd gone out not expecting us back until seven, except that I could hear Betsey crying. I needed to get some petrol so I gave up on her, drove to the garage and filled up.'

'Well, she was probably just changing her nappy, or getting Frankie in the bath. She didn't expect anyone that early. I never answered the door around bath time.' I'm relieved to think of this explanation. 'What are you trying to say?'

'That perhaps she *wasn't there.*'

'Oh, don't be ridiculous. Where exactly do you think she was?'

'I don't know. Perhaps she'd popped out for a few minutes. People do all the time.'

'Do they? Have you?'

'Once or twice.' Her tone is stiff. 'Just for a couple of minutes. George is nearly ten, after all, not a baby

123

like Betsey. *Don't* tell Andrew.' She pauses. 'Why, haven't you?'

'No, no I haven't – and Jess would never leave a *baby*.'

'It's not the worst crime in the world,' she mutters. 'I'm sure plenty of people do it.'

I'm dumbfounded. Does that mean that Charlotte did this when George was small? Perhaps I hardly know her, after all.

I dismiss her suggestion. It's hard not to think that it's somehow motivated by malice. She's always been critical of Jess's choices, not recognising why she wanted to stay at home with her children, rather than returning to work. I can see why Charlotte might resent her. They're a different breed, the stay-at-home mums. At the school gate at a quarter to nine and half past three; relaxed and cheerful in their running lycras like exotic birds chirruping away. Distinct from us working mothers, shrouded in navy or black, who drop and run, our guilt firmly compartmentalised; our choices justified by our desire for fulfilment and the demands of our mortgages.

But Charlotte is still *fond* of Jess. Why else would she socialise with her, attending book groups and mums' nights out, dinner parties and barbecues, linked by those first few months of self-doubt and sleepless nights? There's an affinity, built up over a decade. Is her attachment really so fickle that she'll immediately doubt her now the police are involved?

'Liz. Liz! Thanks for holding onto the kids.'

Mel is walking briskly towards us.

'My pleasure,' I say, but my smile slips as I see her expression.

'Did you get my message? Can we talk about Jess?'

'I did, but you know I can't talk about it. I've talked to Ed and tried to reassure him but I can't be involved any more.'

Her face crumples in disbelief. 'Well, that's just great, isn't it? Initiate this whole great mess and then distance yourself from it completely.' She is properly angry with me, not just distressed as I'd thought. 'You didn't have two distraught little boys staying with you all weekend. You didn't have to deal with their questions and their anxieties and then work out what to tell your own children. Four kids I've had this weekend on my own; two of them traumatised, Frankie *completely* hyper, not that Jess will ever accept that. Plus Ed, who's in bits: completely beside himself.'

'Oh, Mel, was it awful?' It's a stupid response.

'What do you think? I can't *believe* you would do that, Liz. What got into you?'

'Do what?' Charlotte is quivering with interest.

'Do you want me to tell her, Liz, or shall I?'

I'm taken aback by how aggressive and uncharacteristically *brittle* Mel is. I've only seen her this angry once before – back in May when she discovered Rob was leaving her for his twenty-four-year-old personal assistant, a woman who had no intention of burdening him with children.

'Liz is the one who decided that police and social services

should be involved,' she tells Charlotte now. 'She's the one who unleashed all of this upon them.'

'Come on, Mel.' I am not going to just take this from her. 'The whole team thought there were safeguarding concerns. *You'd* act if you had concerns about something one of my kids had said.'

'I guess.' She looks uncomfortable. 'But that would never happen and I'd set that against my knowledge of you.'

'But if one of mine alleged something – or you saw something that worried you in a child of a friend – you'd have to do something, wouldn't you?'

She nods ever so slightly.

'That's what happened here. I couldn't guarantee one hundred per cent that no one had harmed Jess's baby girl.'

'You can't think that of Ed, surely?' Charlotte draws herself up.

'Nor of Jess.' Mel glowers at her.

'I don't want to think it of either of them – but their baby is lying in hospital with a skull fracture.' My voice starts to break. 'I'm sorry. I've said far more than I should; this is *really* unprofessional. Please, can we just drop it?'

We walk in somewhat frosty silence to the school gate, and I try to think of how to steer the conversation in a different direction. But it's clear that Mel isn't finished with me. It's as if the trauma of the past eight months has been given a fresh focus. This isn't just about Jess and the fracturing of her family, but about Rob and his apparently casual wrecking of theirs. I sense this but it doesn't make her criticism sting any less.

'Come on, Liz. We should be sticking together,' she says, as we near the school gates, where our children are waiting for us. She stops, and drops her voice to a hissing whisper, though we're still out of earshot. 'I know people can surprise us – and my God I've learned *that* in the last year – but we have to trust our instincts. You must *know* that Jess would never lay a finger on her children.

'She's always been completely emphatic about that, hasn't she? She's never even smacked them. Don't you remember that dinner party, years ago, when Rob was a prick – oh yes, *what* a surprise – and her response to him? How icy she was when he told you all that he'd smacked Mollie?

'Don't you remember her saying there was never, ever an excuse for smacking your kids?'

LIZ

Saturday 26 January, 2013

Fourteen

'Well, we've done it. Here's to surviving five years of parenting!' Ed holds his glass of champagne up high.

'Hear, hear!' Andrew agrees, loudly.

'That sounds particularly heartfelt.'

'God, but it's hard, isn't it?' Andrew looks over his shoulder to check that Charlotte isn't listening. 'We hadn't a bloody clue, when we first met at that awful antenatal class, had we? Not a *bloody* clue.'

'Come on, George isn't that bad,' I say.

'He's the devil's child.'

'Oh, Andrew!'

'Oh I don't really mean it. Mustn't let Charlotte hear me say that. But he wants so much attention, and you've got to watch him all the time – as this week's antics showed. Sometimes I just feel too ancient for this – and as if I'm the world's most inept dad.'

'You're a wonderful dad.' I put an arm around him and give him a quick hug.

'One whose son is running away from school at the age of five?' He pulls a wry face. 'Charlotte's livid.'

Nick grins. 'I think you'll find our daughter had something to do with that, too.'

'She initiated it,' I admit. 'Told him they should make a run for it at first break.'

'Yes, well. I'm sure they're just as bad an influence on each other,' Andrew harrumphs, trying to walk the impossible tightrope of not criticising a friend's child for something while simultaneously damning his own.

The eight remaining members of our antenatal group are at Ed and Jess's house, supposedly celebrating our children hitting that five-year milestone. But conversation has so far been dominated by the scandal of Rosa and George's truanting, during yesterday's first playtime at St Matthew's primary school.

I've a sneaking admiration for my daughter, though I wouldn't admit it to Andrew or even Nick, who's particularly risk averse when it comes to the children's safety. Four months into reception, Rosa realised that school was boring and persuaded George to take advantage of the button at the school gate, which, being wheelchair-friendly, was also at a conveniently child-friendly height.

The headmaster, Mr Fox, embarrassed by the ease with which two small pupils had flouted school security, has disciplined them with a week's suspension. It's excessive, enormously inconvenient, and Charlotte and I are appealing against it but I really hope it doesn't continue to dominate tonight. After all, they barely reached the main road before being spotted by another parent, no one was run over, and no one was abducted. They were gone less than five minutes. Obviously it's far from ideal, and it's concerning that no one immediately noticed their absence, but I'm not allowing myself to catastrophise about what could have happened. It could have been far, far worse.

'We don't mean to sound flippant,' I try to reassure Andrew, who has already mentioned using a solicitor to appeal against the suspension. 'We've talked to Rosa. We're seeing it as a wake-up call for us, and for the school to improve their security. It was a very lucky escape.'

'Sounds a sensible approach,' Ed says, topping up my glass, and lightening the conversation with the social ease at which he excels. 'They're hardly Bonnie and Clyde.'

'Exactly.' I smile at him warmly.

'Shall we join the others? Jess says it's time to eat.'

The conversation swirls and settles, over five-hour lamb, on the topic of our children. It's the thing that binds us, even if Rob briefly succeeds in steering us in the direction of the Bank of England's fiscal policy, and Charlotte – making a concerted effort not to discuss 'Schoolgategate', as Ed has dubbed it – grows animated as she discusses the rise in house prices in our area, always a source of glee.

Rob is irritated when Mel begins a lengthy anecdote about something Mollie, their eldest, has done.

'It's always the kids!' he says, his sensuous mouth sliding into a sneer.

I don't like him, I suddenly realise, a fact not unconnected to Jess confiding earlier in the kitchen that he tried to play footsie under the table. ('Really? Are you sure?' 'I'm not *that* clueless at reading the signs.' 'Poor Mel. Will you tell her?' 'Of course not,' she says.)

'Well, they're a pretty central part of our lives,' I say, now, looking at him directly across the table. I'm feeling combative. Rob takes a traditional view of parenting in which he is the authoritarian father while Mel does the bulk of the childcare. 'It's inevitable we want to chat about how they're doing. They make us so proud.'

'Though not when they're being naughty?' He raises his wine glass and looks me in the eye.

'I think we've already discussed that at length.'

There is a slight frisson. I've been sharp and committed a dinner party faux pas in saying something to sour the atmosphere.

'More wine, Liz?' Ed asks. Charlotte and Andrew murmur in appreciation, and the tension slackens as he tops up our glasses with generous amounts of Bordeaux. Nick and I don't go to many dinner parties and few where the wine flows this freely. I have three glasses – for champagne, white wine and red wine – and have drunk far more than usual. Tiredness and the excitement of going out for once have combined to make me tipsy and a little reckless, and so perhaps that's why I choose to goad Mel's husband, now.

'But, tell me,' I say. 'What should Nick and I, and Charlotte and Andrew, do? How would you discipline Mollie if she'd behaved like Rosa and George?'

'I'd give her a short, sharp smack on the back of her legs.'

There's a collective intake of breath.

'Rob!' Mel flushes, and I wonder how often this happens.

'What?' He snaps at his wife then turns back to us. 'Don't judge me! I've smacked Mollie twice in her life. It may not be *politically correct* to do so,' he spits, as if the phrase is distasteful, 'but it's quick and effective and she won't do it again.'

'That's interesting. That's how I was parented – and at boarding school of course, where we still had the cane,' Andrew says, deflecting attention from Mel, who looks close to crying. 'I hated the latter – but I'm not sure the odd smack from my father ever caused me any harm.'

'Everyone gave their kids the odd wallop in the Eighties, didn't they?' Charlotte concurs, in a brief show of marital harmony. 'Not that we've ever smacked George, of course.'

'God no. I'm far too much of a softie,' Andrew laughs, then undermines his argument. 'Though perhaps that's where we've been going wrong.'

Nick starts to talk about how corporal punishment is never the answer, and the difficulty of trying to curb violence among secondary school boys who've experienced it meted out by their parents. 'The cycle of abuse continues. They see violence as the way to impose authority because it's all they've experienced,' he explains, a vein in his forehead pulsing as he becomes animated. 'We see it all the time.'

'We're not talking about *abusing* our kids but one short sharp smack, when they've done something really bad.' Rob leans forward, his expression intense, his tone unrepentant. 'You can't tell me psychological or emotional abuse isn't just as damaging. God, when I think of the sort of things my old man said to me ...' He pauses, momentarily distracted, and I wonder at the phrases he's recalling: whether he is dwelling on the most savage. 'At least this way, it's all over fast.'

There's a short silence: the kind that comes when someone you thought you knew relatively well lets slip something that makes you see them in a fresh perspective.

'What's your take, Liz?' Ed asks and then, before I can answer: 'We don't do it – though like Andrew, I was caned frequently.'

'Oh, it didn't happen *frequently*.'

'Perhaps my school was more draconian, or I was a more difficult child.'

'I can't imagine that,' says Charlotte, almost flirtatiously. Her tone, with its gravelly undercurrent, sits oddly. 'I imagine you were high-spirited, as you were at uni. Perhaps a rebel but never difficult or *demanding*. I bet you're being too hard on yourself.'

'I think my parents would disagree,' Ed demurs, though he looks a little embarrassed. 'As far as they, and my school, were concerned, I was a bit of a nightmare. But what do you think, Liz?'

'We've never smacked our children,' I say, trying to quash the rage that threatens to bubble up inside me. 'And yes: I've seen some horrific cases. Not really the stuff of dinner party conversations, but enough to know that, although there is a vast difference between a smack and abuse, they're on a continuum I don't want to be part of, and I will never, ever hit my kids.'

I look at the faces of my friends, drinking wine and eating expensive food, and for a moment I want to shock them out of their complacency. To tell them about two-year-old Jake Summers, and the red welts striated around his neck I'd assumed were a viral rash until my registrar explained someone had tried to strangle him. Or fourteen-month-old Louis Smythe, admitted with multiple fractures caused by his mum's boyfriend. Or about the case that still haunts me at night: of eight-month-old Caitlin Clarke, who a colleague discharged in her first job in A&E, thinking she had a virus but who was brought back, fitting, a few hours later. In the intervening period, one of her parents – the courts could never prove which – had shaken her so severely she sustained life-changing brain damage.

I swallow the hard plum at the back of my throat. Good old Liz. I've already changed the tone of the dinner party by being angry and earnest. No one wants to be harangued and no one wants a guest to cry either, as I feel embarrassingly close to doing now. Only Nick knows the more personal reasons for my never smacking our kids. My mother's anger and the trauma of my brother's accident, which means I already feel as if I've caused enough harm. I feel Nick's leg press against mine in silent solidarity as I concentrate on trying to calm myself and on stilling my breathing. Know he probably hopes I'll drop the issue, too.

'Fair enough. Sounds like a pretty good reason.' Ed is watching me, his expression sombre. His eyes crinkle. *Are you OK?* his look seems to say. *Did I push you too far?*

'Sorry for being so serious,' I manage, though I don't feel apologetic in the least.

'No need to apologise,' my host says.

I look around the table. Rob gives me a curt nod, as if acknowledging I have a point; Mel offers a watery smile: she's still staving off crying. Nick takes my hand under the table and gives it a squeeze.

But it's Jess who seems to feel the strongest connection. She is looking at me as if she understands my motivation; as if she too has experienced a volatile parent, though she never talks about her background and I'd always understood her parents were benignly absent: her upbringing the sort of upper-middle-class one where parenting was largely contracted to boarding school.

'Quite right,' she says, raising her glass. Her gaze is too intense, and I wonder if she's also a little drunk. She pauses and there's a peculiar tension: as if there's something she is poised to reveal. Jess has the capacity to shock. On the two occasions when I've seen her drink too much, she's said or done something outrageous, something that belies her controlled image. On a mums' night out ordering tequila slammers and dancing sensually with a group of delighted male students; more recently, challenging Andrew into limbo dancing with her at a school fundraiser. Now, she lowers her glass as if thinking better of it and I wonder if the moment has passed.

'None of us want to be on that continuum,' she says, eventually. 'And what was acceptable in the Eighties really isn't now.'

She takes a swig of her red wine, a drop beading at the corner of her mouth. She swipes it away with her tongue. Eventually she looks up, and there's no hesitation. Her voice is icy and calm.

'There are different types of destructive parenting. Mine might have been called benign neglect. My parents didn't care for us much – we were rather an inconvenience. My father rarely smacked us but there was always that potential if we stepped too much out of line.

'It was what was done, as you say. And perhaps an emo-tionally robust child bounces back if it doesn't happen frequently: my brothers certainly did. But a child who's less resilient, who's scared? For her, the threat can stir up all sorts of anxieties.' She looks at us, frankly, and it's as if everything's stripped away.

'So I can't think of any circumstance in which it is acceptable to smack a child.'

LIZ

Monday 22 January, 2018, 8 p.m.

Fifteen

'Is that Liz Trenchard?'

The voice at the end of my mobile is unfamiliar, nervous, and just a little excited. I sense this just as I understand that the speaker is ringing with bad news.

'Yes,' I reply. 'That's me.'

'It's Sandra Rhys. I'm a neighbour of your mum's? She's all right, but there's been a spot of bother,' and here Sandra pauses, and I hear the delicious trepidation in her voice: she's been looking forward to imparting this information.

'What sort of bother?' I ask.

'Well, it's a bit delicate . . .' I imagine her pursing her thin lips. From memory, she's in her sixties: a small, neat woman with a small, neat Jack Russell my mother thinks is vicious. 'But she's a bit *incapacitated*.'

'*Incapacitated?*' I repeat, not understanding.

'It was lucky I was in Tesco, really, because that's where

she was being, well, "drunk and disorderly" is how the young police officer described it.'

'Drunk and disorderly? In Tesco?' My heart stutters: a physiological response to something I've feared a long time. 'And the staff had to call in the police?'

'Well, a PCSO, really. A police community support officer,' she says, spelling it out. 'Tim, he was called. A lovely young man. Luckily, he was on the high street at the time, dealing with some teens. The staff called him in because she was being ... well, *aggressive*. She wanted a bottle of vodka and she refused to leave when they wouldn't sell it to her. Then she sat down on one of those stools they use to stack shelves – you know the ones I mean? And she refused to get up. Luckily, I'd just popped in with my Dave.'

'Oh good Lord.' I lean my forehead against the cupboard in the kitchen, imagining the scenario only too clearly. Memories of her rage kaleidoscope: her hand striking at the back of our thighs until they were whipped red.

'I'm so, so sorry,' I say. 'But she wasn't arrested? You're not calling from a police station ...'

'Well, no. PCSOs don't have the power to do that. They'd have to have called an officer.' She is keen to impart her knowledge. 'My Dave's strong, though, and the officer was only too grateful when we said we'd get her back home safely. The only thing is: I don't like to leave her alone ... I'm worried she might vomit in her sleep.'

'Of course.' The poor woman has done enough. 'Look ... my husband's just got home so I can leave the children and

138

come straight away. Depending on traffic, I should be with you in twenty minutes. Would you be able to stay with her until then?'

'Of course.' Her voice sings with relief. 'Though she doesn't like having us in her flat.' Her tone turns conspiratorial. 'She seems to think we've been cosying up with the police ...'

'Yes, I can imagine. I'm so sorry. And thank you for bringing her home, and for calling me.'

Sandra is brisk when I arrive at my mother's ground floor flat in a Victorian terrace. She's clearly had enough of my mother.

'We'll get going, if we may.'

'Please *do*,' my mother says.

'Mum. Sandra and Dave very kindly brought you home,' I intervene, speaking in the sort of over-bright voice that I've used in the past when treating elderly or hard-of-hearing patients. I must stop it. She's not that old and she's not my patient. She's drunk and she's my mum.

'Get her away. And get *him* away,' she says, gesturing to Dave, a mountain of a man, as huge as his wife is petite. 'I don't want him here.'

'Well that's charming,' he tells her. Though it's January, he's wearing a polo shirt that rides up to show a strip of hairy stomach. He pulls it back down, giving his flab an itch.

'They were with that police officer. In *cahoots*.' My mother glowers and I'm reminded quite how much she detests authority figures. She has always been like this: resisting parents' evenings and doctors' appointments; ensuring Mattie failed to receive adequate care.

For a moment, I'm back at the hospital burns unit as my mother turned on a plastic surgeon who explained my brother would need regular surgery.

'I don't *want* him to come back to hospital,' she'd said, and her eyes had flitted to the door as if searching for an escape. 'We need to get on with our lives.'

'Mattie needs the adducted scar tissue to be cut so that his arm can develop its full range of movement.' The kind young doctor had pressed on, perturbed by her lack of understanding. 'It's crucial for his rehabilitation.'

She had snorted with what looked like contempt but I now realise was fear. Stubborn and self-absorbed, she failed to take Mattie for each necessary operation so that he required more aggressive surgery once he turned eighteen. Her apparent disdain for someone trying to help was the point at which I realised she was fallible. Watching the snarl on her face, a snarl replicated now, I knew I wanted to be a different mother to this.

'Thank you so much,' I tell Sandra and Dave. 'I'll stay with her until she sobers up or I can get her to bed. Make sure she's looked after.'

Sandra folds her lips neatly against each other. 'Well, I think we've done our bit.'

'I'm incredibly grateful,' I add, conscious that they rescued my mother from a possible arrest.

'Get him *away* from me!' My mother bats her arms in Dave's direction. The nape of my neck prickles, and I remember her doing the same thing to someone in uniform; not a nurse but I *think* a policeman. It's a weird déjà-vu, and I feel unsettled as I bustle them away.

My mother calms down as soon as they've gone, stops shrinking so I can look at her clearly. I scan her face, appalled at what I've missed. Her eyes are bloodshot and her skin, sandpaper rough. I want to soothe it. To drench it with moisturiser and ease away the wrinkles that criss-cross her brow and run from nose to chin.

There's a nasty gash on her cheekbone, dotted with flecks of tissue where she's tried to stem the bleeding.

'Is this where you banged your face?'

'What are you talking about?'

'Your eye. Can I see?' I manoeuvre her so that she's turned towards the light, tilting her chin to see the extent of the bruise which mottles the socket and spreads up towards her hair. She is shorter than me. Five foot two to my five foot six, and I am conscious of how our roles have changed: how I'm caring for her, though in truth I've long been a carer, long been someone who acts as a mother, particularly to Mattie. She smells of cigarettes, cheap white wine, and the grub of unwashed skin.

'I dunno how it happened ...' she says at last, and she sounds genuinely taken aback.

'Oh, Mum. You've been drinking.' I'm tired of the pretence, of my pussyfooting around her. 'Can you tell me what happened?'

Like an obstreperous teenager, she shakes her head.

'Has this happened before?'

'What?'

'Your drinking this much.'

No response. Then a sullen mutter: 'Stupid little bitch.'

The insult slides off me like water slipping from a Vaselined back. As a child I imagined myself as a long-distance swimmer, the jibes beading and streaking away. The irony is, that if she spoke to me like that in a hospital, I could have her removed. Here, I can hardly walk away.

'Let's get some water into you and a cup of tea; would you like that?' I grasp at the props of ordinary life. My mum used to inhale tea: orange-hued and so steeped you could smell the tannins. I go into the kitchen, crouch down and swing open the door of her small fridge. The seal's dirty and the holder in the side has snapped so it can't hold any milk but the light bleeds into the room. There are just a couple of bottles of wine on their sides, an onion, a cracked heel of cheddar cheese, half a wizened lemon, dusted with mould. The milk has turned, the sour smell kicking the back of my throat. I fill her a pint glass of water, which she ignores.

'You need to try to drink this.'

Still nothing.

'Coffee,' I say. 'Let's have a black coffee.' There's a jar of instant coffee in the cupboard and I fill two mugs, taking my time as I stir the granules and inhale the steam. I need to discover whether this is a one-off or a regular occurrence,

142

and if it was precipitated by anything in particular. To work out how I can help her.

But by the time I take the mugs through, she has fallen asleep.

Two hours, three, I wait, listening to her heavy snores as she lies on the sofa, covered in a blanket. She looks even more vulnerable, now she's asleep. Sugar once sustained her. Now her skin hangs in loose flaps below her arms. Her face is mottled and topped by a fuzz of dark brown hair. Many women lighten their hair as they age but my mother is having none of it. Her determination to remain the colour she was at sixteen – but a harsher, chemically induced version, with none of the lighter streaks that might have appeared naturally – is typical. *Why should I go grey*, her insistence on reaching for the hair dye every four or five weeks seemed to say. But now her one concession to vanity has vanished. Two centimetres of silver run along her parting, like a seam of quartz running through slate.

I shift in my upright chair. She moved here three years ago. This has never been my home and it doesn't feel homely. Her old electric fire emits little comfort or heat. The fabric on her armchair is worn and I'm struck by how sparse and impersonal the room is: with its stark ceiling light, its small, mustard sofa devoid of cushions, its wallpaper with damp lapping at the bottom. There's nothing to indicate she has grandchildren and just the one childhood photograph of Mattie and me.

I stare at the mantelpiece again. There's a dog-eared post-card of Hastings Pier, and for a moment I am back there – or more specifically at Sea View, the cafe she ran when Mattie and I were children, right up until it closed five years ago. That's all it takes: one photo and I am transported to that space. Hungry workers rammed themselves onto benches against Formica tables; the air rang with the sound of male laughter and knives scraping against plates.

You rarely see caffs like that these days in such prime locations. The sort that serves sliced white bread and butter as standard, and too-stewed tea in individual metal teapots, the handles scalding, the liquid a thick stream. The sizzle of eggs frying in a pan and the smell of hot fat was ever-present, and everything came not just with bread and butter but chips. It didn't occur to me for years that potatoes came in any other form. There were burgundy bottles of Sarson's vinegar and fat plastic towers of salt; cheap brown sauce and ketchup, jammy around the cap, which dripped and splodged in smears of blood.

We didn't always live there. We moved when I was four and Mattie, two. After my father left us and my mother suddenly found herself on her own. I don't remember much about our previous home, a Dartmoor cottage down a steep-banked lane, except that it was isolated. My mother hated it, and moved to a seaside resort when he'd gone, craving somewhere less desolate and insular; less judge-mental, too.

Sea View – or the flat above Sea View – holds difficult

memories, not least of Mattie's accident. They come at me in a rush: Mattie's screams, of course, but more generally her explosions of anger: her wrenching Mattie so that his shoulder dislocated; the dull clout to the side of my head that left me deaf for two days. It wasn't that we were regularly beaten, but we knew not to push it. Because, when our mother lost it, it didn't feel as if she was frustrated: it felt as if she *hated* us.

Did Jess feel like that? Even now, faced with a mother so drunk the police were called, I keep coming back to this question. Did she ever feel so angry with her baby that she lost her customary self-control? Jess, who crouches down whenever a child falls over to look them in the eyes and tell them they'll be OK. Jess, who used to set up painting sessions, despite Frankie's short attention span and her love of order. Jess, who decided to have a surprise third baby while the rest of us only felt relief at having left babyhood behind. I just can't see it somehow.

Just after midnight, my mother stirs. Sleep has sobered her up a little and she fumbles her way to the bathroom.

'Do you need any help?' The toilet seat bangs and she's violently sick. I fetch a cloth, a fresh glass of water, find some tissues in my bag, amid the detritus of dusty Haribos and bits of Lego figures, and try to wipe her forehead dry.

I pull a band out of my hair so she can tie hers off her face but she refuses and plonks herself down on the sofa. As she does, her leg catches the pint of water I'd left her.

'Look what you've made me do!' she screeches as she's drenched.

I find a towel and dab at the floor and her bare legs. Her legs are threaded with varicose veins, her toenails yellow and gnarled. I am so conscious of her ageing, but her anger makes me recoil. I resist apologising; feel irritation. It's close to midnight and here I am, the dutiful daughter, the conscientious medic, literally kneeling at my sozzled mother's feet.

I just want to go home; but the shock of the water, and of her being sick, means that she is becoming sober. Her speech is no longer slurred; her gaze no longer glazed. She makes a curious sound and I'm surprised by a flood of tenderness. My mother swipes at her right eye angrily. She is crying, and she never cries.

'Do you want to tell me about what happened in Tesco?' I ask, sitting back on my heels.

'No.'

'OK.' For a moment I am so tired I feel like giving up on her. She has always treated her body badly, piling on the pounds to become clinically obese after we left home, risking type-2 diabetes, until I scared her into doing something; then starving herself as she veered to the other extreme.

She no longer smokes but she drinks. Just a couple of glasses a night. She has never admitted to the gin. I've told myself not to be judgemental; have mentioned that the government now recommends no more than fourteen units a week. *Nanny state*, she's said, scornfully, and I've known not to push it. But I've clearly shut my eyes to a problem.

Being drunk and aggressive in public takes self-destruction to a new level.

'Can you tell me if something in particular made you drink so heavily?'

She fiddles with the edge of the sofa, prising apart the weft. 'I'd been thinking of Clare.'

'Clare?'

'Your sister.'

For a moment, I'm bemused and then there's a dawning realisation.

'You mean . . . the baby who died in a cot death?'

'Yes.' She swallows. 'That was her name. Clare.'

I fixate on the texture of the fabric, a heavy, ugly weave. I knew she experienced a cot death. It was part of our family mythology and yet it was never discussed. I'd never been told the baby's name, how old she was, or even if it had happened after I was born. There were no pictures and the one time I'd asked about it, my mother had refused to speak to me for three days. The message was clear: I was never to discuss this child.

Shorn of any details, her life and death were just cold facts; nothing that preoccupied me until I had my own children and the risk of cot death was something about which every parent was warned. And now my mother, who has resolutely refused to discuss her, has been thinking of her as she drinks herself into oblivion.

'It was thirty-five years ago today.'

'Oh, Mum.' I want to reach out to her.

'Don't.' She pre-empts me.

'Do you want to talk about it? Tell me what happened?'

'What is there to say? Eleven weeks old. I put her down to sleep. She never woke up.' She shrugs, dismissing her grief with this abrupt gesture, and yet the impact is clear to see.

'I'm so sorry.' I want to put my arms around her but she has always resisted affection. 'I wish I'd known the importance of today. We could have spent it together ...' I stop, realising the mother–daughter relationship I'm evoking is pure fantasy and probably the last thing she wants or needs.

'You think it's just a baby,' she says at last. 'Not a real life. Not worth getting upset over. But perhaps it is.'

I try to think of something suitable to say. There is so much I want to know. Thirty-five years ago, I was three, and Mattie one. I have a recurring dream of being a young child and spying on my mother through the chink of a bedroom door. She is holding a baby and I'd assumed this was a projection of my subconscious yearnings: that she is holding the child I longed to be. But perhaps it was Clare and this is a long-suppressed memory of my mother holding this baby in the immediate aftermath of her death?

'Did you talk to anyone about this at the time? Did you have any support? Is her death connected to Dad leaving?'

The questions tumble from me but my mother has clammed up. It's as if, having given me a glimpse of her inner life, she can't risk further closeness. 'I'm tired,' she says, crossing her arms in front of her tightly. 'I want to go to bed.'

148

'Are you sure?' This is typical but I'm discomfited by this sudden desire for distance.

She stands abruptly, her voice querulous. 'I just said so, didn't I?'

On her doorstep I try to put my arms around her to give her a quick hug but she stands tense inside them, characteristically resistant. Perhaps this death coloured her mothering of my brother and me? Did it numb her, and does it explain her lack of affection; her emotional detachment; those unpredictable bouts of anger that came from nowhere and were never mentioned afterwards as if, once the bruises had vanished, they had never occurred?

'Well, bye then. Take care,' I say as I drop my arms, my words inadequate and inconsequential.

She nods, refusing to look me in the eye.

'Will you at least let me put you to bed?' I try again.

'I'm not one of your patients.' Her anger flares, sharp as a lash. She busies herself with the latch, her movements jagged.

'Well, goodbye, then. Bye.'

JESS

Tuesday 23 January, 10 a.m.

Sixteen

Jess stretches her hand tentatively over her baby's pudgy fist and strokes the back of it. Beside her, Lucy Stone stiffens. Does she know that she fears causing her baby harm?

She moves Betsey's rabbit away from her face. Lucy is watching closely; her breath caught in anticipation, as if wondering quite when she will lash out.

She catches the social worker's eye, withdraws her hand and nods towards her baby daughter.

'I just want to hold her.'

The desire to do so is overwhelming but so is the need to appear like a normal mother: someone who can be trusted with her baby girl.

Because her mind is playing tricks on her, she knows this even while she is sucked into its stories. When she reaches out her hand, she sees her palm smack flat against Betsey's downy cheek. When she strokes Betsey's back, her fist strikes down on it, the punch reddening the delicate flesh. When she lifts the toy rabbit, she thrusts it into her baby's nostrils, depriving Betsey of air.

Bad thoughts always escalate when she's stressed, and there's no environment more stressful than this hospital. Just being here reminds her of Betsey's labour: the manhandling and the obstetrician's fear.

Her breath is high and light. She mustn't think of that now; must focus on Betsey and appearing rational and compassionate. But it's impossible to act naturally, when every single tic or movement is being observed.

'It's all right, sweetheart,' she tells Betsey, and her voice sounds unnatural and saccharine. 'It's all right, baby. Mummy's here.'

Nothing from Betsey. What was she expecting? A smile? A 'mum-mum'?

'Do you think she can hear me?' she pleads with the social worker. She sounds pathetic.

'I expect so,' says Lucy – but it's clear she's humouring her.

She sits on her hands so there's no risk of her touching, let alone smacking or punching, Bets. Will Lucy smile at her to acknowledge the risk has passed? *She must really dislike me. Must think I'm the lowest type of individual.* There is no one more morally suspect than an abusive mother.

It would be better if she went home, she thinks. She is just creating extra work for Lucy and the nurses, who watch through careful, narrowed eyes.

'I don't think I'm helping,' she says. Betsey is asleep;

it makes no sense for her to be here. 'I'm wasting all of your time.'

She makes her excuses and gathers her coat and bag, almost dropping them to the floor as she scrabbles to get ready.

'Are you sure? You've only been here half an hour.' The young woman looks surprised.

'No, really. She's asleep and you must have so much to do.' Her voice singsongs, the cadences light and carefree as if this is a social visit.

And Lucy's relief is palpable; Jess can see that, she hasn't imagined it. Her smile is less forced and her posture eases as Jess rushes away.

'You're back already?' Martha comes into the hall as Jess enters the house, rushes forward to try to hug her. She feels her sister's full breasts flatten as she presses against her own slight chest.

'How was it? How was Betsey?'

Her sister's face – a wider version of her own with a more unruly mass of curls – furrows in concern. Warm and no-nonsense, she's a more generous version of Jess: expansive where Jess is closed, ample where Jess is slight. When they were children, Martha would stand up to her waist in the sea, feet planted in the shingle as Jess clung to her, letting her legs swirl around her like seaweed. Thirty years on, Martha is rock-like, still.

'Just the same,' Jess says now. 'Still wearing that bandage

and I still can't hold her.' Her voice cracks with self-pity and she busies herself tidying the clutter Martha has created: the slumped handbag; the battered boots, good quality but uncared for, that she's failed to put away.

'That will change. She *will* get better.' Martha, pragmatic and unremittingly positive, is desperate to instil some optimism. For a moment, Jess remembers how fiercely she missed her big sister when she went away to school. Left at home, she would plunder her drawers for empty bottles of Body Shop White Musk or a tennis shirt, infused with the soft, sharp scent of her. At night, she would creep into her sister's room and remember curling up to her instead of watching moonlight spill across a cold, empty bed.

Now, she is deeply grateful, and simultaneously resentful that Martha is permitted to do all the mothering, while Jess aches for her baby girl. It's the warmth of Betsey's small body she craves, its compactness, and the way she would nestle into her in those few rare moments when she was happy to be still. Her head would loll on Jess's shoulder while she clutched her rabbit and sucked her thumb, and if she were particularly tired her body would sag so that she almost melded into her. All too briefly, Jess would let herself enjoy her smell of warm, sweet skin and clean cotton but she never relaxed properly. She'd be too conscious of all the things she should be doing to maintain order, to preserve her baby's safety, and would have to put Betsey down.

Now, those things don't seem so important. There is

none of that intimacy in hospital. They might as well have an armed police officer guarding her bed, as they have elsewhere in the hospital where a drug dealer is recovering from a gangland shoot-to-kill. The faces of the doctors and nurses are sharp with suspicion. *We have to look at the possibility someone harmed your little girl.*

'Are you OK?' Martha is looking at her carefully.

'Yes, yes.' But she isn't. 'I just need some time on my own.' She retreats to her bedroom, unwanted thoughts already crowding her head. She sees Betsey in the hospital, lying on her back, drowsy or asleep; she creeps towards her; Betsey's eyes fly open as she presses a pillow down, the heels of her palms crushing the fabric against her cheeks.

She's being ridiculous. She left Betsey half an hour ago and she was alive. And yet what if she wasn't? What if she has tricked herself into believing this because the alternative is too painful to bear? What if the images that fill her mind are real? She can feel the heft of the pillow as she leans over Betsey; hear her struggling, legs furiously kicking, as she fights for breath.

Her insides turn to liquid. She needs to ring Ed. They are barely speaking but no one else is as tightly entwined in this nightmare. She can't confide in Martha, still less in Mel or, and here she nearly gives into self-pity, in her previous confidante, Liz.

He answers quickly, his voice a whisper, his manner hurried. He's in a world in which her anxieties must be kept separate.

'Is Betsey OK? I'm on my way to a meeting. Running late.'

'Ed – I know it sounds stupid … but …' Her fear spills in a burbled rush. 'They're not keeping anything back about her, are they? There's nothing they haven't told us?'

'Like what?'

Her fear is caught high in her chest like something she can't swallow. 'She's not *dead*, is she?'

'What?' His voice cracks like a gunshot, causing her to flinch.

'I mean, the hospital would tell us, wouldn't they, if anything had happened to her? They wouldn't hide it. They would tell us if she was already dead? If she'd died in some way?'

'Jess.' His tone is sorrowful. 'What are you *talking* about?'

'I know it sounds mad …'

'Yes, it does. Haven't you just been to see her? You know this isn't true. Don't say things like that, *please*. She's suffered a skull fracture and I know that's horrific, but they would have told us if she was getting worse or it was more severe. She's not in intensive care. There's no reason to think she won't get better. She's just in hospital to give her the chance to mend – and, I guess, to give us all some breathing space.'

He pauses. He thinks she's mad, but surely *he* is? *She's in hospital to give us some breathing space?* They don't need breathing space. They need Betsey to get better, and for them to be allowed to get on with their lives.

'Look,' he continues. 'I have to get to this meeting. We

can talk about this later but please don't think like this. You *know* this isn't the case.'

He sighs and she realises that she has become a problem Ed wants to be rid of. He has never had to think of her like this previously. She has always been so careful to hide the anxieties that nibble at the edges of her brain. But she can't do that any more. She has broken a self-imposed rule: left the calm, contained Jess behind and let the anarchic version leap out.

'We'll talk later,' he repeats, effectively dismissing her and leaving her alone with her vortexing anxieties. 'I'm sorry but I really do have to go now, OK?'

She spins her rings; cleans the kitchen; tries all her usual rituals. But of course she can't keep her thoughts at bay.

She sees it so clearly. Can feel the softness of the goose feather pillow, its heft, solidity and substance as she pulls it taut between clenched fists. The white pearls of her knuckles bead and she hears Betsey's hiccupped crying: the cry of a baby who's beside herself with distress. Her skin is slick, her face red, her pupils dilated as she stares back at her mother. And Jess sees herself leaning forwards and pressing down, as her baby's tiny hands, with their shell-like nails, flail at her, trying to force her away.

She must ring the hospital. She needs to check. But when a nurse picks up the phone she is silent. How can she verbalise these fears?

It's Jess Curtis. I just wanted to check that my daughter isn't dead. That she's only suffered a skull fracture. That she hasn't been smothered. That I haven't killed her, and no one's noticed or mentioned this to me?

'Paediatric ward. Can I help you?' the nurse repeats.

'Um. Yes.' Some shred of self-preservation kicks in. 'It's Betsey Curtis's mother, Jess. I wanted to know how she was since I left her?'

But the nurse's bland detailing of her daughter's condition is far from reassuring. *How can she know? How recently has she seen her? How can she be one hundred per cent certain that nothing has happened since she last checked?*

'Please could you check on her again? Check she's OK?' She is aware she has stepped beyond the boundaries of normal behaviour but it doesn't matter because the alternative narrative is so compelling. The vision consumes her. She strokes Betsey's right cheek and brushes her hair oh-so-tenderly before pressing down. Betsey struggles – legs kicking, torso straining, surprisingly forceful against the pillow – until finally she stops.

The nurse wants to get rid of her. Jess can hear her rustling papers; hear, too, the note of over-bright reassurance. But Jess isn't going to be fobbed off. Only a parent – only a *mother* – really knows what is happening to their child. The thing to do is to go to the hospital because all other reassurance is meaningless. There's only one person she trusts, and that's herself.

'Just popping out. That's all right, isn't it?' she shouts to Martha, and she is out of the door before her sister has a chance to object.

The traffic flows, for once, and as she nears the hospital, what might seem ludicrous becomes a certainty until she knows that not only is Betsey dead but that she killed her baby girl. Her palms moisten and her vision blurs; her chest burns as if she's pushed herself in a sprint and can't gulp the air down fast enough. And her longing to see her daughter is tempered by a cold, sharp fear.

She half-runs along the corridors, darting around patients on trolleys or in wheelchairs. At the entrance to the paediatric ward, she catches up with a couple pressing the buzzer and follows in their slipstream, throwing them a quick smile. The nurse looks surprised by her second visit of the day but there's no time to explain, to concede that she knows she's not meant to just turn up. Her smile — the smile of Jess Curtis at her most composed, her most confident — will smooth over any confusion. At least, that's what she hopes.

She leaves the nurses' station behind and walks briskly towards the six-bay ward and Betsey's bed, hoping that she's got it wrong and her baby's alive and getting well. That she is just asleep, her cheeks no longer flushed with a high tempera-ture, but their usual healthy colour. Or perhaps she's awake. The bandage will be off and she'll be smiling: she'll give Jess her sunniest, most beatific beam, and gurgle, as she some-times does for her, in her delicious, irrepressibly joyful way.

But something's wrong. As she rounds the corner of the ward, she sees a junior doctor and nurse gathered by Betsey's bed, the one nearest to the entrance. The SATs machine is pinging, the blue wiggly line on the monitor dropping dramatically, and a tube snakes from this to the small body on the bed. The floppy-haired young doctor is looking down at his mobile phone. They're shielding her baby from her but she can hear the most terrible noise: a rasping as if Betsey can't breathe properly.

'OK, my lovely,' the nurse, who she thinks is called Zoe, says. The fetid stench of a suddenly filled nappy mingles with ammonia, cloying the already stale air.

Jess steps forward, and manages to glimpse Betsey's face. This doesn't look like her child. Betsey's eyes have rolled back and her eyelids are flickering, her back is arched, and her limbs are stiff. Her arms start to quiver: quickly, rhythmically, like a butterfly against a window. Then her legs begin.

'What's happening?' she cries, not caring that she shouldn't be here, because this is it, isn't it: the prelude to her dying? But the junior doctor is looking fixedly at his phone. 'Please, can you tell me?' she tries again.

'Mrs Curtis,' Zoe begins. 'You're not meant to be on the ward.'

'What's wrong with Betsey?' She sounds shrill, her voice babbling.

'It's nothing to worry about,' the nurse takes her by the arm. 'She's just having a seizure ...'

'You shouldn't really be here, Mrs Curtis,' the junior doctor repeats. He is far too young. Must only be in his mid twenties: he has *spots*, for fuck's sake!

159

'But I can't leave my baby. I can't leave my baby ...' She scans his unlined face. How can he not see? And where's Liz?

'Where's Dr Trenchard?' she asks. 'And why aren't you stopping this? Why are you looking at your bloody *phone*?' Her gaze flits back to her daughter: Betsey's eyes still freakishly flickering; her body stiff — like the corpse of a cat Frankie found in the garden one frosty morning. She can't look away.

The doctor turns his phone towards her. 'I'm timing Betsey's seizure, Mrs Curtis. It's only been two minutes, fifty-two seconds, as you can see.'

She sees the seconds flying: two minutes fifty-three, two minutes fifty-four, two minutes fifty-five.

'It hasn't yet been five minutes. A short-lived seizure is upsetting but safe. If it reaches five minutes, we'll give her medication.' He remains eerily calm. 'But we do need you to go, Mrs Curtis. You're not meant to turn up unscheduled like this ...'

'But she *needs* me.' She struggles to remain controlled. And then something breaks inside her. *If I leave, she will die.* She is absolutely certain of it. She cannot risk stepping away because if she does, who knows what will happen? She was meek and obliging and trusted Betsey would get better on their watch and *this* happened? She needs to remain here, to be vigilant, because when she isn't terrible things occur.

'I'm not leaving. I'm not leaving her.' She makes her legs heavy and tense; braces herself against Zoe, who is not just plump but surprisingly strong, she realises as the nurse tries to shift her, her muscles honed by years of handling difficult patients or rolling them onto beds.

'Five minutes,' Dr Smith notes to the second nurse, who picks up a syringe and moves towards Bets, then prises open her jaw and squirts the contents of the syringe into her cheek. And Jess wants to cry, out of relief that something is being done, and outrage that they can all touch Betsey while she is being forced away.

There's a rush of footsteps and Zoe drops her arm. Jess senses the shift in the atmosphere. Someone more senior has arrived.

Neil Cockerill is bearing down on her, his height imposing and his gaze severe.

'Mrs Curtis.' The look he gives her before turning to her baby is filled with contempt. She understands now why Liz might find him intimidating. 'What the *hell* are you doing here?'

LIZ

Tuesday 23 January, 12.45 p.m.

Seventeen

'Your crackpot friend's been in.'

Neil is fizzing with bad temper as he checks some records on the computer. I am exhausted. Preoccupied by my mother's behaviour, for a moment I think he's talking about her.

'Do you mean Mrs Curtis? Jess?'

'Hmm?' He looks up, irritated. 'Betsey's mother? She's your friend, isn't she?' He hammers away at the keyboard. 'I had to call security. She turned up unannounced – just came onto the ward – and her daughter was fitting at the time.'

'Is she OK now?' My heart clutches like a fist. Fitting is a risk with any head injury and the longer and more numerous the seizures, the greater the potential for damage.

'It went on longer than I would have wanted,' he says, with characteristic understatement. 'The midazolam didn't work so Rupert tried lorazepam and then the phenytoin. She'd been going nearly twenty minutes.' He finishes typing. He is absolutely furious. 'The point is, quite apart from the mother contravening everything we'd agreed with her, having her waltz in like that was *hugely* distracting. Can you imagine if we'd had to intubate?'

'We would have removed Mrs Curtis pretty swiftly, just as we would with any other parent,' I say, trying not to imagine this worst-case scenario in which an anaesthetist would have put Betsey into a coma that would then be managed.

'My point is: we shouldn't have to deal with this.' He batters the keyboard some more, two fingers hammering his point home. 'She needs to comply with what she agreed with the police and that namby-pamby social worker, what's her name?'

'Lucy Stone,' I supply. It's a waste of time trying to counter his assessment: he dismisses social workers as indecisive; believes only doctors have the gumption to make decisions.

'The drippy girl, yes. *Christ!* I'll have to call *her* now, won't I? Or the police.'

'I think your calling security will have scared Mrs Curtis enough,' I say, hoping to dampen down his reaction. His anger's so strong he seems to have forgotten I'm not meant to be discussing this. 'She'll have got the message pretty clearly. And she'll have hated being man-handled.'

'She didn't seem very happy.'

'I'm not surprised.' One of the guards, fat-necked and with a snake tattoo curling around his forearm, is particularly intimidating. Jess will have felt revolted, and humiliated. 'Did they escort her off the premises?'

'I think they directed her to the concourse.'

'She'll have got the message and gone home,' I seek to reassure him, though I wonder if that's the case. Jess will have been unlikely to leave, having seen her baby in the throes of a seizure.

'Just grabbing some lunch,' I say.

She is sitting at a table at the coffee shop, hands cupped around a mug of black tea, shoulders hunched as if trying to become invisible: a study in despair. The queue's long and it takes a while before I'm given my double-shot Americano. All the time I watch her, sensing her sorrow, wondering how I'll be received.

She doesn't look up. Around her, the tables are filling up as elevenses slips into lunchtime and customers begin to fuel up on paninis. A heavily pregnant woman slumps at the next table, stuffing a plastic folder of hospital notes into her bag. Her hapless partner arrives with two coffees and she berates him: 'Oh, Chris. I can't drink that. It's *caffeinated*. Of *course* it matters.' But Jess only gives them a cursory glance before drawing a paper napkin from her lap and beginning to play with it.

Watching her, I wonder quite why I've always perceived Jess as such an exemplary mother, never seeing her flaws as I did with Charlotte or Mel. Perhaps it was because she made motherhood look so easy. But then Kit was such a good baby, who would fall asleep at prescribed times and spent months sitting placidly on his bottom, unlike Rosa who refused to sleep, was toddling at ten months, and soon pushing all the boundaries as I tried to fathom her out.

Riven with anxiety, I tried copying Jess's parenting techniques for getting Kit to sleep and even her recipes – which Kit wolfed down greedily, while Rosa squirmed in her high chair, her mouth a tiny moue of disdain. Sleep deprivation refracts your thoughts, and in those early months, I saw Jess as some kind of baby whisperer: capable of lulling her child to sleep, and keeping him docile while mine thrashed around and woke me repeatedly. It was only when I returned to work and regained some sense of who I was that I remembered that babies aren't machines that can be programmed to behave in a certain way and that all sorts of things – viruses, teeth coming through, growth spurts – can unsettle and disrupt them. And yet, my early admiration continued despite this epiphany.

Jess isn't looking serene now but agitated as she fiddles with her napkin. Disgust skims her face as she screws it into a ball and shoves it deep into her bag.

'Jess …' Coffee in hand, I gesture to the chair opposite. 'May I?' My voice comes out wrong: business-like and perhaps a little aloof because I'm anticipating that she'll be angry. I haven't seen her since we alerted social services, and she will know, from Ed, that I was partly responsible for this.

She nods and I sit, conscious that this cuts against all professional mores but justifying it because it might help her, and it should certainly help Betsey.

'How are you doing?' I ask.

She rolls her eyes; a hint of the old Jess who would do this behind Charlotte's back whenever she said something particularly socially awkward. But her attempt to be sardonic is undercut by the fact she is close to tears.

'I've just been on the ward,' I begin, 'and they said you've been up there . . .'

She shrugs.

'You do know you can't just turn up, don't you?'

'Of course.' Her eyes are hard, now; her voice determined. 'But I had to see her. I had to check she was OK.'

'Lucy and the police will be able to stop you seeing Betsey altogether if you do this again.' Beside us, the pregnant woman looks over, intrigued. I lower my voice and wish we were somewhere more private. 'No one wants that to happen. It's in neither of your interests for you to be banned from here.'

'I had to check on her. I had to see that she was OK,' she repeats, somewhat sullenly.

'Oh, Jess. We do know how to look after your baby.'

'But you didn't, did you?' she hisses, suddenly irate. 'She's never had a seizure before.'

'It's happened because she has a skull fracture. And it's far better that it happened here where we have the medication to manage it,' I say.

The colour drains from her cheeks. Perhaps I've been too harsh but it's frustrating, and *arrogant*, this failure to accept we can treat her baby girl. For a moment, I'm reminded of my mother's open hostility towards the doctors who treated Mattie: the blithe assumption that they didn't know what they were doing. That seminal moment when I realised my mother wasn't always right.

'Is she OK? Is Betsey OK?' Jess is suddenly meek, and my irritation putters like a damp firework. Jess isn't my mother. She's my friend who's desperate for information about her sick baby.

'She had another seizure but she's been given a different drug and she's stabilised. We'll ring you if things deteriorate but there's no reason why they would do so. The best thing that you can do is go home and try to get some rest, or spend some time with the boys.' I look at her closely: there are dark shadows under her eyes, and her hair's unruly. 'How are they?'

'Oh, you know.' Her voice cracks. 'I didn't think you'd care.'

'Of course I *care*. I'm just not meant to discuss it.' I want to take her hand, but I've already stretched the boundaries of my professionalism too far. Besides, I doubt she would take it, anyway.

I sit there for a moment, searching for something constructive to say.

'You do know that if you wanted to tell me anything, you could, don't you?' I try eventually.

She looks at me with utter derision and it's as if she's punched me in my stomach. This defensive, shifty Jess isn't her. I remember weeping in her arms when I returned to work

167

and Rosa wouldn't sleep, terrified I was incapable of functioning with that level of exhaustion. She had held me close, shushing me like a baby, and it was a revelation, for someone who couldn't remember experiencing warmth and intimacy from my mother, to be soothed and comforted like this.

My phone buzzes with a text message from Fousia: 'Jacob Brooks wants to say goodbye. U around?'

It's hardly an emergency but I'm relieved at having a legitimate reason to leave.

'I've got to go.' I stand, but then I prevaricate, reluctant when there's clearly so much we need to discuss; when I haven't managed to smooth things down. 'You will head home, won't you?'

Jess gives a tiny nod.

'Please. I promise I'll ring if there's any change.'

She crosses her arms and won't look at me. Closed and defensive, she views me with suspicion, just as, if I'm completely honest, I view her.

I head back to the ward, relieved that I can focus on another child, and desperate to shake off this sense of mutual ill feeling. Jacob's recovery is the tonic I need. Three days ago he came in unconscious, suffering from life-threatening diabetic ketoacidosis. Now his blood sugar levels have stabilised sufficiently for him to be discharged.

His mother, Sonya, is exhausted but effusive.

'We just wanted to say thank you *so much*.' She looks as if she wants to hug me.

'My pleasure. It's what we're here for.'

Jacob gives me a shy smile and steps closer. 'Thank you, Dr Liz.'

'You're very welcome, Jacob.' I hold my hands up for him to high-five. He's delighted.

'Up above,' he chants, as we go through the various movements. 'Down below, in the middle, you're too slow.'

'I was, wasn't I?' I say, pretending to be confused and letting him win.

They leave, Sonya clutching Jacob's hand as if she will never let him go. I turn back to the nurses' station. Thank-you cards fan across the wall and I read a new one from the Fitzpatricks, whose three-year-old, Chloe, was admitted with a kidney infection last week. She was hallucinating before we administered IV antibiotics, and her mother Rachel was frantic. Now, she writes: 'We can't thank you enough for all you've done,' scattering kisses in a fat, cursive script.

The Fitzpatricks have sent a huge box of Heroes. ('Heroes for our heroes,' Rachel's card says.) There's always a steady supply of chocolates from grateful parents. I usually resist but my willpower deserts me when I'm tired or stressed. The caramel stickiness coats my tongue, and I'm irritated with myself for giving into such emotional eating – prompted by my sadness that Jess, who once chose me to confide in, can no longer do so.

I'm only gorging chocolate because I feel so sad for, and *troubled by*, Jess.

LIZ

Friday 7 October, 2016

Eighteen

'You needn't have gone to such an effort, Jess.' Charlotte leans over the plate of blinis Jess has put out and pops one straight in her mouth. 'These are divine but *honestly* we'd have been just as happy with a bowl of crisps.'

We've gathered at Jess's for one of our erratic book club meetings – more of an excuse to get together than an attempt to discuss literature since Mel usually fails to open the novel, to Charlotte's irritation – and Jess has gone typically over the top. There are blinis with smoked salmon and crème fraîche; homemade cheese straws; green and black olives; white and red wines; and elderflower cordial or water for Mel who has given up alcohol in an unnecessary bid to shift some weight.

'This is so kind of you though,' I add. 'Thank you so much for spoiling us.'

Charlotte catches my eye as she picks up another blini.

No need to go overboard as well, her glance says. But I feel the need to counter the acid in her remark: the implication that Jess has tried too hard and that Charlotte, with her important job – she's now a partner in her law firm, who's come straight from work – wouldn't have the headspace or the time to do more than open a tub of Pringles. Charlotte rarely hosts, but the last time she did there were trays of canapés bought from Waitrose or M&S.

Jess doesn't seem to have picked up on Charlotte's implication because she's too preoccupied with making everything perfect: flitting in and out for napkins, putting another log on the log burner, lighting an extra candle so that the beautifully dressed room glows with pools of light.

Now she's fumbling with the prosecco cork, not quite managing to twist off the wire.

'Could you do this, Liz?'

'Of course.' I ease the cork out like the proverbial mid-wife delivering a baby. The drink froths and spills into the glass. 'There you go, Charlotte,' I say as I hand it to her. 'Mel, you're not drinking, are you?' Mel shakes her head. 'Well, Jess, you have this one.' I nod towards the delicate flute.

'No, you have it,' she says, refusing to take it.

'Don't you want one? It seems a shame to open it just for Charlotte and me.'

'I'll just have some sparkling water.'

'OK.' I'm slightly surprised. Jess tends to drink at social events: she recently told me she needed a bit of Dutch courage when having to contend with Charlotte, 'just to give me a bit of sparkle.' ('You always sparkle,' I'd said. 'Not with her. I never feel very sharp when she's around.')

'It's just you and me then, Charlotte,' I say now, raising the glass and giving her a broad smile to try to smooth over any low-level friction. 'Cheers, everyone!'

'Cheers!' Mel clinks her tumbler of water against mine but Charlotte's distracted: though she mouths the toast, she is watching Jess intently.

'Are you sure you're feeling OK?' she asks. 'It's just you look a bit peaky.'

'Don't hold back, will you?' Mel snorts into her water.

'Sorry.' Charlotte is frosty. 'I'm just concerned.'

But now that I look more closely at Jess, she does look a little off-colour: pale beneath the remains of the tan she acquired during a Corsican holiday in late August.

'I'm fine, really,' she says, looking round at us all. 'I'd have cancelled if I thought I was coming down with something. I'm just feeling a bit tired: it always happens about this time of year.'

I'm not convinced but she clearly doesn't want us to make a fuss so I take my book out of my bag and start the pretence that we're going to try to discuss it.

'So, *Jane Eyre*, which I last read as a teenager. What did we all make of it?'

'I didn't finish it.' Mel, as always, gets her excuse in early.

'Did you read *any* of it?' Charlotte is in a particularly formidable mood. She has taken up half the sofa, and whether it's because she's so much taller than petite Mel, because her posture's so upright, or because she has such a deep voice – an authoritative voice, I always think; one used to being listened to – we immediately pay attention to her.

'I *did*.' Mel is a little defensive. 'I read quite a lot of it – and I've seen the film. But I gave up when Bertha started setting fire to things. I know we're meant to feel sympathy for her, and that Rochester's a shit – and he is a shit, isn't he?' We all agree, knowing there's a certain amount of projection going on. 'But I just don't have the energy at the moment to deal with female madness.'

'Oh, Mel!' I laugh at her lack of sisterly solidarity.

'What?'

'I think the madwoman in the attic's the best bit. Bertha Rochester's my favourite character.'

'I agree actually,' Charlotte says. 'Well, I'm not sure about "favourite" but I found her sympathetic. Can you imagine what it must have been like to be locked away like that – and to know that your husband's chosen a younger, more biddable model? Her jealousy's understandable.'

'Well, I get *that*,' Mel says, somewhat bitterly. 'Christ. I don't need to empathise with that.' Rob has recently admitted to a one-night stand with a colleague that, according to him, 'meant nothing'. 'Oh, fuck it. I need a drink.'

I pour her a glass of the prosecco, and check that Jess is sure she doesn't want any.

She shakes her head and stands up abruptly. 'Actually I've forgotten I made a pudding. I'll just get it. It's in the fridge.'

'A pudding?' Charlotte says in her most Lady Bracknell of tones.

'Just a chocolate torte and some raspberries. It was really simple.'

'Oh, Jess, we do love you,' says Mel, visibly relaxing now that she's drinking. 'There's nothing simple about making a chocolate torte.'

'I'll come and help you carry the plates,' I say.

'Would you?' She gives me a grateful look.

'Just keeping the warmth in,' I explain to the others as I reach for the snug door. *Find out what's wrong with her,* Charlotte mouths – theatrically and somewhat unnecessarily – as I close it behind me, but I pretend not to understand.

Something is definitely up, though. Jess is twisting her rings, a tell-tale sign that she's nervous, and darting around her pristine kitchen.

'Is the torte in the fridge?' I ask, opening the vast stainless steel doors. 'And are these the raspberries you want us to use?'

'Yes, yes.' Her head is buried in a cupboard. 'There's some double cream, too – I'll get a jug, and some cake forks.' She dances lightly and I want to grasp her by the shoulders and tell her to calm down.

Instead, I wait for her to stop flitting around. I've learned with Jess that you have to be patient. Unless it's a rare occasion when she's properly drunk, it takes time for her to tell you anything personal and you can't hurry her along. So often in life, I feel I've too little time to talk: children, work,

Nick pulling me in different directions. But for once there are no other distractions – just two friends, alone in a quiet kitchen, one of whom has something to divulge.

'Charlotte seems a bit sniffy,' Jess says eventually, as she counts out cake forks. This is a typical Jess manoeuvre: discussing something tangential before she gets to the heart of what's bothering her.

'Charlotte's Charlotte.' I am dismissive. Sometimes I wonder why we still include her. She would never have been a natural friend had we not met while we were all going through the same, life-changing experience, but that shared history, and her kindness to me at the time, means we can't just drop her. Besides, I sense she'd be devastated. She doesn't have many close girlfriends, and has indicated she needs us. 'Her sharpness isn't a reflection on you, you know, but on her.'

'I know. But have you noticed she's only like this when it's just the four of us? When Ed and Andrew are around, she's sweetness and light: she seems to rein in her archness, or at least dilute it.' Jess lets out a heavy sigh. 'She's guessed as well. She's so clever, so sharp. Did you see her watching me, assessing? And she's the one I've been dreading telling all along.'

'Telling her what?' For one moment I wonder if she's leaving Ed: not that there's been any indication that they are anything other than happy. Their relationship seems among the most solid of ours: certainly more than Mel's, but also Charlotte's, since she always seems dissatisfied with Andrew.

('A good man but not someone to inspire deep passion,' as Mel once said.)

But of course Jess is talking about something far more obvious. She leans back against the surface of the counter and looks down at her slightly convex stomach. 'I'm pregnant,' she says, and fiddles with her lips as if trying to coax a smile.

'But that's wonderful!' I pull her into a hug. She feels slight: too insubstantial to have a baby. I draw back, noticing how pinched she looks, how uncertain. *Never assume anything.* 'It is, isn't it?' I scrutinise her expression. 'Is it good news?'

'Yes, yes, of course it is.' She gives me her cubic zirconia smile – dazzling and artificial – then starts arranging the raspberries in a neat circle. Her hands are trembling. 'I'm *slightly* apprehensive about how I'll cope with three of them ...' A small laugh. 'But I'm sure I'll muddle through.'

But muddling through isn't something Jess does. Everything – from the food she produced this evening, to the candles and fire in the snug – will have been considered over the past few days; will have taken an inordinate amount of time to organise. The trick is to make it look easy, and of course she does, but babies and very young children – as she well knows – can be erratic and changeable. The order she achieves once the boys are in bed will be disrupted even more.

'Forget I said anything,' she says now, perhaps reading my mind. 'The boys will be at school all day so I'll have plenty of time with the baby, then, and they sleep when they're little, don't they?'

'Yes. Not sure about Rosa but your babies did. Why do you dread telling Charlotte though? You're not worrying about her liking Ed again, are you?'

When our first babies were tiny, Jess was convinced that Ed had slept with Charlotte at university. It almost became an obsession, and clouded those first weeks of Kit's baby-hood as she fretted that her husband might find Charlotte more attractive and leave. Mel told her she was mad. Subsumed by Rosa, I didn't pay it much attention; perhaps was too dismissive. Anyone could see Ed adored Jess, and that Charlotte – attractive but socially awkward – could only ever have been a fling. I wonder if this pregnancy could be stoking the embers of that age-old fear.

'No!' She laughs and I'm relieved. 'I'm dreading telling her because she had to have all those courses of IVF to get pregnant with George, and she hasn't managed a second child. I feel so guilty getting pregnant, particularly since we did it almost on a whim.'

That surprises me. Jess is so controlled and careful that I can't imagine her taking a decision like this recklessly.

'Well, you don't need to tell her it wasn't really planned. That's something quite intimate. Were you going to tell them tonight?'

'Yes, now that she knows. I'm three months already and we want to tell the children so I'll have to tell everyone soon.'

'Then just make sure you're really positive when you tell them. Don't leave any room for her to imagine doubt.'

'*Thank* you, Liz. You're very wise.'

'I've just dealt with a few Charlottes,' I say, thinking of some of the pricklier women I've come across in medicine. 'You never know. She might even be excited.'

And yet of course, Charlotte isn't.

They know something's up as soon as we go back into the snug. Mel is delighted, hugging Jess, and asking about dates: almost going overboard – at least in contrast to Charlotte, who looks, in her black work clothes, like the bad fairy at Sleeping Beauty's christening. Her lack of response, let alone her lack of enthusiasm, becomes embarrassing.

'Did you hear? Jess is pregnant,' Mel turns to her.

'So I guessed.'

I glance at her sharply. 'You OK?'

'I'm a little tired, actually. I think I might go home. How lovely,' she tells Jess, but her comment comes a little too late. 'It seems to be quite a common thing, doesn't it, if you're a stay-at-home mother? To have another baby, or a puppy, once your youngest is at school.'

'Charlotte!' Mel and I say in unison. Jess tried having a puppy last year: it only lasted three weeks before she handed it back, too distressed by its excessive incontinence to continue with it.

'I'm sorry – that wasn't meant as a dig ... I've had a horrific week. I'm tired, and a little, well, surprised. You've never given the impression you wanted another one, particularly after all your difficulties with Frankie ...' She pauses. 'Is Ed thrilled?'

'Yes, of course he is. It's me who's a little more apprehensive.' Jess falls into the trap of playing up her ambivalence to make Charlotte feel better.

'Really?' Charlotte raises an eyebrow. 'Well, a baby's not something to be apprehensive about it. Some of us would love one ... But of course I'm pleased for you,' she says.

She suddenly looks exhausted: the only one of us in her forties, her extra four or five years seem abundantly clear.

'I *will* go now, though,' she says, gathering her bags together, her voice strained and unnatural, and I'm reminded of quite how much she wanted her second baby. 'Let's email about the next date and book.'

'OK, let's do that,' I say, feeling a rush of sympathy despite her spiky hostility; and relief that she still wants to meet.

Jess gets up to see her out, and is gone some time.

'Bloody hell!' whispers Mel when they've left the room. 'That was a bit below the belt about the puppy, though I guess she had a point.' Mel had a dog from the same litter, and has never quite understood Jess's speed in getting rid of it. 'She hated it. Couldn't wait to hand it over to someone else.'

'A baby's not a puppy. You know how much she loves her children. She won't want to give this back.'

'I don't know. I've often wanted to get rid of Connor.' She takes a big swig of wine.

'You don't mean that.' Mel is smitten with her boy.

'Not really.' She tops herself up. For a while, we are silent, perhaps both contemplating the upheaval of a newborn baby: the joy of its existence coupled with the anarchy of sleepless nights and disjointed days.

'I suppose babies wear nappies, so the chaos is more containable than with a dog,' she continues, philosophically. 'Babies are just as needy, and there's more sleep disruption, but it's not as if they chew everything or shit all over the floor.'

'I think the best thing we can do is be hugely supportive.' I raise my glass and drink deeply, imagining the alcohol working its magic and flowing through my bloodstream.

Hindsight's a wonderful thing. Did I consider why Jess might be anxious about having another baby? I think I dismissed it as a perfectly normal apprehension: the jump from two to three tilting them into the realm of being a 'big' family. I don't think I dwelt on her behaviour; or gave it much more attention. Lulled by the warmth of the fire and my wine, I let myself relax.

JESS

Tuesday 23 January, 2018, 1 p.m.

Nineteen

Liz couldn't get away fast enough.

And who can blame her? She thinks – they *all* think – that Jess is at best a hindrance, at worst someone sinister: a mother who needs to be controlled.

Jess rubs her upper arm. It hurts where the security guard gripped it. 'Kick up a fuss and we'll call the police,' he had said. His size, his burliness, his implied authority in his faux-police uniform, even the red and green snake curling around his forearm suggested he meant it. She thinks of the shorter, squatter of the two, who grinned, his piggy eyes narrowing; shivers at the memory of the curved bicep bulging beneath his shirt.

She can't risk going back to the ward. Not while Dr Cockerill or Liz are there and not while the security guards are prowling. Instead, she must just sit and wait, her legs vibrating with fear. Breathe deeply: in for five, out for eight, she tells herself, as she tries not to obsess about the germs on this table but to focus on the hiss of the coffee machine; the cries of the baristas. Accept you are in limbo, unable to see Betsey; equally unable to leave.

Think of something else. But all she can see is her baby in the grip of a seizure: the flicker of her eyes, the quivering of her limbs. The images spool and her mind spirals with fresh questions – *What if this kills her? What if she is having another fit while I'm sitting here?*

She can't rid herself of the sound of that terrible rasping from the back of Betsey's throat that sounded inhuman. Should she just race up there? It's only her fear of being denied any access at all that makes her behave as Liz suggested; and that makes her cling to the idea that she has still got a grip.

Focus on something different. Next to her the pregnant woman is delivering a monologue to her partner. A well-rehearsed birth plan: birthing unit, no pain relief, a water birth, no Syntocinon to speed up the delivery of the placenta once the baby is delivered. Jess gives a yelping laugh: she'll be eating the placenta next. The woman looks at her, again, and she wants to tell her that, while she may believe she is in control in her final trimester, it's all an illusion. She will lose any autonomy once the baby decides to arrive . . .

The memory comes in a flash, as it always does, knocking her off balance. Betsey's labour: the horror of her head getting stuck; the terror as the registrar tried to ease her out. His intense concentration as the waves of pain intensified and Jess forgot how to breathe. A catheter inserted in her bladder; her pubic bone pushed down; her legs yanked into an excruciating position; two failed attempts to draw Betsey's arm out. Then the most horrific sensation of her life. More manhandling, as she became a ragdoll – limbs pulled this way and that, and her body an appliance to be delved into – and then sweet relief as her baby burst free, and wetness. A rush of blood and a slipping from consciousness towards darkness and sleep . . .

Later, after the blood transfusion and the surgery to stitch her up, it wasn't the pain that made her yelp when she peed, or the throbbing ache of her womb contracting that most distressed her, but her overwhelming sense of inadequacy. She hadn't been able to have a natural birth; one of the key things her body was designed to do. Without massive intervention, she would have killed her longed-for baby. She was potentially destructive and powerless, all at the same time.

She feels that same crushing impotence here in this coffee bar. There is nothing she can do to help her girl. She is not allowed to see, let alone mother Betsey, or be left with Frankie and Kit. And she feels so very alone: an irritant to the hospital staff, confusingly superfluous for her children, distant from her husband. Someone from whom Liz, once her dear, dear friend, was desperate to rush away . . .

And perhaps she has good reason.

Because Betsey would never have had her skull fractured if it wasn't for her.

JESS

Friday 19 January, 6 p.m.

Twenty

Friday. Early evening. Jess thinks this might be the worst part of the week. The time that, in a previous life meant drinks and celebrations and the anticipation of a fun week-end, but now means being stuck alone with the children while Ed chooses the company of his colleagues over coming home.

Kit is at football practice. It will be an hour before Charlotte drops him back and she can have a couple of minutes of adult chat. She's never particularly relaxed with Charlotte – the question of the extent to which she was once involved with Ed has always niggled. ('Is that how Ed put it?' Charlotte once asked, when Jess referred to their being old friends, and the qualification 'with benefits' – too crude a phrase for Charlotte ever to use – had hung unspoken.) But she clings to the chance of any conversation. If she can just make it until seven, then there's only another hour before they're all safely in bed. If she can package up her evening, then perhaps she can manage to keep her thoughts checked, her children unharmed.

Because it's been a long hard afternoon and early evening: the sort that would make her question her ability to parent even if Ed hadn't come back and compounded her sense of inadequacy. Yet another day when she feels she hasn't mothered well.

The rain hasn't helped: the sort of relentlessly heavy rain that stopped her leaving the house, except to dash to the car for the school run, and barricaded her behind a curtain of water at home. After Ed left, she'd spent an hour peering out of the window, trying to ignore Bets's whimpering, and watching rivulets trickle down the glass.

The heavy rain means Frankie has been fizzing with energy. 'Careful!' Her voice rises to a shriek when he decides to use his skateboard inside, streaking up and down the hall and across the kitchen before bounding off and haring upstairs.

Betsey, too, has been out of sorts. A sudden squall meant they'd abandoned their morning walk, rain seeping under the buggy hood and making Bets inconsolable; then she didn't sleep at lunchtime. Of course Jess is to blame. As the afternoon has progressed, she's been clingy then erratic, pulling herself up on Jess's legs but resisting being cuddled. She stares, her gaze incredulous and dark.

She'd be better off without me. The thought builds, only confirmed by her daughter's renewed crying. At teatime,

Betsey is too tired to eat. Food is hurled on the floor – softly steamed carrot and a puree of cod and mash; then fingers of toast, offered to placate her because her rage now is that of a small tyrant, her exhaustion and hunger vicious when combined. All Jess wants is to get her to bed early – by six-thirty, not her usual seven. If she can do that, she will have an extra half hour in which her fears about this child's safety – near the kettle, near the pans, near the knives, being strangled by the straps of her high chair – can be contained.

Bugger it. She'll start her bedtime routine, now. But the wailing intensifies as she picks up her little girl, who lashes against her, anger making her wriggle and squirm. She's as slippery as a salmon, one arm striking out, her tiny fist surprisingly strong.

'Stay still. I only want to get you to bed. I'm only trying to help. I'm *only trying to help*!' Her voice crescendos and rises in pitch until she is shouting at her baby. She catches sight of her own face in the kitchen mirror and is struck by how ugly she looks: her face twisted, her hair wild. *I don't know you any more*, Ed had said – and nor does she know herself. She has lost all self-control.

Frankie, who has been kicking his foot against the leg of the table repetitively in a quick, fast rhythm, stops and stares.

'Mummy,' he says, and it's as if her behaviour has shocked him into stillness. 'Mummy, please don't shout. Don't shout, Mummy. Please.'

She crumples, putting Betsey back on the floor and

kneeling down. He puts a thin arm around her shoulders, imitating the way in which she comforts him. 'Don't shout, Mummy,' he repeats, as she buries her face into his small torso, feeling the firmness of his rib cage, the rapid thudding of his heart.

'I won't,' she manages to promise. 'I'm sorry. I won't.'

'That's all right, Mummy.' He strokes her hair, continuing this curious role reversal. Even Betsey seems to have stopped crying. 'Shall I play with Betsey for you for a few minutes while you wash your face?'

She stares as he parrots words she might use and mirrors her ideal parenting.

'No. No I can't,' she says, but her voice trembles. She is caught in a bind: she needs to be vigilant and keep watch over Bets but she doesn't trust herself with her. She sees herself slapping her daughter, really slapping her, the flat of her palm sounding against Betsey's soft, plump thighs.

And then she sees – oh God, her familiar thought; the one that keeps recurring – she sees herself smashing her against the marble mantelpiece then dropping, no, *flinging* her away.

Frankie looks at her and she sees his trepidation. He is properly *scared*.

You're meant to leave the room if you think you're at risk of harming your baby, aren't you? Put her down, close the door, and walk away. Remain elsewhere until you feel calmer, that's what the health visitors and the baby books say. But that's always felt counter-intuitive. Why would you abandon your baby when she needs you the most?

'I can't,' she repeats, and yet she has two children who are fearful of her. Who watch, trying to anticipate her next move. She remembers feeling that way with her father: wishing he would leave so that there might be some reprieve. The thought makes her breathless, so she aligns and realigns her rings. *One, two, three, one, two, three.* And again, to make it the correct number: *One, two, three.*

She could just walk around the block, couldn't she? She needs some milk for breakfast and she can hardly ask Ed to fetch some. How long would it take? Not much more than five minutes if she ran to the corner shop and back. The cloudless sky might give her some perspective. Might calm her though she won't see any stars through the orange smog of this light-polluted suburb, and the traffic will be hurtling along the main road. But it doesn't matter. It's 6.11. If she goes right now, she has time.

Betsey is calmer already. Sitting on her play mat and smiling weakly as Frankie plays peek-a-boo behind a teddy, her eyes widening as she's captivated by his exaggerated expression; the humour in his own eyes. He's better with her than Jess; and Bets seems happier, too. She'll be safer with him than in this atmosphere of muted threat.

'Frank . . .'

He looks up at her, his face pale.

'I need to go out to get some milk. I won't be more than five minutes. I promise. I've got my phone. Do you remember my number?'

He recites it perfectly.

'Look, I'll dial it now.' She picks up the landline and does so. 'Now you just need to press redial.' She shows him. 'And you're not to open the door to anyone at all.'

He nods but he's not listening. It doesn't matter. He knows all this: don't answer the door to anyone; don't talk to strangers; keep away from the road. She has been reciting this list of warnings since he was tiny. If he just stays here in the kitchen with Betsey, they will be fine.

She's in a hurry to leave now. Excitement builds at the thought of leaving the room with its tang of disappointment, of unwanted dinner and tear-streaked children and constant reminders of her inadequacy as a mum.

'Just stay here, OK?' she says. 'Just play with her and don't lift her up.'

'OK, Mummy.' Frankie nods, rocking back on his heels then zooming in towards Betsey to make her smile. He doesn't look up; wants to be rid of her as soon as possible.

'Right. Well, I'll just be five minutes.' And she is still repeating herself, still calling reassurances, as she slips from the door.

The night is cold. The temperature is meant to drop to minus two later but the crisp air is welcome: something to freeze her cheeks, and distract her from her thoughts. She walks briskly, but when she gets to the down-at-heel news-agents, she hesitates. She never normally uses this shop: the windows are grimy and she always imagines rats scurrying down the aisles. A dishevelled man shuffles out with his

Tennents four-pack, and this decides her. She'll use the mini supermarket further down the road, as usual. If she runs, it should only take about three minutes more.

She scurries along, trying to avoid the puddles pooling after the intermittent downpours. But the shop is nearly an extra five minutes, by foot: far further than she thought. At the door, she hovers, heart hop-scotching out of synch. She checks her phone, again. 6.19. She's already been away too long. But she must get the milk, and she craves a word from the shopkeeper, who always asks how she is and looks as if he's genuinely interested – though she will cry if he asks her now.

'Are you going in?' A man in a suit is irritated with her dithering and forces her to make a decision: she ducks her head as she slips through the automatic doors. She moves quickly, picking up some organic full-fat milk and a bottle of wine Ed likes that's on special offer, then joins the small queue. Too late, she realises that the woman two in front lives three doors down: Penny, a divorcee whose children have left home, and who has too much time on her hands. Exactly the sort of person she doesn't want to see.

'Oh, hello,' says Penny.

'Hello,' she mumbles.

'How are the children and you – all good?'

She nods and gestures towards the checkout, focusing on looking busy, furious at risking being seen. Penny hovers, perhaps surprised by her brusqueness. But Jess puts her basket down and scrabbles in her bag. 'Just forgotten something,' she whispers, hoping to convey, with her tilted head, that she's far too preoccupied to chat. The customer in front of her shuffles forward and Jess moves ahead, picking up her basket to place it on the counter. Penny, looking somewhat disgruntled, takes the hint and moves off.

Though she's clearly in a hurry, the shopkeeper tries to involve her in the chat she thought she'd wanted.

'Your children not with you today?' he asks with an amiable nod. 'Husband home early?'

Does he know that I've left them? She reads judgement in the most innocuous of lines.

'Yes. Friday night. He's with them now.' The lie slips from her as she holds her hand out for the change.

'Well, have a lovely evening.'

She nods, and hurries away.

But as she leaves, she notices a girl in her early twenties, leaning over a buggy and playing peek-a-boo. The baby is barely older than Bets, but there's something about the delight in her eyes and the utter trust she places in this young woman – an au pair? No, her mother – which pierces Jess's heart. Betsey never looks at her with that unquestioning love, and Jess, with her need to be constantly vigilant, has never managed to be so unselfconscious and playful. The young woman, who bends and touches the baby's nose with her lips, is only a few years past childhood; must remember how to play and laugh herself. Has Jess ever experienced that? Yes, long ago, with her siblings; moments of bright sunshine, away from the shadows her father's volatility cast.

191

She smiles at the young mother and rushes from the shop, head down to hide the tears that are welling. It's raining. Her feet scuff through puddles, her boots grow wet. A car drenches her with spray and blasts its horn, indignant. How long has she been out? Thirteen minutes, she realises, glancing at her phone. There's a missed call: 'Home'. The place she rushed to avoid and yet the word drives her forward. She presses the number but it rings out: Frankie must be too scared to answer, or perhaps something's gone horribly wrong?

She starts running: feet pounding the pavement, the bottles, in her tote bag, thudding heavily against her shoulder. Her breath is caught in her chest: fluttering high. She slips but manages to right herself before smacking down on the pavement. *You're a bad, bad mother.* The thought threads through her mind until the fear of why he might have rung thrusts all other thoughts away.

ED

Tuesday 23 January, 7 p.m.

Twenty-one

It strikes Ed that the other football dads might be keeping their distance when he and Kit turn up for the evening training session. He's not the sort to be paranoid but they seem to be huddling together and he's not sure he can blame the bitter cold.

It doesn't matter. He tends to chat with Charlotte. George is nifty with a ball; has recently been scouted for a trial with an academy – but Andrew is uninterested in his son's footballing prowess and it's usually his wife who brings him to the sessions. At least once a week they find them-selves chatting on the touchline.

To Ed's surprise, Charlotte loves it, cheering effusively when George heads a goal into the top but resisting scream-ing advice like the dads who act like would-be Gareth Southgates. 'They're *so* frustrated,' she once whispered when Tom and Louis's dads were particularly vociferous, and it was so unexpected he had had to laugh. 'All that pent-up desire just waiting to spill out,' she continued *sotto voce*, and he'd been reminded of the old, irreverent Charlotte from his student days. 'Go on,' she'd said, and there'd been a frisson of something he wasn't quite sure how to handle. 'Tell me I'm wrong.'

Now, though, he is intensely relieved to see her.

'Hello,' she says softly, and her quiet sympathy is deeply comforting. Jess thinks she's spiky but he has always found her clear-sighted, empathetic and warm. Perhaps he could confide in her now? He needs to talk to someone. Perturbed by Jess's call earlier that day and the laptop discovery, he wants to discuss the former (he can hardly discuss the latter) with someone who knows his wife well. He's recently mentioned Jess's anxiety and Charlotte seemed reluctant to chat, but maybe she was being loyal. Things have moved on since then. Perhaps she will be more open to talking about it now.

Tacitly, they move sufficiently far from the other parents not to be overheard.

'I'm so sorry,' she says, touching his forearm. 'How *are* you? It must be horrific.'

'Well, yes.' It is such a relief to admit it. 'It's a bit of a nightmare, to be frank.'

'Jess being under suspicion – and having to consider, impossible though it seems, that she could have done this,' Charlotte carries on.

He freezes. He didn't mean that. He was referring to the fact that Betsey is in hospital, and more generally the police investigation. He wasn't acknowledging that he might suspect his wife of doing this to her, and yet Charlotte is assuming he would think the worst.

'I'm not considering that she's done it. I *don't* think she could have done this,' he says, sounding more unequivocal than he feels. Perhaps he would have inched towards the idea if Charlotte had not assumed it so categorically but he never likes being told what he thinks.

'Oh, OK.' He can hear the confusion in her voice; knows he's being unfair, turning on her like this. 'I just thought . . . because you'd mentioned you were worried about her before . . .'

'There's a big leap between worrying about her and suspecting that she's hurt Betsey,' he says, his voice quiet and low. 'I'm not allowing for the possibility, I *can't* allow for the possibility, that Jess could have done this to our little girl.'

She is silent. Kit scores a goal from the cross bar: a spectacular shot and he knows he should cheer but he lets the other dads do it for him, their cries ripping through the night air. His son looks over in his direction and he gives him a thumbs-up, face spliced in a rictus grin. He can't carry on like this: so concerned for his baby girl that he can't feel joy on behalf of his older kids; snapping at a friend, who is only trying to be well meaning, whose support he has sought and who he values. He can't afford to be frosty, particularly when they might need their friends.

'God, I'm sorry,' he says.

She gives him a small, sad smile. 'No, *I* am. I didn't mean to jump to conclusions. But no one would judge you, you know, if you found yourself thinking what the police, and other people, might think.'

He focuses on Kit, pushing up the pitch, a long pass to George who dribbles past three players before crossing to Ben.

'Is that what *you* think?' His throat is tight but he makes himself look at her.

'I don't want to consider that she could have done this. Of course I don't. Jess is my friend and she's a wonderful mother. But the police, and Liz, clearly have some concerns. I'm just saying it would be perfectly normal if you felt some disquiet, some doubt, and if you do, however disloyal that seems, you mustn't beat yourself up about it.'

He turns back to the game, incapable of formulating a response.

'Wonder if we should go and be a bit more sociable?' he manages, eventually, and she nods in an admission they should drop the subject. They edge back towards the other parents where he chats about the team's position in the local youth league and gives the impression of being enthused about their prospects at next Saturday's game. One of the would-be managers discusses the weakness in their defence, and Ed makes a lame joke that everyone laughs at a little too heartily. Throughout, Charlotte remains silent and detached, a little to one side.

'So sorry your little un's poorly,' Jake's dad says, almost as an aside as the boys start to leave the pitch. There are a couple of gruff nods from the other dads that move him more than he'd imagined. No one mentions the involvement of social services or the police.

But he realises, from Charlotte's assumption, that he cannot express even the slightest equivocation. To mention any concern would amount to a betrayal. It was foolish of him to let Charlotte get close, and his fury simmers, with himself and with her for her disloyalty. But perhaps this was a good reminder that he mustn't let anything slip that might somehow implicate Jess.

It's an important lesson. When he gets home, the social worker is there to discuss Jess's unauthorised appearance at the hospital.

He listens bleakly. Jess hadn't mentioned that she'd done this and he finds himself wondering what else she is keeping secret, how little he knows his wife.

Lucy chats away, trying to build up a picture of the family as she does on her daily visits.

'Could Jess have talked to anyone about this? Does she have a good support network?' she asks, as she did at the start, and he repeats that Martha moved in without a quibble, and mentions Mel and Charlotte.

'And what about you? How does she find it with your working such long hours?'

He takes a deep breath and concentrates on not sounding defensive. Once, he might have quipped that Jess knew that was the deal: it's the payoff for his fat salary and for her not working. Instead, he mutters: 'She's very understanding,' and wonders if it is an adequate response.

He is walking a tightrope, editing each thought; trying to ensure he says nothing that's not supportive. But this means he can't be honest about his fears. He can't tell Lucy about the laptop. He'd considered skirting around the issue of Jess's anxiety – maybe admitting she has found this third baby hard; even that she's seemed a bit *low*. After his experience with Charlotte, there's no way he can imply this.

Now, he runs his hands over his head, fingers lightly scanning his brain as if for the right answers. Lucy watches him intently, as she chats away.

'Does Jess go to baby groups and see other mums?' she asks, leaning forwards, hands clasped together, and he looks at her, bemused.

'Um, baby swimming, I think.' She used to do that with Kit. 'A music class, perhaps?' That sounds wrong: Betsey's too little. 'I don't know, I'm afraid,' he concludes. His baby is in hospital with a skull fracture that is causing her to fit and Lucy's interested in her social life? How ludicrous that sounds.

'How did you meet?' the social worker continues, in her warm, conversational tone, and he wants to tell her he is too tired for this; that he doesn't want to talk. But of course he doesn't.

'A smoky cellar bar off the Embankment. Not particularly original or romantic, I'm afraid.'

And yet it had been to him. He was twenty-six; Jess,

twenty-three, and working in events after graduating, like so many girls he seemed to know. But she was different: someone who listened after asking you a question, and who had this surprisingly sexy laugh that hinted at an earthiness you'd never have guessed from her slightly standoffish exterior. He was captivated. Completely infatuated from that first meeting. He can't remember when she last laughed like that.

Nor can he remember the last time when she properly relaxed so that her shoulders weren't hunched and she didn't vibrate with tension. When she last got tipsy or was spontaneous; when she wasn't preoccupied with everything being calm and controlled, or focused on the kids. He wants the old Jess back. Of course he wants a wife who doesn't consider harming their child – *Christ!* It doesn't get any easier the more he contemplates that Google search – but he also wants one who doesn't worry all the time.

Because she hasn't seemed happy for quite a while. Certainly not since she's had Betsey, the baby they'd created in a moment of romantic spontaneity. And perhaps she hasn't been herself for even longer, because Frankie's hard work, and though Jess parents him brilliantly, it drags her down. And, OK, he's not exactly bursting with happiness himself, but he'd persuaded her to have a third baby to try to recapture that excitement, that sheer joy, of early parenting. How fucking *stupid*. He's only made things worse.

Of course some of Jess's anxiety is inevitable – Betsey's birth had been horrific. But Jess was only in hospital a couple of days afterwards; had got her figure back within a fortnight; and Betsey was thriving – or so it seemed.

It has only been in the last month that he's started to realise that Jess might have been more affected by the birth than she claimed. He'd been fumbling towards an understanding, but he only realised quite how miserable she had become when they argued, on Thursday night.

Ed

Thursday 18 January, 6.30 p.m.

Twenty-two

It is the pile of neatly folded vests that triggers their row, or rather, the contrast between this and their tear-streaked baby.

Ed has never seen such an ordered stack of clean washing, or known that it might exist. Bone white cotton bodies are folded and piled on top of one another like shirts in a Jermyn Street tailors. Then there's a second pile of Babygros, folded to the same height and width, another space and a third pile of tops folded in the exact same way.

Ed doesn't deal with the children's washing. (To be honest, he doesn't deal with any washing.) He vaguely knows where he might find a clean item of clothing for the children but he couldn't say in which particular drawer. And so it's a revelation, discovering these piles. He pulls out the second drawer: the same, this time for tiny dresses; and the third, for leggings. In the bottom drawer, there are stacks of disposable nappies, and on the top of the chest, a white wicker basket filled with cotton wool pads, neatly tessellated.

The irony is: he wouldn't have been aware of this extreme neatness had he not been trying to make life easier for Jess. Conscious of quite how little he's been around, he'd been aiming to get home for bedtime all week, finally managing it on Thursday night.

'Darling, I'm home,' he calls, as he walks through the door at 6.30 p.m., and, though he knows it's unrealistic, he hopes she'll run out to kiss him. There's no response apart from the ragged anguish of Betsey's cries. His sons, curled up in the snug, are focused on their gadgets. 'Hi, boys,' he tries. Frankie blanks him, thumbs jabbing away at the control on the Xbox, because part of him always needs to be fiddling, to be doing *something*; Kit looks up and gives him a brief smile.

In the kitchen, Jess doesn't acknowledge his presence: is too busy wiping down the fronts of the kitchen cupboards and the surfaces, which are spotless with no sign that she's recently prepared whatever's in the oven, or the children's tea.

'Betsey sounds upset,' he says.

'She doesn't want to sleep.' Her eyes are fixed on the floor, which she's scanning for any rogue crumbs that have escaped her notice.

'Well, shall I get her up? She doesn't need to be in bed this early, does she?'

'I put her down because it's easier that way. It means I can get this sorted.' Jess bends to brush a pile of dirt into a dustpan; gives him a mirthless smile as she tips the dirt into the bin.

He feels deflated. He was so eager to help: had been quite excited at the thought of giving Betsey a bath and proving to Jess that he could be a more hands-on father.

'She sounds like something's wrong,' he ventures because Bets doesn't sound close to dozing off. She sounds desperate.

'She just wants attention. We need to ignore her. It works best if I do it this way.'

She puts an empty glass in the dishwasher; reaches under the sink for a cloth and starts spraying the glass of the bifold doors with the window cleaner. He can't see the smear she seems to be cleaning. All the time, the crying continues, a soundtrack of distress.

'I'm just going to get changed,' he says, but she doesn't respond. Unable to just stand by and listen, he bounds up the stairs and pushes open the nursery door.

Betsey has obviously been left for some time. Her face is puce; her skin hot as if she has overheated through the effort of sustained screaming; her nappy is sodden against her red raw skin. The nursery is pristine: white wooden furniture that's unchipped, clean sheets, soft animals arranged in a basket, those ordered drawers that send a strange chill through him. There are no toys in her cot apart from her favourite, a velveteen rabbit that Bets chews, the ears grey and soggy with spittle. But there's a jarring disconnect between the perfect setting – and the immaculate kitchen downstairs, and the ordered snug where the boys are confined to their gadgets – and the anarchy of his baby's wretched, frantic crying. He changes her nappy, and tries to soothe her, his chin resting on the top of her head.

'Shh, shh, it's OK, baby,' he murmurs, his palm patting her back in an imitation of a heartbeat, self-conscious at first, but then less so as she starts frantically sucking her thumb. 'Shh, shh. It's OK.'

It calms him, realising that he is capable of soothing her like this; that he is not so redundant as a parent.

'Shh, shh. It's OK,' he repeats.

But his heart constricts a little because he is not so sure it is.

Later, over dinner, he tries to suggest that perhaps Jess has become a little obsessive about the housework.

'Obsessive?' She puts down her cutlery. She has barely touched the lamb tagine.

'Well, not obsessive, just conscientious,' he backtracks. 'Betsey's drawers, for instance: it must take ages to make them like that?' He catches sight of her expression and stops. 'All I mean is, I'd far rather the children were happy and the house messy. I hate to think of you worrying you need to make everything perfect for me.'

Her face closes over as it does when she's hurt.

'Have the children said they're unhappy?'

'Of course not. No.'

'Then I don't understand the problem.'

He feels the words dry up in his mouth as he tries to capture his unease.

'I don't want some sort of Stepford Wife,' he blunders on – and where had *that* come from? 'I mean. I don't care if the house isn't pristine, if the toys aren't put away, if there's a bit of mess. That's not what matters, is it? I hate to think that you're making the place immaculate while Betsey's screaming upstairs.'

Her face is like a mask: bland, unresponsive, her way of staving off further criticism. He's gone too far in implying she has neglected the baby and yet he is reluctant to drop the issue. They need to be honest about this.

'I just . . . I'm worried that things feel out of balance: that you don't seem happy or even content at the moment. Not in the least. Not like you used to. That you don't seem fulfilled – or even *happy* with the kids.

'This should be a precious early year with Bets, shouldn't it?' he ploughs on, unsettled by her silence but determined to get the words out now his sense of what is wrong is crystallising. 'All those milestones, all those memories . . . She's our last baby, and I thought you wanted to spend time just enjoying being with her?'

She looks at him as if he is speaking a different language, and he's blurrily aware that he might have an idealised vision of motherhood: one that doesn't fit with her experience, at all. He never thinks about what they get up to, though he vaguely imagines Jess pottering around, or going for brisk walks, or relaxing with friends in cafes. He has never considered it as a particularly *arduous* day . . .

But he can see, from her reaction, that his perception is skewed.

'Have I got this all wrong?' He laughs a little nervously. 'I don't mean to criticise: I want to help make things better. I don't think your experience of motherhood needs to – or *should* – be this way.'

She looks at her lap, twisting her rings. If only she'd look up. He wants to catch her eye; to reassure her that it will be OK, and that, though he might not understand her, he loves her more than he can possibly articulate. He has always felt like this about her. He reaches out a hand but she snatches hers away.

'Jess . . .'

'Don't.' Her voice is savage.

When did she become so prickly? He thinks of that cliché about walking on eggshells, usually said of an abusive partner. He feels like this and has done for the past few months.

'Jess – please.'

He thought he had snared the problem, and that raising it would make things better. But he only seems to have heaped on more distress.

He gets up and goes to put his arm around her, to try to make everything right, but she recoils, twisting her face away from him. Feeling stupid, he returns to his seat. If he waits long enough perhaps she'll eventually see this as an opportunity to tell him what's wrong. But, instead, she starts clearing away. The bin lid clatters and there's an angry hiss as she squirts the sink with antibacterial spray.

'Will you please just stop,' he says, because this is part of the problem and she doesn't see it: can't even stop when he's trying to get to the heart of the issue. She carries on and he sits there, his words bouncing off her back.

'I just don't know you any more,' he adds, and he doesn't really mean to say it out loud but there it is: the fact of the matter, squatting in the space between them. Her shoulders round, almost imperceptibly, and he wants to hold her; to tell her that he doesn't mean to wound her; that, in his clumsy way, he is only trying to help.

'I don't want to talk about it,' she says at last, and her voice is as curt and clipped as a post-war broadcaster's; her profile as coldly perfect as a cameo brooch.

And then she says something she has never said before, not even after Betsey's birth when sleep was at a premium and he would have completely understood if she felt so fragile she couldn't bear another body lying close to hers.

'I'm going to sleep in the spare room.'

The next morning he leaves early for work without saying goodbye and their conversation – their argument – keeps nagging at him, his comments ragging his thoughts. This isn't like them. They don't row, Ed having discovered early on that Jess hates conflict: a legacy, no doubt, of a childhood with her father. Neither of them shouted last night, he reminds himself, but he suspects he sounded pious. Judgemental. *I hate to think you're making the place immaculate while Betsey's screaming upstairs.*

207

And so he does something spontaneous, and entirely out of keeping. He excuses himself from a meeting and tells Jade, his PA, he'll be taking the afternoon off. Then he travels home, unease growing exponentially with each Tube stop, bemusement at his behaviour increasing too. Nursing a bunch of white roses, he tells himself he just wants to make it up to her. At the very least they might talk, unimpeded by exhaustion and the demands of small children. But, early in his journey – somewhere between Holborn and Tottenham Court Road – he forces himself to admit to a more dubious motivation. Because isn't there something underhand about his behaviour, too?

It isn't purely his desire to smooth things over with Jess that has forced him from his desk but his concern for Betsey: this creeping realisation Jess's treatment of their daughter isn't massively maternal; is maybe a little detached. It's not that she is cruel, but she's not as engaged as she was when the boys were small. When Betsey's little body had shuddered against his chest, he'd felt her relief at being picked up, and he wonders if this distress was atypical or if it frequently happened. Out at work for fifteen hours a day, he has no idea what goes on at home when he's not there, and, for the first time, this perturbs him. And so this seemingly loving trip home is powered, in part, by a need to find out.

Of course she sees straight through him, when he arrives home to find her, sitting at the kitchen table, immersed in something on her laptop.

'Are you spying on me?' A raspberry spot flares in the centre of each cheek as she slams the MacBook cover shut.

'Of course not.'

'You've never popped back like this before. Do you think I'm neglecting Betsey?'

He doesn't know what to say.

'Can you hear her?' She pauses, a hand to her ear. 'If you're wondering where she is, she's in her cot. She isn't crying. She isn't distressed. This happens at this time of day, every day, because it's naptime. There's nothing unusual, or odd.'

He is thrown by her tone: this curious mix of triumphant and defiant. It's so different to her usual manner that he almost wonders if she's been drinking. He moves closer, trying to detect a hint of white wine.

'What are you doing?' Her voice is querulous, and the too-loud sound pollutes the space between them. The house is quiet, though he knows logically that Bets is asleep.

'Go and check up on her if you like.' She reads his mind, her tone as sardonic as a teenager's – and it's this that drives him to bound up the stairs.

Betsey is lying on her back, staring at a mobile of suspended ducks, kicking her feet ineffectually, apparently not in the least perturbed at being put to bed.

His relief is immense.

'Hello, Bets,' he whispers and she turns her huge forget-me-not blue eyes on him and stares, surprised to see him there. Her face crumples and her mouth turns down, her bottom lip protruding. Before he can do anything, she is bawling: cheeks red, eyes spilling outraged tears.

He lifts her awkwardly, determined to quieten her as he managed the previous evening. She has a healthy set of lungs on her, as his late mother might have said. He doesn't want to give Jess any ammunition to criticise him and so he needs to stop this outburst, quickly; needs to reassure Bets, too, though he doesn't seem capable of doing this.

'Shush.' He presses his lips to the top of her head, where her curls grow damp with sweat. She squirms, twists, thrusts her feet down, arches away from him; does everything she can to express her distress.

All he wants is to soothe her, and make her quiet, so that Jess can't be disparaging and he won't feel even more inadequate. But her cries grow louder until he is staring down her throat at her tonsils, mesmerised by how *angry* she appears. There's none of the shuddering relief of last night; nothing to suggest he's calming her down, that he'll make things better. What sort of a dad is he that he can't stop this and that she carries on, irrespective of whatever he is doing?

He puts her back down, a little clumsily, and this seems to shock her out of crying. She stares at him again and he sees that she is startled: her mouth forming a tiny O, her outrage tempered with a look of disbelief.

He stands at the end of the cot, surprised by the abrupt silence, and feels utterly lost. Is parenthood meant to be this bleak? He's doing so well in his career – earning well, excelling professionally – and yet life at home is one long struggle:

the benefits outweighed by the frustration, the tedium, and now this fresh fear that something is seriously wrong with Jess.

So many of his colleagues have three or four kids. It's the ultimate status symbol: a sign you can provide for that many children; a sign of your virility. He'd wanted a little girl, because he thought it might complete their family and bring fresh happiness, particularly to his wife. But life, even with Frankie's needs, was so much *easier* with just the boys. Now they've upset the delicate balance and there's no room for lightness, or selfish enjoyment, any more.

What the fuck have we done? He bends over, crouched on the floor of the nursery, the enormity of their mistake coalescing in his mind.

He doesn't realise he's spoken aloud until he sees Betsey, watching him furtively, through the bars of her cot. She's clutching Liz's rabbit, no longer grey but washed and dried since yesterday evening, and sucking hard on her thumb.

And the thought comes to him, cool and clear; so sharply defined he can see it.

She is a lovely little girl but, just for a moment, he wishes she had never been born.

211

LIZ

Wednesday 24 January, 2.45 a.m.

Twenty-three

It's the sound of a baby that wakes me. The unrelenting, pitiful cry that tears through my sleep and shakes me from a nightmare so engrossing I can't tell where the boundary between my subconscious and reality lies.

My top is drenched with sweat, my heart castanetting as if I've physically tussled with sleep – and, yes, my duvet's twisted, the cover wrenched from its feathery heft and there's something pressing down on my face. I thrust the pillow away and knock a half-empty glass off the bedside table. It spills, chill water spreading all around.

I spring out of bed, disorientated as I adjust from the vividness of my nightmare to scrabbling around in the darkness, mopping up a puddle, and trying to locate this ragged cry. No longer a screech but the wearying sound of a baby being soothed by its parent, a child who will still take some time to fall asleep. It's Max Gibson, our neighbour's three-week-old baby, who seems constantly befuddled by this strange new world in which he's found himself. The sound, curiously intimate, seeps from the house next door.

I rifle in a drawer for a dry T-shirt; get back into bed; pull the duvet close around me to stop my shivering and block out this sorrowful lullaby. But the pillow's cold and lumpy and I toss and turn. Nick stirs in his sleep and reaches out to give me a cursory hug, arm flung over the curve of my waist, hand cupping my left breast. 'Go to sleep,' he murmurs, his voice just audible from the depths of his drowsiness. Then he rolls over, dragging the duvet back to destroy the warm cave between us before I give it a quick, assertive tug.

Max's cries are slowing now. But if he is slipping into sleep then I doubt I will. I glance at the clock radio. 02.47: the worst time of the night to be awake. Insomnia, which plagues me given half the chance, sees an opportunity. I think of Betsey: not technically worsening but far from stable, given the three lengthy seizures she suffered yesterday; and of my mother. Ponder, not just on her drinking but on her reasons for remaining so secretive about my baby sister, to the extent that she's always refused to divulge her name.

Clare.

I roll her name around in my mouth then whisper it out loud, feeling a rush of tenderness for this unknown sibling; unremembered and only spied through a chink in a door. I'm back in that cottage, peering at her now, or rather spying

on my mother. Her expression's still impenetrable: a mixture of anguish – that's not too strong a word for it – and a
flicker of something else. Horror? Or is it fear?

Other memories crowd in. Slivers of a story that splinter
against each other. I am three and sitting on a rag rug in
next door's cottage. Nathalie, one of the hippy neighbours,
is trying to plait my hair. Her fingers nip my scalp but I
don't complain. Her breath reeks of garlic, and the cottage is
sickly sweet with what as an adult I will recognise as a mix
of joss sticks, mould and weed. Still, I don't say anything
because I sense that I need to keep quiet. This situation's
unusual. Nathalie has never looked after me before.

I dig my fingers into the weave of the rug, trying to separate the thick strands of red and purple and green – bright
flashes of colour all the more exotic because those at home
are muted: mud brown, bottle green, the off-white of terry
towelling nappies that will never be pristine. My left hand
clutches a plastic Tiny Tears doll. Baby wees water if you fill
her up and press her tummy. She's orange and hard; doesn't
break if you throw her. She's not like my baby sister at all.

Jed, Nathalie's boyfriend, is peering out of the window.
'They're still here.' He gestures with his head and I see that
a car – white, mud-splattered, with writing on the side of
it; something I'll later recognise as a police car – is parked
out in the lane.

'Shh,' Nathalie says in her fairy voice, and she rolls her
eyes towards me. I don't like the look on her face. I want
Mattie; I want my daddy. I want to know where they both

are, and my mother. Somehow I sense that my being kept here has something to do with her.

I roll against Nick, unsettled by this memory and trying to stop the images that seem to have been unleashed from my subconscious.

Another fragment, another shard that must come later that day. A man has left our cottage. An older man in a tweed jacket and rust-coloured trousers with grooves like ploughed furrows. Dr Moore, our local GP. His head's bowed and he's talking to my daddy outside, though it's dark and it's been raining: droplets drip from the thatch of Nathalie's roof and gleam like jewels in his hair.

He looks worried, Dr Moore. I watch his expression, caught by the light from Nathalie's old oil lamp. A look of pity, and a trace of sorrow. He's talking quickly, telling my father something important, something my mother mustn't hear, because otherwise why aren't they in our cottage but outside with water sliding down my daddy's neck? My father's broad shoulders heave, once, then twice, and I know with a child's intuition that he is crying.

And in a flash, I am slipping into the cold. My feet are wet – I haven't thought to put on wellies – and I'm shivering as I clutch my father's large, calloused hand. He won't look at me, but Dr Moore bends down and places one large hand firmly on my shoulder, his eyes serious and kind. He smells of clean clothes and tobacco. I'm reassured: here is someone who might make things better. It's the first time anyone, other than my father, has made me feel this way.

'Your daddy's sad but he'll be all right. Your mummy will be too. Will you look after them for me?'

It's too big a burden to ask a child but of course I nod. I'm Daddy's good girl even if my mother doesn't see me that way.

He leaves us then. My father keeps his face turned so that I can't see the grief that is clawing at him; can only see the tear that is rolling down his left cheek.

I sit upright. My heart is hopscotching now; my mind wired and frantic. 'Go to sleep,' Nick, sleep-addled, repeats, pressing against me. We tessellate like spoons, his thighs toasty behind mine, his groin soft, his shins a warm ledge for my feet. His breath is hot on my neck and I try to melt into his warmth, as welcoming as his hug at the end of a long weekend on call. But my mind won't be stilled. These memories jangle me.

Why is it that, in the still small hours of the night, our fears are more heightened, and our deepest anxieties swim up from our subconscious? I lean against Nick, but am quite alone while he is lost to sleep. My mind skitters and whirls, flitting from Clare to Betsey and then to the nightmare that wrenched me awake.

And though I can rationalise it, it doesn't make it any less potent or vivid.

I was that screaming baby, writhing and grappling, and someone was holding a pillow to my face.

'You were tossing and turning last night,' Nick says when the alarm goes off at 6.30.

I feel drugged with exhaustion: my limbs dead weights that seem impossible to move.

He rolls towards me and pulls me close. I want to drift back to sleep but I'm aware, despite my closed eyes, that he's watching me intently.

'What?' I pull away, peeling open my eyes.

'Were you thinking about your mum?'

I groan.

'You don't have to talk about her,' he says, treading carefully, 'but perhaps it would help at some point.'

'I haven't the time.' I move to the side of the bed and swing my legs over to force myself up.

'We can't ignore the fact she was so drunk she caused a row in Tesco . . .' he begins.

'I'm not ignoring it,' I snap. 'Of course I'm not. It's just that I haven't the headspace to think about it when I've got to get to work.'

He smiles at me and I feel my bad temper ease like a knot prised open. He's a good man, who cuts me plenty of slack whenever the topic of my mother arises, and I shouldn't take my irritation out on him.

'I'm sorry,' I say, gesticulating hopelessly. I was drawn to his emotional stability, his calmness, the fact he experienced a relatively easy childhood – the wonderfully solid basis his parents, Pam and David, gave him. But the flipside is that sometimes he's too bloody *reasonable* about everything.

I move towards the bedroom door and the bathroom, but Nick's still trying to be helpful.

'Is it worth calling Matt about your mother?'

'What good will that do?'

My brother has made it clear he has no desire to hear about, let alone help, the woman he insists on calling Janet.

'Liz: your mother started to open up about your sister. There's some serious stuff going on here.'

'There's no point. He won't want to know.'

'Try him. It's not fair that he should absolve himself from all responsibility. If he won't help on a practical level, he should at least listen and know what's going on.'

'I guess.'

Nick will never understand the depth of Mattie's antipathy or the extent of the pain he experienced: how can he when he didn't witness what happened, or the painful aftermath? And yet perhaps I'm protecting him too much. As Nick has pointed out before, when I've been exasperated by his self-exile, he's thirty-six – not eight.

'It does feel as if there are gaps,' I admit. 'Things I can't make sense of that he might be able to remember, bits of a broken jigsaw – though he's so antagonistic towards her, he'll hardly have a positive view.'

'Well, it's up to you.' My husband pulls on his boxer shorts as I make for the shower, hoping the water will blast me awake and wash away these emotions. 'But I'd try him. He might surprise you.'

I call Mattie as I near the hospital entrance, knowing that if I put it off until this evening my resolve will crumble. The street is filled with the noise of cars and the sound of hospital staff walking briskly, impatient to get on with the day.

'He-llo?' His voice is hesitant but clear. I picture him, five hundred and thirty miles away, against a backdrop of tussocky grass and snow-capped mountains. 'Lizzie, is that you?' The wind swirls in the background and his voice holds a trace of a Scottish accent as if he's been only too ready to shrug off his Essex vowels. Then again, he's lived in Scotland for over twelve years.

'Hello, you.' It's such a relief to hear this voice I know as well as my own, despite these relatively new inflections. I pick my way carefully. I want to appeal to the man who teaches underprivileged teenagers on outward-bound courses, not the one who clams up whenever I try to bring up the topic of our mother, but then I realise I haven't the time.

I tell him about her drinking and the intervention of the police; about her naming Clare and revealing that her death happened when we were tiny. 'We didn't know about this when we were kids, did we?' I check.

'We didn't,' he says.

'I'm worried about what might have triggered her talking about it, beyond the anniversary of Clare's death. Whether she senses she's ill; if it's been a regular cause of this heavy drinking.' Once I start, the anxieties flow from me. 'And I'm concerned about the impact on her mental health of keeping this a secret for so many years.'

He snorts with derision.

'Matt . . .' I feel protective on her behalf.

'Look, I can understand you being concerned about her drinking. But I can't fret about whether the auld bitch is going crazy. Let's be honest, she's always been a bit on the edge.'

'Matt, please. Her baby died and she shut the fact away and refused to acknowledge it. But suddenly she's thinking about her and it's triggered a drinking binge. Any idea why she's brought this up after all this time?'

A long pause and I wait, hoping for some eureka moment: an answer that will make sense of this development. Only a sibling can understand the unspoken fears about a parent: the connections I've not yet made but which might be hovering within his grip.

'I don't know,' he says. 'And to be honest, I need to get her out of my head. Perhaps she's got a guilty conscience? Or perhaps she hasn't been bothered by it?'

'That's a bit harsh.'

'She wasn't bothered about me.'

And here it is. The sticking point that means Mattie is as stubborn as our mother – and as cruel, perhaps, in his refusal to forgive her for her parental failings.

His lack of connection isn't just because of the accident, though the scar tissue is a constant reminder: sullying his left arm and torso, and creeping up his neck like a textured stream. It was every single thing, he once told me, his face twisted with hate. The fact she avoided going to the hospital if possible; that he didn't get all his operations; that she behaved as if what had happened was an inconvenience. The impression that her life would be preferable if neither of us had been born.

'Look, I'm sorry but I've got to go to work,' I say, now. 'I shouldn't have rung but I'm not sleeping, and you're the only person I can talk to properly about her.'

He grunts, non-committal.

'I also thought you might know something about Clare, too; something I didn't recall.'

'Sorry, sis,' he says, brushing his hands of the conversation – and, it feels, of me. 'I know nothing – but you know what?' and his voice manages to combine sadness and bitterness; is hard and cold but tinged with a quiet longing. 'Nothing about that woman would surprise me.'

We say goodbye, and I rush to the ward but his tone perturbs me. It's customary for him to be dismissive when discussing our mother – it's an obvious protective mechanism – but I sense a strange knowingness there. He must have memories, like me. Not of being eighteen months old but later in childhood: inklings that might explain her current behaviour. Or has he managed to suppress it all?

LIZ

Friday 25 August, 1989

Twenty-four

I was irritated with him. That was what I felt just before it happened. Acute irritation that my annoying little brother wouldn't leave me alone when all I wanted was to finish my book from the library. An Agatha Christie. Not even a good one, at that.

I was lying on my stomach on my bed, listening to the rain and finally warm after a trip to the pool where we had been caught by a sudden downpour: a proper, late August torrent that meant my toes squelched in my Freeman, Hardy and Willis sandals as I raced through the puddles, and our T-shirts and shorts turned transparent as they clung to our skinny frames.

We were shivering when we got back. Proper, teeth-chattering shivering: Mattie's lips a curious bluey-purple before I found him some jeans and a worn sweatshirt, then made some sweet mugs of tea. He was happy for a while, dipping a pile of broken custard creams into his mug, then deconstructing them by dislodging the top from its fondant middle and licking off the icing.

I picked up my mug of tea and left him to it. There were only hard, straight-backed chairs in the kitchen and the only place with room to stretch out was next door, on my bed.

'Where you going?'

Where did he think I was going?

'Just reading.'

'You're always reading.'

'You're always annoying.'

This comparison was weak. Being annoying was hardly an activity like reading, but he was only eight, compared to my nearly ten, and not as good at arguing as me.

I sank deep into the bed and counted my remaining pages. Only ten. I had at most five minutes' peace before he came to find me.

He lasted about two.

'C'mon, Lizzie. C'mon.' He tugged at my T-shirt, the thin cotton cutting into my stomach as he tried to man-handle me off the bed.

'Get *off*! Leave me a*lone*.'

'No.'

'I *mean* it.'

'But I'm bored. I want you to *play* with me.' He pounded the bedding with his fists.

'No. Leave. Me. A-*lone*.'

I shifted to the other side of the bed, pulling a blanket away from him with a growl.

'You *never* play with me.'

'I do.' I turned a page.

'Not properly.'

'Yes I do.' I rolled off my stomach to face him. 'And I take you to the pool and I make your packed lunch and I cook for you. I do *everything*, just as if I was a mum.'

'I could do all that.'

'No you couldn't. You're too little.'

'Am not.' He punched down on the blanket hard, pent-up frustration and testosterone fuelling his fury, though he looked as if he was trying not to cry.

I turned back to my book, ignoring the ball of anger wedged in my chest and rifling through various responses. I picked one that was suitably dismissive. 'Yes. You. Are.'

'Well I'll show you,' he said, getting up. 'I'll show you that I can cook and do our clothes and all the things that you say *you* do. That I'm not the stupid little one.'

'Yeah, you do that.' I didn't as much as glance at him. Made a great show of turning a yellowing page.

'Will, too.'

'Oh-kay!' My voice was a mocking singsong and it seemed to do the trick. He shoved himself off the bed and stomped back to the kitchen, banging the door and making a great show of his feet thudding on the worn carpet. There was no way he'd do anything. He'd be back in three minutes. I'd play with him then, or cook us something. Pot

Noodles, or Cup-a-Soup. My watch – a red Casio I'd been given for Christmas – said ten past twelve. If he could just give me until quarter past, I'd be finished and then I'd go and look after him.

I was so immersed that when the smell of frying fat seeped into the bedroom, I barely noticed. The salty tang of fried eggs and bacon always filtered up from the caff so nothing seemed out of the ordinary.

My nostrils twitched. *Mattie's cooking*, I half-thought, as I turned the last page. My brain, filled with the coincidences of Christie's plot, was soupy, and it took a while to register the fact. Mattie was cooking – and frying eggs from the sounds of things, because I could hear the crisp sizzle of fat, the muffled crack of shell against bowl.

I ran from our bedroom and wrenched open the kitchen door to see the gas on far too high, a slick of oil simmering with fury, and great globules of fat flicking from the pan.

Mattie was standing on a chair, reaching towards the kettle. 'I'm cooking.' He looked wired and defiant. 'It's all all right,' he said.

'It's not all right,' I screeched. The flames licked around the frying pan, and the handle was sticking out at a jaunty angle: he could knock it over at any moment. 'You'll set us on fire.'

I shoved the handle away, my head turned aside as a wall of heat flared up and fat spat at me. Hot shivers rippled through me as I reached for the dial at the front of the hob. The flames were sucked back down and I dropped the frying pan into the sink with a clatter, the water fizzing, a puddle of boiling oil slopping out.

But the relief was short-lived.

'Don't touch anything. It's scalding,' I shouted, not looking at Mattie but turning on the tap and thrusting my arm beneath the cold running water. My scalp prickled; my forearm seared with pain.

'I'm not, I'm not,' Mattie said, his voice rising, but I wasn't really listening. All my focus was on the molten water, the hiss and the steam as it hit the pan. 'I'm just making you some tea.'

I turned to see a great cloud of steam rising from the plastic jug kettle; could hear the water ferociously bubbling. *He's filled it too full*, I thought, as he tried lifting it high with both hands, before listing and pulling one hand away.

There was a thud: Mattie lost his balance, slipped on the chair, tilted the cheap kettle whose plastic lid clattered off. And the full two and a half pints of boiling water cascaded all over him.

I'd never heard such a horrific scream. As shrill as a vixen mating or a woman in the last stage of labour. A cry that senses death is near. He was drenched, the water splashing his face and bathing his neck, torso, arms, stomach, groin; even the tops of his thighs, in those heavy jeans I'd insisted on him wearing; his skin turning a vicious red.

I flung cold water at him as he writhed on the floor, and I screamed for our mother, working in the caff below us. She didn't come, and it was Leah, the sixteen-year-old who manned the till, who blundered up the stairs a minute later, panic plastered across her face.

She was the one who called 999; who screeched at our mum, who'd popped along the seafront for an extended fag break and arrived moments before the ambulance. The one who told Mattie, over and over, he wasn't going to die.

He was lucky not to. He spent months in hospital. Endured numerous skin grafts. His torso now resembles a patch of sand where the tide has ridged and rippled. His neck is shiny and there's extensive damage around his armpit where the scar tissue had to be cut after he failed to get sufficient corrective surgery. His hair doesn't grow properly around one ear.

And though I blamed myself, Mattie has always blamed our mother for putting him in a situation where his body was permanently scarred and disfigured; has blamed her too for not getting to him sooner and for not visiting him more frequently in hospital – once a week, as his stay lengthened, and no more.

'It was an accident,' I used to remind him. 'She was a single, working mum, with me to deal with. She was only trying to do her best.' I've tried to rationalise it for myself too. The specialist burns unit was twenty miles away, she didn't like to drive, and didn't have the money for the petrol; she was exhausted after working; perhaps felt intense guilt at what happened to her boy.

With my compassionate, health professional's hat on, I continued to make excuses. Her absence – because this is the part that has hurt him the most – didn't indicate a lack of love. She wasn't particularly maternal and clearly found the hospital distressing. By her standards, she did her best.

And yet, now that I've seen scores of families visiting their children in hospital, I've realised that my mother's behaviour wasn't typical – nor is it how I would behave.

Faced with the pressure of working, and with another child, wouldn't I still do my utmost to be with my child as much as I could? And wouldn't I try to ensure that they never felt that visiting was a burden, as Mattie did, our mother clearly uneasy at being in an environment where she was surrounded by so much suffering and pain?

Those visits to the paediatric burns unit inspired me to be a doctor. As I watched my brother's rehabilitation and saw the skill with which he was put back together, I knew I wanted to atone for my part in his accident and to try to pay back his care.

But my mother found it far more disturbing. And I can't shrug off the feeling that her detachment, her lack of care, was intrinsic to her personality, and is somehow mirrored in her attitude to Clare.

JESS

Wednesday 24 January, 2018, 8 a.m.

Twenty-five

'Is your husband in?' It is 8 a.m., and DC Rustin is standing on Jess's doorstep.

'Um, no . . .' She is caught off balance by her sudden appearance. 'I'm sorry. He stayed at the hospital last night and he'll be at work, now.'

'We'll catch him there.'

The police officer gives her a smile that says she doesn't trust her and walks away. A curtain in the window of the house opposite shifts. Her neighbours view her uneasily: Jane fumbling for her front-door key, yesterday; Annie shielding eighteen-month-old Lucas in his buggy, as if Jess was capable of harming not just her own but other babies, too.

'It was the police,' she tells Martha, coming back into the kitchen. 'They say they want Ed but I don't know what for. Why do you think they want him?'

'I don't know.' Martha is brisk. 'Look: why don't we keep the boys off school and take them out? They're worried about Betsey and you could do with some distraction. There's no point in sitting around here.'

'Are they checking up on me? Perhaps they're questioning his statement? Why would they doubt him? I'd better text.' She jabs away at her mobile phone. Maybe she should just call him, but what if *he'd* contacted the police? She'd avoided him when he got in from football last night; too ashamed to mention her impromptu visit to the hospital which she suspected Lucy would be discussing. When he set off to spend the night at the hospital, she pretended to be asleep.

'They must want to talk to him about *me*.'

'Come on. Let's go,' Martha repeats. She has been a source of support, though her presence makes it impossible not to feel redundant. Increasingly, Jess finds herself withdrawing. 'What did you think about keeping the boys off school?' Martha prompts her. 'Are you happy with that?'

'Yes, yes.' She is so distracted she barely takes it in.

'Did you hear that, boys? We're going to skive for the day!'

Frankie punches the air and starts running around the room; Kit smiles at his aunt's rebellion.

'Some fresh air will do them good.' Martha starts filling water bottles. 'We're not going to stay in, cooped up. We're going to explore.'

*

They set out for Richmond Park. Jess manoeuvres her four-by-four through the London traffic; her driving by turns reckless and tentative.

'Careful!' Martha sucks in her breath. 'Bit close to that car!'

A horn blasts. 'Watch where you're fucking going!' The driver of a white Ford Transit gives her the finger, his aggression spilling towards them; startling the boys into being quiet.

She sees danger in every direction: cars ploughing into her; her children shrieking; her bonnet crumpling. Her breath flutters. She barely knows what she is doing: the vision of a van swerving off course and smashing into them is so strong.

Another blast of a horn. She rams on the brakes and pulls into the side.

'You OK?'

She screws her eyes up tight. Their car hares to the right, her boys scream over the screech of tyres and the thud of metal. But the car's not moving. Her hands are shaking but somehow she has stopped and wrenched on the handbrake.

'Not really. Could you drive?'

In the passenger seat, she shrinks into herself, letting Martha's conversation wash over her. She didn't crash the car. Of course she didn't crash the car. They are all safe, Frankie chanting, 'Look where you're *fucking* going,' Martha driving sensibly, eyes flicking to the mirror, hands at ten to two.

She must focus on the boys. 'OK, both of you?' she asks, twisting around.

'OK, Mum.' Kit is her brave boy: conscious, with a ten-year-old's newfound maturity, of the need to reassure her.

Frankie is preoccupied with his Blu Tack: folding it over and over then rolling it between his fingers like over-worked pastry. The 'fucking goings' have finally subsided.

'OK, Frank?' She wills him to look up at her. He gives a quick nod.

They tramp over rough grass and push into the centre of the park, as far from the roads and civilisation as possible. Kit loves it. He bounds ahead, evidently relieved to be free. Frankie is more hesitant: stumbling over the uneven ground, spinning his fidget spinner that catches the light, until he spies a herd of deer grazing beneath a tree.

'Oh my gosh, oh my gosh, oh my gosh. Look, Mum, *look*!'

'Shhhhhh.' A shot of adrenalin races through her. 'You have to be *quiet*, Frankie.'

A stag raises his head and she grips his hand, squeezing it tight. Will it lower its head and charge at them? He is regal. Imperious. Coldly assessing.

She sees Frankie tossed as effortlessly as a pile of laundry; watches the stag gore him, antlers sinking into his abdomen, his jumper bleeding vermillion red. The herd joins in and Frankie is thrown high into the air: dark hair flying, neck snapped, limbs hanging at obtuse angles. Then they dance on his body: bones crushed, kicked, cracked.

'Jess!' Martha is racing through the grass towards her; grabs her arm; pulls her and Frankie back. 'What are you doing? Move! Now!'

'I . . . I'm sorry.'

'Christ. What's wrong? You were standing there frozen. Don't you know you should never just stand stock-still like that?'

'Why not, Martha? Why not?' Frankie, sensing danger, skips along.

Her sister ignores him, so he shifts his attention: 'Was he going to get us, Mummy? He looked as if he would get us.'

'Shh, Frankie,' Jess manages, and then to Martha, 'Of course I didn't, no.'

How can she explain that she saw her son being disembowelled; that she sees death and danger all around her: when driving the car, when using a knife, when pushing a buggy, when walking down the stairs. That Betsey's admission was the point when she tipped from a state where she could just contain her fears into an abyss where they spill out, limitless. That anticipating danger is her default position. That she fears she may be going insane.

'Come on,' Martha links her arm through hers. Jess feels her sister's warmth and weight against her ribs. 'Let's catch up with Kit.'

Where is he? She strains to see a figure heading for the horizon.

'Kit. *Kit* . . .' Her voice betrays her fear. What if he's

been abducted? What if he's being abused? Who knows what might be happening now he's out of sight? There may be paedophiles hiding behind the trees, ready to bundle him into a van, the crook of their arm locked around his neck, hands fumbling with their flies in anticipation. Fear catches in her throat like an irrepressible tickle; she begins to run.

'It's all right.' Martha lumbers to catch her up. 'He's not going to come to any harm.'

But how can she be sure?

'He'll be fine – look, there he is.'

And so he is. Bending over to do up a shoelace. She rushes up to him and hugs him close.

'Muu-um.'

'Are you OK?' She peers into his face, searching for any sign that he's been harmed.

'Of course I am. This is brilliant, isn't it? Can we come more often? Why haven't we been here before?'

Because the place is riddled with danger, she wants to say. *Because nothing here is certain.*

'I'd forgotten this was here.'

'So we can come again?'

'I guess so ... if you really want to.' She tries again, though it's so very difficult. 'Yes. Of course we can.'

But her ordeal isn't over. They have come to a small copse of oaks, the tree trunks sturdy.

'They look quite scalable,' Martha is saying. 'I bet you like climbing trees, don't you, Kit?'

He glances at his mother. 'I haven't really climbed one.'

'Jess!' Martha half-teases then stops, incredulous. 'Really? Well, why don't you have a go?' She gestures to a particularly fine oak, its bark mossed with green, imprinted with whorls, and studded with the stubs of branches on which to get a hold.

'Wait a minute, he can't do this,' Jess manages, as her insides turn molten. He can't trust that the branches will be strong and evenly positioned; that he'll have the spatial awareness and fearlessness to get to the top. 'I really don't think he should,' she adds, but her voice is weak and the words float away.

'Jess.' Martha puts her hands on her upper arms and looks her in the eye. 'I know you're under a lot of strain but he needs to enjoy just being a little boy. He needs to challenge himself. To be allowed to live in the moment. Otherwise you're doing him a disservice. You're not preparing him for life.'

'I can do it, Mum. I know I can.' Kit buzzes with energy. 'Dad would let me do it . . .' And, before she has a chance to concede that yes, Ed might let him but this isn't on his watch, he's not here; or to tell Martha that she needs to keep Kit and Frankie close, and out of harm's way, he has pulled himself up onto the first rough stub of branch.

'Go on, Kit,' Frankie calls, jumping with excitement, as his brother searches for the next handhold, the muscles in his calves straining as he eases himself up and away.

'To your right, Kit, just above you . . .' adds Martha, her face flushed with the excitement of it all.

'Do be careful, Kit-bob.' Jess reverts to his baby name. 'Just concentrate, won't you, Kit?'

'I'm fine, Mum,' he says as he pulls himself up to the next level, eyes searching for the next foothold. 'Look! I can do this!' and he turns his head and smiles.

Don't look at me! she wants to scream. 'Just concentrate,' she hears herself say. 'No talking. And don't look down.'

'O-ka-ay!' His voice drifts: cocky, carefree, the voice of a boy who has no concept that he might fall.

This is what being a mother is about, she thinks, not wanting to look yet mesmerised by his agile body going higher and higher. Letting your children take little steps until they abandon you completely and you are left quite alone. Learning to relinquish control from the moment they begin to crawl until they are scaling trees, cycling to school, leaving home. Out in the big, wide world where she can no longer control what's happening or offer any protection at all.

She does not think she can do this. Live without managing to keep them safe, or knowing they are safe. Look what happened with Betsey. That one, stupid decision to leave them has upended her world. Her baby's in hospital, the police are crawling all over them, and she thinks back to DC Rustin on the doorstep, her stomach cramping with anxiety. She would do anything to reverse what she did now.

And so she mustn't take her eyes off her boys but focus all her energy on keeping them safe. If she concentrates intently, perhaps she can keep Kit from harm. She is shaking, though, knees quivering as she wills him to make each move safely, to test each branch and not shift his weight until he's absolutely sure he can go on.

He's going too high. He's going too high. He's going too high.

'You're going too high, Kit. No more please.'

'Jess, he's fine.'

Martha puts her arm around her shoulders and she wants to shrug her off. *It's not like when we were small. When you could dare me to swim across the cove, or scramble up a cliff and I would do it. The stakes are so much higher. These are MY children.* Instead, she keeps very still. 'Don't move,' she hisses at her sister. 'Don't do anything that might distract him at all.'

'You're going *reeeeaally* high, Kit,' Frankie calls. 'He's really high, isn't he, Mummy? Go higher, Kit. High as a kite.'

'Shh. He's too high, Frank.'

He has stopped climbing. His body, in its skinny jeans and Puffa jacket, is splayed against the bark, unmoving. His toes have found a crevice; his arms stretch wide.

'Are you all right?' Jess asks.

'I think I'm a bit stuck. I don't know where to put my feet . . .' Kit's voice floats down, high-pitched and suddenly too young.

'That's all right, darling,' she says, moving closer. 'You're fine. You're absolutely fine. You just need to come down now and not go any higher.' She focuses on keeping her voice strong.

He must be eighteen feet up. How did he get so high? High enough for a fall to prove fatal? 'I'll help you,' she calls out – and of course she will. She can do this. She has to do this. To get him safely down.

She skims the trunk with its ancient grooves and ridges, its furrows and dips that might prove steady if he presses his weight against them.

'If you move your left foot – no, not that one, your *left* one – if you move it down a bit there's a hollow. That's it . . .' Relief as his sneaker finds it. 'Now, if you move your right hand you can put it on the tufty bit there.'

'Here?' He nods towards a whorl of trunk with fresh shoots sprouting from it, and she sees that he is blinking back tears.

'That's it. Well done.'

He eases half a metre down.

'Brilliant.' Her voice sings with relief. 'Now, if you put your left one down a little, that's it, yes—' He makes the step down, again, his foot juddering against the bark and causing her heart to skip. '—and your right there . . . yes, there . . . you've got it . . .' He is now just twelve feet from the ground. Not much further and she'll be able to touch him, help him down. 'If you can put your left down a bit – on that branch there . . . yes that's right, that one . . . then you'll be fine.'

Her anxiety is a helium balloon held in her chest but she can feel it rising from her, floating up, up and away the closer he comes. Twelve feet. Eleven. Ten. So tantalisingly close. Any moment now she'll be able to pull him into a hug. She doesn't hold him often enough, these days. Not since he's turned ten. Not since she had Betsey. But she will hold him in a second, if he can just move down.

He stops, his freshly confident movements stalling.

'Kit?'

'I can't ... I don't know where to go now.' He is pained by the situation, poised between embarrassment and the hope this could all be turned into a joke.

'Nearly there, Kit,' Martha breezes in. 'Just put your right foot there and then we'll catch you ...'

'Where? There?' He turns to look at them – his foot slips, he slithers, and then he is tumbling, body falling to the earth as he lets out a guttural roar.

'Kit!' She reaches him as his body hits the ground, with a flat, definitive thud.

Later, she will rail at Martha: 'Why did you tell him we'd catch him? You confused him.' But at that moment, blame is superfluous. Her boy is broken as he lies at the base of the tree.

He's dead. He's dead. He's dead. He's dead. He's dead. He's dead ...

It is the near silence that frightens her the most. She hears the distant roar of traffic, a rustling in the grass, the pounding of her heart. Even Frankie is so shocked he resists screaming for a moment.

And then Kit begins to cry.

ED

Wednesday 24 January, 9 a.m.

Twenty-six

'DC Rustin and DC Farron to see you, Mr Curtis.' Jade Bridge, twenty-four years old, smart, streetwise, unapologetic in telling it as it is, leans her torso around Ed's office door.

'DC Rustin?' Ed stands automatically. 'Has something happened to Betsey?' It is his unacknowledged fear. That his baby will slip away, her head fracture, unseen, incorrectly diagnosed, more sinister than any of them realised. She's been having further seizures. None lasting more than five minutes, none clustering together, but still unsettling. He was with her when she had one yesterday: saw for himself the roll of her eyes, the fluttering of her limbs; experienced the sensation of being in limbo as he willed her to jerk back out of it; to behave normally. He feels sick thinking about it.

'There's no change to Betsey's condition as far as I'm

aware,' DC Rustin says. But his relief is short-lived. His thoughts tip towards Jess: are they here because of her? That discovery on her laptop has skewed everything. He knows that something is seriously wrong: that she needs help, though since she won't talk to him, refusing to communicate since that erratic phone call, he can't see how he can help her. It's surprising how swiftly having a child in hospital, and being the subject of a police investigation, makes everything unravel so that your thinking is clouded and you feel as if you're losing your grip.

'And Jess – is she all right?' The words trip from him despite him not wanting to prompt questions about her.

'It's not Mrs Curtis we're interested in talking to at the moment but you,' DC Rustin says.

'Oh.' His skin goose pimples and sweat licks the back of his neck.

'We wondered if you could answer a few questions for us to help with our inquiries?' DC Farron adds.

'Of course. What, now?'

'There's just something in the statement you gave us that we'd like you to clarify.' He gives that reassuring smile, as if to say this is just a low-key chat.

'That's right,' DC Rustin says. 'I'm wearing a Body Worn camera, just so there's no dispute about what's said, by the way. And we'll need to take a written statement.'

'Do I need a lawyer?' He had discussed this with his criminal lawyer friend when the scenes of crime officer visited their home but dismissed the idea as a panicked overreaction that would look suspicious. Now he wonders if he has been naive.

'Not at all,' DC Rustin says, doing a good job of looking nonplussed. 'You're just helping us iron something out.'

Ed gestures to a couple of chairs and sits back at his desk. The detectives take their seats, DC Rustin perching on the edge of hers, as if primed to leap up at any moment; DC Farron leaning gently back.

'In your statement, taken at your house, you said that on the day Betsey was injured you were "at work all day and then out with work colleagues for a drink". That's right, isn't it?' begins DC Rustin.

'Yes.' He thinks he knows where this is going. He didn't tell them about popping back for lunch in his original statement because he didn't think they were interested in that time period, and he didn't correct it because he didn't want to draw attention to his reason for doing so. But it's been bugging him for a while.

'But we've a statement from a witness who says they saw you arrive back home, at Kneighton Close, just before one-thirty?' The detective wrinkles her nose, apparently bemused. 'They checked the clock because they thought it unusual. We're just wondering if there was anything you could say to explain this?'

What should he do? Deny this outright? The witness must be a neighbour. Probably Jane, next door: a widow, in her late sixties, she has indicated that she'd love to be more involved with their family. Jess has never been keen:

believes she's too preoccupied with the comings and goings of everyone in the close, from the relationships of the teenage children living there, to an affair she is convinced poor David Frampton, four doors down, is having. Now, it seems her interest has been of use to the police.

'Mr Curtis?'

'I'm sorry ... I popped home briefly for lunch. I wasn't there for more than twenty minutes. Half an hour at the most.'

'Our witness says they were listening to the Archers, which runs from two to two-fifteen p.m., when you left, so it would be at least half an hour.'

'I wasn't timing it.' He feels a burst of frustration. 'If you say it was thirty minutes then it must have been, but no more.'

'Was it usual for you to pop home for lunch, Mr Curtis?' DC Farron eases forwards from his settled position to pick up the baton of the questions.

'No. Not really.' There is no point pretending.

'But you did on that day? The day Betsey was hurt?'

He doesn't like the implication but tells himself to remain even-tempered. 'Yes, I did. Yes.'

'It's quite a commute for you, isn't it? At least an hour and a half, possibly two, there and back?'

'Taking into account delays on the Underground it can be that, yes.'

'So I suppose we're wondering why you decided to do something so unusual?'

Ed shrugs. He isn't going to help them out and tell them that he'd intended to take the afternoon off but changed his mind after Jess's frosty response.

'I imagine you're a busy man, Mr Curtis,' the detective continues, 'and there's no shortage of places to eat around these offices, so why did you think to go home in the middle of the day?'

'I wanted to see my wife.' They have goaded him into admitting it. He doesn't want to lie and perhaps complete honesty is what is needed to get them all out of this mess. But he can't admit to everything that happened: can hardly tell them he lost his temper and shouted, when he went downstairs after checking on Betsey, though there's a risk Jane might have heard. He compromises: offers the truth about returning home and a lie about returning to the office. 'I'd intended to take the Friday afternoon off for once but on my way home I realised I just had too much work to do and I'd have to go back; I knew that even before I arrived.'

'And was there any particular reason for going home for lunch?'

'We . . . we'd had a disagreement the previous evening. I just wanted to check she was OK.'

Something passes over DC Rustin's face. She has what she was after, and he feels snared.

'Was there any reason she wouldn't be OK after a "disagreement"?' She does a good impression of looking both surprised and concerned and Ed, at that moment, hates her. What must it be like to be so immune from emotional frailty?

'I just wanted to see her. We very rarely argue and I wanted to put things right.'

'And how did it go? Your attempts to put things right?'

'I'm sorry, I'm not sure how that's relevant?'

'It may be relevant because you and your wife are the subject of a police investigation into how your daughter sustained a head injury,' DC Rustin explains. 'If you'd argued and you continued to argue despite your best intentions, then that may be relevant to what happened to your daughter next.'

The temperature seems to drop a couple of degrees. How completely stupid could he be? Or should he be honest? Admit that their conversation *did* deteriorate. That he'd left without saying a proper goodbye? That he'd slammed the door after she'd given him the silent treatment, when he'd gone downstairs, rather than telling him what was wrong, as he'd so desperately wanted? Jane *would* have heard that slammed door; would have heard his raised voice, too; would, no doubt, have mentioned all this to the police. With horrible clarity, he imagines the detectives' narrative. A row, raised tempers, and the baby bears the brunt of it at the hands of one – or both – of her parents. And yet that's not what happened here.

You've got this all wrong, he wants to tell DC Rustin. *We would never hurt anyone; we would never touch our little girl.* Instead he admits: 'It didn't go very well.' And then, because

Jane will be bound to have heard male footsteps trudging up the stairs and he cannot trust that Jess won't tell, he bows to the inevitable. 'I went to give Betsey a kiss in her cot. She was awake but gurgling. Was perfectly happy. And then I left.'

DC Rustin eases back from her out-of-the-starting-blocks position and watches him, carefully. She has some of what she wants. She can take her time now. Ed glances at his desk: everything is as it was when they entered – even his coffee is sufficiently hot to be drinkable – and yet the atmosphere has irrevocably changed.

'Why didn't you mention any of this before, Mr Curtis? When we asked where you were that day?'

'You asked where I was that afternoon and evening. Where I was earlier in the day didn't seem to be an issue.'

'We are investigating how your little girl was injured,' she reminds him. 'It would have been helpful if you had been more forthcoming about this.'

Silence stretches, tense and taut. All he can think of is Jess's laptop. Though he deleted the search history, any expert could retrieve it, couldn't they? Better to distract Rustin with his failure to admit to this impromptu visit. And yet he doesn't want to implicate himself.

'There was no reason for me to mention it since I have done nothing wrong,' he manages eventually. 'You didn't seem to think it relevant at the time and it didn't occur to me to mention it.'

DC Rustin looks dissatisfied and glances at her colleague.

'You've been most helpful, Mr Curtis,' says DC Farron. 'I'm sure you'll appreciate that we need to iron out any inconsistencies in statements. So we're now clear that you returned home to Kneighton Close at one-thirty p.m. on Friday lunchtime and left between two and two-fifteen?'

'It would have been straight after two. I was back at my desk by three p.m. You can check with my PA, Jade.'

He no longer feels rattled; is nudging towards being his usual, urbane self, confident of managing any situation. It is a relief to have cleared this up, to be honest, but he wants them to go now. The strain of having to pretend that everything is fine with Jess is intense, and he doesn't know if he can maintain it much longer. The more DC Rustin digs, the more likely he is to say something that implies he is concerned for, or no longer understands, his wife. Work has been a sanctuary but now their inquiries have spread into the one place he thought he could briefly escape from his anxieties. He stands abruptly, eager to initiate some change and conscious of looking assertive as he pulls himself up to his full height.

'I don't mean to be rude but if that's all, I really should get on with some work.'

'Of course.' DC Rustin gathers her bag together but takes some time doing so. 'There's just one thing that keeps bugging me,' she says, and he sees that it's deliberate, this prevarication. 'I can't help thinking about what a distance it was for you to go back home, that lunchtime, and how disruptive. How it would have been easier for you to speak on the phone.'

'Possibly. But I wanted to see her. I'm better at apologies face to face.'

'I understand you took her flowers?'

'Yes.' Is there nothing Jane didn't see?

'Must have been quite an argument to do all that,' she says, tilting her head.

She moves back into the room and perches on the edge of his desk. He resents her doing this. It's a clear imposition: a means of asserting she isn't leaving. He wills her to move that bony bottom as he concentrates on not saying anything sharp.

He loves Jess and he is not going to implicate her. There is no way he is going to say anything that might increase their suspicions because of course he has considered that she might have snapped. 'Why do I want to harm my baby?' Christ, that phrase has been rattling around his head since he read it in the early hours of Sunday morning, and that conversation yesterday with Charlotte hasn't helped. What was it she had said? 'It would be perfectly normal if you felt some disquiet, some doubt.' Do they all *sense* he mistrusts his wife?

He is keeping these thoughts quite private. These people will never detect the slightest disloyalty to her, however hard they try.

And yet DC Rustin is tenacious. Here she is now, her bottom shifting on the edge of the desk and provoking irritation. She knows she is in control, knows that he will have to give her an answer. Perhaps for this reason, there's a flicker of a smile on her face.

'So,' she says, with a look that says she has all the time in the world, and they both know it. 'Perhaps you could tell us what this row was about?'

JESS

Wednesday 24 January, 7 p.m.

Twenty-seven

They are back in hospital.

Kit has broken his arm. A forearm fracture. They've been here for over four hours, waiting in A&E then getting it X-rayed, manipulated and put in plaster. Now they're in Radiology, waiting for it to be X-rayed again.

At first, Jess was riddled with fear.

'They'll think I've hurt him, too. They'll think it's too much of a coincidence, having two children injured. They'll take the boys from me.'

'It doesn't look *great*,' Martha admitted. 'But I'll tell them *I* encouraged him to scale the tree.'

'But then they'll think I can't parent,' Jess fretted, paralysed at the thought of how Kit's injury might be perceived.

In the end, the doctor didn't seem unduly perturbed. It was a nasty but standard forearm fracture and Martha was there at the time.

And as the hours ticked on – two, three, four – and no police officer arrived, Jess's fear that the boys would be physically taken from her began to ease.

Martha's uncharacteristic nervousness diminished too, and segued into boredom.

'I'm gasping for a cup of tea.'

The air is cloying and Frankie frustrated, as he kicks away at his chair leg with a dull, rhythmic thudding. Martha can't take him home because she has to remain with Kit, and Jess can't take him because she can't be left alone with any of her children. Her sister gives a long, heartfelt sigh. 'I'm sorry,' she says, though she doesn't look apologetic; she looks fed up. 'It's all catching up with me.'

'I'll get you a drink.' Jess springs up, desperate to make amends and to do something to break this stasis. 'There's a vending machine near A&E.'

'Oh, don't worry. I can't bear that crap.'

'Or I could get you a proper cup, or a decent coffee – at the shop on the concourse.' Martha hesitates: she runs on caffeine. 'We're going to be a while here, and then we'll have to wait to be discharged and given a date for fracture clinic,' Jess says. It's not that she wants to leave her boys but the opportunity to escape for a moment is suddenly hugely appealing.

'Well, if you're sure? Then a proper coffee would be lovely.'

'Of course.' She is gathering up her bag and coat; suddenly cannot get away from there quick enough. 'It shouldn't take too long, depending on the queue, and I've got my phone with me.'

'I'll call you if they tell us we can go before you get back.'

Jess smiles apologetically, knowing they're unlikely to be discharged any time soon. Four hours will stretch to five, then six. 'I'll try to be quick,' she says.

She doesn't mean to make a detour but she gets lost on the way to the main hospital concourse. She's trying to take a shortcut and then she sees the word: 'Chapel'. Of course, she takes it as a sign.

The room is empty. All the trappings of religion are here: the stained glass window, the brass candelabra, the plush red velvet cushioning, the tapestried footstools, even a table of candles to be lit for loved ones in desperate hope. She takes a pew, hoping for a rush of warmth or certainty, some reassurance that Betsey will be OK. (Kit's fracture, though further evidence of her poor parenting, is a more containable, familiar worry.) But none is forthcoming. 'I don't know what to do,' she whispers, over and over. 'I just don't know what to do.'

She reaches into her bag for a small ragdoll she's been carrying around like a talisman; holds it to her nose to catch Betsey's smell. But it's incense she can detect, and that potent mix of ammonia, bleach and fear that burrows inside her nostrils. Her throat thickens. She's so tainted by this place she can't even conjure up her child.

Panic flares and she aligns her rings in her own troubled

rosary but none of her usual rituals are helping. Perhaps lighting a candle might calm her down? She strikes a match, watches as the wick catches and the flame spits into life. But why has she only lit one? She needs to light three. She fumbles with the matches. Now they will last for different lengths of time, Betsey's burning out before the boys'. Will that mean her life is more fragile than theirs? Her hands shake as the match flares and the flame nips her flesh, her nail blackening. 'Ow!' The smell of singed skin; a shiver from the burn and she is trembling with fear.

How can she get out of this mess? Should she just be honest? But no one will believe her. Not DC Rustin. Not Liz. Not Martha. Not even – and this is the thing that distresses her the most – Ed.

She sobs and swipes her mouth with her hand, wipes her nose with a clagging tissue, snot bubbling from her like a child. She is broken. Completely hollowed out.

For some reason, she thinks of the puppy: yet further proof of her maternal failings. The boys had clamoured for one and, ignoring her desire for calm and order and a day that was suddenly hers from nine to three, she eventually gave in. They chose an apricot cockerpoo, who the boys named Teddy: a bundle of fluff; less dog, more bear. She had intense misgivings in the run-up to picking him up but the joy on Frankie's face when they collected him on Christmas Eve reassured her this was a good thing.

How wrong could she be?

She had tried to love it. And it wasn't just its neediness

that stopped her but the grim reality of being responsible for a tiny creature that pissed and shitted everywhere. Life became an endless cycle of disinfecting floors and washing its bedding at ninety degrees. Then she would have to clean the stupid creature, which would trample in the poo in its excitement and distress, and jump up at her – meaning she had to start washing herself, the floor, and *it*, all over again.

Everyone said things got easier after two weeks but at three weeks she was still trapped. Her hands so raw they started bleeding, her chest tight, her throat sore from inhaling the smell of bleach. Her thoughts were of germs, and blindness caused by shit smeared in her children's eyes. It frightened her, the force with which such thoughts could cascade. She'd been anxious about germs when the boys were small, but never at this intense level. Now her fears delighted in rushing back in.

One night she had stood in the frozen garden for half an hour with a puppy that refused to poo but did so as soon as it bounced inside and she realised she couldn't cope. Mel had a puppy from the same litter and was managing admirably, and its softness and eagerness to please would constantly highlight Jess's failure to be a similar owner, and by extension, mother: someone competent, capable, fun. But she knew, standing there in her kitchen confounded by that tiny, encrusted creature, that *it* – she no longer gave it its name or thought of it lovingly in the least – had the potential to break her.

Perhaps there is something wrong with her that means

she fails to do what's right – whether it's persisting with a puppy, or confessing she is overwhelmed by motherhood. A fatal flaw that made her resist taking her baby to hospital; made her fudge her story; made her lie to the police.

But the truth has become so tangled that she no longer knows how to make things right. She watches the flame of Betsey's candle, mesmerised by its brightness until the light brings clarity. If she can only rely on herself to be vigilant, then she has to do one thing.

The paediatric ward is quiet when she arrives there a little after 8.30 in the evening. She hasn't called Martha to tell her what she's up to; has closed her mind to the fact she was meant to be getting her a coffee. Her phone has vibrated in her bag a couple of times but she ignores it, just as she ignores the fact that she shouldn't be here.

To her surprise, she gets in easily: a parent who recognises her from the previous day buzzes her through and the night staff are preoccupied at the start of their shift. The woman at the nurses' station is unfamiliar. A bank nurse, perhaps; someone employed through an agency who hasn't seen her before, who doesn't usually work here.

'Who are you here to see?' The nurse's English is abrupt and fractured. Jess hopes her understanding of the agreement forbidding her from visiting without a social worker is equally rudimentary.

'My daughter, Betsey Curtis – she's in that bay.' She gestures in the direction of her bed. 'I just wanted to drop off a toy of hers – and to say goodnight.' She pulls the ragdoll from her bag and the nurse nods, convinced by this badge of parenting. 'Thank you,' Jess whispers. 'Thank you very much indeed.'

Betsey looks so tranquil as she sleeps. The pressure bandage is still in place and a tube snakes from a cannula in her finger but there's no evidence she's recently experienced a series of seizures. Her limbs are still and her eyes closed, not rolled back in her head.

Jess strokes one plump cheek, savouring its soft peachiness, then brushes her forehead with her lips. But Betsey's smell is masked by that of the hospital ward and the fabric of her bandage.

She sinks into the blue plastic chair by the side of the bed. She hasn't thought about what she will do next. All she had wanted was to sit with her baby girl, unquestioned and unnoticed, and then, somehow, to spirit her away. *I need to take my baby away from here.* That's a mad idea, isn't it? Not in Betsey's best interests since it contravenes what the police, social services and the doctors have said. She knows this, just as she knows she should have returned to Martha, but it makes no difference. Perhaps her maternal instinct – never as strong with this baby as with her boys – is finally kicking in?

She places a hand on her daughter's fragile arm, circling her wrist with her fingers. The tube protruding from the cannula in the back of her hand can be unscrewed from the drip and from the cannula so easily. And once it's gone, there will be nothing to bind her to these machines. Her coccyx prickles as she thinks of the needle piercing her baby's skin. She has long since resisted medicalisation, preventing Betsey from being vaccinated, trying so hard to give her a natural birth – and how she failed there! Now, she can spare her any further intervention and take her away from this.

She just wants to hold her. To feel her: warm and surprisingly solid, but no longer straining against her in anger; her heart beating in close harmony as she lies against her chest. Betsey hasn't rested like that since the night before her accident and every memory is of her exhaustion and fury that afternoon, and then, after it happened, of her pain. All Jess wants – and this is how she will justify it to herself later – is to hold her baby close.

She unscrews the tube from the IV bag, like disconnecting two pieces of Lego; puts a hand either side of her baby, and lifts her up, her torso like a squat bag of cereal; her head far heavier than it appears.

'Mummy's here,' she whispers into the top of her bandage, which rubs roughly against the base of her chin – and how she wishes she could remove this and kiss her properly. She sits back in the chair, hardly believing she has managed this; tries to preserve this moment. 'Shh, shh. Mummy's here.'

But they're too exposed. A curtain hangs around each bay and she eases this across, breath held tight as she prays the rings won't clack on the runners. Now they are cocooned in their own private world. Betsey's chest rises and falls and this connection, with their chests touching and breath mingling, reminds her of a closeness she hasn't experienced since she was pregnant with her. This is how they should have been from the start! It's all Betsey needs: a mother content to sit still, listening to the patter of her heartbeat, attuned to her tiny snuffles, breathing the same air. She drinks her in – and she was wrong: despite the stench of antiseptic and bleach, and the grub of her bandage, she still smells like Betsey. And Jess knows she can mother her.

Or can she? The truth is she can mother a child who doesn't wriggle or strain. Who doesn't resist. Are the two things connected? Betsey's resistance and Jess's busyness, her failure to ever sit with her and be still?

You're a bad mother. The familiar mantra kicks off. *A bad mother, a terrible mother.*

But no, I'm not, she thinks. *For the fragile moments that Betsey is content, I am a good mother, now.*

And perhaps this could continue? She could manage to be a good mother if she somehow managed to maintain this calm. If she takes the time just to sit quietly with her, at home – not in a hospital, with its fluorescent strip lights and bleeping machines, its brutal way of doing things, but in the quiet of Betsey's nursery.

She is going to try. Her baby shouldn't be here. Look at her. She's fine detached from that machine. She doesn't need this equipment. All she needs is a mother who loves her – and her love flows through her veins like melted chocolate, hot and dark and intent on scalding anyone who suggests she shouldn't take her baby home. She unclips the other end of the tube from the cannula and wraps a hospital blanket neatly around Betsey's limbs, swaddling her up to her neck. If she swings her tote over her shoulder and bunches her light Puffa jacket in front of her, shielding Betsey, she should be able to make it. If she is careful now ...

She peeks around the curtain. The nurse is still bent over the work station, and so she sidles out, walking softly for the first tentative steps, and then quickly, each footstep increasingly decisive now that she has turned the corner and left her behind. Jess's heart swells. She has done it! She has managed to whisk Betsey from her bed and all she need do is get her down this corridor and then out of the ward.

She picks up speed and almost trips. She must slow down; mustn't attract attention. Betsey is heavier than she remembered, or she is holding her cack-handedly, the jacket flapping against her baby's legs, the polyester threatening to slip. Her bag vibrates, an insistent buzzing, but she ignores it and hitches Betsey higher. 'It's all right, darling,' she wants to whisper, but she daren't. She must be as quiet as possible. Betsey wriggles, and she clutches her tight, her fingers digging in. A tiny, protesting mew. 'Shh. Mummy's here now. Just a moment,' she whispers, and her voice is savage in its anxiety. 'Almost there.'

'Jess. What are you doing?' The automatic doors to the corridor have swung open to reveal Liz, in her coat, and carrying her bag, perhaps having forgotten something and coming back for it, at the end of a long day.

For one long moment, they just stare at each other. Then Liz shatters the silence.

'Is that Betsey you've got there?'

Jess's throat is dry.

'Please, let me take her from you.' Liz moves forwards, unnaturally calm, as if she thinks Jess may do something erratic. 'Jess? You can't take Betsey away from here. Do you understand? She needs to be kept under observation; we have to keep a very close eye on her.

'Here let me take her,' she repeats, because Jess isn't relenting, isn't releasing her grip at all, and has absolutely no intention of handing her baby over.

'Jess.' There's a real steeliness to Liz's voice. 'Betsey is still very poorly. Do you understand? She needs to stay with us.'

Jess tries to sidestep around her, to make her way along the corridor, towards the exit and freedom, but Liz is too quick and blocks her path.

'Please. Just give her to me,' she says, like a mediator in a hostage situation. And then the threat comes, the steeliness explicit. 'If you don't, I'll have to call the police.'

'No.' Jess shakes her head fiercely. Could she make a run for it? She is fitter than Liz – three HIIT sessions a week; a weekly run – and she is more driven, her fight-or-flight instinct tuned to its highest pitch. Clutching Betsey tight, she darts to the side of Liz, desperate to race away.

'Oh no, you mustn't,' Liz says. And then she cries: 'Security!' and everything ratchets up a gear. An alarm sounds and fast-paced nurses seem to dart at her. A nurse

barks orders – 'Just give her to me; give her to me now!' –
and there is something about her directness, the economy
of her language and her no-nonsense tone, that makes Jess
falter, that makes her vulnerable, and in that moment the
nurse swoops.

'Nooooo!'

Her baby is snatched from her arms. Within a split second
Betsey is being carried back along the corridor at a fast,
clipped pace. She tries to reach for her but she can't go anywhere. A security guard has her held fast.

'I'll have to let Lucy know about this, and DC Rustin,'
Liz says, and there is pity in her eyes as well as frustration –
and yes, she thinks she can read it, anger. She pauses and her
voice softens. 'Oh, Jess. Do you understand?'

'Of course I bloody understand.' Jess never swears but fear
has turned her into someone she no longer recognises. Her
arms are too empty: her body yearns for her child. She turns
her head, not wanting to acknowledge the reprimand; not
wanting Liz to see that she is so close to crying. *What have
we become?* she wonders. *What have I become?*

'I know you want to be with your little girl but this isn't
the way to do it,' Liz says.

'How else can I be with her?' Defiance surges
hot and fast.

'Not like this.' Liz's voice dips to a near whisper. 'Not like
this at all.' She pauses, then, and puts her hand on Jess's arm.
'I need you to come back with me to the ward.'

'Why?' She knows why. She has broken all the rules.

'I'm afraid we'll have to ask for police protection again.'

'And what does that mean?' The phrase is familiar: uttered when Betsey was first admitted but she is tired, so very tired, of the jargon with which they all speak.

'It means the police can arrange for Betsey to be kept here in hospital but without you having any access to her. It means you'll be banned from coming here and the police will stop you seeing your child.'

LIZ

Wednesday 24 January, 8.30 p.m.

Twenty-eight

Neil is incandescent, of course.

I've come back to the ward to relay what's happened. He is unequivocal: calls are to be made to Cat Rustin, and to Lucy Stone. 'What the fuck was she playing at? She could have killed that baby. Is she insane?'

He quivers with rage, but it's an anger tempered with fear. Fear of what could have happened to Betsey; fear too of how we as a hospital might be deemed negligent for almost allowing a parent to abscond with her child. The bank nurse on duty is admonished, Neil lambasting her in terms that contravene all employment rules and confirm him as due for retirement. I intervene. She's tearful and profusely apologetic; then, out of Neil's earshot, extremely defensive. I think of the clinical incident forms that will have to be filled in; the potential inquiry into how this could have occurred. But my main concern is for Betsey, transferred back to her cot, and Jess,

263

being held by security in the doctors' room while Neil phones the police to relay this recent breach of her visiting conditions.

It's not DC Rustin who arrives but two uniformed officers: those who happen to be the closest, and can get to the hospital fastest. They only took ten minutes to arrive – it's a high-priority call – and their speed means they're not on top of the details of the case.

Jess looks terrified as they approach. She's shrunk into herself so that I get a glimpse of what she will look like as an old lady: fine-boned, delicate, vulnerable, with none of the spirit she showed when we first met, or the defiance shown minutes ago when she refused to hand over Bets. This diminished Jess reminds me of my mother, and the ghost of a memory shimmers: a Dartmoor lane; rain licking the windows; and a young police officer turning his head as he ducked into a panda car, keen to be away from us, embarrassment blotching his face.

The memory distracts me; I need to focus on the present. The officer taking the lead – blond, confident, just the right side of burly – is indicating that Jess must go with them now. His manner is perfectly considerate but there's a disconnect – his words, sharp as a paper cut, don't seem to make sense.

It's because he doesn't know the minutiae of the case, I tell myself; because he's been radioed to get here as quickly as possible; because Rustin's not working tonight and there's no time for this officer to process why a mother might want to snatch her baby from a hospital.

But, as he places a pair of handcuffs around Jess's slight

wrists, her alleged crime seems to bear no resemblance to the reality of her situation.

'I'm arresting you on suspicion of child abduction,' he says.

'You can see why I had to do that?' Neil says, when the police take Jess away. Before their arrival he was quivering with self-righteous indignation, huffing and puffing about whether she had the faintest idea of the ramifications of her behaviour: in the aftermath of her arrest, he is uncharacteristically subdued. When Betsey was admitted, he made it clear I wasn't to be involved with the case in any way but now he seems to be asking me to validate his decision, just as he did when we discussed whether it was a safeguarding issue. Perhaps he finds the sight of a mother being manhandled by two police officers discomfiting, too.

'Yes ...' Barely thinking, I tell him what he wants to hear as I try to process what's happened. 'Parents can't just come in here and deny their children care.' And yes, I can understand his fury and I can't condone the selfishness of her behaviour: the sheer recklessness of trying to remove Betsey, and her arrogance in thinking she knew best. But I'm flailing, my frustration undercut by incomprehension and a deep sadness for a friend who seems a distorted version of herself, like a figure in a fairground mirror. Just how *desperate* must she be to believe that snatching her baby would be a better option than allowing Betsey to be treated here?

The truth nudges me through the fog of my thoughts. This isn't *rational* behaviour and contacting the police – though inevitable from the hospital's viewpoint, and according to the trust's protocol – doesn't seem appropriate for someone not behaving as if she's in robust mental health.

'I don't think she could have been thinking clearly.' I edge my way nearer to this idea. 'Perhaps we should talk to Lucy Stone about whether she has undiagnosed postnatal depression. See if she can be assessed.'

I anticipate a snort; a harrumph; a dismissal because Neil is less sympathetic towards people with mental health issues than physical conditions. Not that he would ever admit it (he's at least aware of the need to appear politically correct) and not that he thinks this about conditions such as schizophrenia that are extreme. But a bit of postnatal depression in an affluent, married mother? In a world in which he treats terminally ill children, he has limited sympathy.

'It might help explain this behaviour,' he concedes. 'But it doesn't excuse it. I'm not having her on my ward. She's a liability, and she only has herself to blame.'

It's the inevitable response: our duty of care is to Betsey and to our other patients, and we can't risk a repeat of this behaviour. What would have happened if Betsey had started fitting or banged her head while in Jess's care? And yet, Jess isn't well. It's a revelation like discovering, aged twenty, that I needed glasses: the edges around my thoughts are no longer blurred; everything begins to make sense.

I begin to argue her case but Neil raises a hand to silence me, like a policeman stopping the flow of traffic, and I am so stunned by this reversion to his old self – the self-regarding, dismissive, openly contemptuous Neil who keeps me firmly in my place – that I am quiet.

But I'm not going to doubt my judgement on this. Because it tallies with something Jess suggested three years ago. Something I told myself I'd misheard and that she couldn't have meant, but which now makes perfect sense.

LIZ

Friday 5 December, 2014

Twenty-nine

I'm getting old, I think, as I collapse on a sticky leatherette banquette having finally escaped from the dance floor. We're having a mums' night out and somehow a nice, quiet meal has segued into a full-on night of tequila shots and dancing at a dodgy club.

It's 1.30 a.m., and though I've gyrated enthusiastically to a string of Nineties anthems, my feet ache and I'm hoarse from trying to make myself heard above the music. Mel and Charlotte are dancing flamboyantly – arms reaching for the ceiling or flung around each other, lyrics shouted lustily – but, unlike everyone else, I'm working on Sunday. I've stopped drinking; have moved onto the Diet Coke.

'Don't be so *boring*! Come and dance!' Jess flops next to me, and smiles up into my face. 'Even Charlotte's going for it.' She gestures to our friend, now swaying to Oasis. Eyes closed, she couldn't be more removed from the mother who creates highlighted spreadsheets when organising extra-curricular pick-ups and harangues us for not concentrating at book club. Her expression is dreamy, as if she's remembering a particular kiss. 'Look at her,' Jess says, gesturing to Charlotte, amused and indulgent. 'I don't think I've ever seen her this drunk.'

'Wonderwall' came out when I was fifteen: when I had yet to experience romantic love and doubted anyone would ever feel about me in that way. It was a miserable time – except that, by this stage, I knew, from watching Mattie being put back together, that I wanted to be a doctor: a plastic surgeon, I thought initially, though I later realised I was more suited to medicine than surgery.

I managed this by studying obsessively and being academic and I'd imagined Charlotte was similarly bookish. But seeing her, lost in the music, I realise she might have had a far more balanced adolescence than me. There's a surprising sensuousness to her dancing, and I can suddenly see a younger Charlotte falling deeply, obsessively, in love.

'You OK?' Jess shouts over the music.

'Just looking at Charlotte.'

'Oh you don't want to do that. Come on. Let's go and dance.' She takes my hand as if to pull me along. The music is building to its climax; in a moment the DJ will cut the sound and everyone will start chanting.

'Just a minute. I need to get my energy back.'

She looks at me reprovingly. I relent and shove on my too-high heels.

'Fab. I need my disco diva.' She leans forward and gives me a kiss on the cheek and her curls brush against my mouth. When she draws back, her pupils are dilated, and for a moment — a moment that stills because I'm not sure how I'd react if this happens — I think she's going to lean in for a kiss.

'I love you, Liz,' she says, her limbs so languorous they are almost floppy.

'I love you, too,' I say. She is extremely drunk.

'Isn't this lovely?' She flings her arms out and points to Mel and a posse of other mums from Rosa's class who are belting out the chorus. She rests her bottle of beer against her forehead, and smiles at the pearls of condensation trickling from her hair.

'Yes — yes it is,' I say because what's not to like? I may have felt tired and bored but it's good to see a group of friends letting their hair down. 'It's a relief to know that we can behave as if we're teenagers again.'

'It's good not to be a *mummy* all the time.' She takes a swig from her bottle.

'Well, there is that.' I'm mildly surprised. Of our immediate group of four, she's the only one who's chosen to be a stay-at-home mum and she's never expressed any opposition to doing this before.

'I mean, I love my kids—'

'I know you do.'

'—but sometimes I just need a *break*. They wear me down, you know? I love Frankie dearly but I feel like I have to be on high alert all the time. And Ed's never, ever there. It's just me who's responsible *all* the time. There's no let up from always having to look after them. Always having to make sure they're not doing something wild and impulsive; always being vigilant, and checking they're all right.'

She swigs savagely. I'm not sure what to say. This isn't a standard, gentle moan, made half-apologetically with the knowledge she's bloody lucky, but is riddled with resentment. Perhaps I'd underestimated her level of frustration, secretly thinking she has it quite easy, having a rich husband and not having to work. Or perhaps the boys are far harder than I'd thought: Frankie's behaviour must grind her down, however adept she seems at dealing with him. I pull her to me in a hug.

We should chat properly about this when we're both sober, I resolve. I'm not sure either of us will make much sense at the moment. I mutter something about motherhood being much undervalued. That I couldn't do what she's doing and stay at home with the children; that it's the hardest job in the world.

'No one tells you that, do they?' she says, her face just that bit too close. She wants me to understand this. 'You think you'll learn from your parents' mistakes, that you'll be a completely different mother to your mother, but no one tells you how *hard* it is. How there's just so much to consider. So much to think about all the bloody time. That there's so much that could go wrong.'

'So you won't be having another baby then?'

I don't know why I say this. I think because I'm tired and it's late and I don't want to hear my dear friend pouring out her mothering woes on this one night when we're supposed to be forgetting about our children. Perhaps it's because I don't want to hear this: not from Jess, the friend who I've always thought is more skilled at motherhood than the rest of us, and certainly more so than me. And so, like a fool, I don't listen but use humour to try to deflect her anxiety and, in doing so, I only make things worse.

'Christ no!' she says, and I know she's slipped into the stage of extreme drunkenness where she'll say outrageous things – where she'll no longer sound like the Jess I know – but where she'll also speak frankly. 'Ed thinks it would be lovely: that a baby girl would "complete our family". That it's what I'd like, coming from a family of four children.' Her tone tilts from mockery to sadness. 'But a, I can't guarantee I'd have a girl, which is what he wants; and b, I don't think I could cope with it.'

She rests her head back against my shoulder. I reach over and stroke her curls; drop a kiss on the top of her head. We sit there, and as I watch Mel dance as if she's driving something from her, and Charlotte, swaying trance-like, Jess says something so quietly I have to lean closer, unsure if I've heard her properly.

'What did you say?' I check.

'Just that I don't want the responsibility of having any more children.' She is looking at me intently. 'I think I'd probably kill them if I did!'

'You don't mean that!' Her tone is wrong: too vehement; a joke delivered oddly. I must have imagined it; or, with the pounding music, have heard it wrong.

'No, not really.' She laughs, and gets up, holding out a hand. I take it and she pulls me up so that we're facing each other. I smile, trying to feel relief.

She smiles, too, but there's not much joy to it, and her tone is pragmatic.

'But I think it might just push me over the edge.'

Liz

Wednesday 24 January, 2018, 9.55 p.m.

Thirty

It's nearly ten by the time I make it home, my body sagging with exhaustion; my mind reeling with the thought of what Jess must be going through, being questioned by the police.

Nick makes me a mug of tea and I slump in front of the television, watching a dysfunctional couple arguing about an exorbitant house build on some property programme, but not taking any of it in. I think of Jess trying to dart past me. Remember her erratic movements; the glint of desperation in her eyes.

'Coming to bed?' At half ten, Nick pulls me up and we start getting ready. As usual, I peek into the children's bed-rooms, tucking their duvets around them; dropping a kiss on their heads. Rosa sleeps in the foetal position; Sam splays like a star. I linger, conscious that Jess won't be kissing Kit and Frankie tonight; that Betsey won't have a parent check-ing on her either. What a mess; what a bloody mess.

I put my mobile on charge, but as I do so it vibrates. It feels ominous. My mother? Who else would ring at this time at night? I glance at the screen. Of course, it's Ed. I can't discuss Betsey, and I probably shouldn't have any contact with him at all, but what friend would refuse to speak to him in a situation like this?

'Ed? Are you OK?'

'Jess has been arrested.' His voice breaks. 'She's at the police station, now. She gave Martha the slip and tried to take Betsey from hospital.'

'Oh, Ed, I know. I'm so sorry.'

'She said you stopped her and called the police. You let them arrest her – and you didn't think to call me? To tell me what had gone on?'

His aggression winds me. Before I can start to explain that the matter was taken out of my hands, he seems to realise he has gone too far.

'I'm sorry, Liz. Sorry. It's just such a shock. I just – I can't make sense of this.'

'I know,' I say, abandoning any pretence that I can maintain some professional distance. 'I know.'

'I don't think she could have been thinking straight. She's behaving like one of those parents who snatch their kids from hospital to get different cancer treatments. She can't have thought you were treating her properly. Or did she want to harm her? Are the police right? Have I got her wrong?'

'Of course she didn't want to harm her. And of course you haven't got her wrong.'

'But what was she thinking? What would have happened if Betsey had had a seizure when she was out of hospital, or if she fell down at home and the bleed got worse?'

She could have suffered irreversible brain damage, I think. 'The important thing is that neither of these things happened. I know it's hard not to imagine the worst but Betsey's still in hospital; she wasn't harmed by what happened; and she's stable despite all this.'

'Yes.' He sounds despondent and I realise he's completely out of his depth.

'I'm so sorry, Ed,' I repeat. 'I know her behaviour must seem bizarre. She's clearly been struggling a bit and needs some help. I'm just so sorry I haven't seen her much recently. If I had, I might have picked this up.'

He is silent for a moment. From what I know of him, mental illness isn't something he has ever had to contemplate: like Nick, his was a relatively uneventful childhood and adolescence. And, while he knows Jess can be anxious, he had no reason to think she might do something as erratic as this.

'You mean *psychiatric* help? Or just a bit of counselling?'

I hesitate, conscious this isn't my specialty and not wanting to perturb him further. 'Look, I don't know. But perhaps the trauma of Betsey's birth affected her more than we realised. Perhaps that's triggered this. Made her unwell.'

'You think she's mentally ill? Do you think she's suffering from postnatal depression or something?' His voice escalates.

'I can't diagnose her, Ed. She's not my patient. But ... I think she needs to be assessed to see if she's suffering from that, or postnatal anxiety.'

'But mothers with postnatal depression can kill their babies, can't they? There was that management consultant's wife in North London who smothered her kids, and that mother who jumped off Beachy Head with hers recently ...'

'But Jess didn't do either of those things. Those are two examples that are in the news precisely because they're so very rare.'

I try to reassure him that now there has been this crisis we can get Jess a diagnosis and treatment. But he barely listens, his attention flitting to what's happening to Jess currently, and how her behaviour at the hospital might impact on her treatment by the police.

'What if they have evidence that she harmed Betsey before she took her in? Or they see this as proof she could have done it?'

'You don't think that, do you?'

There is a pause that goes on for too long. I'd expected an immediate denial but it's as if he is contemplating telling me something incriminating. I wait, increasingly sure I've worked out what's happening, and increasingly concerned he's unconvinced.

'I don't know,' he says at last, as if he's embarrassed to admit this, and his tone speaks of grief and incomprehension and a relationship stretched to near breaking point. 'This morning the police questioned me about my movements and I was relieved because I thought at least they weren't focusing on her. But now she's done something this mad, this disturbing, and – Christ, I feel horrendous admitting this – now, I don't know what to think.'

JESS

Thursday 25 January, 8 a.m.

Thirty-one

The interview room is stark and intimidating. A grey table sits slab-like between two sets of plastic chairs and the one, high-set window allows a faint shaft of wintery light.

On one side of the table sit DCs Rustin and Farron; on the other Jess and Liam McFadden, a solicitor acquired by Ed. He's a thickset man, whose sturdiness seems designed to reassure and yet she shrinks from his presence. When they met, he gripped her hand and told her intently, 'You're not to worry, Mrs Curtis.' But he might as well have told her not to breathe.

DC Rustin unwraps a DVD and explains that the interview will be recorded. 'There'll be a buzzing noise for a few seconds and then we'll start.' She states the time and date and all of those present, and Jess notes the calm, apparently untroubled look on her face. Beside her, DC Farron is unreadable. She remembers his relative sympathy in that first interview: her hope that he might view her as a decent mother. Now his gaze slips over her like running water: not a hint of a smile.

They go through what happened at the hospital.

'Why did you try to take Betsey from the ward, Jess?' asks DC Rustin.

'Because I love her.' The answer is simple.

'But taking her away meant she couldn't get the right treatment.' A line appears between DC Rustin's eyebrows as she tries to get this straight.

'I ... I wasn't thinking,' Jess tries to clarify. 'She didn't seem to be in danger. I just wanted to hold her – and then, I suppose, I wanted to take her away from those machines, all that intervention. That's why I tried to get her away from there.'

'Do you always try to keep Betsey safe?' DC Farron leans forward. His gaze has shifted; is now warm and encouraging. For a split second she imagines being completely honest and telling him everything. But that's impossible.

'Yes.' She is grateful for his use of the present tense. 'Isn't that what mothers are supposed to do?'

'But you didn't in this instance. You took her away from the environment and medical expertise she needed.'

'I wasn't thinking clearly,' she says.

'You didn't keep Betsey safe on the day she went into hospital either, did you, Jess?' DC Rustin leans back in her chair, her pale blue eyes resting on her.

'Yes I did.'

'You took quite a while to bring her into hospital. Over six hours if she sustained her injury when you say she did.'

'I didn't want to overreact.' The police officer's suggestion that she lied about the time frightens her: what else does she think she lied about? 'I've explained all this before. I didn't realise it was any different to a tumble my boys might have taken when they were toddlers. She cried at the time but' – and she's embarrassed by how ineffectual her explanation sounds now that her baby remains in hospital five days after being admitted; now that she's had a series of seizures; now that the situation has escalated beyond anything she could have imagined – 'I don't think I realised how serious it was.'

'You didn't bring her in even when she had been sick in her cot – a clear sign of concussion?'

'I hadn't realised she was sick. I was asleep.'

'You were in bed, with the duvet over your head, according to your husband.'

'I . . .' Her lungs feel emptied. Had Ed said that? That she was trying to block out the sound of Betsey's screams? *I was scared to go to her in case I hurt her.* How can she admit this? Shame engulfs her body, heat spreading up her neck to her cheeks. 'I was dozing; was trying to get back to sleep; I was so exhausted I don't think I properly registered her crying, or the *extent* of her crying. But if I knew she'd been sick, or was so distressed, of course I'd have gone to her. I wouldn't have *ignored* her then.'

'By all accounts – your husband's, your neighbour's, your sister's – you're usually an attentive mother,' says DC Farron.

281

She is flailing in the quicksand of their conversation. An attentive mother is the opposite of what they think.

'Your children are always well dressed and well nourished; there was no sign of any of them being harmed when your boys had their medical examinations and Betsey her skeletal survey,' the detective says, and he smiles as if to say: it's fine, you can agree with this.

'Yes. That's right.' She glances at her solicitor for confirmation. He shifts in his chair and nods, indicating that this isn't a trick question, but the coil in her stomach still doesn't ease.

'And so what I'm struggling to understand, Jess' – and here DC Farron's face morphs into something approaching compassion, though Jess knows it's a mask – 'is what happened that night that made you dismiss Betsey's injury as something that didn't need hospital attention, and then ignore her as she lay screaming in her bed?'

She doesn't know what to say.

'Because when an attentive mother sleeps she is always aware that her baby might wake up crying, particularly if she's banged her head, isn't she?'

She cannot answer.

'An attentive mother doesn't lie there, ignoring her, with the covers pulled over her head, does she?'

'My client has said she was exhausted,' Liam McFadden interjects, and she is grateful, and suddenly thankful for his physicality, and all the trappings – woody eau de cologne, starched shirt, designer watch, too ostentatious for these dour surroundings – that lend him weight.

DC Farron raises his eyebrows as if Liam's comment is barely worth a response.

'What did your husband think of your relationship with Betsey?' he continues.

'What?' She is confused by this conversational swerve.

'Did he think you were "bonded"?' He says the word self-consciously. 'That you were in tune with your daughter?'

The air is punched from her. Has Ed told them he was concerned she seemed detached with Bets?

'Was that why you argued on the Thursday night and why he came back to see you on the Friday lunchtime?' DC Rustin joins in. 'He was concerned about your relationship with your daughter?'

'I . . .' She shakes her head. 'He was worried, yes.'

'And how did it make you feel? Your husband checking up on you like this?'

Has he told them everything? Something dissolves inside her: the residual belief that he will support her. Her eyes burn with tears.

'Did it make you feel angry?'

'No,' she manages eventually. *You're a bad, bad mother.*

'So angry that you took it out on Betsey?'

'No!' *You're a bad mother. An evil mother.*

'So angry that you were a bit brusque, a bit cack-handed when you changed her nappy? A bit frustrated, perhaps, so that you accidentally banged her head?'

'No, no, no,' she insists.

DC Rustin pauses, leans back and watches her again.

You're such an evil mother you slammed your baby on the changing table so hard you split her head open. It's what they think, and how can Jess convince them of her innocence when her own thoughts whisper this? Her rings were confiscated – along with the rest of her jewellery, her keys and her belt – and so she crosses and uncrosses her fingers, over and over. *Let this be over. Let me convince them. One, two, three. One, two, three. One, two, three.*

'So you're an attentive mother.' DC Farron interrupts her internal monologue.

'Yes.'

'One who didn't ignore her baby when she was crying but was too exhausted to hear her?'

'Yes …' That's not quite right – she heard her, of course she did, but she didn't go to her because she feared she would hurt her. 'I didn't register the extent of her crying.'

'You're an attentive mother – but you delayed bringing your concussed baby to hospital?'

'My client has said that she didn't realise the severity of the injury. She thought it was a fall of the kind experienced by her boys as toddlers.' Liam's tone suggests such repetition is tedious.

DC Farron ignores him. 'But if you're this attentive,' he says, and his tone is suddenly suffused with sarcasm; a shift that grates and pulls her up short, 'then you're not the sort of mother who would ever leave a small baby alone in the house, are you?'

The atmosphere is freighted with expectation. Jess's insides turn fluid. *They know. They seem to know.*

'I think you know Mr Yadav, don't you? Nihal Yadav?'

'What?' She is blindsided. Nihal Yadav? 'I ... I don't think I know anyone with that name. No. I'm not sure ... Is he a parent at school?'

'Nihal Yadav runs Superb Deli Stores, a mini supermarket and off-licence seven minutes' walk from your house.'

Her solicitor clears his throat and edges forward as if to intervene but Jess knows what is coming. Blood thuds through her head. *You're a bad, bad mother.* They have her here.

'We have a witness who recognised you in that shop, and we have CCTV footage showing that you were there, buying a carton of milk and a bottle of wine at six twenty-three p.m. on Friday, nearly two and a half hours after you say your baby daughter sustained her head fracture. Far from being attentive, you are on your own.' A pause. 'We know Kit was at football training but where were Betsey and Frank while you were there?'

'I must object to this evidence being sprung on my client like this without our having a chance to discuss it. I would like a few moments with my client alone,' says Liam.

'No, it's OK.' They know she is a bad mother and now they have the evidence to prove it.

'Then I would advise you to make no comment.'

'It's OK.' *They will take your children away from you, just as you've feared from the very start.* Her throat constricts and her thoughts turn to liquid. She mustn't cry; she mustn't cry.

DC Farron pushes a photocopy of an image towards her, with the date in question and the time – 18.23 – in the corner. It's a grainy black and white, but the woman in the picture is unmistakably her: same hair, bag and coat; same sharp slant of her cheekbones as the camera catches her dipped face.

'That's you, isn't it?'

There's no point denying it. She nods.

'For the tape, please.'

'Yes.' She swallows. 'That's me.' She looks down at her hands in her lap. She has ripped a cuticle and it's now spitting a scarlet pearl of blood. She itches for a clean tissue to smear it away.

'You look rather distressed in this picture,' DC Farron says eventually.

'That can't be deduced from this image,' says her solicitor.

Oh, but it can. Her posture screams anguish: shoulders hunched, head bent as if she wants to hide herself away. *I said I'd be five minutes*, that's what she was thinking as she stood there. And: *Penny's seen me; what was I thinking?* But that figure caught on CCTV footage wasn't thinking straight.

'We've also talked to a Jill Baker, who dropped your son Kit back from football practice that night – getting to yours at around six-forty p.m.,' DC Farron continues.

Her heart contracts in anticipation of a fresh blow. She doesn't know Jill well: not well enough to have asked her what she might have said to the two detectives, though she desperately wanted to; not well enough for strong ties of loyalty to bind.

'Football training finished earlier that night because there was a problem with one of the coaches, and so she was with you earlier than usual,' says DC Farron. 'You couldn't have been in long?'

Jess nods. 'About five minutes.'

'She says you opened the door and she saw you for sufficiently long to be struck by your manner. She described you as "distressed and distracted". You "looked as if you'd been crying". She said, "Her eyes were red." Had you been crying, Jess?'

'I might have been,' she admits.

'Is it fair to say you were distressed?'

'Possibly.'

'Possibly?'

'Probably.' Her voice catches, and she wants to scream at him that of course she was distressed.

'The question,' says DC Farron, and he leans forwards, 'is what happened that was so *distressing* it made you, an attentive mother, leave your ten-month-old baby and eight-year-old son to go out on a cold and wet night to buy wine?

'Did you leave her after doing something you hadn't intended: after growing frustrated and losing your temper?

'Did you leave her after harming your little girl?'

Thursday 25 January, 6.50 a.m.

Thirty-two

'Where's Mummy?'

Frankie's face is a pale oval, hovering above him in the gloaming of the bedroom.

'Frankie ...' Ed glances at the alarm clock: 06.50. He switches on the bedside light.

His youngest son stands, shivering, in his pyjamas.

'Dad?' Kit appears behind his brother, one arm – Ed had momentarily forgotten – in a heavy hunk of plaster; brilliantly, incongruously white.

'Hey, Kit, how did you sleep?' The pallor of his son's face, drained from the trauma of the past eighteen hours, distracts him from his younger boy.

'Where's Mummy?' Frankie repeats, his voice spiking until it's a near falsetto. A pause, and his tone is more querulous. 'Where's Mummy? Where is she? Why isn't she here?'

'Frank ...' Ed throws back the covers and tries to hold

him. Last night, he and Martha fudged Jess's absence, claiming she was staying at the hospital to be with Bets. Kit, characteristically trusting, had swallowed the story, and even Frankie, blank with fatigue, had accepted it at face value. Now, there's no way he can fob them off.

'Where's Mummy?' Frankie's eyes are wild, and the explanation Ed managed to formulate in the small hours of the night momentarily eludes him.

'She'll be back very soon but she's not here at the moment . . .' he says, stating the bloody obvious. But the boy is already hurtling down the stairs.

'Where *is* she?' He races through the kitchen and darts into the snug; ducks into the utility room and the downstairs toilet, his movements increasingly frantic; his voice at fever pitch as his panic grips.

'Dad?' Kit follows more gingerly. 'Muuuum?' He is looking for her bag – a slouchy, metallic leather tote always kept on a peg by the door – and for her coat. 'Daddy?' He regresses to the form he uses when he's apprehensive; looks at him as if he believes he will have the right answer. 'Where is she, Daddy?' He is bewildered. 'Why isn't she here?'

'She's helping the detectives with a few questions about Betsey. It's nothing to worry about.' He gets the words out in a rush. He and Martha had agreed they'd sit the boys down and talk them through it calmly but they've woken earlier than he expected and ambushed him into an explanation. Martha's still asleep, and he knows he's dealing with this badly on his own.

He is shaken by the scale of their distress – though he'd feared this might happen ever since discovering that search on her laptop. Kit, always so stolid, so apparently unflappable, is inconsolable in a way he hasn't been since he was a toddler. And Frankie? His anguish is in a different league.

'Naoooooohhhhhhhhh!' The roar fills the kitchen. Frankie's body shakes convulsively, and when Ed goes to put his arm around him, to hold him as Jess instinctively and expertly would, his son strikes out wildly, batting him away.

'Hey! No need to hit me. We don't do that.' The reprimand is automatic.

Frankie turns his back, wriggling away. *We don't do that? Why the hell does he sound so uptight?* Under normal circumstances his kids shouldn't lash out, of course they shouldn't, but there's been nothing normal these past six days.

He tries to batten Frankie's hands to his sides, but his son wriggles and flails, head twisting from side to side, body jerking, hips squirming against the restraint. A foot strikes Ed's shin and surprises him with spiking pain. 'Lemme go, lemme go. Get off me. Get *off*!' Ed does as he is told, his helplessness increasing until he feels as if he is completely out of his depth.

He sinks on the sofa, head in his hands, eyes on the floor, incapable of looking at either of his sons. Kit slumps down too and leans against him, tears wetting Ed's sleeve. He slides an arm around his eldest boy, taking some solace in the fact that Kit still looks to him for comfort. In front of them, Frankie has crumpled to the floor and is rocking in a foetal position, screaming shrilly.

'Come on, Frankie. Get up!' He can't bear such melodramatic behaviour and goes towards him to try to pull him up and break the hysterical wailing. But Frankie's eyes are wild and his cheeks streaked with tears. The corner of his mouth bubbles with spit, and when Ed bends down to explain that everything will be OK, that Mummy will be home soon, that he needs to stop this crying right now, Frankie cowers. Inching away, the boy pulls himself upright and sits, arms wrapped tight around his knees, head bent downwards, still not looking at him.

'Look. I can't help you if you're going to be like this,' he says, lamely.

What would Jess do? He has always relied on her when Frankie gets stressed. Should he ignore him? Pretend his tantrum isn't happening? Too late he realises how well his wife parents their middle child.

There's a clunk upstairs. The sound of a shower starting. Thank God. Martha must be awake; will be down eventually to help try to ease their anguish, and to take Frankie to school. Last night, they had decided to try for some attempt at normality. What would they usually be doing this time? Breakfast. He should get on with that.

'Let's get us all some drinks. Hot chocolate? A milk-shake?' He's being noisily jovial; slipping into his Daddy Day Care routine of treats all round and general jokiness, indulged by Jess because it happens so rarely. 'Come on, Kit. Why don't we make a monster smoothie with ice cream?'

The boy nods mutely and sniffs.

Incapable of knowing what else to do, Ed starts pulling ingredients from the freezer: vanilla ice cream, frozen cubes of fruit and ice cubes; takes milk from the fridge. Frankie's soundtrack of fractured sobs continues. He should ignore him: just ignore him. But, though he tries to block out the ragged cries, something keeps filtering through.

'It's all my fault. My fault. All my fault,' his son hiccups through his sobs.

'Don't be silly, Frank.' It's typical that he blames himself.

'It is,' Frankie is insisting. 'It's all my fault she's going to prison.'

'She's not going to prison. Of *course* she isn't.' His denial sounds excessive: he lowers his voice, trying to make it all sound perfectly normal. 'She's just having a chat with the nice policewoman you've met.'

'She might though, Dad.' Kit watches him, craving reassurance. They needn't know that Jess has been arrested. It's bad enough that they're aware she is talking to the police.

'She's just helping the detectives,' Ed repeats, and how he hates trotting out that line. He clears his throat; tries to minimise the drama. 'All that means is that she's answering a few questions about how Betsey got hurt and it's much easier for all of us if she doesn't have to talk to them here.'

Kit nods slowly but Frankie's cries redouble.

'My fault. My fault . . .'

He's not going to be able to deal with this except through distraction.

'Right. Let's make that milkshake, shall we?' The ice cubes clatter around the blender as the mixture blasts for twenty seconds. A pause. Then Ed quickly blasts again. Kit puts his unbroken arm around his waist.

'Here's your drink, Kit. Straw?' He reaches into the cupboard for a paper one. 'Don't worry about Frank. He'll cry himself out eventually.' He pauses, uncertain. 'That's what Mum would say, isn't it?'

Kit sniffles. 'I don't know, Dad . . .'

'If we ignore him he'll have to stop,' he says, not feeling the least bit confident. 'Now. What do you want for breakfast? Eggs? Cereal? Porridge?' What do they normally have on a weekday? He hasn't a clue. There's not much bread in the breadbin: not the usual array of spelt sourdough, English muffins and granary. And the contents of the fridge, despite an apparent supermarket delivery, are uninspiring. Everywhere, there's the sense of the usual order of life being abruptly abandoned. Of Jess losing her grasp on things.

He wishes Martha would hurry down but she was so distraught last night, he suggested she have a lie-in. She was contrite, too; blaming herself for suggesting the boys miss school. He is all too aware of her selflessness in moving in and the importance of not taking advantage of this, but still, he's at a loss. He pulls out his phone. Mel would know how to deal with this, and even Charlotte would be a help. No one would describe her as particularly maternal but she'd be no-nonsense: George would never behave like this because she wouldn't allow it. But he doesn't want to contact Charlotte, and Mel will be preparing for work. Besides, he ought to be able to deal with this himself.

And yet he can't bear to look at his youngest son, thrashing around in a rage as he repeats that phrase over and over. He is failing him as a father. Falling so badly short. If he's closed his eyes to what's happening to Jess – and Liz's suggestion makes sense the more he dwells on it – then he's been just as blinkered about Frankie: has been since the day he was born.

He wrenches open the fridge, and peers into it, trying to pull himself together because the last thing the boys need is for him to cave in to this recrimination and self-pity. The very last thing they need is for him to fall apart. The cold air hits his face and he peers into the brightness, not taking in the fridge's contents but just trying to shock himself into getting a grip. His wife is being questioned for abduction; their baby remains in hospital; one son's just been discharged from there while the other lies prostrate and inconsolable, and he has the *audacity* to think about himself?

The doorbell jolts him alert. 7.10 a.m. He is suddenly frightened. No one, apart from the police, ever comes to the house at this time.

What has Rustin found out? Will she tell him they've charged Jess? Or has Jess somehow, erroneously, implicated him? If she's capable of imagining harming her baby, who *knows* what else she's been imagining?

'Just a minute, boys – I'll get that,' he tells them.

He strides to the door and with more vigour than he'd intended, flings it open wide.

LIZ

Thursday 25 January, 7.10 a.m.

Thirty-three

'Hello! Can I come in?'

Ed looks shaken.

'Sorry – perhaps I should have texted, I know it's early but I can't stop thinking about Jess and how you're all doing.'

He blinks and I wonder if he's still angry and whether it was completely stupid to drop in on my way to work.

'No, no, it's fine. Of course.' The colour comes back to his face. 'Christ! It's good to see you. The boys are distraught and I'm being a bit hopeless, to be honest. Come in, come in.'

I drop my bag and scarf in the hall. From the kitchen, I can hear Frankie crying. I glance at Ed, surprised he isn't rushing to his side. He shrugs. *Ed's never, ever there. It's just me who's responsible all the time.* Jess's words have never been more pertinent and I think of how she's shouldered the burden of three kids all these years. It's not sustainable and I

296

feel irritated by his little-boy-lost act, though I suspect Jess once found it attractive. Not any longer. This is crisis point.

I shove my frustration to one side: now's not the time; he's also due some compassion. 'I don't suppose you heard anything?'

He clears his throat. 'I haven't, no.'

'I just wanted to say I'll do whatever I can to help Jess now. I'll talk to Lucy about the possibility of getting a psychiatric assessment and, because I think the impetus will have to come from Jess herself, perhaps you could get her to go to the GP when this is over, as well?'

He looks at me blankly. Perhaps he thinks I'm being too forthright but I'm desperate to make up for not realising what might be wrong. 'Do you really think it will be that easy? That Rustin will let her go with a rap on the knuckles? She doesn't strike me as the sympathetic type.'

'Jess isn't well, Ed. The police will have to see that.'

His face crumples in on itself and his mouth does an odd sideways twist as if he's trying not to cry.

'It's OK,' I say. 'It's going to be OK.' I touch his arm. 'Oh, come here,' I say, giving him a quick hug and feeling the tension coursing through him. 'Now: shall I try to talk to Frankie? What have you told them?'

'That she's helping the police with some questions down at the station.'

'Does he think she's going to prison?'

'Yes.' Ed rubs his hands over his face. 'Christ! How did we get to this?'

'Ed, listen to me.' I place my hands on either side of his upper arms and look him firmly in the eyes. 'It's going to be all right. We're going to help her get through this. But first of all we need to help Frankie. I don't like seeing him this distressed.'

I go into the kitchen, relieved I can finally try to help this child, whose face is puce as if he's tantrumming like a baby. 'Hello, Frankie.' I kneel down and put one hand gently on his stomach. He's surprised and his hysteria lessens just a bit.

'It's my ... it's my fau ...' he tries to say through hiccupped sobs.

'That's OK. Take your time. Can you try to breathe for me? In for three ... out for five ... That's it. Try to calm yourself a little ...'

He nods, supping at air.

'There you go ... that's better. I'm sorry Mummy isn't here. I can see that's upsetting ...'

A rush of renewed sobs and my heart aches for him. I remember being just eighteen months older and dealing with questions about Mattie's accident: knowing something absolutely horrific had happened over which I had no control. He reminds me of my terror; my conviction that I was responsible; my understanding that the person I loved most in the world was in peril. I thought Mattie would die. Prison isn't quite as permanent a separation as death – but for a child, it comes close.

I take Frankie's hand. He grips it and manages a watery smile. I smile back. *We understand one another*, my smile says. *We can do this together.* 'Now: what were you trying to say?'

'It's all my fault, my fault ...' Frankie manages, more clearly now.

'No, it's *not*,' Ed interjects. 'Everyone thinks that they're to blame when something scary happens. It's perfectly natural but none of this is your fault, or Kit's.'

'It is. It is.' He catches Ed's eye and there is something about the sharp terror distilled in his pupils that forces Ed to be quiet.

'OK,' Ed lowers his voice. 'All right.'

'OK,' I repeat, giving Ed a look that I hope conveys that I can get Frankie to open up if only he'll leave me to it. 'Just try to keep breathing, Frankie ... that's right ...' He sits up, our faces so close, our breath is intermingling. 'Can you do that for me?'

He nods, his sobs quietening.

'Now ... can you tell me why you think it's your fault?'

He screws his eyes up tight: that childish trick of believing that if you can't see someone you're invisible.

'Mummy didn't hurt Betsey,' he manages eventually. A pause and a snuffle. 'The police have got it wrong.'

'Oh, Frankie, we don't know what the police think.' Ed can't restrain himself. 'But whatever happened, we know it must have been an accident. She wouldn't have meant to harm Betsey at all.'

'It *was* an accident.' Frankie looks from Ed to me, wide-eyed. 'Mummy didn't do it.'

'Oh, Frankie . . .' Ed begins, and I can see that he believes his wife is capable of harming their baby: that, gripped by postnatal depression, she could have caused the injury after all.

'Ed,' I say, and my voice is a warning that we're at the tipping point and he risks silencing his son altogether if he doesn't shut the fuck up. 'Let's just listen to Frankie, shall we? Frankie – why do you think Mummy didn't hurt Betsey?'

'Because she wasn't even there!'

From Ed, there is silence, and from me the memory of another pair of siblings left alone together; another accident that could have been fatal. Something shifts in my brain. *Two children left alone. And Frankie, like me, believes he's responsible.* I have a sudden inkling that I know what happened here.

'This doesn't make sense!' Ed bursts out. 'What do you mean, she wasn't even there?'

He bends down and tries to put his arm around the boy but Frankie shrugs him off, his body vibrating with tension. He does not want to be held. He wants to be *heard*. It has taken him almost six days to get this secret out and his relief – the relief of a child burdened with too much responsibility, too big a secret – is palpable.

She wasn't even there.

'Can you tell us where Mummy was?' I ask and Frankie visibly softens, his body slumping as if he can relax now the truth is nearly out.

'I don't know.' Then a shrug, his voice almost sulky. 'She went out somewhere.'

'And did Betsey get hurt when she went out?'

A tiny nod: his mouth tight, his face pinched.

'It was an accident, wasn't it, Frankie?'

Another nod.

'And can you tell us who else was involved? Who caused this accident?'

A sharp intake of breath from Ed as he gets there too, as he understands where my questions are leading. Frankie leans towards me and I put my arm around him, letting him burrow deep into my shoulder. I have never felt more affinity for a child; or more sorrow for him.

And Jess's son nods, his face parchment pale, and in little more than a whisper, he finally manages to say it:

'Yes ... Yes, it was me.'

JESS

Friday 19 January, 6.31 p.m.

Thirty-four

Jess senses that something is wrong the second she opens the front door. The children are not in the kitchen, where she left them. 'Frankie? Frankie?' Panic grips her voice as she runs from room to room and races up the stairs.

The sound hits her almost straight away. A full-on, anguished wail, followed by Frankie's pre-emptive cry: the noise he makes when he knows he's about to be told off, coupled with something darker. It is this that terrifies her more than anything else.

'What happened? What did you do?' The accusation flies from her as she bursts into the family bathroom and sees Frankie crouched between the changing table and the roll top bath. Betsey is lying on the marble floor next to him, staring at the ceiling, tears streaming down her face.

She scoops her baby up, cradling her to her chest, feeling

the rapid heartbeats. 'Please be OK, please be OK,' she whispers her reassurance over and over again.

'I tried to change her nappy. She rolled over. I didn't see it ...' Frankie is gabbling as he rocks forwards and backwards. A soiled nappy is strewn on the floor; the stench makes her want to retch.

'It's all right. It's all right.' It isn't, not in the slightest, but she can't be angry with him: her guilt overwhelms her. 'She's all right. Look at her: you can see she is. She's OK,' she shouts as she gestures to her baby, who is screaming, her face filled with fear and pain.

Frankie's burbling segues into a shriek. 'She's not OK, she's not OK,' he yells, over and over, his voice rising in volume.

'She will be.' She needs to minimise his hysteria. There is only one person to blame. *A bad mother who* knew *you shouldn't leave your children.*

Yes, but not to him, she wants to shout. *I'm not a bad mother to him.*

'Shh, shh,' she repeats, holding the two of them close, kissing Bets over and over. The top of his head is damp: he reeks of fear.

'You were so stressy,' he manages, and his words are unbearably sad. 'I wanted to make things better. I just wanted to make you happy.'

She bites back a sob. Of course he did. He has no ability to foresee consequences: is the opposite of her with her constant catastrophising, her continual *what ifs?* He would only have been trying to help, couldn't have predicted his misplaced enthusiasm would result in this disaster. She tries to gain some composure, to calm this voice that betrays her terror. 'I know. But you need to tell me what happened. You need to tell me what you did.'

And so he does, as she kneels next to him on the bathroom floor and Betsey's cries become more erratic, the initial pain not subsiding but ebbing and flowing until her shrieks dip to a ragged lament.

In broken sobs, he tells her how Betsey had been lying on the changing table. How he'd managed to remove her nappy and then reached over for a wipe to clean her. He hadn't held onto her, of course – she doesn't need to ask him the question; stops herself from asking: 'Why didn't you?' – because he never considered she might roll over like this.

'I don't know what happened, Mummy. I turned and she was screaming on the floor . . .'

His eyes are huge like those of the baby in the Superb Deli shop and she knows he expects her to make everything better. Knows, too, the impact on him if anyone discovers this happened because of his misguided desire to help.

It will break him, her boy who doesn't quite fit in; who feels his inadequacies so intensely. He is eight years old and he acted out of love. It was an accident that only happened because she left them, she knows that. Knows, too, that she must bear that responsibility. Betsey is crying lustily – a sign that she isn't concussed, because it's silent children you need to worry about, isn't it? – and so her priority is to protect him.

Her baby's cries slow and she feels a cold sharp fear at the thought of her negligence being discovered. What will happen if anyone discovers her baby fell because she left her alone with an eight-year-old boy? *They will take your children away. They will take them away.* It won't matter that she had the best of intentions. That she thought that by walking away, she was keeping them safe . . .

She pulls the children tighter until Frankie starts wriggling, disturbed by this excessive closeness; kisses both of them, keeping them close. Kit will be back any moment and she needs to calm them down quickly; must quieten Frankie, in particular, so that her elder son and her husband have no idea.

She looks at Betsey's crumpled face. And she checks the back of her head. There's no bump, thank God: no egg like the boys had when they fell. It feels a little tender, and Betsey screams more furiously when she touches it, but there's nothing obvious; nothing dramatic to be extra anxious about. Her heart flutters like a bird banging against a window; cold spreads from the pit of her stomach and up through her chest. Perhaps she should get an icepack? And she is just about to do so when the doorbell rings, a disconcertingly melodic chime.

Frankie jumps up and starts running on the spot, screeching.

'Calm down. You *have* to calm down.' She grabs him by

the shoulders and tries to hold him still, her fingers digging into him more forcefully than she intended, as she tries to stare into his eyes. Her fear is so extreme it's as if her mind has fused and all other emotions – compassion, empathy – have been short-circuited. For once she is forensic, decisive, clear about how she needs to be.

'Who is it? Who is it?' He is frantic. She needs to stop him shouting.

'It will probably be Charlotte. With Kit.'

He gives the most tortured scream.

She binds him tight in her arms, not allowing any resistance, feeling his wired body turn quite, quite still.

And then she whispers to him: 'I promise it's going to be OK. But if anyone asks what happened, here's what I need you to say.'

LIZ

Thursday 25 January, 8.30 a.m.

Thirty-five

The call from A&E comes just as I arrive at work, and my thoughts are still clouded with Frankie: the burden of this secret, his inconsolable distress.

Jess's behaviour swims into focus, too. *This* is why she lied: to protect her boy, to discourage questions about her poor judgement in parenting. *She left her baby alone with her eight-year-old child.* I remember dismissing Charlotte's suggestion and being so blithely disparaging of the idea she would do this. If I'd ever given Jess that impression, no wonder she couldn't open up to me.

So I'm preoccupied when my mobile rings and though a call from the hospital is hardly unusual, still, it jangles my thoughts.

It's about my mother, of course.

The words of the A&E nurse filter through: 'Called an ambulance . . . waiting to be admitted . . . very poorly.'

And all my guilt at my problematic relationship with this woman I love out of a sense of duty but don't understand or like very much, floods together with a sense that this is it: the end. Something she might have sensed was encroaching.

The reason she's been thinking of Clare.

She doesn't look well: jaundiced eyes, a spider's web of mottled blood vessels on her cheeks. Her eyes are dulled above dark shadows and her tummy's oddly distended: she's gaunt apart from this fluid-filled stomach. Not pancreatic cancer, I automatically think.

She's lying on a trolley, her skin sheened with sweat, her fingers gripping the sides as if this grounds her. The junior registrar has pulled the curtains around her bay; in this small, blue world, her fear is heightened and intense.

'You came,' she manages, and my guilt sharpens that this was ever in doubt. Then I think of the times when she's called and I've been working. Of the cancelled visits, when on-call rotas have been changed or Sam and Rosa have been ill, of promises made and broken. I've been so much better than Mattie, but then that's not saying much, is it?

'Of course I came,' I say, but she can't reply. A look of something close to terror skims her face and prevents her from speaking. I wait for it to pass.

'You're in the right place. We'll get you some help.' I utter familiar blandishments but I feel impotent. She's frightened, and it's little wonder. Her distended stomach suggests acute alcoholic hepatitis. She is horribly ill.

She smiles at me, or she tries to smile, because suddenly she is lurching forwards, spurred on by the force of something bursting from her. The blood takes all of us by surprise. She is vomiting up the stuff. Crimson. Prolific. Angry. As dramatic as water bursting from a mains.

The registrar, in scrubs that are soaked through, can't move for shock. I grab a basin but it's useless as the blood splatters the curtains, the bed, his face and body, and my mother. It soaks my hands and arms, pools on the bed and floods the floor.

'Variceal bleed. You've got to stop it,' I bark at the junior doctor. He introduced himself but I've forgotten his name: his youth and inexperience the only thing that's relevant at this moment. 'You need to get a Sengstaken tube down.'

He seems paralysed with fear.

'Can we have some help?' I wrench the curtain of the cubicle aside and call out. 'She's got probable portal hypertension,' I tell him. My voice breaks and rises. 'We've got to do it *now*.'

My mother is making an awful noise. A choking and gurgling, a belching and bubbling as a fresh rush of blood spews from her. Somehow, a tube is produced along with a more senior registrar and he and this junior struggle to force it down her throat. I want to tell her everything will be all right, but there's no time, no room, and I stand aside, knowing I need to trust my colleagues. God, but it's hard. I close my eyes for a second, trying to block out the anarchic chaos of my mother's bucking body; the senior registrar's raised voice as panic grips him; the fear that he might not get this patient back.

JFDI, as Neil might say. His imagined yell stirs me into action. Together, as my mother starts choking on her blood, we get the tube down and exert pressure on her oesophageal veins. She falls back on the bed. Spent. Barely conscious. Alive, for the moment, at least.

I'm in the hospital canteen. The Chill Out Zone, as it styles itself; a place in which relatives and staff can temporarily escape from the death and pain, the blood and chaos being experienced in the building elsewhere. It's not particularly relaxing with its tables bolted into the floor, pine seats padded with plastic and a 1980s decor of mustard and brown, but it's relatively quiet at this time of day and I need a moment to think through what's happened before I go on the ward.

I sip a bitter black coffee and taste self-disgust. My mother nearly died. She will probably die soon. She has end-stage liver disease. But the fact that I diagnosed it ahead of the poor junior doctor who treated her is of little consolation. I should have recognised it, and tried to do something about it, long before now.

It doesn't always take much to contract this disease, although in her case the couple of glasses of wine I'd told myself she had each night was probably more like half a bottle, supplemented by vodka in her orange juice, and gin sloshed into her mugs of tea. I should have guessed when I saw her empty fridge; when I noted the dramatic weight loss and those swollen ankles and legs; when I ignored the yellowish tinge to her eyes; when I told myself her reddened cheeks were due to rosacea and – and it sounds so bloody ludicrous – the biting winter air.

I should have seen, but I didn't because sometimes we only see what we want to see, don't we?

It's the same way I responded to Jess. I should have known from watching her atypical behaviour at the nativity that something was wrong; should have guessed when she brought Betsey in. I should have suspected, not necessarily that she was lying to protect someone, but that she was mentally ill. But, because I'd let our friendship slip, I hadn't picked up on this after Betsey was born. I'd not taken the time to listen; to ask the right questions; to try to secure the help that could have prevented her from leaving her children and Betsey being hurt. Because I'd dwelt on the Jess I'd known – the woman I perceived as a 'better' mother than me; who I'd thought of as highly competent – I missed what should have been obvious.

And if I haven't been a good enough doctor, I haven't been a good enough daughter or friend.

Time to try to put this right.

Because, if my mother's going to die, I have to try to persuade Mattie to come down. To show some of the compassion that I know runs through his veins, because he shows it to the teenagers he works with, and to my children and me.

Conscious that he'll be resistant, I pull out my phone.

*

It doesn't go well. The line's bad: I can hear wind whistling in the background and Mattie's preoccupied. I've caught him at work, just before he discusses orienteering with thirty urban children who have never scaled a Munro before.

He's serious and a touch curt. The fact that our mother's in hospital because of her drinking doesn't elicit much surprise, and I find myself turning towards the wall of the canteen, my voice a tight whisper, my eyes burning as I try to convey the severity of what's going on.

'There's a risk that if you don't come down, you won't see her again.' A pause while I wait for him to jump in; to reassure me that of course he'll rush down to see her on her deathbed. 'Matt. Do you understand what I'm saying? If you don't come down in the next couple of days, I really think it might be too late.'

'I don't know what good my coming down would do.'

'It might help her. To know that you forgive her.'

'I'm not sure I can do that,' he says. His voice quietens and I strain to hear every word. 'You're not the only one who's having nightmares about our early childhood, you know.'

'Really?'

'Yeah. I don't want to talk about it but you've dredged up all sorts of things.'

'I'm sorry.' I don't know what else to say.

'Yeah, well. I've got to go.' His voice dips again as he prepares to make his escape and I feel desperation and a quiet, focused rage.

'You can't just wriggle away from this. I know you can't bear her but you could do this for me, if not for her . . . Matt, please.' I'm aware that I sound pathetically childish. 'I don't want to have to deal with her death on my own.'

'I'll think about it,' he says softly. 'Look. It's busy here. I can't just leave on a whim: I've got commitments; we've got strict student–staff ratios . . .'

'OK. I understand.' It's a convenient excuse but that doesn't mean it's not true.

'Will you let me know if she gets worse?'

'I'll ring you later; tell you if there's any change. And please, think about it. I'm not crying wolf.'

'I know.' I can hear his love for me in his voice; the age-old loyalty of a sibling who has shared a problematic childhood; who knows of horrors we daren't tell others. 'I know you'd never do that.'

I finish the call. I need to get back to work. To shrug on a new role: Dr Trenchard, paediatrician. But I find it hard to stop thinking about the pain my mother caused us, and continues to cause my brother; and the secrets – half-known; some still to be guessed at – too.

I drain my coffee, mentally ticking off the ways in which I've been obtuse, or in denial about my mother:

I closed my eyes to the fact that she has a drink problem.

I repressed any memories about my baby sister, Clare.

I ignored the fact that her detachment when Mattie was in hospital, and her failure to ensure he had corrective plastic surgery every other year, either suggested depression or amounted to neglect.

And all of this makes me wonder if there is something else I've been closing my eyes to that is even more horrific.

Something I can hardly bear to contemplate.

LIZ

Saturday 10 June, 2017

Thirty-six

I should have realised the barbecue would be a disaster even before we decided to hold it. Nick and I never hold large get-togethers. We're both busy; neither of us are extroverts and I'm painfully conscious we have neither the biggest house, nor the deepest wallets in our group. I'm embarrassed by the scrubbiness of our garden compared to Charlotte's manicured lawns and my mere competence as a chef compared to Jess's culinary prowess. Still, it's easy to make excuses, and I reasoned that no one would be expecting barbecued crevettes, like the ones served by the Curtises. And, if I didn't get everyone together, the children would be a year older, and another summer would have slipped away.

Besides it is a glorious summer. The hottest since '76: the grass parched to straw; the sky a cornflower blue; no hint of rain for weeks and weeks on end. The children have changed colour: as brown as nuts, their limbs growing faster than the shoots of the tomato plants rampaging through our ramshackle greenhouse. *It's almost too hot*, I think, as I light the barbecue and wait for the flames to lick the coals until they are dusted ash white. A bank of heat rolls up, but even without this the air is oppressive as if a thunderstorm is brewing. The husks of delphiniums stand still; a bullet of an apple drops. There isn't so much as a whisper of a breeze.

I check the food; lay out rugs for the children to sit on; fill the paddling pool in anticipation of water fights. Sam stops bouncing on the trampoline and lies, spread-eagled, gazing at the leafy canopy above his head.

Everything is set, and yet my stomach twists. I want it to be perfect, I guess because it's something I never had. I didn't grow up in a world of barbecues and family get-togethers and so I romanticise that sort of childhood and want to create it for my kids. But I also want to spoil my friends and try to compensate for my failure to be sociable. And if I need this celebration to reconnect – to remind myself that our friendships are strong despite my being subsumed by work and making little recent effort – then so do they.

Mel needs it in particular. It's been three weeks since Rob left, and I want to show her, Connor and Mollie just how much we love them: that they will always be welcome; that she's not going to be a single mother who's ostracised now her family is no longer a neat, easily assimilated gang of four.

Jess probably needs a bit of cosseting too. I've only seen her properly twice since Betsey was born three months ago: once, when I dropped round a present, and then for a quick coffee – curtailed because the baby needed feeding. I'm surprised at how quickly the time's gone. When they arrive, I half-expect to see a seven-pound newborn rather than this solid three-month-old infant – still intensely vulnerable; still incapable of doing anything as simple as sitting up by herself, but nevertheless a creature with thighs so plump they dimple and a shock of thick dark hair.

As for Charlotte, well, I'd invited her because not doing so risked being hurtful. She might not be at the school gate that much but one of the children would be bound to mention it to George, and I would hate her to discover that she'd been left out. I'd wondered if she'd avoid it: to my knowledge, she's had little to do with Jess since discovering she was pregnant. But they would be delighted, she told me, in an elegantly written email, concluding with the sort of throwaway line that heaped on the pressure and couldn't help but sound ominous: *It might even be fun!!*

Mel arrives first. She isn't in a good state. The combination of the end of the school year and her twelve-year marriage looks as if it's threatening to break her: she's lost so much weight so rapidly that the sundress that flattened her chest last summer now gapes to expose sharp clavicles and what she dubs her 'chicken fillet' breasts.

'He wants the kids to meet her, can you believe it?' she

spits. 'Says she's such an important part of his life they need to get to know her. I am fucking livid.' She shakes with rage.

'He can't rush them into meeting her like this,' I say, calculating that we have ten minutes of intensive chat before the others arrive. 'How are the children?'

'Connor's started wetting the bed and Mollie's sleepwalking. Most nights, we end up sleeping together.'

No wonder she looks so exhausted.

'Drink? White wine, red wine, beer, gin? Pimm's, elderflower, still or sparkling?'

'Something alcoholic. Maybe a gin.'

Wordlessly, I add ice, lemon, cucumber and tonic to a generous shot, decorating the glass with mint to make it pretty.

'Thank you,' she says as she takes a deep slug.

The doorbell rings and there's the bustle of another family arriving: a swell of noise that seems disproportionately intrusive.

'Hello, hello, hello!' Andrew bowls into the kitchen, Charlotte and George in his slipstream.

'Andrew!' I try to shield Mel as I fold him into a hug.

'No Rob?' he asks, looking around as though he might find Mel's estranged husband lurking in a kitchen cupboard. 'Where is he? What have you done with the blighter?'

I glance sharply at Charlotte. I told her about Mel in my email and had assumed she would share this with her husband. She looks uncomfortable.

'He's not working on a glorious day like this, is he?'

Andrew continues, his smile slipping as he registers Mel's expression.

'No.' She takes a fierce swig of gin. 'Rob's shagging.' And then, because Andrew looks so thrown by her uncharacteristic language: 'Not me, obviously. A younger model: he's left me for his PA.'

After that, Jess's arrival, complete with baby, pram, parasol, changing mat, and a bag bulging with bottles of sterilised water, is a welcome distraction.

'Jess!' Charlotte air-kisses her on both cheeks. 'You look lovely. And, Ed—' Here, her kiss lingers, as if she's primed to whisper something intimate. 'Gosh: a newborn isn't taking its toll on you! You look as gorgeous as ever. What's it like coping with one again?'

She draws him off towards the garden, one hand on his arm. I suppose they're old friends, and this monopolising of him is nothing new, but it seems designed to exclude the very person who gave birth to this baby and whose life has been most affected by it.

'What's it like for you, Jess?' I ask, expecting a wry roll of the eyes in Charlotte's direction but she's distracted.

'Is there much shade in the garden? I'm wondering if we wheeled the pram into the shade of the house and used the parasol, would she be completely covered?' Her eyes dart around, looking for the perfect spot.

'I'm sure she'll be absolutely fine in the shade.' I help her manoeuvre the huge pram and set the parasol at a jaunty angle. Not one part of Betsey's skin is exposed.

Jess sits by the pram, sipping a sparkling water, but she clearly can't relax: she keeps checking that the sun isn't slanting onto her baby. Betsey bleats: the tired cry of an infant getting herself to sleep.

'Actually – do you mind if I take Betsey inside?'

'Of course. You could put her down in Rosa's bedroom. That's probably the coolest.'

'I think I'll stay with her, in your front room? I don't like leaving her alone when it's as hot as this.'

'The part towards the French windows is probably best.' I walk her back through. 'If we draw the curtains, it should be dark enough.' I shroud the room in gloom as Betsey's crying cranks up another gear. 'Shall I bring you some food?'

She shakes her head. 'I'm fine really. I'll come out in a while.' She looks embarrassed and I want to reassure her that the crying sounds far more intense to her than anyone else; that she needn't hide herself away; that we can all take turns in soothing Bets, giving her a rare break. But she turns her back on me, and curls herself around her baby, the movement exclusive and intensely intimate.

At least everyone else seems content, apart from Mel who is staring into the middle distance as she nurses her gin and tonic. Nick is still sweltering over the barbecue, and the children are fed and watered: Kit and George chomp on hot dogs while the others loll on rugs, apparently sated. Only Frankie bounces frenetically on the trampoline.

Charlotte is saying something that's made Andrew and Ed laugh and has prompted Nick to wave his barbecue tongs around as he joins in. She's sharp and clever, her arguments precise and well formulated, and I admire her self-assurance – her belief that her views are at least as important as anyone else's – even if I find her difficult at times. Perhaps she's just a man's woman: more at ease in their company than with other women, I think, as I watch her, basking in their attention. For a moment I want to be part of their conversation rather than hovering between one friend who mourns her relationship and another who frets over her crying child.

From the front of the house, Betsey's cries continue: a slowing *waah-waah-waah* now. I pour myself a drink and wonder if it will occur to Ed to swap with his wife so that she can eat.

'I really should check on Jess,' he murmurs at one point, and makes a desultory effort to rouse himself, but he's easily persuaded to sit back down.

'She'll be fine. She'll probably be getting the baby down to sleep. The last thing she'll want is you disturbing her,' says Charlotte.

'You're probably right,' he concurs and swigs his beer.

'One thing I've learned,' Andrew adds – sounding like a smug traditionalist who excuses his own failings by dressing them up as a concession to his spouse – 'is that it's never worth interfering in childcare. Always best to demur. Isn't that right, my darling?'

The look Charlotte gives him could freeze hell.

'The problem is,' says Ed, reflectively, 'that the kids are used to us doing separate jobs. Jess does the practical stuff – and all the stuff with Betsey, of course. I – well, I do the fun stuff . . .'

'You could try doing the boring stuff?' Nick half-teases.

'Yeah. I suppose I could . . .' Ed looks briefly uncomfortable. Then he turns it into a joke: 'But why would I want to do that?'

So this is the state of play when the doorbell rings: one anxious woman, whose husband has no intention of helping her; one tearful one; and one feeling a little fraught that this barbecue is not turning out to be the relaxed get-together she hoped at eight o'clock this morning when she was fiddling around with pomegranate seeds.

That will teach me not to micro-manage; not to hope I can ease everybody's problems with the very best of intentions and a few homemade *sodding* burgers, not to mention the blowsy pavlova that no one will want to eat in this heat. I think of the solar-powered fairy lights I'd strung in the tree above the trampoline, conscious as I did so that it was precisely the sort of thing Jess would do. Why do I have to strive to be something I'm not? Why can't I curb this incessant desire to be the sort of professional woman who makes coriander-and-red-onion burgers while mending marriages and easing her friends' anxieties? Why do I have to constantly fix things as if I – and here's the irony – have all the answers? Why can't I accept myself, and my limitations, more readily?

As if to prove my provenance, my mother is standing on the doorstep, red-faced and uncomfortable, her top exposing a greying bra strap and sunburned flesh. The fabric is damp under her armpits; she is clearly wilting in the heat.

'Oh – hello!' My mind goes blank. My mother never just drops round. 'Come in, come in,' I say, recovering, but I must look bemused. She is instantly on the defensive.

'You said you were having a barbecue when you rang me. Lots of people. I didn't get it wrong, did I?'

'No, no, of course not.' I can't possibly knock her back. Besides, she looks vulnerable: the wrong sort of mother at the wrong sort of event. I have a vague recollection of suggesting she join us. A throwaway line at the end of the phone call, made because I never thought she'd take me up on it. *You could drop round if you're at a loose end.*

'Do you remember my friend, Mel?' I ask, bringing her into the kitchen where Mel is opening a bottle of Pinot Grigio. 'I think you met at Rosa's first or second birthday party? Mel's my teacher friend, Mum; she's got a girl and a boy the same age as Sam and Rosa,' I gabble, conscious that my mother is barely interested in her grandchildren, though I've given her little opportunity to know them.

My mother is unimpressed.

'Let's get you a drink, shall we?' I add, handing her a glass of iced water.

She looks at it disdainfully.

'I'll have what Mel's drinking.'

'Of course.' I fill a wine glass. 'Sorry. I'm obsessed with us all remaining hydrated.'

She nods curtly. I'm let off but I mustn't patronise her, or try to control her behaviour, again.

'Can I get you a plate of food? Nick's still got plenty on the go. Nick!' I gesture to him, as I walk her through the kitchen to the patio. 'Look who's arrived?'

'Janet,' he says, bending down and kissing her on the cheek. He is so good at hiding his true feelings, never making her conscious of his ambivalence towards her. 'Lamb, burger, chicken? The kids have wolfed all the sausages, I'm afraid.'

She blinks in the sunlight and I'm subsumed by a sudden tenderness. This is discombobulating: there's too much choice, too many unfamiliar people; the heat is too intense ...

'Lamb, please.' She turns to me. 'It's a bit hot, Lizzie. I think I'll sit inside.'

'Of course. Let me bring you some salad.' I bustle through. Has she noticed Charlotte's eyes on her? *A poor person. In Liz's garden!* I imagine her storing up this detail; feel a shudder of revulsion at her and at myself for exposing my mother to this. My two worlds have met and jarred but as I glance at my mother, she isn't interested in the company. She's distracted, listening to something upstairs.

'Whose is that baby?'

A high-pitched wail has started: a thin ribbon of sound that soars, becoming louder.

'It's Betsey. Do you remember my friend Jess had another baby? I thought she was sleeping in the front room – but obviously not.'

'She's been crying on and off for the past fifteen minutes,' Mel says. 'Keeping me company.'

'Fifteen minute's nothing,' my mother says, sharply.

I'm surprised: she never talks about our childhoods. 'Did I cry a lot?'

'You weren't the worst.'

'Poor Mattie. Was he a difficult baby? I was too young to remember . . .'

She shakes her head. She's not going to be drawn on this.

The cry grows louder as Jess slowly navigates the stairs, one hand on the bannisters, one cradled around her baby. Her hand cups her head; her forearm props Betsey's body against her as if she is made of hand-blown glass.

'I'm so sorry. I can't get her to stop.'

'Why don't I take her for a bit so that you can get some food?' As I say it, I realise she's never let me hold this baby.

'Trust me. I'm a doctor,' I joke, and then: 'Just for a few minutes to give you a break.'

After some hesitation, she hands her baby over. Betsey looks at me, a bubble of spit forming between her lips.

'Hello, Betsey.' I beam, desperate to coax a smile. The

shock of contemplating someone new has silenced her, momentarily. Tentatively, she reciprocates.

'Look, Mum – isn't she gorgeous?' I turn to her. 'Do you want to have a look?'

'No. You're all right.'

'Oh go on.'

'No, really. I'm fine,' she snaps, then clears her throat, perhaps realising her reaction seems excessive. 'Don't want to set her off crying again. I haven't seen a baby that young in a while. What is she? Three months?'

'Thirteen weeks,' says Jess coming back into the kitchen with a small plate of food. 'You're exactly right. I thought things were meant to get easier at three months, but not with this one.'

As if on cue, Betsey's bottom lip wobbles and she starts to wail, arms outstretched now that she's registered her mother's presence. The sound builds and swirls; so raucous that the adults in the garden stop talking and look in our direction, perturbed.

Jess abandons her plate of food and grabs Betsey, her face flushed with embarrassment as she shushes and jiggles.

My mother seems fixated. She can't stop staring at Betsey as if appalled that a baby could make this noise.

'You OK, Mum?'

'No. I ...' She pushes her plate away, spilling beads of pomegranate and couscous. A smear of crème fraîche clags the edge of her thumb but she hasn't noticed. 'I shouldn't have come. I want to go. I need to go now.'

She struggles to her feet, gathering her bag, her movements jagged; and all the time, her eyes are on Betsey, her expression fearful.

'I'm so sorry, Mrs Trenchard.' Jess's voice clots with tears. 'Liz – I'll take her home. This isn't pleasant for any of us. You've gone to such an effort and we're ruining it for you.'

'No, don't.' I won't have Jess hounded in this way. 'She's just a crying baby. We've all experienced it. She'll be settled in a few minutes. There's no need for anyone to leave.'

But my mother has crossed the room and is almost at the front door, head down, her pace determined.

'Mum. Please.' It feels important to salvage this. To prove to Jess that she's always welcome and to my mother that she mustn't storm off because of something as innocuous as a baby crying. I put one hand on her forearm but she shrugs it off, violently.

The familiar response kicks in. My heart jolts and old memories domino: a yank of an arm; a grip of a forearm; those whip-sharp slaps, furious and incessant, against the pale backs of my legs.

I stand back now, chastened. 'Mum – I didn't mean . . .' What did I mean? The apology is automatic but the words peter out.

In the privacy of my hall, she gives me the look that says there is no room for negotiation.

'Don't you *dare* try to stop me going.'

She fumbles with the Yale lock, increasingly irate as it fails to open.

Sarah Vaughan

'How do you do this fucking thing?' Her voice cracks, on the edge of tears.

There's a trick to it but I know better than to offer to help. Eventually she manages to yank it. Sunlight streams in, and with it comes relief that she can go now.

Without another glance, she heads off down the road.

JESS

Thursday 25 January, 2018, 9.30 a.m.

Thirty-seven

The interview has been going for an hour and a half, and Jess's brain is starting to ache with the strain of not implicating herself further when DC Rustin's phone buzzes against the table. The detective glances at the text message and shows it to her colleague.

'Shall we take a comfort break? Fifteen minutes?' Her expression inscrutable, she suspends the recording and escorts Jess from the room.

Given some privacy, Jess runs the hot tap, the water chafing her palms, a cloud of steam rising up from the chill basin. But the shock of the scald does nothing to distract her from her looping fears.

They know she left them but has Frankie told them something? Or perhaps the text was from the hospital and something has happened to Bets? Panic claws at her as she imagines another seizure: her baby's eyes rolling back, her limbs stiff. Perhaps the anaesthetist has intervened and induced a coma, as they've been warned he may do. She sees Betsey lying in paediatric intensive care, ringed and wired with tubes. *Is this how she dies? Is this the ultimate complication?* She leans over the toilet bowl to retch.

'What happens now?' she asks her solicitor, when she is led back to the interview room twenty minutes later. A white polystyrene cup of tea with a sheen of scum sits in front of her, untouched.

'We wait,' he says.

'Something's happened, hasn't it? Something's happened to Betsey?' Or perhaps it's happened to Kit: perhaps she's been too dismissive of his fracture and he's suffered a concussion no one detected? She can't mention Frankie. Can hardly bear to think of him, cocooned in his distress.

'I'm sure it hasn't.' Liam glances at his watch. Her chest constricts, her breath becoming shallower until she is light-headed. Her throat is dry, her mouth bitter with fear.

The door opens abruptly. DC Rustin looks flushed and DC Farron almost angry: she hasn't seen him look like this before now. Beside her, Liam sits upright, his expression more alert. DC Rustin scrapes her chair across the floor with a sharp grate and presses the button on the DVD recorder, stating the date and time and introducing them once more.

'Why didn't you tell us the truth from the start, Jess?' she begins.

'About?'

'About what really happened.'

She is cornered. Glances down at her twisted fingers, automatically reaching for her absent rings. Her hands feel naked and she sits on them. *You're a mother who neglected her children and told one of them to lie for her.* There is nothing she can do to make things better; nothing she can say.

'Our duty sergeant has just taken a call from your husband which puts a different slant on events. We're about to go and interview him and Frankie. But we wondered if you could tell us what happened, before we hear what your son has to say?'

They mustn't put Frankie through this; she must continue to protect him. What was it he said, in the bathroom? 'I didn't mean to hurt her. I was only trying to help.' *You're a bad, bad mother.* But she must have done something right to bring up a child this intuitive and sensitive; a child who can empathise like this.

'It happened like I said,' she lies, and she winces at the flimsiness of her explanation. 'She must have banged her head after pulling herself up on the side of the fridge.'

'Why don't you stop playing games, Jess?' DC Rustin's voice is cruel. 'We know you left your children alone together while you went to the shop. We have the CCTV footage and your receipt to prove you were there. According to your husband, it was Frank who was involved. It was a genuine accident that you've lied about from the start.'

'I ...'

'Your husband's just told us that's what happened. We need to keep you here while we go and talk to him and

Frankie. I'm going to ask you one last time: is there anything you'd like to tell us first?'

And all Jess can see is Frankie's concern as he tried to protect her, suggesting she took a break from him and his screaming sister; and his extreme wariness, his body cowering when she shouted in that cloying, claustrophobic room. She thinks of how she can't bear him to look at her like that again; and how she needs to shield him from being interviewed by the police. Because, despite there being a specialised child protection officer, he will still find it terrifying; an experience, in a week of disorientating experiences, that will rip him out of his comfort zone as forcefully as a digger hurling rubble. And she knows that if there is anything she can do to mitigate the ordeal, to make it easier for him, she must do it now.

'Yes.' She bows her head, the word slipping from her like a sigh. She is broken; can sink no lower; her maternal failings will be picked over and judged as she listens in shame.

A mother who left her children to go out and buy wine; who was slow to take her to hospital; who lied to doctors, her husband, her sister, even the police, until the lie – told for the best of reasons, to protect her boy, and the less noble one, to protect herself – became too big to row back from. Became so big she had long crossed the point at which she could admit what really happened and say: 'I am so sorry.'

But though she feels intense shame, the relief is

overwhelming. Her voice is a murmur and she makes herself repeat it. 'Yes,' she says.

'You'd like to change your account?' DC Rustin asks, leaning forward to catch what she says, but really there is no need.

Jess looks up and meets the detective's eye; forces herself to speak clearly.

'I'd like to tell you what happened,' she says.

LIZ

Saturday 3 February

Thirty-eight

'I need to talk to you.'

Nine days after her variceal bleed, my mother is lying propped up in her bed in the hospital. She's in the gastro ward but it's relatively quiet for a moment: the neighbouring bed is empty and the other patients preoccupied or asleep.

I think she is going to die. She might not, of course. It's possible she could recover if she stops drinking, though both of us know that isn't going to happen any time soon. She's always been cavalier about her health: first the fags, then the sugar, and now this. One way or another, my mother has been killing herself for as long as I can remember. And if I sound flippant, I'm not. I'm so saddened that if I dwell on it I'll start crying. My mother won't want to see my tears, though. They are a waste of time, and she may not have much time.

She isn't speaking: is just lying back, breathing heavily. It doesn't make for an easy silence, knowing that death may be near. And so I start talking about Jess: about her arrest, and her release now the truth has emerged. I tell her about how I rang yesterday, and how Ed told me she isn't talking to anyone, though I suspect he was being diplomatic and she's only reluctant to talk to *me*. And I tell her of my guilt for not realising she was struggling; for being so stupid I didn't consider that she could be one of those mothers who claim to be fine only to shed tears in private. 'All good,' they say at the baby groups – until they're pushed to crisis point.

Of course I'm apologising to my mother, too, for being blind to the bleeding obvious; for not asking the right questions. 'She seemed so competent. I didn't realise she might be finding parenthood so tough,' I say.

My mother rasps something. I didn't think she was listening but her eyes flicker open and she searches for my gaze. 'It is tough,' she manages. 'I made mistakes.'

'You don't need to talk about it,' I say, suddenly apprehensive. There's nothing like a sense of an ending to clarify what's important. To voice the stories left unsaid. 'You don't need to say anything,' I add because there's a peculiar tension like that moment on a diving board when you've committed to plunging forwards but wait, almost suspended – and I sense that what she might say will change everything.

'I do,' she insists and then she's gripped by a racking wheeze. I ease her forwards, one hand circling her back, and feel how the weightiness that made her so formidable when I was a child has melted away, leaving a woman who is vulnerable. Her cough subsides and I hold her hand. It's thin, with liver spots and raised veins, and a faint scar across the top, the trace of a burn caused when she caught the back of her hand on the grill. It was when Mattie was in hospital and I suddenly wonder if she branded herself on purpose. *It's nothing*, she said at the time, *compared to what he's gone through.*

I won't try to placate her again, or to fob her off. I owe it to her to listen. I squeeze her hand then release it immediately. She won't want to be encumbered by my desire for affection. I must let her tell this in her own way.

'What happened ... with Clare ... wasn't as I said.' She pauses and her dark eyes fix me like pins holding fast a butterfly. A cold sensation creeps up my spine.

'The policeman who came to the house was so callow. Not the sharpest tool in the box. I don't think he had a clue. It was his first death. He was overwhelmed, embarrassed, too, by Pete's crying; by the extent of his grief ...

'The doctor was trusting, as well. A cot death: that's what he put on the death certificate. There was a post mortem but it wasn't forensic. People didn't probe then like they might now ...'

She pauses, apparently exhausted by this torrent of words that hint at a truth without grasping it by the neck.

'Should someone have probed?' I make myself ask.

But she ignores my question. Her eyes are rheumy and her breathing's light. 'I felt so very alone. Pete was out so early, working on that farm, and he didn't want to listen.

Thought I should just get on with it. Day after day, it was just me and the three of you. And she cried all the time ...'

Her eyes rest on something in the middle distance as if she is watching her life, thirty-five years ago, her expression one of utter bleakness before a sheen of horror passes over her face. She snaps back to the present and turns to me, her gaze characteristically direct. It's a look that demands I pay attention; that I understand her.

'Do you remember her crying?' I nod, tentative, but I'm not sure if it's Clare's cries I recall or those of my own children: that relentless wailing that's irrational and inconsolable and once made me put Rosa down and walk away, convinced I was a deficient mother.

'I just wanted to make her stop.'

Her words pull me up short. Is this some sort of confession? An acknowledgement of a truth I've been shuffling towards but avoided admitting? My stomach roils, my body sensing the truth before my mind.

A cot death. That's what he put on the death certificate. I just wanted to make her stop. She cried all the time.

'Are you saying what I think you're saying? That Clare's death wasn't an accident?' I want her to say the words. I want her to take responsibility if she is telling me – and I can hardly believe I am thinking this, though it seems the only credible explanation – that she killed her baby girl.

She refuses to look at me but her mask starts to slip and her face convulses with sorrow. She presses her bottom lip tight, as if to keep any confession in place.

'She cried all the time,' she repeats, shaking her head. 'She wouldn't stop. On and on and on she went . . .'

But some babies do, I want to say. Perhaps she was hungry or ill, had reflux or a neurological issue. It's their means of communication. They don't intend to antagonise. They're in distress.

But I stay silent. I mustn't judge her, daren't risk her not talking now we've finally managed the most honest conversation of our lives. I imagine her, isolated and without support, in that damp, dark cottage. And then I see her screaming at us: a torrent of abuse I told Mattie she couldn't possibly mean as his expression became pained, and he seemed to diminish in front of my eyes.

She is exhausted and yet she still wants to be understood. 'She wouldn't stop . . .' Her voice drops to a whisper. Her eyes are moist and I think I spy humility in them. *I didn't mean to do it.* That's what her look seems to say.

Or perhaps I am desperate to read this because the alternative is too horrific to contemplate.

'All I wanted was to make her stop.'

JANET

Saturday 22 January, 1983

Thirty-nine

The cry builds. At first it is pitiful. A creak and a crackle. Tentative, tremulous, just testing how it will be received.

The doubt quickly flees. The whimper becomes a bleat; the catch hardening as the cry distils into a note of pure anguish. 'Shh ...' Janet pleads, reaching into the cot and holding Clare at arm's length as the sound buttresses the space between them. 'It's OK, baby. Mummy's here now. Mummy's going to make it OK.'

Clare stares at her. Eleven weeks old; in the fierce grip of inconsolable colic; her eyes two beads that glower, incredulous and intense. *Don't be ridiculous*, these eyes say. *I am livid and I'm livid with YOU.* Her face folds in on itself and her Babygro dampens as if the rage that is turning her tiny body into a white-hot furnace is so intense it must escape.

'Shh, shh. It's OK,' Janet repeats. She is suddenly wary. Sweat licks her baby's brow and her fontanelle pulses like some alien life form, golden-red just beneath the surface of her skin. Evidence of her pumping heart, of the blood that courses through her veins and could burst through this translucent spot, as delicate as a bird's egg, so fragile, she daren't touch it in case it ruptures. The beat continues, insistent, unrelenting. Like Clare's uncontrollable rage.

The cry cranks up, the sound now brazenly assertive. Nought to sixty, in two seconds. She draws her baby close and feels stifled: only wants to thrust her away.

'Shh, shh. Mummy's here for you.' One hand presses Clare's padded bottom close; the other splays up the back of her neck. She cradles her head, trying to convey her tenderness but the baby arches her back so that she writhes against her, fists balled, torso rigid with anger or pain.

Why does she hate me so very much? The thought consumes her as she tries to jiggle the child to sleep while pacing the damp, chill bedroom. The early afternoon light seeps through the thin cotton curtains: cruel, since the rest of the cottage is dark. Shadows pool in the corners, mould festers on the walls, and the furniture is oppressive: iron beds, a stained oak dresser and table. The ceilings are beamed and the wood chipped walls are painted not just white but rusty terracotta and turquoise in a warped distortion of a hippy's dream.

She craves light and brightness: summer days when the washing can blow on the line, not steam inside, turning the room damper and colder; when the older children can potter in the garden and not make constant demands on her time. When she can stand with the sun on her face, and just for a moment feel that things might get better at some point. Where she can laugh off the self-loathing that blankets her so that she can't see a route out of this life with its narrow lines, its drudgery, its endless washing and feeding and cooking, its constantly screaming baby – because Clare, through gasps of breath, is still sobbing. And, oh dear God, *surely* she must be close to giving up soon?

'Shh, shh,' she soothes her but it's counterproductive. The baby ratchets up the volume and redoubles her cries. Janet's pacing becomes more frenetic, her rocking fevered, as Clare tries to spring from her, wriggly as an eel. 'It's OK.' Desperation creeps into her voice, as she grips her more fiercely. 'It's OK, really. It's OK.'

But it's not OK. Clare flails at her and Janet can't help but take it personally. *I hate you*, her daughter's lashing body says.

'Shh, shh,' she pleads but she's wracked with self-doubt. *You're a hopeless mother for letting her cry like this. For letting your baby suffer.* 'I am *trying*.' Her voice fractures into a scream. She presses her damp face against the top of her baby's head but Clare just wriggles and strains away.

'Shh, shh.' Her tears are flowing now, of self-pity and an exhaustion so extreme sometimes she just wants to lie down and never get up. *Please be quiet, just for a minute. Just SHUT UP!* she wants to say. Somehow, the thoughts become words and she is shouting. And in this act of rebellion, she finds her voice and it feels good to respond like this: to fight a cry with a cry.

341

And then some sense of self-discipline kicks in. Mattie's having his lunchtime nap and won't stir, but Lizzie's downstairs: she mustn't hear her. And yet the outburst has shocked her baby girl. Clare stares and for a wonderful moment, the crying stops: a tiny reprieve. She holds her, hoping her pounding heart will reassure her, rather than betray her fear.

'I'm sorry. I'm sorry! I didn't mean to shout. There, that's better. That's better, isn't it?' Her daughter wriggles, and she realises she is pressing her too tight.

She releases her grip, and as she does, Clare's lungs expand and the noise resumes: a blast of fury that turns her body rigid, fierce energy pulsing up from the tips of her toes. And she knows she can't do this any more. She can't deal with this continual, soul-destroying noise that wakes her each night, that dominates her days, that summons her from sleep so that her mind-fogged body stumbles from the dark bedroom where Pete is dead to the world and she huddles in the cold, letting this *parasite* of a baby drain the spirit from her as she sucks her dry.

She isn't the mother she thought she would be when she agreed to swap the busy coastal town she grew up in for this rural hovel. She isn't even a competent mother: just one who bitterly regrets having three children because Clare, and she has always known this, was a mistake. A baby conceived in a rare moment of optimism that fizzled out by the time a crying Mattie woke her. She remembers going for a wee and praying, as she douched herself, that the sperm hadn't taken; that she wouldn't be pregnant this time.

She and Pete are falling apart. The hairline cracks that ran through their relationship from the start have widened until they can barely speak civilly. Communication is kept to a minimum. They don't live, let alone love. They exist.

He doesn't want to know. So full of enthusiasm about this alternative lifestyle, so naive, so *selfish*, he doesn't listen when she tries to explain how mind-numbing she finds it and how she's achingly lonely with only the children to talk to each day. One of six, he will never understand her ambivalence towards her kids. She can't tell him of the frustration that's so intense she fears she might hurt them before he gets home, or explain that she fantasises about leaving them: just tramping up the lane, the fierce wind drowning out their screams. She tried doing it yesterday. Left around five o'clock and was out for twenty minutes, before the guilt – or rather the fear of what Pete would say if he came home early – drove her back to them.

This room is filthy. A fly struggles in a spider's web strung from the light bulb to the ceiling and she fixates on this as she grips her baby. She is like that caught insect: bound tight in a trap from which there is no escape. She doesn't want this life. She doesn't want this baby. But, despite knowing this quite clearly, she doesn't mean to kill her. She just wants to shock her into silence.

'Shh, shh, shh,' she says, as she squeezes her tight.

LIZ

Saturday 3 February, 2018

Forty

I am swimming. It's something I rarely do; that I only manage at moments of high stress or intense anger. Up and down the hospital pool I go: thirty lengths, thirty-one, thirty-two, thirty-three.

I'm not a particularly fast swimmer and I'm unfit: my body soft and unwieldy, my hips rolling from side to side. I'm two stone heavier than the skinny teenager who swam obsessively in the university pool, trying to work through her insecurities under the chlorinated water. But if I'm out of shape, I'm dogged and today I'm more driven than ever: goggles on, head down, arms windmilling in slow, considered motions. The water sloshes over the side of the pool as I tumble, turn and plough back on again.

My mother killed her baby. My mother killed her baby. The mantra thrums through my head with every stroke. *My mother killed her baby.* I surge through the water – *windmill, turn, slosh* – as the realisation persists. By this stage of my swim, the endorphins have usually kicked in. But thirty-five, thirty-six, thirty-seven lengths in and there's no hit of wellbeing and none of the usual intoxication that comes as my brain empties. *She killed my sister. She killed my baby sister, Clare.*

Compassion, I tell myself, as I try to kick away my disbelief and anger. *View your mother with the same understanding as you've viewed Jess. Treat her as if you were her GP.* Undiagnosed postnatal depression. Isolation, lack of support, marital breakdown: the risk factors were all there. This wasn't as widely recognised in the Eighties. If she'd experienced it now, it might have been prevented. Though – and here I kick particularly forcefully, using my anger – even then it's missed, isn't it? *I* missed it. I missed it with Jess.

Windmill, turn, slosh. Another length, but it's no good, this cool, clinical analysis, when what I feel is a toxic cocktail of sorrow, anger, shock and shame. My mother smothered her eleven-week-old baby because she *wouldn't stop crying.* I up my speed, putting on a brief sprint, as I try to force this fact away. And then – and here's the thing that seems to chime with her cruelty towards us – she left it thirty-five years before confessing: not seeking help or not using this experience to temper her behaviour towards Mattie and me.

Stop being so bloody harsh, I tell myself. She'd have been terrified of being found out; confounded by what she'd done; perhaps *fearful* for us? Better to bring us up than to have us placed in care. She'd have felt that more intensely once our father left: that big bear of a man who didn't want to listen and walked away. Did he know what she'd done – and if so, how could he abandon his children? Or was the thought so monstrous it was something he couldn't conceive?

I think of our slapped thighs and dulled heads. Of her detachment when Mattie was in hospital. The fierce, hard heat of her gaze. I remember how we learned to read this from a very early age; how I instinctively knew to pro-tect my brother – lying on his behalf; physically standing between them when she raged; taking the brunt of the blows on one occasion – and I've suppressed that memory of hands raining down on me, karate-chopping. And I think of how I've carried the guilt for his accident ever since it happened, and how my mother did nothing to dissuade me.

I up my pace, arms whirling, buttocks clenching as I exploit this anger. *Parcel up those memories; pack them away.* I must think logically. Just because she could be aggressive towards us, it doesn't mean she meant to kill Clare. The postnatal depression would have clouded her reason for that brief moment in time.

Images kaleidoscope of this baby bucking against our mother. Remembering my nightmare, I feel Clare's panic as she grappled for breath. I forget my rhythm and suddenly my lungs ache. I swallow water, the chlorine burning my throat and nose, my chest sharp with pain. Fear grips me as I start spluttering; momentarily imagine I will choke to death.

Bursting out of the water, I clutch the side of the pool as if I've swum the Channel. *Breathe*, I tell myself, as I might to Sam or Rosa. *Stop being so melodramatic. You're fine.* Wrenching off my goggles I sink below the surface, scrubbing away at my nose and eyes. Down here my tears can flow. My vision's clouded, the water murky and opaque, but I can think more clearly. When my mother smothered Clare did she know what would happen? She wanted to silence her, but did she want her to die?

I surge back up to the surface; put on my goggles. An anaesthetist in the next lane raises his hand, poised to strike up a conversation. I give him a tight smile and push off from the side. I need to distract myself, and I need to address the questions I know will otherwise dog me in the still of the night; questions that circle around the notion that Mattie and I are lucky to be here; that we might have been at risk yet somehow we survived ...

After sixty lengths, I pull myself out of the pool, shower, and contemplate going back to the gastro ward to see my mother. I'd left abruptly. She'd been exhausted and I'd needed time to process what she'd said.

I towel myself dry, wondering whether to present Mattie with this news, but knowing it would hardly persuade him to come down. He will always think the worst of her, and this will only confirm his suspicions, whereas I want to believe she was ill rather than malicious. That she never intended this child to die.

I pull on my tight jeans, noting my soft stomach, silvered with stretch marks, and the broken veins at my ankles: the legacy of carrying two children. In the past, I've been critical of my body, wishing I had the time and self-discipline to have a figure like Jess. While other women have staved off middle age, I've seen myself hurtling towards it. But now I can't believe I cared. My body may not be honed, but my *mind*? My mind is sharp and I take my mental health for granted. What a luxury! I've never experienced the despair that must have dogged my mother, or tormented Jess.

It's nearly nine. My mother should be asleep, or trying to sleep. We'll achieve nothing now by talking: far better to visit in the morning when I've worked out what to say.

I walk briskly to the hospital multi-storey, retrieve my car and head for the only place I want to be at the moment: home, and more specifically Nick.

He listens. Eleven o'clock at night and he's still listening as I pace around our kitchen, turning the same thoughts over and over again. I rail, I question, and finally I cry, not just for my sister but for Mattie and me.

He folds me in his arms and it's the steady beat of his heart that calms me. That lets me voice the suspicion that throbs like an intractable splinter: tiny but so invidious, it can't help but dominate.

'The thing is,' I say, not meeting his eyes, because it's something I'm finding hard to think, let alone voice, 'I want to believe she was ill when this happened. That it was a clear case of postnatal depression. But I can imagine her being so angry, so frustrated, that in the heat of the moment she knew what she was doing. I know she's capable of lashing out: that she feels emotions intensely and doesn't seem able to moderate her temper. I'm scared that she just snapped – and it wasn't just because she was ill; it was that she had the capacity to do this.' I pause, and then whisper, 'She killed her eleven-week-old baby – and if it was conscious, or deliberate, how can I excuse or forgive her for it?'

'Could you forgive her if you were convinced she was mentally ill?' Nick looks at me intently and for a moment I wonder that my husband could doubt this.

'Of course I could, yes.' My tone's no-nonsense. I'd have a rationale, a neat medical diagnosis. 'If she was suffering from severe postnatal depression there would be a reason for her doing what she did.'

'I guess all you can do is wait and see if she's capable of talking about it any more? Not much help, I know, but I can't see that there's another option.' Nick gives an apologetic shrug. I'm asking his opinion on a question to which even my mother might not admit the answer.

How can we know what she was thinking when she killed her child?

JESS

Sunday 4 February

Forty-one

When DC Rustin confronted her with the news that Frankie had confessed to what happened, Jess initially felt a hot flush of intense embarrassment swiftly followed by an acute longing to hold her youngest son and reassure him everything would be OK.

Then came relief. It had taken her by surprise and engulfed her like a fake fur coat, making her feel momentarily safe and almost giddy. Because though the fear remained that they viewed her as a negligent mother at least she no longer needed to lie about everything.

For too long she had been living this double life, and the strain of pretending everything was fine, while ignoring the riff that made a mockery of this – the voice that constantly sought to trip her up – was unsustainable, and proving more than she could bear. The officers knew almost everything: that she had left her children alone; that Frankie was involved. But perhaps, and it was the faintest glimmer of an idea, perhaps now she could finally admit that she was in the grip of something perturbing. Something that had taken over her mind and was so compelling it felt like her reality. Perhaps now something might change.

And so she told them what happened, braving DC Rustin's evident irritation at her having wasted police time.

'I thought I would be five minutes. I can't believe I could think that: I clearly wasn't thinking straight.'

From the other side of the table there was silence, the officer appraising her like a stalking cat. And, prey-like, Jess froze. She couldn't admit that she had left the children because she feared she would hurt Betsey: that she had seen herself taking her baby by the legs and slamming her against the mantelpiece. That such scenarios machine-gunned her mind.

It was DC Farron who opened the way for her to indicate that perhaps not everything was well.

'Do you often feel like that? As if you're not thinking straight?' he asked, with a hint of the empathy she'd detected when they'd met in A&E.

Her throat closed over and to her horror she started crying great ugly sobs, her hands fluttering to her eyes as she tried to shield her wet, red face.

A *tsk* from DC Rustin. Jess could imagine her contempt. But from DC Farron, she sensed more sympathy. He watched her quizzically, trying to fathom her out. There was a mention of Lucy Stone, of social services offering support, but she couldn't take it all in and focused, instead, on the thing that seemed tangible.

She was going home.

That was ten days ago. She was released after Frankie was interviewed and now they are all trying to pick up their lives – impossible, really, while Betsey is in hospital in a still vulnerable state. She's in paediatric intensive care, hooked up to wires and drips and machines, and all the medical paraphernalia Jess thought she distrusted and despised. She's with her, now, braving the paediatric nurses' wary gaze.

Of course, she still can't hold her. While Jess was being questioned Betsey experienced another seizure that topped twelve minutes and led to the anaesthetist inducing a coma so that it could be managed. Now she has been eased out of it and is waiting to be transferred back to the ward. And though Jess longs for this, she is terrified. At least here Betsey is safe. She baskets her fingers together, imagining the bones in her daughter's skull knitting tight.

Let her get better soon. It's all she wants – well, that and her family life to return to some sort of normality; for the thoughts that sabotage her to end.

She can't imagine how that will occur. Lucy has talked about an 'early help plan', and suggested she see a GP for a psychiatric referral. Ed rang the surgery on Friday for an emergency appointment: she is seeing someone tomorrow first thing. But though she is grateful, she is passive, Ed and the social worker bandying terminology, arranging appointments, conspiring to make things better when to her this feels impossible. How can she change her thinking and move on from this?

She needs to focus on her children and on Ed, who is trying so hard to understand but is clearly struggling. Their relationship has been strained to near breaking point this week.

Last night he admitted trawling through her laptop. He had found her search, made on Friday afternoon as Frankie and Bets competed to see who could cry loudest and the walls of the house – and her life – had constricted. *Why do I want to harm my baby?* Her chest tightened as he repeated the phrase.

'And you've known about this since Sunday, and you didn't think to mention it before now?' she asked, swallowing her anger.

'How could I admit I'd spied on you? You'd have been incandescent: even less likely to talk to me.'

'And you didn't tell the police?'

DC Rustin hadn't mentioned it. The police had only taken her laptop after she was arrested on that terrible Wednesday night.

'No. I was worried for the children, of course, but they were never left with you unsupervised. And I guess I couldn't imagine you actually doing it.'

Her relief is immense. So he didn't betray her. He didn't even confide in Liz or Lucy.

'Did you tell anyone? Charlotte perhaps?' Her old anxiety flares.

'Of course I didn't! How could I risk incriminating you? I didn't even tell your sister. It's been horrific, to be honest, wondering why you'd written that. Now it seems so bloody obvious you were unwell.'

He is typically relieved there is an explanation for her behaviour. 'We'll get you some help now. We can sort this,' he said, and he'd stroked her cheek as if she was a small child to be humoured. 'I'll try to be around more, and do more to help.'

She doubts this will happen. The culture in which he works doesn't allow for flexible working. And yet it is something: this recognition that he needs to be more involved with the children; that he understands she is less resilient, more fragile than she has always pretended to be.

She thinks of her boys. They've been unconditional in their love, though Frankie has been emotional, even by his standards. 'It's my fault. I'm so naughty. All the teachers say I'm naughty . . .' He was inconsolable when she tucked him up last night.

Something about his behaviour still doesn't make sense and so she approaches the memory in ever decreasing circles. Imagines him lifting Betsey, hauling her up the stairs, excitement building with each step. He wouldn't predict that he might drop her, that she might wriggle, that he would need to put a hand on her body as he fumbled for a nappy: few eight-year-olds would, and none with his lack of impulse control. She had told him not to leave the room, to go upstairs or lift her and she is surprised that he completely ignored her words; that he chose to blindly block them out . . .

She closes her eyes. Tiredness overwhelms her and yet she can't relax: her habitual jitteriness courses through her. Her eyes snap at the sound of footsteps. Someone's walking towards her. A gentle tread.

'Can I join you?' Liz stands beside her, apprehensive. Underneath the unflattering strip light, she is haggard. A patch of eczema flares below her left eyebrow and the eye area looks inflamed.

Wordlessly, Jess nods. Liz pulls up a chair and perches on the edge of it. It irritates her, this *carefulness*. She *should* be bloody hesitant. She wishes she had the strength to tell her to go away.

'She's doing well.' Liz nods towards Bets.

Jess doesn't want her talking about her; feels instantly protective. Betsey has contracted an infection in her groin, requiring antibiotics, and has experienced intermittent seizures. She'd hardly say she is 'doing well'. When she gets back on the ward she'll have to be weaned off the morphine and sedative administered for the past eight days: she can't go 'cold turkey'. And she still faces a week in hospital.

'And how are you doing?'

Jess shrugs. She cannot articulate how she is feeling; can barely admit the extent of her distress.

'How's Frankie?' Liz ploughs on. 'Is he any better?'

She has to say something. To concede that Liz was the one

who winkled out the truth that led to her being released by the police, even though she helped alert them.

'He's still pretty distressed. But thank you for getting him to open up ...'

'I was just so relieved I could help. If I couldn't get him to do that, well, I might as well give up ...' Her voice tails off. 'It's what I'm meant to do, isn't it? To work out what's going on ...'

'You didn't manage it with me.'

'I didn't, no.' Liz looks immeasurably sad. 'My job was to look after Betsey, and we're always conscious that children can be harmed. But I should have realised what was going on. I didn't marry my knowledge of you with what I was being presented with. I should have realised you might be unwell ...'

'You were my friend and you failed to help me.' Her voice is balled up tight. 'You thought the very worst of me: that I would *batter* my baby.' Anger spreads up her throat and through her head and she fears she will explode.

Liz shrugs, and it's as if there is an immense burden on her shoulders she cannot lift. 'I don't know what more I can say. I should have understood more quickly; should have thought beyond the obvious.' She pauses. 'I'm so sorry, too, for being so absent after Betsey was born. I keep thinking that if I'd made more of an effort I'd have seen you were finding it so difficult this time round ... But you didn't help by not being honest about what happened when you came in.'

'I couldn't betray Frankie; and I couldn't risk losing them

by telling you I'd left them. I didn't know you'd call social services, anyway.'

Liz is tender. 'I imagine it felt impossible to admit how you were feeling, as well.'

Her kindness threatens to undo Jess. She swallows the pebble in her throat; only manages a curt nod.

They sit in silence for a while, Jess's antipathy still simmering beneath the surface but complicated by a desire to rekindle their former closeness. She has missed Liz, despite her self-justification and earnestness, her tendency to sound a little pompous. She has missed her warmth and her desire to do the right thing.

She admires her conscientiousness, too. It's nearly 9 p.m. 'Why are you here this late, anyway? You didn't come to find me?'

'No.' Liz shakes her head. 'My mother's on the gastro ward; I've just been to see her. I think she might die.'

The admission startles Jess but Liz doesn't seem to notice. Eyes focused on Betsey, she murmurs: 'I think she's been drinking herself to death.

'I didn't pick up on it,' she continues, in the same flat tone, 'just as I didn't realise you might be struggling. Seems I'm not such a good doctor. And you know the worst thing? However much I try, I can't feel the same compassion for her as I would for a patient.'

'Oh, Liz.'

'Yep.' She scrubs at her eye. There's a stye forming on her lower left lid and Jess wants to ease her hand away.

'Why's that?'

'She told me about something horrific.' There's a long pause. 'Do you remember me telling you she lost a baby to a cot death? A baby sister, though my mother would never talk about her, wouldn't even tell me her name.'

'You mentioned it when Rosa was tiny. You worried about the togs of her Grobags.' A flash of a memory: Liz agonising over whether Rosa would overheat in a winter bag in spring weather; her obsession with the baby monitor and keeping the room a chilly eighteen degrees.

'I did, didn't I?' Liz's mouth twists, her bottom lip jutting out, as if she's concentrating on not crying, but her voice is citrus bright. 'Well, my mother told me she smothered that baby because she wouldn't stop crying. Christ! I'm sorry.' She rubs furiously at her eye.

Jess feels the revelation as a sharp wrench in the pit of her stomach. The shock is intense but so is the relief that she never acted like this. She imagined shaking Betsey, or throwing her down the stairs, or shoving her into the road in her buggy – but she never followed up on these fears. It was as if her mind flaunted the worst possible scenario, pushing her to be increasingly vigilant until there was a vast disparity between what she imagined and her reality.

But Liz's mother did this most horrific thing. White stars cloud Jess's vision and she feels as if she might retch. And then her condemnation is muddied by sorrow. 'She must have been so lonely.' She can see it so clearly: a mother with a screaming baby in one small room. People think you don't have the time or headspace to feel alone with three energetic children, but there is little that's more lonely than being at home with a distraught baby and an unravelling mind.

Liz looks at her, and her expression is raw with pain. 'Yes. She *was* physically and emotionally isolated . . .' She pauses, and there's a clear caveat in her speech.

'Liz, she couldn't have been thinking clearly . . . She must have been so scared, so lost.'

'I know . . . I know that, *rationally*. It's just . . . Oh, she wasn't *kind*. She could be physically abusive; neglected us; was sometimes cruel. We weren't regularly battered but we feared her, and we knew never to push things.'

'Like me with my father . . .'

'You too? I'm sorry. I've often wondered . . . Anyway; it's made me a suspicious person. A necessary suspicion's a good thing in medicine but it means I'm prone to suspecting the worst of people, just as I did with you.'

'She doesn't have any power over you now,' Jess says, and she takes Liz's small, sturdy hand in her own slim fingers. 'You said you thought she was dying?'

'Yes.' Liz swallows. 'Yes. I think she is.'

'So she can't hurt you now. Would it help to see that she must have been in a very dark place to behave like that?'

'I think she's been in a dark place for most of her life.'

'Then perhaps it's time, not to condone her, but to try to forgive.'

LIZ

Monday 5 February

Forty-two

My mother is drifting in and out of consciousness. The consultant tells me she could have a matter of days, but in the end it's just a matter of hours left to live.

I sit by her bedside, watching her thinly veined eyelids; willing them to open. I am nervous. Not of her death – I've witnessed deaths before – but of what I should ask her.

There is so much, and too little, I can say.

She's been barely conscious in the forty-eight hours since she told me about my sister. It's as if the effort of unburdening herself has depleted her resources, and my visits have been brief: at the start and end of each day. I run through my questions – about her intent; about why she harboured this secret for so long; about her state of mind – and I visualise them as bullet points, as if I am preparing for an interview or the sort of assessment I'll have to take to become a consultant. But I know I'll never ask them. I can't quiz a woman who is *dying*. And, although it matters to me, the simple fact that Clare had her life snuffed out can't be altered. As Jess said, now is the time to forgive.

I look at my mother and I see she is a collection of bones: a shadow of the woman who would power up the stairs as she screamed that she hated us and wished she'd never had us. The hospital gown grants her anonymity. Poor life choices, I'd guess if I was her doctor: a smoker, a drinker, someone who lives in relative poverty and will die young. The balance of power has shifted so completely that I see – and the thought blindsides me – I could mirror events: put a pillow to her face and, with her breathing this shallow, there'd be little struggle. *She can't hurt you now.* Yes, that power has gone.

Instead, I take her hand and trace the fine white line where she was branded; try to imagine these fingers doing something mundane or even loving: buttoning my coat or cooking, her movements deft as she lifts a pan or cracks an egg. I see the same hands combing my hair, perhaps moving it softly to one side, but it's a memory I've made up. She would tug a comb through my tangles, speaking sharply in the pre-school rush; slapping the side of my head with the paddle of the brush on more than one occasion. I imagine the same hands holding Clare in that dark, damp room, and clutching a little too tightly; imagine her knuckles clenching, these same fingers tightening their grip.

I drop her hand; note the rattle of her breathing, the faint rise of her chest. She's close to death now. Perhaps it will be gentle, and I do wish that for her, though the irony of Clare's being anything but is not lost. I see that baby through the chink of the door and know for my own sanity I need to stop obsessing. Though she was cruel, I can't believe, or let myself believe, she meant to kill Clare.

I close my eyes and, as so often when I'm with my mother, I think of Jess. And I find that I am weeping, in sympathy for what she has experienced since Betsey was admitted and since her birth. Then I look at the figure lying in the bed, her breath shallow and laboured, and finally, *finally*, and it's such a relief to do so, I feel the same compassion for my mother as I do for my friend.

My tears flow quietly as I take her hand and stroke it gently, tracing her bones, and her too-thin skin. Her pulse is thready. *DNAR* – do not attempt resuscitation: that's what she's asked to be put on her records. There'll be no crash call, no fight to get her back, as there usually would for a woman her age.

My cheeks are wet, now. I ball up my tissue, and reach into my handbag for another. Blow my nose noisily. Should I slip away? People often wait until their family leave before they die, and it would be typical of her to want to do that; to remain that self-sufficient, that independent. And yet there's too much left unsaid. I'm not ready to say goodbye.

I'm conscious of someone walking up behind me, though.
'All right?'

I turn to see my brother, looking diffident, as if not sure he should be here.

'Matt!' I clutch his wiry frame.

His eyes flit to our mother and I see his shock at how she has diminished. 'I thought about what you said and how I wasn't being fair.'

He looks too fit and healthy to be on this ward. A literal breath of fresh air, he smells not of London grime but the chill of the mountains: peat, wood smoke, the fabric of his mountaineering jacket, a hint of neoprene.

And though it's typical of him to leave it until the eleventh hour – *great timing,* part of me thinks – I feel inexplicably teary. 'Thank you,' I say.

We sit either side of her, and we wait. After a while, he gets up and drops a dry kiss on her forehead. Perhaps he also needs to forgive.

'I wouldn't have recognised her,' he says, much later, after the junior doctor has confirmed she is dead, and as we gather up his backpack to return home. 'She isn't as I remember. This isn't the Janet we knew.'

And I nod. *Her power has gone.*

'She went a long time ago.'

JESS

Tuesday 13 February

Forty-three

'What do you do, to keep Betsey safe?' the therapist, Tessa Farthing, asks Jess from across the coffee table between them. It's their first session, and Jess is surprised by Tessa's speed at getting to the nub of things.

'Well ... I ... I do lots of things.'

'Can you give me an example?'

'I ... I don't know where to start.' How to disentangle the mass of measures threaded through her life? To work out which are 'normal' behaviours – the sort of things other mothers do – and which are specific rituals designed to make sure she does no harm?

She knew this would be hard. Cognitive behavioural therapy, that's what she has signed up for. Extreme post-natal anxiety and maternal OCD, those are the conditions she's experiencing, according to her psychiatric assessment last week. She doesn't like being labelled and yet when

Dr Arnold described the characteristics of maternal OCD something in her brain had clicked. *This was a recognised condition? Other people felt like this, too?* The psychiatrist had made it sound as if Jess could alter her state of mind by applying this CBT method. 'You can feel better,' he had told her. 'You will feel better than this.'

Tessa, to whom she had been referred, had been equally clear that she could manage this if she committed to the sessions and worked hard in between them. And now, barely forty minutes into their meeting, she is asking Jess to describe the extent of her safety net.

'Well, obviously I have to remove the knives from the kitchen; remove the pans. I have to make sure there are no soft toys in her cot, and there are no bolsters. I sterilise her bowls and bottles and cutlery three times – and if I think I've inadvertently put neat bleach in the steriliser I have to start again. I disinfect her high chair tray three times, too; and the legs of the chair ...' The details spill out, and it's a relief to explain all this while Tessa sits there, calm and competent, in this vacated office at the GP's surgery. 'And if I'm out and about, and something really frightens me, and I can't wash my hands for some reason, then I need to align my rings.'

'You need to align your rings?' No twitch of a smile. Tessa seems interested.

'Yes. I do it three times. These rings here.' She doesn't demonstrate because then she would have to realign them, three times, just to make it right again.

'And what would happen if you didn't do that?' the therapist asks, charcoal bob tilting to one side.

'Well, I have to,' she says. 'It's not an option.'

'But what would happen if you didn't?' Tessa persists.

Jess stares back; puzzled as to why she *wouldn't* do this, but with a growing consciousness that perhaps her explanation might sound a little ridiculous.

'Then she wouldn't be safe.'

The therapist peers at her over her glasses, her gaze not unfriendly but searching. 'Why don't you try it? It could be your homework.'

'Homework?' Dr Arnold had mentioned this.

'You'd need to take your stacking rings off. Put them in a box at home so that there's nothing on that finger. Take all your rings off, ideally. Then there's nothing to spin.'

The thought terrifies her. What will she do if she thinks the baby monitor isn't working – her current fear now that Bets is finally home – and she is trying not to check it? Spinning her rings is an inadequate alternative but it gives her a brief reprieve.

Her fingers stray instinctively to her right hand now: a quick one, two, three, and the rings are spinned. Tessa notices and Jess flushes as if she's been caught doing something furtive.

'Why don't you try taking them off, now?'

'I – well, OK.'

Cack-handedly, she removes the rings and slips them into the side of her handbag. Her fingers feel naked and she

366

exposed. She reaches for a tissue from the box on the coffee table between them and starts fiddling with it, while blinking back the tears that film her eyes.

'OK?' Tessa says eventually.

Jess nods. She can do this. She has to do this. Learning to think differently – to curb the way in which she has behaved, on and off, since childhood – seems impossible, and yet what choice does she have? Betsey's skull fracture – the result of her acting on sabotaging thoughts – has shown she cannot continue like this. Besides, seeking help is crucial to persuading social services she can be trusted as a mother; is part of her family's action plan.

'It would be good if you could continue to try this,' says Tessa, in her non-judgemental way that is nevertheless quietly assertive. 'And if you could fill out this chart, as we discussed – rating your thoughts, what triggers them, and the likelihood of your thinking they are true?'

Jess takes the piece of paper. She will need more than one of these.

'It would be a good idea to get a notebook so that you can make several charts.' Tessa seems to read her mind.

She has been allocated six CBT sessions on the NHS, and Jess knows she is lucky to have these. She suspects – and she has never felt more grateful for Ed's fat salary – that she will need to have more. Still, she is sceptical about changing something so entrenched. Her intrusive thoughts began when she was ten, ebbed and flowed throughout adolescence, then lay dormant for many years before returning with a vengeance with the puppy and after her traumatic labour with Betsey. She can't imagine existing without them, and yet, and here she feels the tiniest glimmer of excitement, what if she could contain or even silence them?

'You all right?' In the health centre waiting room, she bumps into another mother from Kit's year: Carla's mum – she can't remember her name, she's not one of the mothers she chats to in the playground – a toddler in a buggy, a baby straddling her hip. The woman eyes her curiously: clocking her smudged mascara, the signs of her emotional unravelling. She looks down, averting her eyes.

All good, thank you. That would be her usual response. The reply of a woman hiding her anxieties beneath a spun caramel exterior, her layers of glossiness binding her dark thoughts tight.

But other mothers think like her: that's something she's taken from her conversation with Dr Arnold, and so she is honest. 'Not brilliant,' she admits.

And then she thinks of Ed, who is at home looking after Bets; of Martha, who will drop in every other day; of Liz, who texted this morning to say she was thinking of her. 'But I hope I'm going to get there.'

LIZ

Saturday 9 June

Forty-four

The PTA Summer Fair has been going for an hour and a half and Sam has reached peak levels of excitement, cramming wisps of pale pink candyfloss into his mouth.

'Look what else we won,' he manages through bubble-gum pink fluff.

Frankie, with whom he's pooled his resources, opens a canvas tote to reveal their spoils: lurid chewy sweets, strawberry laces, small packets of Haribos and four Sherbet Fountains. The sorts of prizes his mother would immediately ban.

'That's just the sweetie tombola,' Sam adds. 'We also won a huge bottle of Coke and some bubble bath. The lady on the stall wouldn't let us get you the wine.'

'That's very kind of you – but where's the Coke now?' I ask, amused but slightly chastened that Sam knew I'd choose alcohol over toiletries. My boy belches softly.

'Oh, Sam. You didn't?'

'We shared it with Connor.'

'You drank most of it,' Frankie, ever literal, retorts.

'Drank what?' Jess walks up to us, pushing a sleeping Betsey in a buggy laden with lavender from the plant stall.

'Sam had a soft drink,' I say, because I doubt Frankie would have defied Jess over this. In any case, there's nothing she can do about it. I glance at my son, still folding the floss onto his tongue. 'Sam, you've probably had enough of that now.' I take the candyfloss from him, and wipe his thick fringe from his damp forehead. 'Why don't you help Daddy on the coconut shy?' I nod to a familiar figure in the distance next to a garishly decorated stall.

He brightens. 'I've run out of money, anyway. Coming, Frankie?'

'Is that all right?' Frankie checks with his mother. She hesitates, and it's as if she's running through all potential disasters.

'Of course,' she manages eventually, and the two boys run off.

For a short time we watch them haring across the playground. The site is humming with children and parents and it's a sign that Jess is becoming less over-anxious that she's willing – if not happy – for them to roam free.

I'm flooded with a rare sense of unadulterated joy. Perhaps it's the hard blue sky, or the sun beating down so intensely my hair sticks to the back of my neck. Maybe it's that three hundred children are playing and chattering happily; or that Betsey, now fifteen months, is thriving and Jess seems to be getting better. Perhaps it's that a friendship that fractured is knitting back together: that shared decade of motherhood counting for something, after all. I still berate myself for not recognising Jess might be struggling. But at least the family are now receiving help: Jess is seeing her therapist, and Frankie has been diagnosed as having ADHD and given medication. He's still an intense child, still troubled; but the family seems less fragile, less likely to snap.

'Frankie's doing OK, isn't he?' I turn to my friend.

'I guess so. He still has bad nightmares.'

'It's still early days,' I say, hoping I sound optimistic not dismissive. 'And what about you?'

'I'm getting better,' she smiles, and her tone is less equivocal. 'The CBT's helping, though I don't find it easy to do.'

'And look at Betsey!' I nod at her daughter, flushed in the heat and exhausted after spending the first hour of the fair toddling around. Lolling in her buggy, she is close to falling asleep. Not for the first time I think of how resilient children can be. She spent over three weeks in hospital – a week while her morphine and sedative withdrawal was managed. ('She's become an *addict*,' Jess said in one of her least rational moments.) But you'd never know, from watching her, that less than five months ago she was in PICU with a fractured skull.

'She's still on the anti-seizure drug,' Jess says, 'but Dr Hussain said it's a preventative measure.'

'She should be weaned off it soon.'

'God I hope so. I beat myself up about it all the time. I still can't believe I was so *stupid* to leave them like that.'

'Oh, Jess.' We've gone over this before, in particular her guilt at risking Betsey not getting the right treatment. 'Beating yourself up is a waste of energy: I've had to learn that.'

'I know.' She gives a small smile. DC Rustin isn't investigating her for neglect, it not being deemed in the public interest to prosecute her. But she lives with the consequences of leaving her children every day. She shoves her large shades back down: no one would know she is on the edge of tears, just as none of us guessed this was a daily occurrence ever since she had Betsey. I reach out and touch her forearm, cool beneath my fingers, and she gives my hand a small squeeze.

The chair of the PTA hurries past, brandishing a loud hailer through which she is barking orders. 'The maypole dancing is starting in five minutes!' she intones. 'I repeat. The maypole. In five minutes!' The sound of an accordion and violin drifts from where the pole has been erected on the playground, its ribbons drooping despite the slight breeze.

'Rosa's taking part in that. I said I'd catch her before she went on. Do you want to watch?'

Jess shakes her head. She doesn't like crowds: still worries that people will be chattering about her. She gestures back to the school building. 'I think I'll just sit in the shade.'

Little Disasters

The grounds of St Matthew's are large for a London primary school but I think I spy the girls in the distance, doing balletic stretches by the outer fence. Heading there, I take a shortcut past the preschool portacabin: there's no one here and it's a relief to escape the mass of bodies queuing for hot dogs and fried onions by the barbecue, or for pints of warm Pimm's.

I'm enjoying the quiet, and perhaps that's why a familiar voice catches my attention.

'I don't know how much more plain I can be,' says the man, out of sight but talking in the shade of the preschool building. 'I'm sorry but I have to prioritise Jess. Surely you can see that after all she's been through?'

I stop, uncomfortable, and hover around the corner. Ed's distinctive bass isn't as reasonable as usual: it's tinged with an acid sharpness as if someone has pushed him to the edge.

There's no response at first, and then a clipped, cool dismissal from a female voice I also know.

'You're misinterpreting me,' says Charlotte. 'There's no need to be so bloody *dismissive*. I was only trying to help.'

'I'm not sure she'd view it as that – or that I do either.' He sounds angry. 'Can't you see your wanting to see me will distress her? I've valued our friendship but it can't continue. I don't mean to sound harsh but you need to leave me alone.'

There is silence, and I try to imagine what's going on on the other side of the portacabin. Is he holding her, or has she

373

stalked away? A movement and he is walking off, pace brisk, head bent, not wanting to be seen. What did Charlotte suggest, and was Jess right to suspect Charlotte of still carrying a flame for her husband? He's rebuffed her pretty emphatically, but their conversation unsettles me.

I hang back as Charlotte heads off, too. She's walking in the direction of George and Kit, who have joined the girls and are tossing a tennis ball while they practise their moves for the maypole. (Kit's fracture has long since mended.) This is George's last summer fair before he heads off to King Edmund's prep in September and it will be easy enough to lose touch with the Masons. Perhaps that will be easiest for us all.

I'm reluctant to chat but I promised I'd see Rosa and I don't want Charlotte to think I'm being unfriendly.

'Charlotte – hi!' I overcompensate in case she notices that I've come from the same direction.

'Oh, hello.' She's wearing shades so I can't see her expression but she holds herself stiffly and her voice is strained.

'I'm sorry you're going. We'll miss you,' I say, hoping I don't sound insincere.

'We always said we'd go private: we're just going a little earlier than intended. But I think George will miss everyone more than I anticipated.'

There's an uneasy pause and she backs into the shade of the sycamore almost at the playing field fence. It's hard not to feel as if she's already left us emotionally and is trying to do so physically: either that, or she is trying to hide.

'Charlotte—' I begin, not knowing what to say but sensing that something is very wrong.

'What?' She shoves her shades up and I see raw hurt in
her eyes. Then she puts them back down as if she has given
me more than enough insight. That rare moment of honesty
is all I will get.

'Nothing,' I say, and I cast around for something benign
to say. I start blathering about how the children are growing
and then I have a brainwave. 'Do you remember that photo,
all lined up when they were babies? Do you think we could
try to replicate it, now?'

'Oh, George would love that.' Her smile becomes slightly
less pinched.

'We could even do one with the four of us with all the
kids?' I add, out of some ridiculous desire to pretend we can
revert to a simpler time.

'Oh no. No, I don't think so. I hate having my photograph taken. I always feel so tall and gangling beside the
rest of you.' And then, in an acknowledgement that our
relationships have never been the same since Jess told us
she was pregnant with Betsey: 'Please, Liz. Let's not try to
force things.'

'We've got to do the maypole now, Mum!' Rosa
bounds up, rescuing me from my embarrassment. 'Mel's
there already. *C'mon.* You said you'd see me and we're
late already.'

'I'm sorry, Charlotte – I need to go.'

I'm here if you want to talk, I almost add, troubled by the bleakness of her expression. But she's so private she's never confided in me before and is unlikely to start now. With a feeling of relief, I walk away.

'What's up with Charlotte?' Mel asks, as I squeeze next to her to see our girls waiting by their maypole ribbons. 'Talk about unfriendly.'

'It's nothing,' I say, as the music cranks up for the introductory dance. The girls start skipping backwards and forwards towards the pole before facing each other and dancing in alternate directions. Rosa bites her lip in concentration but still gets ahead of herself, confusing the plaiting so that the PE teacher has to step in and try to untangle their criss-crossing.

'Isn't this lovely,' says Mel as she watches Mollie weave her way in and out with natural grace. 'Look what the *bastard's* missing.'

I squeeze her round the waist. Rob is holidaying in Majorca with his now twenty-five-year-old girlfriend and has a relaxed attitude to complying with his contact arrangements. 'It's his loss,' I tell her. 'You can't recreate a memory like this.'

And suddenly a spasm of grief runs through me for a girl who never lived to run at sports day; who never got to sprint and jump and leap like my daughter. I feel acute sorrow for Clare, my never-known sister, and for my mother – or rather, for the mother and grandmother I would have liked her to be. Janet never came to my school events, let alone my kids'. Did depression dull her emotions, or did guilt cloud everything? She continues to unsettle me, my mother, not least because, in her absence, she is a lacuna. I am conscious that I never really knew her at all.

Later, much later, when the children are puce and the temperature is still in the late twenties, we join the mass of families swarming from the school to queue for ice cream.

'Can we get one, pleeeeeease?' Sam begs, over the sound of 'Greensleeves' coming from the nearby van that chugs exhaust as its owner dispenses fat Mr Whippy's.

'Think you've had enough,' Nick says, indicating Sam's bag of spoils and a box of homemade fudge he has somehow bought.

'You can have an apple ice lolly,' I compromise.

'S'all right. I'll have some water.' We skirt the queue and press on as he glugs from his plastic bottle, a trail of liquid trickling down his chin.

Heat shimmers from the pavement in a thick wall, and the mass of parents amble: it's too hot to rush and, for once, there's no need. The sea of bodies narrows. Nick hangs back with Rosa, who is chatting to Mollie, with whom she has a play date, but I find myself caught up in the crowd, and push ahead with my boy.

In the line in front of us, Betsey is perched on Ed's shoulders like the queen of the jungle. 'You have got hold of her, haven't you?' Jess frets, as she clutches Frankie's hand. Kit walks between them with the buggy. 'Of course,' Ed says – and I see how hard she finds it not to double-check and ask again.

A car backfires somewhere behind me, and the crowd looks around, anxious. The school's close to a Tube station and the thought of a terrorist attack or a shooting is never far from our minds. Jess glances back and catches my eye. I smile, but she's distracted by Frankie who's panicking, dragging her along, as he looks behind us. 'We need to go, we need to get going. Please, Mummy ...' He urges her to walk faster. Jess sweeps ahead, and Ed ends up beside me.

'How are you doing?' I ask.

'Yeah, all right. It's all getting a bit easier.'

'Lovely that you're here – and around more.'

'Well, you read me the Riot Act.' He grimaces.

'Was I that bad?' When Jess was released, I told him she needed far more support.

'You were quite fierce, but to be fair I needed telling,' he concedes. Ahead of us, Frankie is still calling, the sound an almost falsetto cry. Ed gestures with his head. 'Wish we could do something about this. Frankie's still getting freaked.'

'Well, he's had a traumatic time.'

'He's still having nightmares.'

'Yes, Jess said.'

He adjusts Betsey on his shoulders, as if itching at the problem. 'I can't help feeling there's something he's not telling us. Something that's causing this disproportionate stress.'

I catch sight of them up ahead; can hear his anguish quite

clearly. 'We need to go faster, Mummy. We need to go faster.' He shoots that terrified look again.

For a moment I wonder if he's scared of *me*: the woman who, Kit once told Rosa, 'set the police' on their mother. But *I* was the adult who persuaded him to open up about what happened and so helped secure Jess's release.

Besides, he's glancing beyond me, deep into the crowd still clustering for ice creams; way beyond Nick and Rosa.

There's something or *someone* he's spotted who frightens him so intensely he needs to speed away.

FRANKIE

Friday 19 January, 6.20 p.m.

Forty-five

When someone starts knocking on the door, Frankie jumps up in excitement, races to the hallway, and just as quickly runs back to Betsey, whispering to her to be quiet.

Their mum said he mustn't open it. He never does – not for the postman, or the Amazon delivery man or the men who bring the supermarket order, if they come when he's at home. 'I'll get it,' she always calls, with her suspicious face on, and something stops him hurtling towards it. So he knows never to answer it when she is out.

She even reminded him of the fact. He holds onto this rule and the others. *Don't answer the door. Don't lift her. I won't be more than five minutes.* She's been away for eight now. He checks the digital watch he wears on his wrist as the knocking starts up again. His mum likes rules. Likes things to be clear and ordered. But now she's broken her own rule – *I won't be more than five minutes* – and the knocking is going on and on.

Betsey starts her whimpering cry again that means she's tired or has a heavy nappy. He can smell the tang of her wee and something ripe and meaty like a big, fat poo. 'Have you pooed yourself?' he whispers, delighted and appalled. He really needs to do something now. His mum would never let her sit in a smelly nappy. It would sting. So he should sort this and change her. That would make Mummy happy and he'd love to make her happy; she's been so stressed recently, shouting, and making him more het up and jangled than ever – as if her worry is flowing into him and Betsey and they both need to scream it out.

Perhaps that's her at the door? Maybe she's forgotten her key and needs letting in. But if it's her, then why doesn't she just say so? She'll know he'll be frightened. And she said not to let *anyone* in. He tries to call out but the back of his throat is tight and no sound comes out. Maybe they should hide: pretend no one's here, though Betsey is giving the game away with her crying. '*Shhh*, Betsey,' he hisses. Her bottom lip wobbles and she whimpers even louder. He's having no effect.

I'm taking my phone. She'd said that, too, in case he wanted to ring her. He scrabbles for the landline and presses redial. It rings out: a repeated trill – and then her voice asking him to leave a message. He wants to tell her about the person at the door but he's too scared he'll be heard. He hauls up Betsey, hitching her high on his hip;

she's heavier than she looks, and more wriggly. *Don't answer the door. Don't lift her. I won't be more than five minutes . . . I'm taking my phone.*

Betsey is screaming now. She's really angry and he wants to match it, this noise that challenges him to retaliate, to cry even louder, but he's too scared of the knocking at the door. 'Shh, Betsey! Stop crying.' He jiggles her then tries to jolly her along with Rabbie, but the velveteen rabbit flops in his hands; he doesn't get it right.

The tapping comes again. A hard, intrusive sound: someone very much wants to come in. *Rat-a-tat-tat. Rat-at-tat-tat.* There is a metallic clatter as someone lifts the flap of the letter box and it snaps like a monster then viciously clangs shut.

And then he hears a voice – and he's so relieved. Because he knows this voice, and he knows this woman, though he doesn't really like her, and she's meant to be here, dropping Kit off. It's all been arranged. His brother's come home and can help with Betsey, even if this other mummy can't. He'll be able to change her – or carry her up the stairs so they can both do it together. He'll make everything better now he's here.

He races to the door, Betsey in his arms and jiggling as he runs, and fumbles with the catch.

'Hi-iiii!' he sings, excited to see his big, capable brother, the child who makes his parents happy. But there's just one person on the doorstep and it isn't him.

'Where's Kit?' he says. The night is very black and the

woman standing there has her serious face on: the one she wears when she's telling George off for going on his Xbox instead of doing his violin practice.

'Still at football. I popped round to see Mummy.' And then Charlotte smiles, more kindly. 'Can I come in?'

CHARLOTTE

Friday 19 January, 2.20 p.m.

Forty-six

Ed is hurrying towards the Tube station when Charlotte sees
him. She finishes early on a Friday so she can take George
to violin and football. Three hours of ferrying but her boy's
reaction makes it worth it. She craves this pick-up like a
woman longing for her lover after a week apart.

She doesn't expect to see Ed. Hidden behind a flower
stall, she feels the same old sensations: a heart-tug and a
stirring, deep inside. Twenty years on, he still has it: his
looks, but also this ability to provoke strong emotions. *The
one who got away. The one who, for one night at least, was so
very nearly hers.*

Not that anything happened, of course. Not, truly, in
the physical sense, not in the way he would recognise.
He hadn't lied to Jess about it, but he hadn't quite told
the truth. A drunken kiss, post-finals, a stumble into her
single bed and then, before they could really do anything,

he had passed out. The next morning, he was characteristically charming and then he'd asked, 'We didn't, did
we?' and she had seen his apprehension. The fear that
he'd had sex with *her*: his ex-girlfriend's housemate –
good to have around, funny, interesting, but a *mate*. Too
tall, too clever, too assured of herself to be *desirable*. Not
his usual type. Not someone he would intend to have sex
with at all.

How was he to know that she felt closer to him than
any boyfriend? That she'd hankered after him for the past
two years. That she'd watched him all night, memorising
his bone structure, his long lashes, the curve of his lips,
because deep down she feared this was a fluke. That she'd
kept her breathing shallow whenever he stirred in case
she broke the spell; in case he woke and she managed to
scare him off.

'Would it be disastrous if we had?' she'd teased, but she
didn't get the tone right, and he saw quite how much he'd
hurt her.

'No, no of course not,' he'd blustered. 'Look, it's not
you, it's me.' He'd gestured at his beautiful, hungover face.
'Believe me: you wouldn't want to get involved.' And then
he'd trotted out a cliché that made her despise him for a
second. 'We can be friends, can't we?' He'd brushed her
forehead with his lips: platonic, chaste.

'Of course,' she'd murmured, trying to memorise his
smell, to hold it together. She had made it too easy for
him. Within a couple of minutes he was gone.

But of course she couldn't be *friends* with someone with whom she was in love and about whom she continued to think, *if only*. Rejection fanned her infatuation and she became briefly obsessed. Graduation meant she no longer needed to see him and she shunned parties and later weddings she knew he would attend. Eventually the humiliation eased. Time helped, as did finding a man who wanted to have sex with her, who liked and even *loved* her. Not someone who aroused passion, but someone solid, quirky in his own way, and clever. A fellow geek.

Of course she googled Ed; looked him up on Facebook, LinkedIn and Twitter; knew which building he worked in. (She considered finding him on the electoral roll but managed to exercise some self-restraint.) She focused on her career, on getting married, and on getting pregnant, the last more difficult than she'd anticipated since Andrew, the supposed safe bet, turned out to have a low sperm count. And she worked very hard at excising all thoughts of Ed Curtis from her head.

Until that blustery autumn night when he walked into that antenatal class in that nursery and the old humiliation – and yes, a surge of desire, intensified by the pregnancy hormones – resolutely kicked in. She watched as he recognised her, the familiar shame creeping up her neck. 'We must catch up,' he'd said, and in the pub afterwards alluding to what occurred: 'I haven't seen you since ...' He'd had the grace to look embarrassed. 'Since nothing happened?' she'd said, playing it cool. 'It didn't, did it?' he agreed, rather too quickly. 'I was worried I'd upset you, if that doesn't sound arrogant? You disappeared completely. Here, let me take those. I'd love you to properly meet Jess.'

She was proud of herself then; proud, too, of how she managed to be friends with his wife, though they were so different; had little in common except Ed and a child the same age. But she couldn't get over him choosing a wife like Jess: nervous, complicated, emotionally high-maintenance; not stupid but apparently happy not to pursue a career. (She'd worked in events, hadn't she?) Obsessed with creating the perfect home and being the perfect mother to their kids. And that wouldn't matter, except that Ed, though not in the least bit complicated, liked an intellectual challenge, and she sensed he felt a bit lost.

And then Jess announced she was pregnant for the third time, and she experienced the most irrational rage: not just because she had struggled to have one baby and Jess was so effortlessly fertile; not even because Jess *dared* to appear ambivalent about this child; but because, on some barely acknowledged, completely irrational level, she knew Ed could never be free now. Three children tipped the balance: Jess had him well and truly trapped.

She'd had to withdraw from her after that. Still shared their Friday football lifts but had little other interaction. She'd increased her hours in the past year, she explained when Liz mentioned her apparent distance, and had to ration her time. George was moving schools at the end of year five, and she'd moved on: didn't feel she had much in common with someone preoccupied with a baby, any more. She didn't add that she had no time for someone so self-absorbed who had no idea how bloody lucky she was. For her own carefully buttressed sanity, she tried not to engage.

And she had managed it. At the barbecue it had been easy: Jess had spent the entire time fussing inside with Betsey, and Ed had been so warm, so entirely uninterested in helping with this baby girl. And then from September, the boys started Tuesday night training. Andrew had offered to go but she'd said it was only fair to divvy up the football duties, and suddenly she could see Ed most weeks. Of course, there were always other dads around, but they slipped back into a decent friendship, distinct and discrete from anything she shared with his wife or the other women. It wasn't hard to imagine that *if only* could one day *be*.

And now here he is alone, in the spitting rain, outside their local Tube station, and it seems only natural to say hello.

'Hi, Ed,' she says, touching his arm. 'Are you OK?'

Under usual circumstances he might have told her that of course he was fine, but for some reason he doesn't. Perhaps because he is clearly so stricken; or perhaps because they once shared a physical closeness (and before he passed out, he *had* buried his head in her breasts). Whatever the reason, he gives a little laugh and all artifice slips away in that moment. 'Not really, no,' he says.

And he isn't disloyal, he goes out of his way not to be critical, but still he says enough in the three minutes they shelter under her golfing umbrella for her to glean that he has come home because he is so worried about Jess.

'Can I ask: did you ever feel *detached* ... after George?' He looks at her, craving reassurance, hoping she will know the answer: Charlotte, who is Jess's friend. 'I don't think she was like this after the boys but Kit was born during the crash so I wasn't around, and work was still fraught when she had Frankie. I can't remember if it's normal for her to be like this?'

'No I didn't,' Charlotte says, failing to point out that she was back at work by the time her boy was three months old, corporate law being more desirable than the tedium of looking after a baby who scared her. (Those long hours stuck at home with him, sensing that she wasn't doing it right; that she wasn't a good enough mother; the rapid loss of her identity.)

'Maybe we tipped the balance, having this third baby. Maybe I asked too much?'

And then he looks uncomfortable because Charlotte has made no secret of wanting a second child, and had to admit to her failure when she underwent three unsuccessful rounds of IVF.

'No you didn't,' she reassures him. 'You could never ask

too much,' and she gives him a quick, awkward hug, there in the street.

She walks away, cocooned under her umbrella as the rain begins falling more heavily, fixating on his comments and his concern. *Detached. Maybe I've asked too much of her. I'm worried about Jess.*

Poor, precious Jess who has *everything*, and yet it still isn't enough. And yes, she knows she ought to be sympathetic – perhaps Jess is suffering from postnatal depression; she's just the type, isn't she? But perhaps she should bloody well pull herself together, and recognise what she has instead.

And then her phone rings and it's Jill, asking if she would mind swapping and picking the boys up from football next week instead of this – there's some work event she wants to go to – and Charlotte suddenly has an hour to spare.

She would never have done anything were it not for that call, she tells herself later, but it seems serendipitous: having this unanticipated slot of time in which to talk to Jess. She could tell her how she is in danger of squandering everything she has: Ed; three beautiful children; even her looks, because she always makes Charlotte, with her height, her strong nose, her dark brows and eyes, feel physically awkward. *A handsome woman*, that's how Andrew describes her, whereas Jess is dainty; Jess is beautiful. No one has ever described Charlotte as this.

And yes, she might even admit to Jess that Ed was the

one who got away. Not to hurt her – and she won't vent her anger; she has too much self-control for that – but just to make her realise how fucking *lucky* she is.

How her life is the sort that Charlotte sometimes thinks she might like.

That's all she intends when she knocks on the front door. Just to talk to Jess.

FRANKIE

Friday 19 January, 6.22 p.m.

Forty-seven

'Is Mummy in?' Charlotte asks, as she steps into the hall. 'Hello, sweetheart,' she adds, smiling at Betsey. Bets holds her arms out to her and Frankie hands her over to this familiar adult before he realises quite what he has done.

'Where's Kit?' he asks, relief at seeing a mother who might make everything right undermined as he realises he can't see his brother. 'Why are you here?' he manages to ask.

'I came to chat to Mummy but then I heard Betsey screaming. It's been going on for a long time, so I was worried, wasn't I, little one?' She says this last bit in a silly voice as she jiggles Betsey. Then her tone reverts to normal: not unfriendly but bossy – the voice she used when George got out all his Lego – and she asks a question he doesn't want to answer. 'Where's Mummy, Frank?'

He says nothing. He mustn't tell anyone she's gone out. She'd looked guilty when she left them. *I'll just be five minutes. Don't answer the door to anyone.* And he hadn't. Until this moment, he has stuck by her rules.

'Jess?' she calls, when he doesn't reply, and walks through to the kitchen. 'Jess?' she sings up the stairs. 'Is Mummy asleep, Frank? Is that it?' Her eyes are beady, like a black-bird's pecking for worms. He doesn't like it and he doesn't like her calling him Frank.

'Frank.' She bends down to his level, Bets snivelling against her shoulder, and her voice is so soft it's almost a whisper. 'Can you help me? Is Mummy ill – or isn't she here? Did she leave you alone?'

He doesn't nod, he is *sure* he doesn't nod, but perhaps the relief of being able to tell an adult is so intense he moves his head a little. Charlotte straightens – she's so tall for a mummy – and there's a very worried look on her face.

'Right. Well, let's try to stop you crying, little one.' She smiles at Betsey. 'You've got a stinky nappy, haven't you?' She tickles his baby sister under the chin but Bets doesn't like that and her cry cranks up until she's screaming again.

'It's OK. Mummy will be back soon to sort it.' She bounces her on her hip, and Bets starts hiccupping. The movement must jolt her because a brown stain spreads down her thigh.

'Oh!' Charlotte pulls a funny face. 'My. That *is* a full nappy.' She transfers his sister to her other hip, and stops the jiggling. Her special baby voice vanishes. 'Gosh. You do stink. Still, I expect Mummy will be back very soon and then we can get you changed ...'

But Bets is wriggling and screaming, and Frankie knows that if her foul nappy were taken off she would calm down immediately.

'I can show you where to change her,' he jabbers, the words racing from him he is so excited. '*I* was going to change her. Mummy wouldn't want her sitting in a stinky nappy. I could help you. I know where the Sudocrem is.'

He is beaming because it all seems so simple: they can stop her crying and please Mummy. She'll be relieved if Charlotte cleans Betsey. And he could help. He could entertain his sister while it's being done.

But Charlotte looks worried.

'I don't think so, Frank. Mummy might mind and I expect she'll be back very soon to deal with it, won't she?' The poo is spreading up Betsey's back now, seeping through her vest and top. 'Oh! Euurgh.' She stretches her arms out, holding her away so her legs dangle down. She doesn't look as if she's used to holding babies and Betsey, screaming louder, seems to sense this, too.

'She wouldn't,' he says, 'and we've got to stop her crying. Come on,' he races to the bottom of the stairs, his excitement spilling over. 'Come *on*.'

He starts running up as she slips her shoes off. Eventually, he hears her feet padding behind him. It feels a bit strange but Charlotte's been here plenty of times before they had Betsey. He remembers George, always a bit sly, stealing a car from Kit . . .

'Won't Mummy mind?' Once they are in the bathroom,

she looks reluctant to touch the nappy but as she puts Betsey on the changing table, the poo squelches all the way up her back. 'Oh my God,' Charlotte adds. 'Shit.' For a moment, she seems paralysed. 'Well, I suppose we can't leave her like this.'

Betsey's screams are getting louder.

'Let's sort out this nappy!' she says, in an over-jolly voice, as she rips off the tape at one side.

And suddenly this doesn't feel OK. Frankie feels it in his tummy, and he thinks Betsey feels it, too. She is really screaming, despite Charlotte using that increasingly desperate, frantic voice.

'What a mess, Betsey, but I'll make it better, just like Mummy ...'

She holds Betsey's ankles up with one hand and eases away the full nappy. The smell hits the back of his throat and makes him gag, makes Charlotte flinch.

'Oh! That's quite foul. Where's a bag, Frank? A nappy sack?' She is suddenly sharp; her face pinched. 'Come on. Quickly now.'

'I don't know.' He is confused. He didn't know he was meant to be helping: he thought she'd taken over. They're usually on the shelf under the changing table, in a special white box, the vanilla-scented plastic peeking out for easy access, but they're not there.

'Frank, come on! Quickly.'

'I can't see it. I don't *know*.'

'Argh, well, we can't have this mess on the mat.' She makes a parcel of the nappy with her fingers but there's so much poo it bulges. 'We'll have to clear it up later.' And she picks it up between two fingers and tosses it onto the floor.

He stares at it. She shouldn't have done that. It doesn't go there but in a bag and then straight in the black bin outside so that there's no remaining stinkiness, no extra bacteria, in the bathroom. That's what Mummy does, and she won't like this one bit.

'Now, where are the wipes? Ah, here.' She grabs a packet from the shelf and starts wiping Betsey. He can't stop looking at the soiled nappy which squats in the corner like a malevolent, bug-ridden toad.

'Where did Mummy go, Frank?' Charlotte asks as she rips out wipe after wipe, her questions vying with Betsey's crying. 'She's a *silly* mummy, isn't she?' she tells his sister, and her voice has an edge to it as if she's desperately trying to jolly things along. 'A silly, *naughty* mummy.'

Betsey hiccups, and it sounds like a giggle.

'Isn't she a naughty mummy?' Charlotte repeats.

But she's not. She's not at all. She's not a naughty mummy, and Frankie would *never* describe her as silly. Sad, perhaps: she's sad a lot these days.

He hates the word 'naughty': so fat and jolly but with a mean edge. His teacher says he's naughty. It means he's difficult. Mummy's the only one who doesn't think he is. She's been gone twelve and a half minutes, now, and he wants her so much. Perhaps it's this that makes him speak out: this fear for Jess, and his pain at her being mocked like this.

'She's not,' he manages. His fists clench tight.

'Not what?' Charlotte turns, a hand on Betsey's tummy.

'She's not naughty. And she's not silly. She's not stupid!' He is suddenly shouting. 'She's not naughty. That's not a *kind* thing to say!'

'It's not kind to leave your children alone,' Charlotte says, under her breath.

'She is kind. She *is* kind. She *loves* us!' He starts to whimper, distraught and troubled by the stench on the floor, the nappy that just slumps there. Then Betsey starts screaming again.

'Where can I find a fresh nappy?' Charlotte raises her voice above Betsey's cry.

'On the shelf,' he shouts back, hating her now.

She gives him a hard stare.

'On the shelf – here!' He starts to rummage under the changing table, anger coursing through him at her failure to bag up that nappy. Why can't *she* find it? *She's* the adult. The one who should know how to do *everything*. He wants her to go home now. He wants to *make* her go home. And so he shoves her legs *hard* to push her away.

She steps back, taking her hand off his sister's tummy, holding both up in mock-horror.

'Why did you do that?'

She has a hurt face on; seems genuinely puzzled. He's embarrassed and frightened and so he ignores her, searching the changing table shelf, burying himself underneath.

'Why did you do that?' she repeats, bending down so that she peers into his face.

The thud and the wail are almost instantaneous: a scream far more terrifying than any Betsey's made before. Frankie freezes. Betsey lies flat on her back, between the table and the bath, her mouth a perfect O as the sound shoots from her; a look of disbelief on her face.

Charlotte crouches next to her, looking guilty and very scared.

He doesn't understand. How did Bets get on the floor? 'How . . .' he begins.

'Please be OK, please be OK.' Charlotte cuddles his sister to her. Then: 'Look what you did!' she screeches.

'I didn't . . .'

'Yes you did! You distracted me and she rolled off the table. You shoved me aside; you *shocked* me with your naughty, *tricky* behaviour and look what happened to this darling girl.'

'I didn't mean to . . .'

'It doesn't matter if you *meant* to,' she says, as she tries to shush Betsey. She looks very, very frightened and it's her fear that scares him the most.

He shrinks down into the corner of the room, curls as small as he can, head folded into his knees, arms tight around them. If he can make himself disappear then perhaps she'll go away. Maybe this is a bad dream, and he'll wake to discover that Mummy never left. He starts rocking, trying to block out the sound of Charlotte's terror, and perhaps it works because her nasty voice stops as she cuddles his sister. 'Shh, shh, Betsey. Shh, shh, baby. Come on, Betsey, shush. Shh, *please.*'

Suddenly, she thrusts her at him and he is holding his whimpering sister. 'I've got to be back for George.' Charlotte looks properly panicked. 'She's OK. She'll be fine. It's just the shock. That's why she's screaming. Mummy will be back soon – but listen to me' – and here she looks more scared than he's ever seen any adult before – 'when she comes back you mustn't say you saw me.'

'But I *did*,' he whimpers.

'No you *didn't*,' she insists. 'It's *really* important. You were trying to be helpful. You tried to change her nappy and she rolled over. You didn't see what happened. Can you repeat that for me?'

'I was trying to be helpful. I tried to change her nappy and she rolled over. I didn't see it happen.'

'Good boy. Excellent!' She smiles, and he glows under her surprising praise. 'The thing is Mummy will be worried if she knows I was here because *I* know that she wasn't.'

He nods, very unclear.

'Mummies aren't meant to leave their children, are they?'

'No.'

'And she could get in a lot of trouble if anyone else – your daddy or the police, for instance – found out she'd left you here by yourselves.'

'The police?' He is flooded with fear.

'They would put her in prison,' she whispers, looking sad.

'I don't want her to go to prison.'

'I know you don't. And that's why you're not going to say *anything* that would worry her. You don't want the police to find out she wasn't here' – and her face, with its dark eyes and pronounced nose, is suddenly witch-like – 'so shall this be our secret?'

He nods, solemnly.

'It's really important. Remember: you tried to change her nappy to be helpful and she rolled over. You didn't see it. Got that?'

He nods more firmly.

'Excellent. That's all you need to say.'

She goes quickly after that. Leaves him there in that stinking bathroom with Bets and his worst fears: that Mummy has abandoned them and that she'll be taken from them. Sixteen minutes she's been gone. He stares at the digital figures on his wrist as Betsey's cries continue. Sixteen and a half minutes, then seventeen, and she's still not here . . .

Tears streak down his wet face as he repeats Charlotte's words like a mantra. *I tried to change her nappy to be helpful. She rolled over. I didn't see it.* Betsey sucks frantically on her fingers and he lies her on a towel; strokes her tummy; tries to dab her tears away.

At nineteen minutes, he hears the sound of the key in the lock, then the tread of feet running up the stairs. He screams. He can't help it: what if it's Charlotte and not his mummy? It's a dark, guttural sound. The cry he makes when he's desperate not to be told off but here it is anchored by terror. His mother bursts into the bathroom.

'What's happened? What did you do?'

She knows he is to blame: she takes that as read.

'I tried to change her nappy,' he gabbles, drinking in her hair, the smell of her skin, the fact she is next to him and that she is putting her arm around him as well as Betsey, that she is drawing them close together, that he is safe.

'She rolled over. I didn't see it.' The words he has rehearsed spill out in one rush, followed by his guilt that he has somehow caused this.

'It's all my fault. But I didn't mean to. I didn't mean to, Mummy.'

LIZ

Saturday 9 June

Forty-eight

'Shall we catch them up?' It feels wrong to be ambling in the sunshine while Frankie is experiencing some sort of crisis. I spy Jess's curls among the mass of parents; can just see Frankie's dark, silky head.

We walk more briskly, me dragging Sam, Ed and Kit trotting beside us. 'Dada!' Betsey shrieks, jiggling up and down on his shoulders. He raises a hand to grip her torso; consciously slows his pace.

But Frankie drives me on. It's not just his shrill cry. It's my affinity with a child left alone with a younger sibling who then suffered a serious accident. Who was involved in it happening and will think he's to blame. Because however much we reassure him that it wasn't his fault, he'll still feel guilty and responsible.

Frankie, who caused Betsey's serious head injury. Just like

Lizzie, who ignored her little brother until he scalded himself as he made her a cup of tea.

My heart thumps wildly. This isn't about me; it's about this small boy, who still looks deeply troubled. I've lost sight of them, though I can hear his intermittent shrieks.

'It's madness, racing in this heat. Why don't you come back to ours? Have you time?' Ed has slowed right down.

'Great. Good idea.' Still walking, I text the plan to Nick. But though I should relax at the thought, my heart's staccato-ing because Frankie has somehow slipped from my sight.

'I can't see them. Will they have gone up here?'

We've reached the corner of St Albans' Avenue, a curving road of substantial Edwardian semis that's home to Charlotte and Andrew and forms a shortcut.

'No, Frankie refuses to go this way. They go via the main road. Look: there they are!' Ed gestures to a small scurrying figure, still dragging his mother far off in the distance. They're moving at quite a pace.

We take the shortcut, past the elegant houses with their repointed red brick, their smart paintwork, their bay trees in planters, and I wonder why Frankie avoids it. Then I remember making up rules as a child: if I reach the end of the street without stepping on a line, my mum won't be angry; if I walk to the end of the pier without stepping over a plank, Mattie will get well. Like most children I outgrew the belief I could control things if I performed certain rituals – in my case, once the acute stress of

403

Mattie's accident and his period in hospital were over. But Frankie is still clearly affected by what happened. Perhaps that's what's going on here.

The shortcut means we reach Jess's house just after she and Frankie arrive. As Ed turns his key in the lock, Frankie races from the hallway to the kitchen to hide.

'Frankie, it's only us,' Ed calls out, nonplussed.

'I can't get through to him. He completely freaked out,' Jess says, twisting her fingers – she no longer wears her rings. She stops abruptly. 'Frankie, sweetheart.' She goes through to the kitchen and tries to hold the sobbing figure. 'Shh . . . shh . . . it's all right. You're home now. Everything will be OK.'

But Frankie is distraught: the relief of being at home meaning he can give himself up to his distress. It's the same near-hysterical crying I saw when Jess was interviewed by the police.

'It's OK, Frankie. You need to breathe. Can you do that for me? In for three . . . out for five . . .' I try to calm him as I did then, but his sobs ratchet up into disjointed hiccups and tears streak down his flushed cheeks.

'You . . . won't . . .' He is gasping to get a sentence out.

'I won't what, sweetheart?' Jess manages to get both arms around him and he lets her hold him tight.

'You won't go to prison, will you?' The words fight their way through his sobs.

'No!'

'And you won't be taken away from us?'

'No-ooo!' Jess says, her voice swooping in incredulity and sadness. 'Is this about Lucy?' she continues, her voice very small. 'Lucy's still helping us but very soon she won't be involved: hopefully by next month. Because I'm getting better, aren't I? And I'm not planning on going anywhere at all.'

His shoulders quiver with fear or relief, but his noisy sobs tell of the strain he's been under these past five months. And then his anguish cranks up as if a volume dial has been swiped.

'She was there ... at the fair ... and she looked at me. All witchy.'

'Who was there, darling?'

But Frankie clamps his lips tight and shakes his head as if shaking a thought away.

'She. Said. I. Was ... Naughty ... She. Said. I. Was ... *Tricky*,' he manages finally.

'Who did, Frankie?' I ask, touching his hand.

'*George's* mummy,' he wails, as if it should be obvious.

'Well, of course you're not naughty or tricky.' Jess looks at me bemused. 'What an *unkind* thing to say! Ed – do you know anything about this?' she asks, and I hear the unspoken allegation in her tone: *your friend said this about our child.*

'I've no idea what he's talking about. I can't imagine why she'd say that. We've been so clear that it's not his fault. That he's not in any way to blame.'

'She. Said. It!' Frankie looks up at his father. 'I'm not *lying*!'

'Well, she's completely wrong,' Ed tells him. 'You're a good boy, we all know that. Mummy, me; Liz as well,' he says, enlisting my support.

'Absolutely.'

'Maybe you misunderstood her? I can't believe she'd say something like that to you.'

'Ed!' Jess is close to tears.

He shrugs. 'Well, when would she have said it? There must have been crossed wires, or something. Look, I'll give her a call, try to work out what's happened. There's no way she'd have meant to make him this distressed.'

He picks up his phone and moves out of the kitchen, where the sound of the wailing is quieter.

'It's all right, Frankie. Daddy believes you. We believe you, and Charlotte's completely wrong,' Jess says, hugging her boy.

But Ed just made a good point. *When would she have said it?* The families no longer socialise, Charlotte cutting Jess off completely after the involvement of the police. George has had a Spanish au pair since February, so Charlotte's *never* at the school gate.

'He doesn't like George's mum and he's scared of George, too,' Kit offers, as he and Sam watch, wide-eyed. 'He won't come near us in the playground if we're playing with George. He says he *hates* him.'

'Is George bullying you, Frankie?' I ask. 'Is that what's going on?'

He shakes his head.

'Why don't you boys go and play?' I tell Sam and Kit, realising Frankie is unlikely to open up with them there. They oblige, chastened by his anguish. I sit back on my heels as Jess rocks him, trying to fathom the reason for his distress.

I remember him glancing over his shoulder at the mass of parents, as we left school: there were hundreds of us but one in particular terrified him. I think of his refusal to walk past Charlotte's house, and his sudden hatred of George, which chimes with something Rosa recently said.

Then there's Charlotte's behaviour: her clear withdrawal from our group, and her decision to send George to prep school a year early. Her behaviour at the fair, when she kept her distance and refused to be photographed in a group. *Please, Liz. Let's not force things.* It was a perfectly reasonable request, and yet she was shifty: standing deep under the sycamore tree as if she didn't want to be seen.

There's that slight hardness to her, too; something I identified as social awkwardness but which reminds me of my mother. Her defensiveness. Her belief that her opinion is always right. Then, her relationship with Ed. When I overheard them earlier, had she just suggested they become more than friends? Because it sounded very much as if he was rebuffing her. And, perhaps allied to this, there's her willingness to think the worst of Jess: her barely disguised delight when she suggested Jess had left both her children on the night of Betsey's accident. *Perhaps she wasn't there,* Charlotte had suggested – and yes, she had been right.

And yet she hadn't told the police, had she? She'd told

me – perhaps as insurance in case a neighbour mentioned her being there that night. But she kept it quiet despite clearly having an animus against Jess. Why was that? Why hadn't she alerted them? Could it be because she didn't want them to know that she had been there? What was it she'd said? *I rang the door but no one answered. I tried the landline but it just rang out. I could hear Betsey crying.* She'd gone to the garage to fill up with petrol, she said, but what if she hadn't? What if she *had* rung the doorbell and someone – a visibly troubled little boy – had answered it, after all?

The answer comes at me clear and hard like a sudden blow to my solar plexus. And, Christ, if I'm right, he will finally be absolved of all blame.

'Frankie,' I say, and he gives me the smile of a child who is failing to hold everything together.

And I smile back as I ask him: 'When did Charlotte say this?'

Liz

Friday 13 July

Forty-nine

The boy comes hurtling down the school playing field, arms and legs flailing, a look of intense concentration on his face.

He streaks ahead of the other eight-year-olds but the fact he is so clearly in the lead doesn't prevent him from expending every last ounce of effort.

'Come on, Frankie. Come *on!*' Jess shouts. 'You can do it. You can *do* it!' she urges as he flies over the finishing line.

My boy chases after him, chest thrust out, arms flung forwards. 'Well done, Sam!' I yell as he thunders past us, though I'm secretly relieved that Frankie's won.

'Sorry. Did I sound like a hideous Tiger Mother?' Jess asks.

'Just a little bit,' Mel says dryly as Connor arrives in last place.

'I think it's allowed,' I add, noting her flushed cheeks, her palpable excitement; thinking back to the woman with the fearful, closed expression who turned up, six months ago, at A&E.

Beside me, Betsey wriggles in her arms. Jess puts her down and shadows her as she runs around, picking up speed despite her nappy sagging.

'I just can't believe . . .' Mel begins.

'I know. We were very lucky. *I* was very lucky,' Jess pre-empts her, and her expression darkens with thoughts of what might have been.

'Come on. Shall we find the girls?' I suggest as Jess straps Betsey back into her buggy. 'Their relay starts in ten minutes.'

We amble across the playing field, filling each other in with the week's news. Mel and I have made a concerted effort to be more supportive: to text Jess regularly, to talk, however briefly, every few days. At first, we devised a rota, stunned and shamed by what Jess had experienced and we'd failed to notice. But as the habit continued, we slipped back into a closeness we had come near to losing, and had forgotten we might need.

I've been on nights all week, though, and so haven't filled them in on my latest gossip.

'Neil is retiring in September. They'll bring in a locum but if they hold off advertising the permanent job for at least six months I think it could be mine!'

Both seem thrilled and so I tell them that Fousia made a formal complaint after Neil swore vociferously in front of a patient. The department, already concerned about his bullying and uncollegiate behaviour, presented him with a choice: face disciplinary action or agree to step down.

'Of course, the trust will have to advertise, and they might not want me. Might get someone far better,' I backtrack, wary of jinxing my chances.

'Rubbish, you're a good doctor with a great track record,' Mel says as Jess nods emphatically. I shove my failures to the back of my mind – not least my failure to diagnose my mother, or to spot that Jess was struggling – and think of my patients who are doing well thanks to my quick judgement and treatment. And, as we near a group of children who include the younger boys, I think about Frankie.

He's powering towards us, now, having broken away from his classmates.

'Mummy!' His voice is clear and high.

'What's happened now?'

It's clear from his cry, and the jagged urgency of his running, that he's distressed.

'*Mum*-my!' he repeats, his voice spiking as he flings himself around her waist, then barricades himself behind the buggy.

'What's going on?' Jess asks as Andrew walks briskly towards us.

'Sorry, *sorry*,' he says. 'I just smiled at him and he rather took fright. George and I have been trying to keep out of your way but he *bounded* towards me.' He wipes sweat from his forehead. 'I didn't mean to *frighten* him.'

'That's quite all right,' Jess manages. 'I know you would have meant to be kind.'

Charlotte hasn't been seen since the summer fair. The police have interviewed her with a view to prosecuting for neglect but the CPS has made no decision on whether to bring charges. Nevertheless, Andrew has clearly felt the impact of what she did. His air of clownish goodwill has vanished, and he looks quite broken: his cheeks have hollowed and his gently protruding stomach has melted away.

'I'm incredibly sorry,' he repeats. 'Best if we just go now. We'll be taking George out of school from Monday. There's only a week left, and we've no desire to cause any further problems.'

'That's OK, really,' Jess repeats.

But Charlotte's husband is insistent. 'No. I nearly didn't come today but I couldn't let George down. *Please.* Frank has been through too much. Believe me. This is for the best.'

He turns and plods away, and as he does he meets George and puts an arm around his shoulders, holding him in a manner that's more loving, more *instinctive*, than I've ever seen.

'Poor man.' Mel watches them go. 'Living with a partner who's holding a secret like that.'

'Poor Charlotte, too,' Jess says, surprising me. 'It's horrific keeping something like that inside you. Six days was enough for me. We've told the police we won't support a prosecution if it's brought: I've withdrawn my statement. Let's face it: I neglected the children too, and it's the last thing Frankie needs.'

We're nearing the end of the older children's running track. Frankie has calmed down now that Andrew's left and is persuaded to rejoin his classmates for his relay. Jess slows her pace, apparently reluctant to mingle with other parents, or for them to overhear.

'Ed told me what happened with Charlotte,' she says, after a while.

'When they were students?'

'More recently.' Her voice dips. 'He felt she was becoming "too emotionally invested": as if they were having a platonic affair. Then she intimated it could be physical, too. Nothing happened but he knew he didn't want that, and realised how much he loved me. So he told her to back off, and that they couldn't continue being close friends.'

'When did he tell her this?' Mel asks.

'At the summer fair. I imagine he sounded brutal.'

I remember Charlotte's red raw expression. No wonder she looked so bleak.

'Perhaps a fresh break is what they need. New school; new start ... I hope she finds some happiness,' I say, somewhat lamely. I find it bizarre that Charlotte panicked; think it completely irresponsible that she left Betsey; have been furious that she manipulated Frankie – forcing him to carry the blame for five months – and intending him to do so indefinitely. (And I know from my guilt over Mattie's accident how pernicious, how corrosive this can be.) I know Ed's felt furious too – not least about Charlotte encouraging him to suspect that Jess had harmed Betsey. And yet this

413

anger isn't helpful: certainly won't help Jess and her family. It was an accident, I keep reminding myself – and accidents make people act irrationally.

'On your marks . . .' A loudspeaker interrupts us, and we focus on something less intense: the year five girls' relay. Rosa's primed: weight on her front foot, both arms raised.

The starting gun fires and they're off: a flurry of small, light bodies streaking down the track.

'Go, Rosa!' I scream.

'Look at them go!' Mel screeches, as Rosa hands over the baton, then: 'Go, Mollie! Go, *Moll*-ie!' and Jess and I join in, cheering in a manner that's far too competitive for a school sports day but that lifts my spirits high.

The girls come first and collapse in each other's arms as if they've won gold at the Olympics.

'Come here,' Mel laughs, and pulls the two of us into a tight hug as we watch.

In the buggy, Betsey starts kicking her legs.

'Oh – do you want a cuddle, too?' Jess asks – and she lifts the toddler out and into her arms.

Betsey beams. The entranced smile of a child who is adored and who senses she is at the heart of this celebration. She traces our faces with soft fingers before they land in her mother's hair. A smile splits her face and her laughter rises, fat and iridescent as soap bubbles. It's contagious, and soon we are all laughing for no real reason at all.

Or maybe there is. The sun streams down, our children race around, and for a moment I feel nothing but pin-sharp happiness. This is it, I realise. *This. Is. It.* And then I see my mother, alone with a screaming baby, and I wish she had had someone to connect with; to confide in about the lows of motherhood that weighed her down so that she never felt this light-hearted, this joyful, with Clare.

'You OK?' Jess catches my eye, above Betsey's head. These days she's particularly in tune with others' vulnerabilities.

And I want to remind us all to cherish this. These highs of motherhood that sustain us; that buoy us up when we're exhausted, or anxious, or it all feels like a bit of a struggle; these perfect, necessary moments.

But of course, none of this needs saying.

'Yes,' I say. 'Absolutely fine.'

ACKNOWLEDGEMENTS

Little Disasters was written as I waited for *Anatomy of a Scandal* to be published, and in the aftermath of this happening. I am indescribably grateful to Jo Dickinson, of Simon & Schuster UK, for her care, insight and patience in nurturing it, and me.

The entire S&S team has been fabulous: Jess Barratt, Hayley McMullan, Sara-Jade Virtue, Laura Hough, Dom Brendon, Joe Roche, Gill Richardson, Louise Davies, Clare Hey and Alice Rodgers. Saxon Bullock was a forensic copy editor and Tamsin Shelton as thoughtful a proof reader as she was for *Anatomy of a Scandal*. In the US, huge thanks are due to my editor Emily Bestler, of Emily Bestler Books, Lara Jones and Ariele Fredman.

As ever, I am indebted to my agent, Lizzy Kremer, who always pushes me to dig deeper, and to Maddalena Cavaciuti. One of the immense joys of being published has been seeing my novels enjoyed in foreign countries and I'm so grateful to the DHA rights team – Alice Howe, Emma Jamison, Margaux Vialleron, Lucy Talbot, Emma Schouten and Johanna Clarke – for ensuring *Little Disasters* will be read beyond the US and UK.

Unlike Michael Gove, I'm a huge fan of experts and this novel could not have been written without two in particular: Graham Bartlett, former chief superintendent and now police procedural advisor, and Keir Shiels, paediatrician at the Royal London hospital. Both of them showed immense patience in answering my often repetitive questions and, crucially, were quick to respond to emails. They also read certain sections, and corrected facts and terminology when I got things wrong. If the police scenes and the hospital sections ring true, it is largely thanks to them. Any mistakes are all mine.

Other doctors who helped immensely in fields ranging from paediatrics to obstetrics to psychiatry to gastroenterology were: Dr Nancy Morris, Dr Geoff Debelle, Dr Georgina Bough, Dr Manish Patel, Dr Jo Cannon and Dr Roger Marwood. I am so grateful for each of those often lengthy phone conversations and follow up emails. Thank you, too, to Suzanne Biers and Dr Zoe Mead, doctor friends who helped with contacts, and to the press officers at the RCPCH (Royal College of Paediatrics and Child Health) and the RCOG (Royal College of Obstetricians and Gynaecologists).

I am grateful to Maria Bavetta, of the Maternal OCD charity, not least for putting me in touch with Maddelena Miele, consultant perinatal psychiatrist at St Mary's hospital: an interview with her in the early stages confirmed that this was an issue I should be writing about.

Social workers have been harder to find and I'm grateful to my author friend Claire Fuller, for putting me in touch with Paul Shawcross; to Penny Sturt, who I met through Twitter; and to Josie Collier, who, to my daughter's embarrassment, I interviewed after chatting to her on a train. Lucy Stone became a far smaller character than originally intended but it was important safeguarding procedure was accurate.

I drew on several non-fiction books while researching this, including: *Dropping the Baby and Other Scary Thoughts*, by Karen Kleiman and Amy Wenzel; *Direct Red*, by Gabriel Weston; *Your Life in My Hands*, by Rachel Clarke; *This Is Going to Hurt*, by Adam Kay; *Mad Girl*, by Bryony Gordon; and *The Man Who Couldn't Stop*, by my former *Guardian* colleague David Adam. I highly recommend his memoir, and Gordon's, for a greater understanding of OCD.

Writing can be a very isolating job. As ever, I'm indebted to the Prime Writers, who have put up with me whinging, and answered my questions – at one stage debating, at length, whether we'd change the nappy of another mother's baby. Rachael Lucas, thank you for that phone conversation, too. Twitter saps time but the enthusiasm of author friends, booksellers and bloggers I've met through it has helped keep me going. Thank you, in particular, to Shots blogger Ayo Onatade, for answering a quick but crucial question.

Away from the screen, support has come, as ever, from Laura Tennant, my sister, and Bobby Hall, my mother. Laura is the first non-publishing person to read my novels and her points were as kind, perceptive and pertinent as ever. Huge thanks, and love, to you both.

Little Disasters was sparked by a conversation with my husband, a hospital consultant who I met twenty years ago – six weeks after he became a junior doctor. Neither of us could do each other's jobs and I remain amazed by some of the things he and his NHS colleagues put up with and, despite this, still achieve. My love, as ever, to him, and to our children who have taught me everything I know about motherhood.

A final note to the dads I chat to on the sidelines of football and rugby matches: I promise none of these characters are you.